Truth or Dare

THE DOMINATOR SERIES, BOOK 2

DD PRINCE

DDPRINCE.COM

Cover Design: K+A Designs

ISBN# 9781099866869

DEDICATION

This book is dedicated to
the best dog ever --- my Marley.
Marley was my golden retriever and my best friend from 1996-2009.
I miss you, sweet boy
XOXO

Please read book one before embarking on this story.

PROLOGUE

Dario Ferrano

Recently, my father died. He was a hardened criminal and duplicitous liar. He was also a *known* wise guy that was part of something larger and more evil than any of us realized. After he died, I took it upon myself to legitimize and then sell the family business so that I and the rest of my siblings could move on.

But little did I know, before his death he'd started the ball rolling on giving me the same kind of gift he'd given my older brother. When news of this gift arrived on my doorstep, my already chaotic world was turned on its axis.

I had just gotten home from my brother's wedding and I had a to-do list longer than my arm. I told my brother I could handle most of it on my own; I had it under control. I had a few key guys to help me here. He could go, enjoy time with his new bride far away from home, away from secrets and lies and deceit. He'd been my idol and my best friend all my life and shouldering a lot for the last several years. I wanted to ease his burden. In our family, he was the heir and I was the spare so I probably also wanted to prove that I was just as capable as he was.

So after the death of our father Tom Ferrano, my brother Tommy and his new bride Tia were giving a go at starting a fresh life overseas, away from secrets that needed to be kept. My brother decided he needed to be out of sight for a while for a couple reasons.

I, however, was to be back home doing the "laundry" so that we could sell off the empire that my father had spent thirty years building. It was for the best. The empire extended to so many dark and dank areas it was better off for all of us to just start fresh. The kind of businesses he was in, though, made it so that we couldn't just make a clean break. That's why I was cleaning things up first.

Before my father died, he arranged for my brother to get married, gifted him with a girl. After I saw the impact of that girl on my brother's life, I joked with Pop that I wanted a mail-order bride for my upcoming birthday, joked about it with emotions about my now sister-in-law that I should not ever have been feeling.

My father joked back that he was already shopping around and would find me a perfect fit. At least I'd thought he'd been joking. But when I got home from my brother's wedding, I found out that before Pop died, he had gotten that ball rolling. He'd gotten things rolling in a way that could not be stopped and that was going to be a problem. A messy problem.

See, my Pop was deeply involved in a human trafficking ring, one of the many involvements he'd neglected to tell me and my brother about as he prepared us to take over the family business. We never knew that what he'd had in mind for us was just the top skim off a cesspool of filth he'd been too happy to be wading in. We had suspicions but we had no clue just how filthy it truly was.

Pop and I had a conversation when talking about Tommy and Tia and how my brother went from being the non-marrying kind to devoting himself 100% to the girl my father had arranged for him to have. Pop wouldn't tell me his motives behind the choice at that point but it all unfolded over the subsequent weeks. A little less than two months before my birthday he had asked me what I wanted in a bride.

"What's on your wish list, son?" Pop asked.

"Beautiful. Redhead. But she has to want what I want from life. She has to have an insatiable sexual appetite but want kids and a picket fence, too."

"How about if she's all those things because she does exactly what you tell her to do? How about if she's been schooled in all the ways to please a man in and out of the bedroom?"

"That's too good to be true, Pop. Too bad such a woman does not exist." I'd laughed and our conversation got cut short.

I'd always wanted a wife and kids. I wanted the picket fence and enough kids to start my own soccer team. But when I caught my fiancée cheating on me with the DJ we'd hired for our wedding my heart went cold and what my sister dubbed my 'man whore years' began.

After seeing Tommy's life change because of falling in love I decided that maybe it was time to open my mind up to the possibilities of connecting with someone again beyond a one-night stand. But when I got home from my brother's wedding, ready to start the massive job of cleaning up the family business so that I could move on with my life and think about finding my own happily ever after I found out that Pop had already ordered my mail order bride. And I couldn't cancel that order.

Pop's involvement in a human slavery ring, it was deep. We knew the trade existed and we knew he knew people in that trade. Tommy had seen a little more of the inside of it than I had. But neither of us knew that he had partnered with them, that he had an in that meant he could get me the woman on my wish list.

She's waiting for me to pick her up near Bangkok. She's been told she has been sold and is going back to North America. She's about to turn twenty-three, she's a beautiful redhead, and she's been in captivity for two years. There's no way I can accept this gift, keep a woman who was bought for me. I need to pick her up and set her free. Don't I?

Tia Ferrano

Life isn't always what you think it'll be. Sometimes it falls short and sometimes you get more than you ever dreamed was possible, even if it doesn't play out the way you expected. Life throws curveballs and when you sit and dream about an obstacle being in the way of your happiness and that obstacle finally gets moved it's not always smooth sailing like you thought it'd be.

One night just a few days after we got married, my husband had my throat in a crushing hold during the throes of a nightmare and I almost didn't make it out of it. After a huge argument, Tommy agreed to therapy and I don't know yet if it's helping or not. Right now, it almost seems like it's making it worse because he's facing facts and hard truths about himself. It's making him go from aloof and quiet one minute to broody and growly the next. I hope the old adage of "it gets worse before it gets better" is true because that'll mean it will eventually get better.

I also hope I've seen the worst already.

I've tried to reassure him that he had no choice but to shoot his father. Tom Sr. wanted a showdown. He wanted to punish his son for his perceived betrayal and Tom probably would've killed me and maybe would've killed him, too.

But I know Tommy feels guilt even if he won't admit it. He has nightmares that he won't talk about. Sometimes I can calm him down with a cuddle when he's moaning in his sleep and he won't even wake up. Sometimes he gets out of bed after jackknifing straight up, sweaty and hyperventilating, and then he doesn't want to be touched. Sometimes he just disappears to the roof terrace to beat on the heavy bag in the middle of the night or swim a dozen laps. And sometimes he wakes up and takes me…devours me, fucks me hard and rough and like his life depends on it.

Sometimes, when he's really aloof or broody and I can't figure out how to help him through it, I push and pick fights with him until he pushes back and his pushing back usually means that his control snaps and that means extra rough sex. Afterwards, he's always a bit more himself. Sometimes it lasts a few hours, sometimes a few days.

Tom Sr.'s funeral was hard. Lisa was in rough shape and then she found out a week after Tom died that she was pregnant. Tessa and her boys moved in with her and I think they're helping one another heal from the loss of Tom and Tessa's husband James.

Me? I think maybe I need therapy, too. My father, poor excuse for one that he is, the man who sold me to pay a debt to Tommy's father and who thought it'd buy him an opportunity to be a big shot… he's still incarcerated, but he's alive and safe. For now. Last I heard, anyway.

I struggle daily with my situation, with what my life has become. But I can't imagine living without Tommy being the center of my universe. Our relationship isn't healthy; I know this. I also know that I don't want a life without him in it. Hopefully in time we can find our way to a healthier place.

Tommy's moody. I know he's in pain and he feels guilty. He's so protective of me it feels smothering some days. We rarely leave home; I never get to go anywhere without him. And the sex? Even when it doesn't come on the heels of a nightmare it's pretty rough sometimes. But it's what we both need. We both get release. He gets confirmation that I'm his; he gets full control over one thing in his life. And me? I get to be his, get to help him by giving him what he needs and it's not altogether altruistic either, because I get to let go of the crap in my head and for a few minutes I feel totally, utterly, free. He takes control and for those few minutes (or sometimes, those few hours) I worry about nothing.

Sometimes too, it's so gentle I cry when I orgasm because I can feel how much he loves me as it's etched into his features. He worships my body and stares into my eyes whether he makes love to me or whether he's fucking me with this passion, this fire that I will never ever get tired of.

Tommy and his brother Dario decided that Dare is going to transition the company and the subsidiaries and then once it's as squeaky clean as it can possibly get, some or most of it is being sold. Tommy's not out of the loop but Dare is hands-on. They hired a consulting firm to help and he and Tommy talk pretty much daily over the computer.

When Tommy and I got to Costa Rica and got married on a beach at sunset it was almost perfect. It was breathtaking, exactly what I wanted, staring into the eyes of the man I loved with our toes in the sand and the sky a dozen brilliant colors. The only missing ingredient was the people from my life before Tommy, but I came to terms with the fact that it couldn't be helped. We need to be incognito for now and I would never want to put the people I love in unnecessary danger. So, this is how it has to be.

I sent them a letter before we left that said I was taking an extended trip and I plan to get word to them again soon so that they don't worry. I might have Tess mail them a letter soon so that it's not traceable to where I am.

Tommy suggested I visit to say goodbye before we moved and even talked about sneaking them to our wedding like he had to do with his family. But, I'm not the same girl I was a few months ago and I didn't want to bring them into the orbit of the danger surrounding this family. I feel like I've grown into a different person. I've known so much fear and seen so much death and I've felt so much pain that I'd hate to cloud their light and airy lives with that. They probably wouldn't know me anymore. They'd look at me and see I'm different and they'd worry. Or they'd be sad. And if I looked too long at them, I might be sad too. I might be sad for my lost innocence. I don't need that. Regret won't help me.

Tommy got angry when I kept making excuses about not bringing them to the wedding and then I blurted some of what I really felt and he got really upset. He blames himself for this. I blame our fathers. I also can't help but blame my mother, too. She gave up. She gave up on life. She gave up on me. She fixed nothing before she left. She left so many things at loose ends and so many questions unanswered and I know she was hurt and sad and depressed, but I can't help but be angry with her for not thinking about how her actions would affect me. That's what mothers are supposed to do --- protect their babies.

As for our safety, I was hoping that here we'd have a fresh canvas, a place where we could move on and live without Tommy feeling like he's got to be looking over his shoulder all the time. But so far, that isn't happening. Tommy got fake identities for us so that we could slip off the grid for a while. He knows that there's a chance that if what he did is suspected there will be people to answer to that are even more threatening than the cops. He also said that if he goes back, he's afraid he'll just get sucked into the business and have trouble finding his way out of it. He says some day we may move back, he's not sure. He kept the farm for us and has someone checking on it once in a while. The house his father bought him for his 29th birthday was sold and he sold his brother the condo as Dario was living there anyway.

Dario and the girls are all on the path to healing, it seems. No one talked about what happened with Tom at the end and they were all here for the wedding acting like there was nothing but love between them all. I guess the girls are all just quietly mourning him as if he were someone they loved and lost tragically. It was tragic. It was tragic how he revealed his true nature in his last days on the planet and hurt his family so deeply, cost his daughter her husband and the father of her children, put his son in a position where he had no choice but to fatally shoot him.

I get a vibe from the girls like maybe they know what really happened because they and a lot of other people saw what went down just before Tom had me taken. No one's talking to me about anything. The kiss Tom planted on me at his *welcome home* party before he abducted me was never mentioned by any of them. I could be wrong, but I get the impression they're just burying it. It seems like we're all just working at healing. They don't treat Tommy with anger or push him away. If anything, the wedding seemed like everyone was closer, tighter than ever. Moods were quiet and somber when they came for the wedding but there was love and well wishes at the ceremony and reception, and that's what mattered.

Here, we're Tommy and Tia, but on our passports we're Tommaso and Valentina Caruso, names I picked. I chose the surname for Rose's parents. He says we don't have to worry about money, he's got enough put away to look after us for years and once the company's taken all apart and sold we'll never have to worry about money again. He tells me that to comfort me but money probably can't buy my husband what he needs the most --- peace.

In an argument we had a few days after the wedding when he was being moody and broody and refusing to leave the house, Tommy said he wished he could turn back the clock to the day he first saw me and leave me behind that ice cream counter untainted by his poison. I slapped him in the face when he said that to me. In reaction to my slap, he pinned me against a wall with my arms held over my head and scowled at me but I screamed in his face that poison or not, his love is mine and how dare he wish that away. It turned my blood to acid to think that he'd wish what we have away for even a second. What we have is everything to me. It's all I have.

That heated argument resulted in my getting a wicked spanking in retaliation for slapping his face and then sex so rough and so totally amazing that I limped the next day, my body feeling like I'd run a marathon. Sex is a common argument ender for us. It's a common way to share joy or deal with frustration or fear; it's what we do. Sometimes he gets wound so tight that I know it's what he needs, so I push his buttons until he takes what he needs. I've changed. I don't know that I'm stronger but I do know that I find ways to deal with my anger and frustration now. But it's usually through sex.

A few days after that argument, we had another. I wanted to go for a walk and he made an excuse about waiting for a phone call. I waited like two hours but then told him I'd just go and be gone half an hour. He wouldn't let me and refused to bring his phone on the walk with him, mumbling about bad reception and missing the call. So I told him off and left the house anyway. I saw him come out behind me and I said, "I'm going for a thirty-minute walk. Just let me go!" He grabbed me and threw me over the shoulder and carried me back and when we got back in the house he snarled, "Don't you ever do that again!"

I stuck my tongue out at him and took off back out the door toward the water and he followed me so I started running and of course he chased me. He tackled me to the sand. I pushed, shoved, and swore at him, telling him I couldn't spend 24/7 with him without losing my freaking mind and that I just wanted a fucking half an hour walk on the beach to myself. He responded by apologizing for being so overprotective but then he fucked me hard down in the sand, telling me he loved me more than anything, begging me to be patient with him.

I'd often said it was a fantasy of mine to have sex on a beach. But the reality? It's really not all it's cracked up to be. First, there's the sand. It gets … everywhere. E-v-e-r-y where!

I had sand in my vajayjay, up my fanny, everywhere. We were kissing and there was sand getting in our mouths. There were freaking bugs on us, too. It was not as sexy as Hollywood makes it out to be, especially when it's as rough and tumble as it is with Tommy.

But that release of frustration helped us both that day and fortunately or maybe unfortunately, that plus the spanking after the slap in the face meant the start of a cycle of me goading him into rough sex whenever he got moody or broody.

After the beach sex, he took a two hour walk with me. But during that walk we didn't talk. We just held hands and walked, the air heavy with all we were both feeling.

Tommy Ferrano

She's irritating the fuck out of me. She's walking on eggshells with me and mothering me one minute and trying to tell me what to do the next. I fucking hate it. When she gets particularly bitchy it turns me into a fucking animal and I know it's turned into a cycle. She senses that I need release and she knows I hesitate because I worry about hurting her and then she purposely pushes me over the edge so I'll take what I need from her. I know it isn't healthy. Since marrying me and promising before God and my family to obey me and be mine forever it's given me an even more dark and possessive sense of entitlement to her body. But the depth of my love for her makes me feel guilty about it. I'm twisted in knots all the time.

It's like we're both uncomfortable in our own skin or something. Sometimes I don't know how she can look at me after all I've done to her. I have a hard time looking at myself. I thank God that she survived everything

I put her through but now that I'm not Tommy Ferrano, heir to the Ferrano family business, I don't know who I am. And her? She's mine. She's my woman, my lifeline, my life. I'm so obsessed with her that it borders on insanity and I too *frequently* breach that border.

We arrived in Costa Rica and Tia loves the house I rented. It's got a billion-dollar view, it's five thousand square feet, it's private with ocean views and a pool on top of the roof, and it's got every basic amenity we need just a two-minute drive or ten-minute walk away. It has a long dock that she can sit and fish from and we often sit out back around the outdoor fireplace while she cooks campfire concoctions. There's no one but us. No one here knows who we are. I finally have her all to myself and there's no reason why another drama should put her in danger again, but I know better than to become complacent. And I can't handle having her out of my sight yet. I tried. I let her go to a fruit vendor while I was on a patio of a restaurant the day after the family all left to go back home and five minutes later, I had to find her. I was physically ill with anxiety about her being vulnerable.

She wants to explore and shop and try local restaurants and go deep sea fishing and do yoga and take dance classes and live life to the fullest but I don't want her out of my sight for the stuff I wouldn't do and half the time I can't be bothered with the stuff I would do. I go along with her when I can't find excuses not to keep us home. She keeps looking at me with sad eyes and when I catch her… she tries to paint on a smile, a fake smile. It makes me wanna put my fist through a wall.

I'm doing therapy over the webcam. I'd rather just forget it all instead of talking about it. I need distance from home, from the business, from ex-associates and enemies. I need distance from myself, my urges, my needs, my nightmares. That's why we're here. We don't know if I'm in danger, if Tia's in danger. We don't want questions from the cops about any loose ends back home. I don't know if I'll eventually take us back or make a life here or somewhere else, but right now we're supposed to be taking time to breathe, be newlyweds. But I can't *just* breathe.

Every day brings breaking news of shit Pop was into that we were oblivious about. I have a standing weekly appointment with the fucking shrink, which I don't wanna do but which I do because Tia needs me to do it so we both can hang onto hope that I'm not a lost cause. The shrink specializes in helping men like me. Is it helping me? I don't fucking know.

Yeah, I shot my father when he turned a gun on her in order to punish me. But in hindsight, the time between when my father raised his gun to Tia and the time I fired my weapon, I wasn't sure but thought I saw something in his face that told me he wanted to die. I don't know if it's hindsight or just my nightmares haunting me.

I have alternating dreams where his expression changes. Did he raise that gun so I'd kill him with no intention of shooting her or me? Did I save her life and my own life by killing the man who gave me life? Did I pass or fail the ultimate Tom Ferrano test? The fact that I'd killed my own father, did it mean I really was no better than he was, or did I just protect what was mine? His face haunts my dreams.

The blood-covered wedding dress he had someone leave on the balcony outside my bedroom just before he died taunts me, tells me he intended to kill her or at least wanted me to fear that he would. I was relieved it looked nothing like the dress she actually wore and I never told her about the bloody dress or a bunch of other shit that went down because she had enough to cope with. That dress continues to haunt my nightmares. Most of getting her out of that dress on our wedding night was about my desire, yeah, but some of that was probably about those fears and getting her safely out of it while it was still white, rather than stained scarlet.

Dare's doing good back home, really stepping up. He'd always been an asset to the business, mature for his age, serious about being successful, and he and I were on the exact same page about the company and about what we did and didn't want in our lives. He was making my life a helluva lot less complicated and without him dealing with shit back home I don't know how I'd be coping.

Then again, maybe if I was busy sorting that shit out myself, I would have something to focus on to take my mind off what I did, to take my mind off the fact that I'm cracked, damaged, probably irrevocably. But if I go back and that puts my wife in danger…the idea of doing anything to make her vulnerable, therefore allowing anything to hurt her? It's unthinkable to me.

A few days after they got home from our wedding, I sat down at the computer to check emails and saw a Skype notification from my brother asking me to get ahold of him as soon as possible. Finding out about the latest? Shit. The mess Pop left us just keeps getting messier.

CHAPTER ONE

Dare

8.5 YEARS EARLIER

Truth, dare, double dare, or promise to repeat?"

"Double dare," I answered her and leaned over and ran my nose from her chin, along her jawline, to the spot behind her ear.

She giggled and squirmed away, pink tinting her cheeks.

"I double dare you to…" She looked around and then whispered, "kiss someone you have a crush on."

We were sitting under a tree outside our high school, skipping science class, a ways away from the building on the far side of the thick trunk of a big weeping willow. No one would see us unless they were close. I was looking forward to trying to get to second base with my lab partner. I was pretty smitten with her, like Charlie Brown and *his little girl with the red hair.*

"On a dare, yeah, but a double dare? A kiss is way too tame for a double dare," I told her, "Can't you do better than that?"

"Depends where that kiss is," answered a female voice coming from the other side of the tree trunk.

As soon as I saw the source of that voice the redheaded girl in the grass beside me no longer existed. No other girl in the world existed but the tall brunette with the leather jacket and huge tits smoking a cigarette and blowing the smoke into rings. She was the only girl for me for the next six years. And what she did to me ruined me for the following three.

Debbie was a rocker chick. Her style consisted of heavy black eye make-up, tight jeans, *fuck-me* heels, plenty of leather and body-hugging spandex, long nails --- talons, really.

That day we met was her first day at my high school and she and I were inseparable throughout the rest of it. She was wild, she had an insatiable sex drive, she was crazy about me, and the family I was from didn't bother her a bit. In fact, she thought it was a thrill that my family appeared to toe the line between good and evil. She loved to suck my cock, had no sexual inhibitions whatsoever, and she kept me on my toes. She wasn't my first lay, I was a pretty busy 16-year-old when I met her, but she changed the game for me. Back then I thought she was *it* for me.

On her 20th birthday, I gave her an engagement ring. It was logical. We had a great time together. In hindsight, there were things missing, things she didn't give me, but I was young and in love with her spirit and the sex was incredible.

We split when we were 22, four months before the wedding when I caught her on her knees giving head to the goof hired to DJ our wedding reception.

When I walked into her place in the middle of the afternoon unannounced and found Debbie on her knees, I saw black. I got a lock on my rage with her but the guy whose dick was in her mouth wasn't so lucky because he took the brunt. I hospitalized the guy, broken jaw among his injuries, and then I destroyed his life.

I had his and his father's classic car that they rebuilt together crunched at a scrap yard and then returned to his driveway, got him fired from his day job, had all his DJ equipment destroyed, trashed his place, and then took steps that wound up bankrupting his father's business. You could say when I got pissed it meant blowback.

A few times in the first year after Deb and I split, I fucked with the guy just because. I didn't want him to think it was over. I wanted him to keep lookin' over his shoulder. Based on the shit I pulled he was probably *still* looking over his shoulder three years later. Yeah, I'd pretty much *Greg O'Connor'd* the guy.

I wasn't proud of what I did to the guy's father now, and learning about my father's tendencies in the revenge department had me analyzing some of what I'd done to get back at people who pissed me off. But, back then? All I saw was black. He knew she was mine. He knew who I was. He had a pretty good clue who my family was. He was a fuckin' moron for crossing me.

She saw the error of her ways, so she said, but she no longer existed to me. She yelled, she slapped me, she threw things, then she begged and pleaded, tried to use sex to get me back, stalked me for weeks, sneaking into my bed, showing up where she knew I'd be. She no longer existed to me; just white noise. Women in general became white noise, unless I had to have a minor and shallow conversation with them in order to get laid. I had no trouble finding hook-ups.

PRESENT TIME

Fast forward to today, after watching my brother marry a beautiful girl who was perfect for him, I was thinkin' it might be time to settle down, look for someone compatible.

Revenge didn't help me get over what Deb did. Splitting with her was the genesis of what my sister Luciana dubbed the "Man Whore Years" for me. I was cold for a long time. The next few years I got my rocks off in nightclub bathrooms and alleys or motel rooms and sometimes my place with nameless, faceless chicks. I was always focused, driven, but during the Man Whore Years I was focused and driven with a big chip on my shoulder and no desire to trust a female that wasn't a member of my family.

Then one day, my pop says that he's arranged for my older brother to get hitched. Yeah, it sounds prehistoric, but my brother wasn't gonna do things the traditional way and Tommy getting married was a piece of the puzzle in whatever sinister plot Pop had cookin' so Pop said he had to get creative because to him he couldn't hand the business over unless my brother showed he had settled down. A wife and preferably a wife with a bun in the oven said that to my father and his business associates. He wanted Tommy hitched so that he could move on and do other things while Tommy took over as president of the company with me as VP.

Tommy was practically doing all the heavy lifting at that point anyway but Pop dangled the business like a carrot, knowing what buttons to push with my brother. Pop was always makin' us jump over hurdles, both of us. My brother laid eyes on the girl chosen for him and he was interested. More than interested. It didn't take long for him to do a one-hundred-and-eighty-degree turn. It was astounding to watch.

Up until that point I'd never seen my brother in a relationship. He showed up stag to family events, business occasions, never brought women around. He had a rep for being a womanizer and he and I are tight, I knew he got action, women liked how he looked so he barely had to snap his fingers to get laid, but I knew he wasn't interested in settling down. After Debbie I probably modeled my approach to women after my older brother. *Fuck 'em then chuck 'em.*

He was all about power and had a single-minded focus to get to the top of his game in our business, to be someone no one questioned deserved to be in Pop's chair. His love life was something that wasn't discussed much, but he had a rep as a prick who liked it rough. More than a few women who were interested in sinking their claws into him got knocked back or scared off. They didn't kiss and tell outright because they knew better, but there were hushed whispers about Tommy's tendencies, especially after a neighbor's cousin who'd moved to town turned tail and left town after one date with my brother, rumor having it that she pursued him relentlessly until he finally gave her a shot. She learned her lesson. She had bruises around her wrists, ankles, and throat and left town the day after their hook-up. There were a few other stories like that about Tommy, but not much was said. People knew better than to gossip about him. If it got back to him, there'd be hell to pay.

This flesh payment my father took, Tia…she's a real looker, a knockout. And sweet. She worships my brother. He's a lucky fucker. My brother was turned inside out over her. His whole focus, reason for what he did, his motivations … all changed. As I watched their love story play out, I frequently thought about the fact that by that point I should've been married to Debbie a few years. She and I should've been thinkin' about kids.

Debbie really wasn't the maternal type and I guess I hadn't really thought that through when I proposed because I wanted kids. After we split, I found out she had an abortion and never told me. It shook me. If I'd married her, maybe she'd never have given me kids. Maybe she would've kept aborting them. Or maybe she'd have had kids but maybe I'd be raising kids that weren't even mine. Before the "man whore" years, I wanted a wife who'd drive a soccer mom Hummer (No woman of mine would ever be forced to drive a minivan) and fill it with enough sons to make up a soccer team.

I wanted daughters, too, to spoil. I wanted my woman to drive our boys to soccer and our girls to ballet and to do that while wearing lace and garters underneath her clothes for me because she was still a wildcat for me. I was foolish to think Debbie would grow up and mature into something maternal, traditional. She never promised me the picket fence, never promised to grow old together. I just figured it was a natural progression. I pushed the signs she wasn't away until I was forced to face them when I saw her on her knees deep-throating that fucking goof.

I was Dario Ferrano, respected in my field of work. I was a member of an influential family with ties to organized crime but the appearance of loose ties and not a small amount of mystery so I was revered and feared. But I wanted the traditional sort of family that the Ferranos were not. I wanted someone I could have a real connection with.

I'd seen a little of what I'd wanted with my grandparents, my maternal grandparents. My ma grew up in a stable and loving home and when I spent time with her for two weeks every summer, I saw that. I wanted that. She picked the wrong man to have kids with and that choice had far-reaching impact. I didn't wanna make that same mistake.

Anyway, too bad I fell for a non-traditional girl. After I caught her with the DJ, it came to light that she'd cheated plenty. She was wild, willing to try anything in the bedroom, always bringing new ideas of ways to get us off. After we split, I knew why. She'd been doing more than her fair share of wild oat sowing.

My father was married four times, widowed twice. He was in his early 50's when he died. My Pop had not only been married 4 times but he also had a long string of girlfriends and mistresses in between and often at the same time and our upbringing was anything but traditional.

Rarely saw Ma, and when I did, she was timid, broken. My ma's parents lived in Iceland and they were amazing. If I'd have grown up there, I'm sure I'd be a very different man.

My grandfather was Italian, grandmother was from Iceland, and that's where they retired. I visited them in Akureyri for a few weeks every summer until I was in my late teens and that's where I got a glimpse of a normal family life. My ma came from a big family and most of my Icelandic cousins came from stable homes with married parents. My grandparents were married 50 years, my grandmother died peacefully in her sleep and then my grandfather died the same way three days later, because he just couldn't live without her. I wanted that kind of love.

I wanted a woman who was spirited, beautiful, who loved to fuck, and who wanted a family as a means of getting more out of life, not out of settling. I wanted a woman who had substance. I didn't want the Barbie dolls my pop had around, didn't want a shell of a woman like Ma was turned into out of the fear she lived with because of my father. I wanted someone real, spunky, loving, interesting. After Deb fucked me over, I closed my heart off. I didn't see anyone around me who seemed real enough for me to let them in. Maybe I just never gave anyone else a chance.

Pop died after alienating his family. After he died, I was taking stock. I'd been doing it a while beforehand, really, watching my brother fall in love and seeing what he was getting. A girl with fight in her, a girl who was awesome with my sisters and our nieces and nephews. And I wanted it all. I wanted success in my work life and I wanted a family.

I also didn't wanna worry about people kidnapping or shooting at my family. I didn't want my wife and kids to face the risks we'd all faced due to my father's choices, especially seeing what it did to Contessa who'd been widowed and left with two boys to raise on her own. I was spending time with my nephews, trying to be a male figure for them. So was Eddy, my brother-in-law, but those boys would grow up without their father. Jimmy was a good fuckin' guy and didn't deserve to have his life cut short at 26 years old.

And what all the drama had put my brother and Tia through? It was enough to make me do my damnedest to avoid the same thing.

Tia made him better. I wanted a woman who'd make me wanna be better, too. I didn't know if I'd ever get back to resembling who I was before Deb cheated, but after I got back from Tommy's wedding I decided on a new era. I was gonna clean up my life.

New motto: man whore no more.

From then on, I wasn't gonna waste my time with women who weren't likeminded. I'd try to thaw my heart, but figured I'd probably have to settle because if she was wild like Deb, she probably wouldn't want the picket fence. I wanted both, but it wasn't likely so I'd pick picket fences and sensible bikini briefs over the garter belts and thongs if it came right down to it. It'd suck to settle but I'd already had the wild girl and that hadn't worked out so if I had to settle, I had to.

Not long after we were back from Costa Rica, it was my birthday. We had a small family dinner with my sisters, my brother-in-law Eddy, my pop's widow Lisa, and my nieces and nephews. But the next day, I found out what Pop had gotten me for my birthday. He'd arranged it before he died.

I found out that Pop had procured a wife for me. She was almost 23, was a redhead like I'd jokingly requested in memory of my science lab partner who maybe would've had a better outcome for me than Deb. This girl was American, and she'd been in captivity for 2 years, trained to be the perfect slave. Part of the deal was that if I wanted, she'd be put in a 30 to 60-day program to take her from slave material to wife material; some value-added transition service the resort offered for those who wanted their "possessions" to function flawlessly outside of the bedroom. I got the news via an associate of Pop's, a lawyer I hadn't met more than three or four times.

***

"Dario?" he asked when I answered my secure cell line. It was 6:30 in the fuckin' morning.

"That's me. Whoever this is, it's 6:30 in the fuckin' morning so this better be good."

"Stan, Tom's lawyer in Thailand. I'm at the airport, on my way to you. I need a meet. I'm arriving tomorrow night, your time. Where can we meet?"

"We can't discuss whatever this is about on the phone when you get here?"

"Absolutely not."

"It can't wait until day after tomorrow?"

"If need be, but I'd prefer to speak to you sooner if possible."

"You headin' here for any other reason?"

"No."

"Email your flight details to my receptionist. We'll pick you up." I gave him the email address.

I had no clue what this was about. Stan and my pop had a friendship that went back decades. I had shit to do, I was busy, but this sounded like something that needed my attention. Yet another axe about to fall, I could just feel it. But I had no idea how big that axe was until Stan arrived and spilled the beans about my birthday gift.

***

At 9:30 the next night, Dex, a buddy and someone who worked for us doing security and other errands, brought Stan to my place. My place was a condo downtown, just a five-minute walk from the Ferrano Enterprises office.

I told him to wait out front and to drive Stan back to his hotel afterwards. I poured Stan a drink and invited him to sit.

"I'm a busy man. I know you are as well. You spent almost a whole day on a plane to come here unannounced for something clearly pretty important. Lay it on me."

"Your apartment? When was the last time it was swept?"

He was talking about surveillance devices.

"It's clean," I told him.

"Guaranteed?" he prodded.

I raised a brow at him. "You don't know me real well, Stan, but if I say it's clean, it's clean. I do not talk out of my ass."

"Apologies. There are a few matters we need to discuss about business ventures of Tom's overseas that he had me help him with. I'll need some direction in a few areas from you and your brother. On top of that and most pressing, your father, rest his soul, my sincere condolences, he bought something for you before he died and paid me handsomely to arrange it. He said it was a birthday gift. Happy belated. The gift is something less than above board, so I need to be cautious. Very cautious."

I gave the guy the once-over. He was tall, thin, gray-haired, and 60ish with a receding hairline and a ruddy complexion. He looked totally respectable. He was anything but. He handled some shady-as-fuck shit in Thailand and that part of the world for my father. I didn't know all of what they got up to, but we were finding out that Pop had a lot goin' on that he'd never briefed my brother or me about. He had a small import/export business and it was mostly a front for things that weren't exactly legit and he dabbled in some not-so-legal areas in several countries. The good news was that there were off-shore accounts with a lot of dough left to me and my siblings. The bad news? Besides the fact that there were more unsavory businesses and relationships to end slash unload … was the news of what my birthday gift was.

"I don't know how knowledgeable you are about a certain private resort your father profited and partook from," he said cautiously.

"Unfortunately, Stan, it seems that me and my brother were not nearly as knowledgeable in a few areas as we'd like to have been."

"How can I reach your brother, by the way? I called his home but the number forwards to your office."

"He's on his honeymoon. You can speak to me about anything

outstanding regarding my father's affairs. Do you need something related to Tommy directly?"

"No, I can deal with you."

"So, that pressing reason you're here?"

"Right." He sipped his drink. "We'll deal with the matter that impacts you the most first. Your, erm, birthday gift. Your father was rather involved with a certain secret exclusive club that involves entertaining men with females, or males if they prefer. Trained entertainment." He held up air quotes at the word entertainment. "I'm not sure if you're aware of the association."

"Trained females?"

"Let's call a spade a spade, Dario. I'll stop beating around the bush."

"Please do." Like I've got all fucking night to play guessing games.

"Your father was part owner in a resort, an extremely exclusive resort. That resort has human assets on site for erm... entertainment, but occasionally pairs men or sometimes women who want trained slaves... to take off-site. Pairs them with the type of slave they desire. Your father partook. He decided to have one of those assets transferred to you before he died. He told me when he arranged it that it was to be a surprise birthday gift for you and that you'd marry her. That transaction is nearly ready. It just needs a few details from you for that order to be completed. This was a big deal for the resort to do. It was only due to Tom's perceived value to this organization that he was able to acquire this specific asset for you. Perhaps you or your brother should speak to your father's business partners at this club in order to determine the best way to move forward with the partnership in Tom's absence."

"My father arranged a slave for me for my birthday?"

"Yes."

"My father arranged for me to be given a slave? To keep? To marry?"

"That's right."

"I don't want it." I shot up to my feet. The conversation I'd had with him about the mail-order bride came over me then. No fuckin' way. I knew that he knew people who profited from human trafficking. I knew nothing about a resort, knew he did a little business linked with that trade, but did not know he was a partner. To order a slave for me when I'd joked about wanting a mail-order bride? My father had been getting increasingly irrational in the months before he died. How in a million years could he think I'd be cool with this?

"I'm afraid it's not as simple as declining the gift."

"I don't fuckin' want it." I started to pace.

"Dare," he said, like he knew me well enough to call me that.

I shook my head. "I'll need you to facilitate the sale of his shares of that business. Sell them Pop's shares back and put the money in an offshore account. In fact, detail all of what Pop had goin' with you so I can arrange for you to follow suit with everything else. I have a lot of shit to sort out locally and don't have time for overseas businesses to take up my time. I---"

Stan silenced me by taking an orange envelope out of his briefcase and putting it on my coffee table.

When I paused, he said, "It's a complex situation and I think it's one you need to handle delicately. Not accepting her, in fact not letting the partners think you were well aware of this transaction from the start… it would raise some serious red flags to your father's partners." He motioned to the envelope. "This is a tablet and it contains her details. You'll have an hour to look it over once you turn it on and then all details will be wiped. You turn it on with your fingerprint. Have a look and then sleep on this and call me in the morning. I'm staying at the Renaissance hotel down the road---"

Now it was my turn to cut him off. "How in the fuck is this programmed with my fingerprint?"

Stan let out a slow breath and looked at me with a careful intensity. "Your father prepared everything, supplied the fingerprint."

"Fuck, Stan. I need to think." I walked to the door.

"There is a lot at stake. Your father always spoke highly of your business savvy, Dario. I know you're in shock but
---"

"Yeah, I need to think," I told him. "Like, now."

He picked up his briefcase and headed for the door. "I'll leave you to it then. I don't normally get this involved. I know this goes on but I don't partake. Don't ask; don't tell. But your father asked me to handle this transaction personally for him and I firmly believe that if you decline and if you hastily attempt to exit this business, you'll raise some serious red flags with them. These are major players, powerful people, son. Sleep on this."

I didn't like the condescension of the "son" but he was not wrong.

"I'll text you my local cell number. Call me tomorrow after you've thought on this. I fly back out the day after tomorrow. We have other business to discuss as well. I hope we'll continue to have a business relationship. Your father and I made each other a lot of money. I'm sure we can carry on that way with myself and you and Tommy."

I shut the door, barely acknowledging him. I loosened my tie, paced a minute, running my fingers through my hair. He was right. I had to play things out careful-like. I should've been more guarded with him, but what a fucking shock. My pop's business partners would see me as a threat if I didn't play things carefully and in that kind of business they would deal with any perceived threat accordingly. Fuck. I needed this added complication as much as I needed a hole in the head.

***

I'd talked things over with my brother and we agreed I needed to handle this in person. I'd have to play things cool with these partners, do a meet and then figure out the right exit strategy. In addition to buying me a slave for my birthday, Pop had essentially bequeathed us a piece of a human trafficking ring and that was absolutely fucked. It'd make our exit strategy even more complicated than it already was.

The best thing we figured we could do would be to pick this girl up and help her reintegrate into society. We'd probably have to fake her death and help her move on with her life somewhere fresh.

Tommy told me he knew of the place. He remembered Pop telling him about a trip to Thailand a few years ago where he was staying at a resort with sex slaves. Pop hadn't said much back then but Tommy knew of that place as well as a similar place in Mexico. He said Pop occasionally did business with stakeholders in those businesses but Tommy hadn't known he was an actual partner.

Before going to sleep I'd opened the envelope and lifted out a small tablet. Immediately after giving it my print, which I fuckin' hated, I was greeted by a slideshow of photos of a gorgeous girl. Long, sleek hair almost to her waist. Her specs read 5,5", 115 pounds, 34C, 27" waist. It said she had a pink treble clef tattoo on her left hip and a white bass clef on her right hip, pink music note on her inner thigh. Her ears, eyebrow, nose, upper lip, tongue, and belly button were all pierced but it said in brackets she now only wore earrings in her ears and navel. She had never been pregnant and had healed in the last two years from a broken wrist and a fractured ankle, two different occasions.

She was O positive blood type, redheaded, blue-eyed. She had an IUD and as of the transaction close date she'd been taken off the rotation and had since been off limits sexually to anyone in preparation for her transition to me. By the looks of things, Pop had finished the transaction and she'd been taken off rotation just a few days before he got shot by Jesse Romero's crew.

The boudoir style photos I flicked through were black and white except for one, her Alaska driver's license. In that color picture her hair was wavy and wild. It looked auburn with highlights the color of copper or maybe copper with auburn highlights. It was both. She had the piercings in, she had a look of mischief, like she wanted to give the camera the finger, a smile on her face. She barely resembled the straight-haired expressionless girl in the boudoir photos.

They called her "Felicia Sapphire", the quotes telling me it wasn't her real name. It didn't list details about her true identity and the license had identifying details blacked out. At the end of the slideshow was a note stating that if I wanted nude photos, they would be made available. There was an additional screen that said "report" but there was no information on that page, just a blank spreadsheet that said 'error' in the first cell.

Before I crashed for the night, I texted Stan and told him to be at my apartment at seven in the morning, for a conversation and told him there was a missing report from the tablet.

Once that hour was up and I'd seen that the info wasn't accessible any longer, I hoofed the tablet with a pair of boots on and then chucked it down my building's garbage chute.

***

Three days later, I was on a flight to Bangkok. I'd done some juggling and delegating at the office with my staff, a consulting firm I'd hired to help me prep the subsidiaries we wanted to unload in order to put them up for sale, and asked a few of my key guys to be my eyes and ears with everything else.

Business was winding down in a number of areas. I'd sold all the local debts to a factoring company who paid a decent rate to buy the debts, since we'd done them all with contracts under our financial services wing, and those who'd been in debt with us now got to deal with a collection agency instead of bloodthirsty thugs like Tino and his crew if they were late for a payment.

We were in talks to sell a few of the retail and hospitality businesses. Businesses we were part owners in were being sold to the existing partners.

We were keeping the chain of coffee shops, but would be hands-off by hiring a few extra people to run the day-to-day and all the locations would be franchises so it'd just be royalties coming our way. We were talking about gifting Venetia, our Italian restaurant that was run by Eddy, to Luc and Ed.

We'd backed off some of the other shady stuff, too. Not all of it. But it was work-in-progress. There were still people in our pockets but that'd all get slowly phased out as the companies under Ferrano Enterprises were all sold. The construction arm and the nightclubs we owned would take more clean-up before being sold and other than a few associations that all had or would have time limits on the relationships, that'd be the last bit of it. I was trying to take care of our guys, too. Some of our key guys had been offered first refusal on some of the businesses or given our blessing to go onto other ventures. It was all working out. All working out fairly smoothly with just a few kinks now and then until now, when all the Thailand shit had been dumped in my lap.

Stan had gone ahead already with some directions from me on how to handle some of the other business ventures he'd told me about and he would be picking me up at the airport. From there he was dropping me at another location where I'd be picked up by a guy named Gan Chen, general manager and one of the founding partners of Kruna, the name of the resort. He'd said Kruna meant *please* in Thai, and had dual royalty meanings in Croatian. The place was designed to please, to make visitors feel like they'd been crowned royals.

Kruna was on a gated waterfront property outside Bangkok, classified to the public as a private time-share community. Most of what they did involved entertaining on-site with slaves. Stan said it was only very occasionally that they parted with them and that the slave sold to become mine was considered an exceptional asset.

I didn't know how Tommy and I would exit this partnership yet, but for the moment I needed to get in, assess the place and the management, pick her up, get home, and then figure out what to do next. All without arousing any suspicion. This would be natural for me. I often dealt in shady businesses with dangerous people. I could handle myself. But I'd never dealt with human trafficking at this level and I'd certainly never handled a transaction that was so personal --- a female being prepped to be handed off to become my wife slash personal sex slave. I had a plan, not a very in-depth one, but I had a plan and that entailed getting in, making them think I was a friend, and getting her back home.

From there, I'd tell the girl she was out of the sex trade and I'd help her get on with her life. Before I left, I briefed Zack Jacobs, our PI. I'd get him some details and then he'd assess and get us some information to help us determine an exit strategy.

I'd do all this as fast as possible so that I could finish my task of selling off the rest of Ferrano Enterprise's assets. Who knew how cracked this sex slave would be and whether or not she'd be another risk to us. But, I'd see how things went and decide from there. Hopefully she wasn't going to be a problem we'd have to dispose of. Hopefully we were at a point in our lives where we could be past all that.

CHAPTER TWO

Felicia

When Cleo, my handler, told me a little under two months ago that I'd been sold I was a numb walking zombie for hours after the fact, maybe even days. I wasn't sure, at first, if she was playing a game with me. She'd snarled it in my ear and stormed away, furious. A few hours after she imparted this info, she took me from where I'd been left sitting in the slave courtyard over to Rafe's office. He confirmed it.

Rafe was Kruna's warden, in essence, and he was not my favorite person but I was one of his favorites, which worked in my favor. When I was brought to his office where he sat with his boss, Mr. Chen, I was tweaking, not sure if Cleo was playing a game designed to put me off my game, getting me in trouble, or what.

"Felicia, darling, sit," Rafe said. Rafe was a short and bald muscular Spanish guy who looked like a steroid user. He always wore giant princess cut diamond stud earrings that looked totally stupid on him. He was about forty-five, but dressed like he was twenty and on his way to go clubbing. Mr. Chen was a shorter but older Asian in an expensive suit but he had a long salt and pepper ponytail and goatee. He was also physically ripped, with the body of a 20-year-old. He was a Kung Fu expert.

I squatted to go to the floor.

"I said sit, not kneel. On the chair, Felicia," Rafe corrected. I did as I was told.

"Cleo told you that your time here is almost done?" Rafe asked.

"Yes, Sir."

"Myself and Mr. Chen will brief you. You're on that chair because your status has been elevated. You're getting married, Felicia. Congratulations. As of ten minutes ago you are no longer owned by Kruna."

I kept my eyes fixed on the window behind them. Unseeing. My heart sped up. I held my emotions in check.

Mr. Chen spoke up. "Felicia?"

"Yes, Sir?"

"You're very lucky to have been matched for this. Cleopatra suggested it wasn't the right role for you, but a redhead was requested with your sexual proclivities and we had no better match. You've been an exceptional asset to Kruna. You will be missed."

"Thank you, Sir."

"Your future husband is an important man, the son of one of our most valued benefactors and that benefactor is recently deceased so his sons are now partners. As you yourself know, death can change everything. These sons will help us take Kruna to a new level of success, we're sure, so we expect that you will exemplify all that we stand for here. It's vitally important that you do."

"I will, Sir."

My future husband. The words echoed in my head.

"I can't stress this enough, Felicia. You're to be his wife."

"I understand, Sir."

"You are excused. Now that you officially have a Master you are no longer available to patrons or staff. Your collar will be changed immediately. You'll continue to exercise daily and it may be weeks or longer until he comes for you so you may rest but you will not forget all you've been taught. If when he arrives your Master wants additional training, you'll be enrolled in an advanced transition program to complete before you leave. As of now you are no longer Kruna property but we are stewards in your Master's absence."

"Thank you, Sirs. It's an honor to be chosen."

I was escorted back to my room by Cleo and one of the other handlers. Cleo radiated barely restrained fury all the way back. When she closed the door after changing my collar and I was alone, I let out a breath that it felt like I'd been holding in. Holding in for years.

I would have weeks of peace. Weeks. What would come after that could be anything. It could be hell on earth. It could make me wish I was back here (although not likely as I'd lived in this particular hell long enough). But despite the fact that the next phase of my life or my next phase of my hell was unknown, I had weeks of peace to look forward to and I hadn't had anything specific to look forward to in a very long time, so I curled up on the thin mat on the floor that had been my bed for 21 months and 9 days and faced the wall so that the cameras wouldn't see my face. Then I did something I hadn't done in 19 months; I quietly let tears fall.

***

I was going to meet my Master and future husband today. It'd been almost two months. They were weird weeks of not being Felicia. Weird weeks of being no one, just this shadow at Kruna with the black X on her throat.

I'd be assessed through spending time with him for a few days here and then he would either take me with him or he'd leave me here for some additional training wherever he saw deficiencies. Or, he'd reject me and they'd choose someone else for him. This was my one chance. If it didn't happen, I would not get another. Failure was not an option.

I had been sick to my stomach for days with worry. Really, I'd been worried for weeks. The peace I'd thought I'd get was riddled with worries about my future. I knew nothing about him other than the fact that he was a son of a partner in Kruna, an American, and that he'd requested a redhead with a big sexual appetite. I knew nothing about what life would be like after I was taken away from this place.

They had me dressed in a pale flowy peach summer dress, I wore nude, heeled sandals, and my hair was trimmed to the middle of my back and then tamed by a flat iron, like it typically was. I wore minimal makeup. I was given new and larger than usual blue sapphire stud earrings to wear with a matching sapphire tennis bracelet. They matched the jewel on my navel as well. I was dressed very differently from what I typically wore, which rarely strayed from lingerie. I hadn't dressed in clothing designed for the real world for almost two years. Underneath the dress were white thigh-high stockings with lace garters and matching bra and panties.

Cleo removed the blue leather collar with a dangling X of black obsidian gems on the front before escorting me to a guest suite. I immediately got to my knees to assume my standard waiting pose when Cleo snapped at me to sit on the edge of the bed instead. I avoided the urge to frown and internally shuddered that I had to avoid the urge. Being in street clothes must be messing with my brain because I didn't normally show any emotion and at this stage didn't have to tell myself to hide it because it came so naturally to me to keep it all locked away. I was on autopilot all the time. But this situation had me off my game.

Add to that having a naked throat and then being told to do something as simple as sit on a bed instead of waiting on the floor in the pose I'd been trained to wait in were both foreign. I sat and placed my hands in my lap.

Cleo leaned close to my ear and whispered a warning that was soft in volume but the tone was laced with venom. "Fuck this up and that ass is mine, you. I won't be lenient."

Cleo, Cleopatra Jade, was a tall and elegant forty-seven-year-old Asian woman with flawless skin, not a wrinkle on her super skinny face, and zero per cent body fat. She had the temper of a Tasmanian devil. She'd stayed away from me the past six weeks but glared at me every time I was in her orbit. I knew that if I was lucky, I'd never see her again. It wouldn't be lucky, exactly, because I didn't know what was next for me and I didn't dare to hope, but I'd be forever grateful to never be in her evil clutches again.

I remained frozen, waiting for my future husband. I hadn't received another brief, which was strange. I expected to be told what persona to assume, what he wanted from my behavior, but that never came. I was on edge because without directions I didn't know what to do with myself. I had found my way in this world because I always knew what was expected of me, but without any instructions to fortify my armor I was feeling uneasy. All I could do was try my best to hide it.

Dare

I opened the door to the room that had been assigned to me for my stay, which they suggested be two days or longer, as lengthy as I wanted, and I knew that I had to play this carefully. It was a spacious room with a king-sized bed and a desk with adjoining bathroom. I was told that under the bed were restraints, whips, and a chest of sex toys, if I wanted them, and that there was a hatch in the ceiling that contained a swing. It was a nice room despite being discreetly equipped for kink or sexual torture and looked like any typical five-star hotel room. On the edge of the bed sat Felicia Sapphire, my slave.

I couldn't tell this girl what my plans were. She had to think she was being sold to me. I had to get in and get out and then I'd reveal to her that she was not to be my wife or my slave, but that she would instead gain her freedom back under some very specific conditions that would protect her and protect me and my family from blowback. I had to play things carefully because I did not need to be alerting these scumbags to the fact that I was not likeminded. I didn't know if anything here was being recorded or filmed so I had to play this game carefully.

She was on the edge of a king-sized bed, staring at her hands in her lap. Her beauty took my breath away for a second. She had the face of an angel, almost porcelain doll-like, straight shiny copper-toned hair with auburn highlights. It fell to just past her breasts, arranged over one shoulder and she was tiny, but looked toned and fit.

The short, bald, Spanish guy who Chen had left me with when he got an urgent call had offered to escort me to the room, but I said I'd like to meet my bride-to-be for the first time alone. I added a smirk for good measure

He'd smirked back, saying, "By all means; I completely understand. She's been waiting for you." He sent me ahead with a bellboy with plans to have another conversation later that evening or the following morning. The bellboy took my suitcase to the closet and closed the door and then I nodded at him as he shut the door behind himself. I locked it.

Felicia

I'd heard the door open and close and I knew it was the moment of truth. I had no expectations. I knew better than to try to anticipate what would be next. I only knew that I was to not only be owned by this man but was to become his wife, too. That suggested that there would be a certain degree of freedom because the man didn't just want a slave in his bedroom but wanted the appearance of legitimacy and normalcy that having a wife suggested. I might be expected to have children by him. I'd heard he was American and that meant I might get off this continent. I'd get away from *them*, the ones who broke me, who took the person I was and crushed her into dust.

It also meant an extreme amount of responsibility. To hit this level of elite meant that I was expected to be perfection, Kruna personified. I'd represent him to the world. I'd represent Kruna to him. I didn't know if he was attractive, ugly, psychotic, abusive, or what sexual tastes he would have; all I knew was that I couldn't screw up.

All of what he was and what my life would be would reveal itself over the coming days. I knew that being sold to become a wife was a level of elite that some women here aspired to, that most feared due to the level of responsibility, but that precious few actually got. It would be as close to normal as normal could get for us. I'd hit the slave girl jackpot for all intents and purposes. There had only been six in all of Kruna history, which dated back to the early 1970s, that became wives, only thirty-six that had been sold. I would be the seventh wife, thirty-seventh slave sold.

I also knew what it did not mean. It did not mean life like it had resembled just over two years ago when I went to Thailand and bought myself trouble like I'd never imagined in my worst nightmares. The girl I was back then? The fun-loving fearless girl who loved to drive fast, loved loud music, partying, raves, mechanical bull-riding, playing ice hockey, and roller derby? The girl who wasn't afraid to express her opinions and tell people where to go? She was gone. I'd shed that skin and become someone else because that was what needed to happen in order for me to survive.

Since I'd been here, I'd seen girls survive and I'd seen some who did not. I'd also seen that one girl who'd left a few years earlier to become slave number thirty-four get returned when her Master died. She committed suicide three days after coming back. From her story I knew I had to try to get out. What she'd found on the other side probably wasn't exactly bliss, but compared to Kruna it had been for her. So much so that being brought back here was worse than death.

I aspired to achieve whatever might be on the other side, even if it might not be bliss. It was something to hold onto and so that's what I'd worked at. I went on autopilot to do what needed to be done and I'd succeeded. I was about to face the best-case scenario, marriage. But I wasn't exactly jumping for joy because although I'd achieved my goal it didn't mean I was lucky. I'd soon find out just how lucky or unlucky I was. It didn't mean I'd be happy or free.

And this only happened because Mr. Frost died. If he were still here, I might not still be here; I might be dead by now. If he were still here, he'd never have let me leave this place. He told me that daily. But fate was kind enough to take him from my life and now I was looking at Point C.

Succeeding in being sold also didn't even mean I'd never, ever see Kruna again, either, because I knew guests and partners who visited often brought their slaves with them. It just meant a different kind of prison from what I had right now and I didn't know if it'd be better or if it'd be worse, but I knew it was away from here and that was precisely what I had been working toward because that was the only thing I could do, the only hope I had.

I waited until my Master addressed me. It felt like it took a long time for that to happen. I wished I knew what role to play. Did I look up coquettishly? Should I give off a persona of innocence? I didn't know what he wanted. He was standing in front of me, but I knew better than to make eye contact before being permitted.

"Felicia," he finally said. I looked up with what I hoped was a blank expression and saw him for the first time.

He was young. Under thirty. He was dressed in a light gray suit with a cream-colored shirt and no tie. He had wavy blond hair, longish, almost to his collar, flopping over one eye. Bluish grey eyes, full lips, olive skin, and he looked tall from this angle. He was male model gorgeous and wore that suit well. Gorgeous didn't matter in this world because gorgeous could also mean cruel, crazy, or disgusting. But beyond good-looking… he looked angry. No, not angry, he looked pissed. Pissed *right* off.

My heart skipped a beat, worrying about how the anger would come at me. I knew from experience that it could be unleashed in a variety of ways and based on the tension he was emitting and based on what I knew from past experience: I should expect the unexpected. I kept my blank gaze on his face and waited for direction, but he just stood there, staring at me, looking angry.

"Dario Ferrano. Nice to meet you." He extended a hand, finally. I reached out so he could take my hand. He held it for a second, staring at me with something I read as disgust etched in his features. Was I a letdown? Would he reject me and request another? *Please no.*

"It's very nice to meet you, Master. I've been waiting for today for a long time," I answered and his grip tightened almost painfully. His eyes flashed with something scary. I swallowed back the wince I'd almost made.

For another beat there was nothing but intensity in the room, so I tore my eyes away from looking at him and softly asked, "Is there something I can do for you, Sir?"

He crouched low and tipped my chin up with his index finger. "You can look at me when you speak to me for a start. Don't be afraid to look at me."

"Yes, Master."

He straightened back up to standing, flexing his jaw muscles for a moment, and then his eyes traveled the perimeter of the room for a minute. Then he said, "Let me look at you. Up."

I stood up.

"Twirl slowly," he commanded.

I obeyed.

"Your hair," he said. "That's not natural?"

"No Sir. The color is, but it's not straight. It was straightened this morning."

"I'd prefer you not straighten it."

"Yes, Sir."

He was quiet for a minute, assessing me.

"Have you had dinner?"

"No, Sir."

"Is now around the time you'd usually eat?"

"I don't know what time it is, Sir."

He looked at his wristwatch. "Almost 5:30."

"Yes, Sir. I usually eat between five and seven."

"Stop calling me Sir."

"Yes, Master."

"Call me Dare or Dario."

"Yes, Dare." Sensation prickled in me at using his name. But if I was to be his wife I'd have to do that in public. Public. I pushed away my anxiety.

"Where do you have dinner?"

"If I'm not entertaining, I eat dinner with the others who are off-duty. If I am entertaining, I sit at the feet of the patron I'm attending to while he or she eats."

"Where?"

"In the patron's suite or in one of the dining areas, Sir. I mean Dare. Sorry, Sir. I mean Dare." My face heated. I hadn't felt flustered like this in… in I don't know how long. If I wasn't more careful, I was going to be punished for this. It had been a long time since I'd been punished. And even worse, I could screw this up. I directed my brain to forget what was at stake here and to just go on autopilot.

A to B. A to B. That's what I needed to do to get to C. I'm at C now.

Don't mess up.

He moved to the desk beside the bed, lifted a telephone and pushed a button. "I want menus for dinner, please. Right, okay."

He opened a bedside table drawer and pulled menus out. "I've got them. No, we'll dine in the suite. Right. Fine." He hung up.

I remained standing at the end of the bed. He sat down at the head of the bed.

"What's good here?" he asked and I turned to face him. He passed a menu to me.

"What do you like, S--" I blushed again. "Dare?"

He gave me a little smile and my heart spasmed. But I was thinking, 'wait for it…' knowing that the crazy or kinky or evil or a combo of any or all of the above would reveal itself sooner or later. It usually didn't take long. The longer it took the more chances of it being brutal when it came.

"I like everything. What do you like?"

"I…" I swallowed and then stupidly I said, "Pasta."

Damn, why did I give him a personal answer? I knew better than to give anyone ammo that could be used against me. I hadn't had pasta in two years and the answer just slipped. How could I let it slip?

"They don't serve pasta?" He opened the menu and looked. "There's a shit load of pasta."

I shook my head a little. "I'm not permitted pasta." I stopped myself from ending with the 'Sir'.

"Why not?" He cocked an eyebrow.

"Too fattening," I answered.

His eyes roved over me and I knew he was assessing my body shape. I was very slender. I was fit and healthy but definitely 10-15 pounds underweight.

"What sauce do you like on your pasta?"

My eyes widened. "Anything, Sir. Dare." Another blush.

"What's your favorite?"

"Car- carbonara or alfredo." I'd already let it slip so might as well let it all hang out.

He smiled at me again. My belly fluttered at that smile. He was very attractive.

"Sounds good." He picked up the phone and said, "Dario Ferrano. Need a table for two in my room. No, two chairs. Yes, two. Two orders of pasta carbonara. An extra-large order of garlic bread with cheese. Mozzarella. A bottle of red. And a big bowl of Cesar salad. Extra bacon. Bacon, not that bacon bit shit." He winked at me. "Four bottles of water and two bottles of orange Gatorade."

I fought the urge to smile. I fought the urge to relax. I fought the urge to cry out in elation as I hadn't eaten a meal like that in 2 years. But then a chill shot up my spine because maybe he was planning to sit and eat it in front of me and degrade me. Sadly, that game was not new to me.

Dare

She was reserved. She was guarded. She was doing her very best to behave like an absolute angel. She was so careful about every word she said and she'd looked embarrassed a few times, like she'd slipped up, but had never said anything that I could construe as a slip-up other than calling me Sir after I'd asked her not to. She looked healthy but I could see in her eyes that she was far from healthy emotionally speaking. I wanted to tell her she was close to freedom, that we just had to play things out for 2 days here and that I'd get her out of here but I knew I couldn't tell her. I had to remain aloof and at the same time give anyone who might be watching us on camera the impression that I was just like them.

In my brief meeting earlier with three men who had been kissing my ass, knowing I was Tom Ferrano's son, I did not let them think I was anything but Tom's son in terms of my goals and objectives. They said very little about her, stating they wanted to let me meet and assess her and then we'd have another conversation. They assured me that she had been carefully trained and was an exceptional slave with no punishable infractions in more than 18 months. She had not been touched sexually since her last clear STD test when she was put on ice to wait for me.

Stan Smith had suggested to me that it'd be best not to ask questions about her origin and her past. I wouldn't care about that shit if I was just a typical client of theirs. I'd find that out later when I helped her get back to some semblance of a normal life. I remarked to the scumbags that I was looking forward to meeting my bride-to-be but that I needed to get home quickly as we were still sorting my father's affairs out after his untimely death. I texted my brother to tell him I'd arrived safely and texted Stan the same and said I'd call him when I got back home and give him further instructions.

Felicia

When the food came and they brought a table with two chairs I wasn't sure what to do with myself. Usually, once a patron sat, I would wait for him to snap his fingers and I'd move to his feet. But I wasn't generally waiting seated on a bed, I was typically already on the floor on my knees.

When he sat, he looked at me. "You good to eat?"

"May I use the facilities first please, Master?"

He looked annoyed but waved his hand toward the bathroom. I stiffly moved to the bathroom and once behind closed doors I let out a big breath.

When I came back from washing my hands and taking a moment to compose myself, he was sitting, looking broody. I hurried to his side and got to the floor. I didn't want to presume I was to sit at the table with him even if there were two chairs. It was better to be corrected for not taking kindness than to be punished for taking liberties.

I was on the floor on my knees beside his leg.

"Sit at the table." His body was locked tight. He was angry.

I got up and sat at the table and my eyes landed on the mountain of food between us.

"Eat," he said and poured me a glass of wine.

I lifted a fork and twirled a small amount of pasta on the fork, maybe just three or four strands of linguine. Dare heaped creamy bacon and parmesan-coated romaine lettuce with buttery-looking croutons onto my plate beside the pasta and held the platter of garlic bread in my direction with a jerk of his chin.

I took a piece of thick white bread laden with golden crispy cheese. My stomach rumbled at the sight of it. "Thank you," I answered softly, hoping he hadn't heard my stomach. But it was so loud he would've had to have heard it.

He glanced up at the ceiling and rolled his eyes and then drank back half of the glass of wine. I didn't want to upset him.

I put the forkful of pasta in my mouth. It was heavenly. I tried not to show it but wanted to moan, it was so delicious. His anger appeared to soften a little as he watched me eat.

I subsisted on small portions of soup, fish and rice and vegetables without condiments, for the most part. I occasionally got chicken or steak, usually handfed to me from a patron. Once in a while I'd get a chocolate covered strawberry or something decadent but never in copious amounts. I was religiously weighed and if I went up more than a pound my workout regimen would escalate from intense to boot camp rigid.

He ate, watching me as he did. Under his scrutiny I felt very self-conscious about eating but didn't want to insult how generous he had been with the food he had ordered for me.

I took a bite of the garlic bread with cheese and suppressed the urge to moan in ecstasy. I couldn't put away all the food he'd ordered for me; I was used to eating small meals, but hated to waste it so I ate more than I could really manage, enjoying it but starting to feel discomfort. We ate in silence, awkward silence. So awkward that he got up and put the television on, put it on a news channel, and he watched it while eating. I couldn't recall the last time I'd watched news on television, or anything other than porn.

"You look full," he said quietly, wiping his mouth with a linen napkin and stepping away from the table. "You don't have to keep going." He reached inside his blazer pocket and produced a pewter cigarette case and matching lighter.

"I'm stepping out to the balcony for a smoke. Be right back." He gave me a thin smile.

When he came back, he looked at me quizzically. I was still sitting at the table, not sure what to do with myself. If he'd left me on the floor, I'd know what was expected; it would be expected that I'd sit and await his direction. But up here at eye level with him I didn't know what to do with myself.

"How do we get rid of this?" he asked me.

"You can dial 9 for housekeeping. Would you like me to do that…Dare?"

He shook his head. "I can do it." He called for housekeeping on the room phone and then sat back on the bed and kicked his shoes off.

A moment passed where I sat watching the television from the table and he thumbed away on his smartphone. There was a knock at the door.

He put his shoes back on and went to it and opened it. Cleo and Rafe were in the doorway, two housekeeping staff members behind them.

"Forgive the intrusion, Mr. Ferrano, but because you requested housekeeping, I thought it might be an opportune moment to speak with you."

"Come in," Dare said.

Cleo and Rafe both looked to me, sitting at the table with a half-eaten plate of pasta, creamy salad, and cheesy bread. Cleo's eyebrows shot up but she quickly reined in her shock. I averted my gaze and then fixed my eyes on my lap.

Once the door was closed, Dare started with, "What can I do for you?"

"We wanted to ask if you have any requests for Felicia this evening that we might help with."

"Meaning?" Dare looked down at Rafe and he looked pissed off.

"Felicia's attire. Do you have any requirements?"

"I don't," Dare replied and then added, "In fact, I'd like to leave tomorrow after my meeting with Chen so if you can have her things packed and arrange transportation to the airport that'd be appreciated."

"Mr. Ferrano," Rafe said, looking like he was choosing his words carefully, "We highly recommend you stay at least until the day after tomorrow. We'd be happy for you to stay even longer, as long as you like, but we recommend staying at least that long. And we're happy to arrange for transportation when you're ready to go but I urge you to consider staying at least one more day."

"And why is that?" Dare looked down at Rafe and Rafe looked intimidated. I suppressed the urge to enjoy what I was seeing, worried it might show on my face. Rafe wasn't the worst guy around here but who he was in front of patrons wasn't who we was when he was pissed off. I hadn't had a direct punishment from him since being broken but I had seen him give them out and he could wield a whip like nobody's business.

"We find that optimally, Sir, a Master should spend at least a few nights here at the resort with his acquisition. We want you to get acquainted with Felicia while you have an opportunity to notify us of any corrections you want made. We can also help you plan to ensure your fiancée seamlessly transitions into her new life. We usually keep her for thirty days as a minimum and then you return to inspect and then pick her up."

"What if she's fine as is?"

"Many patrons are happy with their acquisition because of the painstaking preparation we've already taken. If the Master prefers to complete his own training, we absolutely respect that. She is already yours. We have no rights to put rules forth regarding your property. She is already your property. But in a scenario such as yours where she will be integrated into your life in a marital capacity… see, she hasn't been off the resort yet and we would normally run a few trials to integrate her into life outside Kruna and find that it's often helpful when masters utilize our services to---"

Dare cut him off, "Oh, I'll be completing her training, all right. I'm looking forward to it."

I glanced at him and saw a glimmer in his eye that made my heart skip a beat. He eyed me from head to toe and then he smirked. His eyes heated and I felt a swish of heat between my legs while at the same time fought back fear. Cleo and Rafe appeared to see it too. Cleo got a sickeningly satisfied smile on her face.

"Very well, Mr. Ferrano. It's your choice, of course; we know you are a very busy man. We just like to see that your acquisition is suitably prepared, so that you'll be happy in every way."

"I suspect I will be." He glanced at me. "Are you worried she won't behave?"

"Absolutely not! Felicia is exceptional. She---"

"Because I'm eager to complete her training. She will behave. No concerns there."

The gleam in his eyes made my blood run cold.

"We have no concerns, Sir, otherwise she wouldn't be with you right now. We chose very carefully and matched her specifically to your needs. We still recommend you stay tomorrow night if possible so that if there are any inadequacies or you have major issues, we have an opportunity to address them or if needed swap out your Felicia for another. If you opt for another, we again recommend at least 48 hours on site for you to assess---"

"Fine. I'll stay the extra day. But that's a maximum. I have things at home to see to. And I'll let you know if any changes need to be made." Dare cut him off again.

"Excellent. So, should you require any assistance this evening please do not hesitate to contact me personally at extension 252. If I'm to be away from my phone I will forward it to someone else who can handle anything that arises for you. Perhaps we can meet for or after breakfast. Mr. Chen would like me to accompany him while he gives you a tour of Kruna."

"Fine." Dario strolled to the door and opened it and then motioned toward the open doorway, making no bones about his desire for them to leave.

Two housekeeping staff members came in at that point and efficiently cleared away the contents of the table and then the table and chairs. I'd risen to my feet so they could take the chair and looked to the floor but said, "Master, may I speak?"

"Speak," he answered.

"Where would you like me?"

"Sit."

I looked up at him and he motioned to the bed. Then he shut the door and locked it. Cleo and Rafe were standing directly outside the door. After the door was locked, he turned and looked at me. His expression was sort of grave.

He loosened his tie, then took it and his suit jacket off. I stared straight ahead and waited.

Dare

There was an awkward tension in the room and I wasn't sure what to do with it. This whole fucking situation was turning my stomach. I was trying to keep it together, not tip them off, not tip her off, in case a) she did something to tip them off due to being suspicious or b) the room was bugged. I just wanted the fuck outta here. It was still early, too early to crash for the night.

"Felicia, wanna take a walk?" I asked and rolled my sleeves up to the elbows and undid the top two buttons of my shirt. I needed air and away from here for a bit. And for some reason I didn't trust leaving her here when those two could come back in. I didn't want them to even breathe on her. Sick fucking scumbags.

She got to her feet. "That sounds wonderful…"

That hung like she was going to add a Sir or a Master. As we left the room, I cocked my elbow and she took my arm.

I hadn't seen much of the resort so far since I'd acted anxious to be alone with my slave. We weren't far down the hall, which looked like your garden variety hallway in any high-end resort, when I spotted a tall and thin redheaded man in his 40's walking with a woman on a leash. She was an exotic-looking young Somalian woman, crawling behind him on her hands and knees, topless, wearing just a black thong. Felicia was oblivious. I tried to hold my expression stoic. I suspected these halls had cameras, too. I didn't know whether my suite did or not but was acting on the suspicion that it did.

I had asked earlier and was told that many suites were outfitted with surveillance equipment only to keep an eye on things but that VIPs and company stakeholders were not included. Because they didn't know me yet I wouldn't trust that was true. I wasn't letting my guard down.

We passed another couple but they were walking hand in hand, dressed to the nines. The woman had a silver choker necklace on her throat with two bands crusted with rubies.

We stepped outside and it was a gorgeous night. The sun was setting; we were on a sandy beach and anyone whose mind was clear enough to notice would've thought it was a breathtaking sight. But me? I wanted the fuck outta here. She struggled a little through the sand with her high heels so we switched to a boardwalk that extended in one direction what looked like pretty far.

"Where did you grow up?" I asked her, "Alaska?"

Her eyes widened.

"How'd you get here?" I asked right after that, not giving her a chance to answer my first question.

She went pale.

"Forget it. We can discuss that later." I quickened my pace. I fought the urge to tell her the truth so I could put her mind at ease.

She kept pace with me.

I was fuming at the whole situation and I couldn't seem to rein it in. We walked for a bit and then we were at the boundary of the property way too soon. I lit a smoke and inhaled deeply, leaning against the fence, looking at her.

She stood uncomfortably in front of me, looking down. I gazed out at the water, taking my time to finish it, and then when I put the cigarette out I grabbed her hand and we walked back to the resort. By the time we were back, the sun had disappeared completely.

Felicia

By the time we got back to the building after our walk, my heart was thumping wildly against my chest because as time wore on Dare seemed more and more angry. I didn't know what I'd done wrong and I was not looking forward to being alone with him. He'd asked me personal questions, which was odd, but he never gave me a chance to answer them. I'd been relieved though, because I didn't want to answer them. No other patrons had asked those sorts of questions. They almost never asked any questions. That would intimate we were people with thoughts and feelings. *As if.*

When we got back inside the suite he said, "I need to make a few calls so I'm gonna step back outside. Maybe you can take a bubble bath or something? Watch TV. I'll be back soon."

"Yes, Sir." *Oops.*

He rolled his eyes at me and then he was gone.

***

It had been a very long time since I'd had a luxurious bubble bath alone. I'd had duties to perform in pools and baths plenty of times but a long bath on my own? It had been too long since I'd had that kind of luxury. It was decadent.

There was a knock on the door. Oh no. I hit the switch to turn the jets off.

"Yes?"

"You okay?" It was Dare's voice.

"Yes, Master!" I called out.

"I've been back ages and you were still in there so I wanted to make sure you didn't fall asleep in the tub or something."

"I'm coming now. Sorry, Sir. Uh, Dare," I called out and quickly pulled the plug.

Darn. There was nothing in here for me to dress with. I didn't know what to do. Normally there were provisions for an evening with a patron or if I was expected to be without clothes for the duration of the assignment, I'd be informed of that. This, however, wasn't an ordinary evening with a patron.

This wasn't an assignment. This was my new Master, a man who I'd been told would become my husband. I dried quickly and wrapped myself in a towel. I stepped hesitantly into the room and saw him sitting on the edge of the bed with his head in his hands, elbows propped on his knees. My scalp prickled.

"I'm so sorry to have kept you waiting, Master. But … I haven't brought anything to wear, would you like me clothed or unclothed?"

He got to his feet and rubbed the heels of his hands over his eyes, looking frustrated. He reached into the closet where his suitcase sat on a stand and pulled out a white cotton t-shirt.

"Will this do?"

"Yes, thank you."

"What else you need?"

"Hairbrush?" I asked.

He reached into his bag and pulled out a shaving bag.

"Use whatever you need," he said impatiently, not looking at me.

"Thank you. You can, if you prefer me dressed, request that my things are sent here."

He nodded, "Tomorrow. I don't wanna deal with anyone else tonight."

I gave him a nod, even though he still wasn't looking at me, and reentered the bathroom. I brushed my teeth with a new toothbrush that was stocked in all the rooms with the other toiletries. Then I swished mouthwash and towel dried my hair some more and then brushed it with Dare's hairbrush. As I did, I thought about the fact that he and I would share things like this going forward as husband and wife.

I got into his t-shirt and it covered just below my bottom. The shirt smelled like fabric softener, like Downy April Fresh, the one I'd used back home. It was a scent I hadn't had in my nostrils since arriving. I closed my eyes as I inhaled it but then the scent soured in my body, reminding me of all I'd lost. I pushed the thoughts away and walked slowly out to the room and he was coming in from the small balcony, putting his cigarette case and lighter down on the bedside table.

"Grabbin' a shower," he told me as he passed me.

"Sir?" I asked.

He gritted his teeth, "Enough with the Sir. Fuck."

"I apologize."

"Stop apologizing."

I clamped my mouth shut, unsure of how to reply.

"What did you need?" he asked, impatiently.

"Nothing, Master."

He rolled his eyes and disappeared into the bathroom. I had been about to ask where he wanted me to wait for him, on the floor, in the bed, etc. But at his reaction to the Sir and the apology I decided to just wait and see.

I sat on the edge of the bed where I'd waited for him when he first arrived and stayed there until he came back out. I wish I knew what he wanted. A few simple orders and I'd easily be able to fit the role. But with no direction and all that was at stake I was afraid I'd muck it all up. I waited, trying to get my head together.

He wore a suit well. But wow, he also wore a bath towel well. That's all he was in, a short towel around his waist and he was muscled: arms, legs, chiseled abs, the sexiest shoulders I think I'd ever seen. He was tanned and he was delicious-looking. My mouth went dry at the sight of him.

It had been a long time since I'd felt any sort of arousal before the act of being with someone. I did my job well during those acts, managed to provide enough moisture to make penetration not hurt at the start, and I always got into it, to fulfill my end. But until right now I don't think I ever, since arriving here, felt arousal before it was time to get into it and had no other choice but to turn my body on with an order from my mind because it knew what was next and what was expected of me.

Despite the fact that I'd been with some good-looking men here at Kruna, some who'd even been kind enough under the circumstances, I had a different and new set of emotions swirling through me at the sight of my Master's almost nude body. After all I'd endured looks typically meant nothing to me. I'd learned that evil came in both beautiful and ugly forms. It didn't matter. A to B. A to B. That's all I did, not noticing looks, not feeling anything but the orgasms, on complete autopilot.

Maybe it was because I hadn't had sex in six and a half weeks, probably the longest stretch of abstinence since I'd lost my virginity at the age of 14. Maybe it was just because this man was the one who'd get me out of here, as long as I didn't screw it up. That body right there could also be my only source of pleasure for the rest of my life and looking at it right now, at least I'd probably never get tired of looking at it.

Dare

She was seated on the end of the bed in just my t-shirt, her hair wet and curling but the length sitting over one shoulder. She looked up at me with piercing blue eyes and what looked like desire. There was no way she was legitimately aroused at the sight of me, not when this poor girl was a sex slave. No fucking way; I must be mis-reading the tint in her complexion, the swallow, the way she'd moistened her lips and was breathing more heavily; the way her eyes had traveled from the floor to my face and then slowly back to the floor again. Or I wasn't misreading it but she was just trained so well at it that it was all part of an act. Pop's voice echoed in my brain.

"The perfect woman. Schooled in all the ways to please a man."

Fuck, Pop. Why'd you do this to me?

Not perfect. Just doing what she was brainwashed to do.

I never wanted to parade in front of her in just a towel but she'd flustered me to the point I'd forgotten to bring clothes into the bathroom.

And in the bathroom seeing her fucking white stockings, garter belt, white lace thong, and bra laying on the vanity… it put me even more off-balance. I reached into my suitcase and grabbed a pair of black track pants with a white stripe up the legs. I went back into the bathroom and got into them, ignoring the pile of lace on the vanity.

Fuck, this next part was gonna suck.

Maybe I should go to their gym and tell her to crash and then hope she'd be asleep by the time I returned. But I didn't know what I'd see out there, what scumbags I'd have to have conversations with. Maybe here was better for tonight. I'd slept like shit on the flight so maybe I could actually sleep. Sleep would clear my brain for the meeting I had to attend in the morning with these scumbags.

When I had left before her bath, I'd stopped into Rafe Ruiz's office. He and that Asian woman were huddled in a deep discussion with a nude blonde slave who was on her knees between them. They halted their conversation and looked at me as I entered.

"I am a very possessive man," was how I greeted them. "Now that I've collected her, no one fucks with what's mine. No one talks to her or approaches her, and especially does not touch her without my permission. Understood?"

"We understand. Absolutely, Mr. Ferrano," Rafe replied.

Then he spewed a bunch of crawling-up-my-ass bullshit appeasing words. I avoided looking at the girl on the floor on her knees. If I looked at her, I'd be tempted to beat the shit out of Ruiz and that bitch standing beside him. I wasn't someone who ever wanted to beat the shit out of a woman but something about her vibe told me it was a case where I could make an exception.

"Goodnight," I said and left it at that and stepped outside for a quick messaging session on my cell with my brother, and then I returned to the suite.

When I came back out of the bathroom, I flicked the light off.

"Might as well get some shut-eye. I'm zonked from the flight."

She hesitated and then said "Okay" softly.

I climbed into the bed under the covers and said, "You can crash." I wasn't sure at first why she was still sitting there at the end of the bed but then realized she was waiting for me to tell her what I wanted her to do. I reached for the lamp but she got up and then laid down on the floor beside my side of the bed before I could get the light flicked off.

"What're you doing?" I looked down at her. She'd put her hands folded in prayer position under a cheek and was laying on the floor without a pillow or blanket. She was in my t-shirt. It had ridden up and I caught sight of the fact that she wasn't wearing panties. I pushed the unholy thoughts away, not looking, determined not to let myself feel anything but disgusted because this girl was clearly behaving the way she'd been brainwashed to behave.

She sat up quickly. "I'm so sorry. Whatever you need, Master; I wasn't sure." She stood up and climbed over me in the bed and while hovering over me quickly whipped the t-shirt off and lay down on her back beside me, spread eagled, totally nude.

"Whoa; what the fuck?" I was completely taken aback. I looked at the ceiling.

"Please enlighten me as to your needs, Dare. I want to make you happy." I could sense her fear and it was escalating.

"I'm tired, Felicia. I'm in need of sleep." She went to leave the bed. I caught her wrist. "Where are you going?"

"Would you like me to return to my room or would you like me to sleep on the floor, or?"

She looked a bit lost.

"It's okay, chill out," I said, looking her in the face, not looking at her body. Trying really hard to not look at her body.

"Sorry."

"Stop fuckin' apologizing!" I bit off.

She flinched and I felt like shit.

"I'm sorry," I told her, looking her in the eyes.

She looked baffled.

"Tell me what's on your mind, Felicia. Talk to me here. We need to communicate."

"I'm just trying to figure out how to please you, Master. I'm accustomed to being directed."

I gritted my teeth. "Just lay down and go to sleep. In the bed. I have no expectations of you right now."

I pulled the comforter back and motioned for her to get under, trying really fucking hard to not look at her nudity. She looked shell-shocked.

"What?" I snapped.

"Am I not…uh…did I do something wrong?"

I clenched my teeth and decided I needed to play things carefully here. I planned to get through this unscathed, to get out of here and then figure out our next move.

"No, Felicia. Nothing's wrong. I'm tired from the trip. We'll have plenty of time to get acquainted better later." There, that should do it.

"Are you sure you don't want me to take care of you, Dare?" she asked huskily and the change in her tone made the hairs on my arms and the back of my neck rise.

"I'm good," I mumbled. "Put the t-shirt back on."

She reached over and found it. I flicked the lamp off and squeezed my eyes shut tight. I rolled over so my back was to her.

Felicia

It didn't take me long to fall asleep. The bed was soft and felt like it was hugging me. And his presence, it did something to me, something I couldn't put my finger on. My mind was almost buzzing but it was like it was all white noise, muffled, unintelligible.

I occasionally slept in beds with patrons but normally when it happened, I was totally exhausted, completely spent by the time I fell asleep. Not tonight. He hadn't wanted any sexual favors. He fed me, walked me, let me take a bubble bath, and then clothed me and let me sleep beside him in a soft bed. He was handsome. He was young and virile. So what was wrong with him? He was angry. What else? He'd have no problem finding a woman so maybe he had very dark carnal tastes. I'd had dark; boy had I had dark. How dark would he be?

As I fell asleep, I grazed with my fingertips, the idea not of hope of a happily ever after but hope of being off this continent. Him taking me away from here could mean anything. He might be twisted and sick. I might end up cold, in the ground and pushing up daisies. But I had worked so hard to get to this moment and I wanted with all my being for it to not be all for naught. Just about anything was better than here.

I didn't dare hope for normalcy; all of that had been programmed away. I wasn't an individual with rights and freedoms; I was a slave. But I hoped that I could, I don't know, cope maybe? Maybe being away from here would make that easier. Maybe not. But maybe.

***

I slept well. I slept like a baby. And when I woke up, he was spooning me. Spooning me, for heaven's sake. It was the oddest feeling to wake up like that. I felt strangely protected, claimed. It was wonderful. I was smiling big, smiling bigger than I could remember smiling in a really long time.

He was warm, his body hard and strong, he smelled really, really good, and he was erect against my naked backside. The t-shirt had ridden up above my navel. I found myself pressing back against him, wiggling in, basking in that feeling of being cocooned by him. He started to rock against me. I twisted my neck to sneak a peek at his face and he was asleep but gently humping my backside. My smile probably got bigger because my cheeks were now hurting.

Okay, so he wasn't impotent. I'd recently had to entertain a much older man who was impotent and who got rather angry when we couldn't get things working. I don't know why he thought I'd be some miracle worker when it was clearly a medical issue. I'd wound up with a black eye after that session because the old geezer was so frustrated with my inability to help him maintain an erection. Thankfully I hadn't gotten punished for that. The Kruna cameras told them the story; they knew it wasn't my fault. It was one of the rare occasions I'd been treated fairly --- if you could call it that.

I knew I was in a room without cameras, a VIP perk, and this lack of being watched was strange. When Dare didn't touch me last night, I wasn't sure if he was uninterested in me and planned to knock me back for an exchange or if maybe there was a medical thing happening. If so, it wasn't happening in his sleep, that was for sure.

One of his hands glided up my thigh to my hip and his other arm slid under me and then around my chest to grasp my shoulder. He pulled me tight against him. I was still peeking over my shoulder, watching him do this in his sleep but as he rolled his hips against me, I started to rock with him and as his cock was directly against my crack, I clenched my cheeks. He was big. Nice.

He let out a little groan and his sleeping face was looking very sexy, very aroused. But then his eyes opened slowly and he glanced at me for a split second and then he winced and backed away.

"Fuck," he grunted.

I was now on my back, looking at him and he was standing up.

Dare

She was lying there looking gorgeous with her copper hair wavy and fanned across the pillow and her eyes sleepy and a sexy smile on her face.

I'd gotten instantly to my feet. Her eyes landed on my groin. I had a raging hard-on. Fuck! I stumbled to the bathroom and slammed the door. Fuck! I punched the wall, breaking the drywall with my fist.

When I came back out, she was still in the bed, blankets pulled up to her armpits and she was looking at me with fear on her face. I hadn't meant to scare her. I needed to get us outta here so I could tell her the truth. But it'd have to wait.

I sat on the edge of the bed. "Don't be afraid." I reached over and touched her face with my palm. Her eyes moved over my face and she gave me a little nod. Then she flung the blankets back and spread her legs wide, took the t-shirt and whipped it over her head. She was naked and spread eagled. Again.

Damn it. This chick was definitely damaged. I was not taking advantage of this.

"Felicia." I looked at her disapprovingly.

Fuck, she was beautiful. Slim and toned. Great tits, long legs, fully waxed pussy, no landing strip. Blue gems peeking from her belly button. I had gone soft as I punched the hole in the bathroom wall but of course at that sight my dick had a mind of its own.

"Please, Master. Let me take care of that for you," she whispered, looking down at my groin. "I'm ready for you." She reached down and spread her folds apart with her hand splayed and her middle and ring fingers parting those folds and she was ready all right. She was glistening. I let out a slow breath.

"Not here," I said, having trouble taking my eyes off her pussy. I tore them away and looked at her face. I was shaking my head and skimming my teeth across my bottom lip.

She moistened her lips with her tongue and looked at me flirtatiously.

"Not here, Felicia. I wanna get us home." I tried to push my anger away.

Something flashed in her eyes and it just about knocked me over. Maybe the word home was having some sort of effect on her. She looked lost, in pain, her lower lip started to tremble and then she seemed to pull herself together.

I took the comforter and covered her up.

I lifted the phone off the base and hit 252. Rafe Ruiz answered on the first ring,

"Mr. Ferrano! How are you this morning? Is everything to your liking so far?"

"Very much so," I said, "Please have Felicia's things sent to my room so she can get dressed."

"Immediately, Sir. Will you be dining in your suite or in the dining room for breakfast?"

"My suite," I said. The less time spent with these scumbags the better.

"When you are finished breakfast please call me and I can take you to meet Mr. Chen for your tour and meeting. We can see to Felicia as well."

"See to her how?"

"D-does she require any care?" he stammered nervously.

"Care?"

He let out a nervous laugh. "Forgive me, Mr. Ferrano. I'm not aware of your preferences but we offer after-care services should your Felicia require anything. Physical therapy for her muscles, any medical care, waxing, etcetera."

Sick fuckers.

"No, I don't want her seen to. I told you last night no one was to fuck with her. She's mine; I'll see to her," I bit off, "She stays in my room during the tour and no one touches her, no one even talks to her."

"Absolutely understood," he said quickly. "Kindly call me when you're ready for your tour."

I hung the phone up and then muttered "fuck sakes" under my breath.

Felicia was staring at me wide-eyed.

Emotion came over me and before I calculated the move, I grabbed her and pulled her against me in a hug. "Not a single one of those fuckers will lay hands on you again, I promise you that." A hand was on her naked back and another in her long silky hair. It was wavy, untamed; it felt good between my fingers.

She was stiff for a beat but then put her arms around me and sank in, then softly said, "Master…thank you." There was a lot of emotion in her voice. Her naked tits were against me. I had to let go. Now.

I shook my head and let her go. Her eyes were big, her lip quivered, and she was trying to hold it together and clearly didn't know what to make of me. I gave her space. I got a suit from the closet and said, "Will you order breakfast and coffee for us, please?"

She was taken aback.

"What would you like, Master?"

"What do you like for breakfast?" I asked her.

"I usually have fruit and Greek yogurt."

"Is that what you like?"

"Uh…it's what I usually have."

"What do you like?"

She shook her head at me, her brows furrowed.

"What?" I said, probably a little too impatiently.

"I… I don't know."

Something wasn't right with her. Was she having some sort of episode or something? She was trembling all over.

I sat on the bed and leaned closer. "What's wrong; you okay?"

She nodded but her hands were trembling.

"Hey?" I took her face into both hands and leaned close. "It's gonna be okay."

She started to huff and puff. She was hyperventilating.

Then she grabbed for me and clutched me tight.

I flinched at first but then put my arms around her and rubbed her back.

"It's okay," I said.

"Master?" she whispered.

I had to get her to stop calling me that. But I'd work on that later. "Yeah?"

"Can I ask you for something?"

"Yeah," I answered and she clung to me. My nose was buried in her hair. It was so soft.

"Will you please take me?"

"Yeah, I'm taking you. You're coming home with me, Felicia."

"Thank you. Thank you so much for that. I'm honored that you choose me. I can't even express how honored that you're taking me with you. But Master, will you please take me now? Please?" She was shaking, her voice was shaking, and my throat was going dry.

"We're leaving tomorrow. No one will hurt you again. They know you're mine so they won't even try." My gut twisted at my own words.

She breathed a sigh of relief. "Thank you. So much. But will you please take me?"

I shook my head. "I'm not getting you, baby. Take you where? Back to Alaska, you mean?"

"Take, fuck me," she whispered into my chest hoarsely, "Please Master, will you fuck me, please?"

Whoa. Motherfucker.

I pulled back. "Not here." I let go of her.

She looked down. She looked crushed. This girl was seriously damaged goods. I felt a pang of sadness for this poor, sweet, angelic-looking girl who was nothing but a profitable piece of ass to these sick scumbags.

"What's the hurry, angel?" I asked gently, wanting to settle her down. "There's no hurry, okay? Let me deal with things and then we're outta here tomorrow. Lots of time, okay?" I cupped her jaw.

The color drained out of her face. Her mouth dropped open. I tilted my head, watching her. She stared off into space looking catatonic. She was still trembling.

"What do you want for breakfast? Bacon & eggs?" I asked gently. She stared straight ahead, like she wasn't even here, like she was in shock.

"Felicia?" I let go of her and snapped my fingers in front of her face. Her attention snapped back to me.

"Breakfast?"

She shook her head. "Whatever you'd like me to have, Master." Her eyes, her eyebrows, they were twitching in confusion.

I picked up the phone and ordered and then went into the bathroom to shave. I heard knocking. I quickly took the last stroke and rinsed and then grabbed a towel and blotted my face as I headed to the door. She was still in bed sitting against the headboard with the covers up to her armpits.

I opened the door and a bellboy pushed a cart in. That woman who was with Rafe Ruiz yesterday was beside him, "Mr. Ferrano," her eyes darted toward Felicia, "Is everything to your satisfaction?"

I was losing my patience with these people. I gave her a dirty look. "I told Ruiz that I didn't need anything. I'd like to eat. If you'll excuse me, please." I motioned for her to leave. She glanced at Felicia quickly and I sidestepped to block her view and raised my brows at her. She quickly retreated. I got the impression she wanted her alone, but that wasn't happening. Something about that woman did not sit well. Hell, none of these people sat well. I shut the door. The luggage rack had a large trunk.

"Get dressed. Rap on the door if room service comes and I'll deal with it. You don't answer this door at all," I told her and was about to step out onto the balcony for a smoke.

"What would you like me to wear, Master?" she asked softly, looking pale, sickly pale.

I stared at her for a beat. "Is there something you'd, ah, like to do when I'm done with my tour?" I asked.

She stared at me blankly.

"Do you want to go to the beach? If so, put on a swimsuit. If you wanna go for a walk, shorts and a tank maybe? It's sweltering hot out there today. We'll do what you wanna do when I get back." I shrugged. Clearly, she was gonna need direction at every turn.

She nodded a little and pushed the luggage rack toward the bathroom while I headed out to the balcony.

When I came back in, there was knocking on the door again. She was in the bathroom so I got the door and it was breakfast on a tray. There was no table and chairs this time so I put the tray on the desk beside the bed and that's when she came out in a fancy blue tank top, more for a nightclub than a beach, and a pair of white shorts. She wore bejeweled flip flops. She had her bathing suit on as well, I could see the white halter ties around her neck.

She looked like she was trying to be casual, but her face was made-up, with smoky eyes and shiny lips with a hint of color, the color of peaches. Her hair was wavy and wild, probably from having slept without styling it after her bath, unlike yesterday when it was board straight. I liked it like this. It was more like the girl from the driver's license, the girl with the fire in her eyes. There was no fire in her eyes, now though. I didn't wanna even think about what they'd done to her to extinguish that fire.

I motioned for her to help herself. I lifted a lid and found a dish with separate compartments filled with bacon, scrambled eggs, fried potatoes, and a stack of toast. She looked at the platter with uncertainty so I dished her up a plate with a bit of everything. I poured her a cup of coffee and handed it to her black. "Not sure how you take it." I motioned to the sugar and milk.

She looked at me with warmth, but guarded warmth, as I passed her the plate and cup.

Felicia

I was feeling more than a little unhinged and I was trying my hardest to hold myself together. I hadn't felt this way in a really long time. I had a system. I found out what was expected of me and I went along with it, fulfilled whatever the duties were until I could be alone again. I had no real outlets other than exercise or reading. When I worked out, I poured everything into a workout. When I read, I got lost in the story. And when I had sex… when I had sex, I poured everything into it. That's how I proved my worth around here. That's how I got to where I was getting married off, getting out of here.

I screwed my assignments good and that kept me going. I'd got off on the sex because I'd go away to this place in my head and that's where my heart and soul would live while my body did what it was supposed to do.

My assignment getting them to orgasm meant I'd done my job and I'd have an orgasm and it'd be done. Usually. It didn't always go smoothly. Sometimes it went really wrong, but I succeeded at not letting it show. For the most part, I always knew what I needed to do to get from point A to point B and that's what I did every day. I almost always knew what they wanted before the session and even if I had to stay in character for days, I was able to deliver. It was all in an effort to get to Point C and now was that time.

This guy, this Dario Ferrano, gorgeous rich guy who inherited partnership in this place could get me to Point C. Once I got there, I didn't know what'd happen. I never thought about what I'd do if I actually got that far. What would I hope for then? I pushed the thought away. I couldn't let my mind go there now or I'd mess this up. Right now, the prize was getting out of here. I couldn't think beyond that. I could barely fathom life outside of these walls.

I'd never seen him before and other owners frequented the club, they frequented with friends, adult sons, one of them with an adult daughter who was a vicious Domme who'd drawn my blood more than once. I wasn't sure who Dario's father was or if I'd ever met him but Dare, clearly, had never been here.

Here I was with a guy that could get me to Point C but he didn't want the A to B business so far. Well, obviously he did when he was asleep but awake, he didn't. I'd tried. God, it was humiliating to be told No. And he'd gotten angry with me. It's all I knew and without giving him that… I didn't know how to proceed. He said he didn't want it here. But I needed to make sure he didn't change his mind and leave me behind.

When he left the suite, he put the 'Do not Disturb' sign on the doorknob so housekeeping wouldn't come. I made the bed and tidied. I worried that someone would come and tell me it was all a mistake, that he really wasn't taking me with him, that he'd changed his mind. I was worried I'd messed up and that someone would come, haul me off, and punish me for not representing Kruna well enough.

I'd been trained, had it drilled into me to please the patrons and I'd been trained that if I was ever lucky enough to be purchased by someone who wanted to be my Master that I'd have to be absolutely perfect in order to please him. Failure was not an option. I was considered an exemplary slave. So why was I doing so badly at this? I was like a fish out of water right now, all but flopping around on the carpet.

He was gone for a few hours and no one bothered me. He'd left the television on while he was gone and after a while, I'd gotten comfortable on the bed. It had been just about two years since I had a room to myself with a television in it. I didn't even have the nerve to change the channel. I simply sat and watched the news for the whole time he was gone, mesmerized by the ability to watch news, to see what was going on outside the confines of the resort.

When the door to the room opened, I scampered to sit on the edge of the bed, feeling like lounging had been wrong.

He frowned at me and shook his head and then sat. He looked pissed. "Did someone come and harass you?"

"No, Master."

"Good. Right, well we have a few hours until we need to dress for dinner. Are you hungry? Want lunch?"

I was still stuffed from breakfast. I swear that the bacon melted in my mouth like manna from heaven. "I'm not hungry, Master. But if you are, I'd be happy to order something for you or to accompany you to one of the dining rooms."

He rolled his eyes. "No, I'm good. But I need out of this…this…" He searched for a word, "building for a bit."

I resisted the urge to sigh. I really had hoped he'd just keep me here until it was time to leave. It felt like if I left this room that things could go wrong.

"Come." He took my hand and led me out to the balcony.

He shut the doors and got close to my ear, making my whole body prickle with sensation. "We have a game to play tonight," he whispered. My nipples tingled at the proximity, at his breath on my throat, at those words. "I don't wanna, but fucking scumbags," he said really softly, so softly I wasn't sure if I heard him correctly. I frowned.

I looked up at him and nodded, not sure what he meant but wanting him to be pleased with me.

He gave me a small sad smile and put his hand on my face again. God, when he did that it gave me shivers.

"So, we're taking a walk, I take it?" He smiled at me and then lifted a lock of my hair and examined it.

"Much better wild," he said.

I smiled, sort of surprised. "I wore both. So, whatever pleases you, Master."

"I'll change. We'll do both."

I was glad he wanted to walk rather than take me to a public area here. I was also glad for the physical contact. It helped me put things into context. Him telling me he was pleased, touching me, it helped me be who I needed to be. It'd be nice to again get as far away from the building as possible. Our walk last night was the farthest I'd been from the building since arriving here. And if I didn't screw it up tomorrow, I'd be on a plane. A plane away from here. My heart wanted to leap with joy and hope. It didn't. It knew better.

He stepped back inside and I followed. I watched him grab a few articles of clothing from the closet and head to the bathroom. A few minutes later he emerged in a pair of navy-blue board shorts and a tan tank top, wearing brown leather thong flip flops. He looked gorgeous. I could practically count his abs, which I already knew from earlier were an eight-pack, through his tight shirt. His arms were cut, chiseled, inkless, beautiful. He grabbed a pair of sunglasses from his bag in the closet and took my hand and we were off. His hand was warm, strong. I felt twinges in my nipples.

When we were as far away from the buildings as we could get before hitting the fence line, he sat on the sand just near the shore, put his feet in the water, and patted beside himself. I sat.

"We're leaving right after breakfast in the morning," he said and for the first time since he got here, I think his face held no anger. He was beautiful.

I nodded, feeling my heart swell. The breeze blew my hair into my face so I pushed it out of the way and the way he was looking at me, I couldn't help it but I think I dared to actually hope a little. Not a lot, but a little.

"Tonight, they're insisting I attend a dinner and I don't want you at my feet but it's what they expect. And I don't feel good about leaving you in the room alone for that length of time." The anger crept back over his features.

I nodded, thrilled that being at his feet was not something he'd expect going forward, but feeling cautious at his expression.

"I get the impression it might get…" His face went sour, "sordid."

I nodded, totally confused. Of course, it would get sordid. It usually did. Wasn't that why he was here? I mean, some of the patrons were more exhibitionists and voyeurs than others, it wasn't out of the ordinary for me to attend to someone who was more private about their sexuality, but with him being a partner's son I guess I was a little surprised that this didn't seem to be all second nature to him.

"Has it been terrible?" He took my hand and rubbed his fingertips across the back of it.

I opened my mouth and wasn't sure how to answer from my heart because I hadn't allowed myself the luxury of digging in there in a long, long time and didn't dare go there now for fear doing that would screw this up for me so I said, "If I get to leave with you at the end of it, I'd do it again."

He frowned at me and then shook his head. His eyes were the color of the sea. He had a handsome, strong jawline, a perfect nose. His shoulders were large and muscular. And his hair looked soft; it was in his eyes a little. I ached to touch it, to brush it away from his eyes with my fingers. I couldn't cross that line, though. I looked away, needing to guard my emotions so just stared out at the water but could feel that his eyes stayed on me.

"Build a sandcastle with me," he said after a few minutes of silence.

I was speechless.

"C'mon." He gave me a little smile and plopped his sunglasses on and then got onto his knees and started pulling wet sand toward us into a mound.

I was like a deer in the headlights.

"You gonna help or what?" He flashed a big smile and I think my heart stopped.

"I… I don't know how."

"I'll be back. Wait here," he said and took off jogging toward the grounds where he stopped one of the gardeners. I sat, flabbergasted. I was still in his sights, but we were far apart. It was weird to be sitting here in the sand alone. I'd never been so far away from a handler or patron. It felt weird and not in a good way. I felt vulnerable, at risk. I felt like I was gonna climb out of my own skin. His shoes were in the sand beside me. I stared at them, focusing, his shoes are here so he'll be back. He'll come back. I clutched my bare throat and took slow breath after slow breath.

Thankfully a minute later he was back.

"I'll take the lead." He pulled me by the wrist until I was on my knees and I mimicked him, started pulling mud toward the mound.

"That gardener is getting me some tools. Let's see what we can do." He gave me another little smile. He had bright white straight teeth, gorgeous full lips.

I wondered what it'd be like to kiss him. Some patrons loved to kiss. Some had been quite skilled at it. Some, not so much. Some were downright sloppy and gross. But until right now I'd never looked forward to a kiss since being here. I was hoping my Master was a kisser and hoping he was good at it. This might be the only man I'd ever kiss again.

Dare

I needed to do something with my hands. I wasn't the type to sit around idle and there wasn't anything to do in this place, this place of excess, sick and twisted fuckin' hedonism. The resort had activities but most of it was either sex-centered or at least stomach-turning from what I'd seen on my tour because guests had women in collars on the floor beside them or whatever while on the treadmill or playing cards or whatever. I didn't want around those sick fucks and I didn't want her alone in that room, why I don't know, but I just didn't. I felt protective of her, that it wasn't just my mission to come here and suss things out, but that it'd also become part of my mission to get her away from them, get her and I outta here without a hitch.

The tour had turned my stomach and I couldn't let it show. I didn't. I wanted to go for a run but not on the treadmill, on the beach. The property was fenced so that wasn't much of an option other than running back and forth on the limited amount of fenced property so instead I poured my energy into building a sandcastle with my hands. Because if I didn't find something to busy myself, I was afraid I was gonna snap.

The tour had shown all the things the guests see. The spa, the movie theatre, the performance theatre, dining room, games areas, lounges, bowling alley and arcade. It was early but there were guests mulling about. Some slaves were nude, some were leashed, there was nothing sexual going on in public areas. But as a new partner in the company I was also shown behind the scenes.

Gan Chen and Rafe Ruiz showed me their intake rooms and there was training in progress. I saw that Asian woman backhand that tiny blonde nude girl who was in the office last night with them for incorrect posture as part of the training process was explained to me. The Asian woman didn't know we were watching so I wasn't getting a show, this was how she handled trainees. The idea of her backhanding Felicia that way? I was furious at that idea.

I'd seen tables and benches outfitted with shackles and cuffs. I'd seen St. Andrews crosses. I'd seen dungeon rooms that looked like filthy shower stalls with a rusty drain on the floor where they kept slaves being punished or during their 'breaking'. The Hole from prison movies where people were held in solitary confinement for misbehaving consisted of better digs than that. When I saw those things, I saw them hurting her in my mind and it made me boiling fucking mad.

I also saw lavish suites that were designed to hold entire harems, suites that had themes, some of them pretty kinky and some of them pretty fucking sick. I could see that their girls could see that they could live in a filthy moldy shower stall with no light or in a palatial suite if they did what they were told and pretended their Master was a Sheikh or assumed roles as little girls with lollipops and pigtails and diapers being given a spanking by their "Daddy". I was all for people having the right to own their sexuality and had dabbled with some kink myself but consensually. This wasn't consensual. Collectively, it was all making me sick.

I was told that the club had a couple thousand members, around a dozen of them were higher profile celebrities and the others were very wealthy men and women from around the globe. Members paid exorbitant membership fees and then additional fees when they visited.

Some members spent months here at a time. Some came a few weeks every year. There were 200 on-site slaves, fifteen of them men, the rest women, and three currently in various stages of their training. A new one would be brought in to replace Felicia and I didn't like that one fucking bit but kept my mouth shut. It had been a few years since anyone had requested marriage material. Then when it was revealed to me who the last customer of a 'wife' was… it took everything in me to guard my reaction.

I didn't let them see emotion. I held a cool and standoffish entitled tone with them, as if nothing surprised me, as if I had every right to be a part of this, as if the very idea of everything they stood for was not absolutely abhorrent to me.

Stan Smith had said that some of their women opted for this lifestyle, applied to join, joined up so that they could be looked after. And he told me that most were drafted via dubious methods. To me that meant they were abducted or that they were traded in, much like my brother's Tia had been drafted into my family as a flesh payment for a debt.

Before my flight, Zack Jacobs the private eye we used told me he couldn't find a thing about them. He had to search carefully so he wouldn't raise any red flags but Kruna did not exist as far as he could tell so far. He gave me a verbal list of things he needed intel on from my trip for him to start investigating. The resort wasn't even visible on maps online as anything other than vacant wooded waterfront property, which didn't even jive with the whole private timeshare thing. That told me they had friends in high places.

Oh, it existed alright. But I didn't ask any questions. It was arranged that the following morning Felicia and I would depart. They invited my brother and I here for their upcoming annual stakeholder's meeting. They called it their Partner Summit. The meeting was optional but they wanted one or both of us to attend, if possible.

As far as anyone knew, Tommy was on his honeymoon. I didn't pick up on any suspicions but was being cautious. In the weeks before Pop's death we were at odds over the direction of the business and due to the reveal of secrets, and I didn't know if Pop had made any of his associates aware of that rift. It was unlikely because it would make Pop look weak as a man, a father, and head of a company, but we had to be cautious nonetheless and because of a few legal actions Pop had taken I knew there were records that would look like there was family trouble if someone looked close enough.

There was extended family there for a showdown between Tommy & Pop the day he died and while we didn't doubt loyalty of anyone who'd been present it was possible that word had leaked that there was a rift and if so, there might be suspicion.

Felicia had no clue how to build a sandcastle but she tried to help. The gardener dropped off a pail filled with gardening tools. We didn't talk, she just watched and tried to help when I was gathering up more sand, tried to mimic my actions. We worked at it for quite a while and then after I couldn't fuss with it any longer due to lack of better tools I said, "How about a swim?"

She nodded, staring at the castle with a weird expression on her face. But then pulled her tank top over her head revealing the white bikini halter top. When she got out of her shorts, I averted my eyes so I didn't look at her body too closely. It was hard not to look at her tiny barely-there bikini bottoms with ties on the sides. Her tits looked luscious in that halter. Her tiny ass was almost fucking perfect but would be better if she were allowed to eat whatever the *fuck* she wanted with carbonara sauce on it every day for a few weeks to mean a little more to grab onto.

I shook that thought off as I grabbed my shirt from the scruff and pulled it over my head and threw it beside the castle and then sprinted for the water, diving in as soon as it was deep enough. I swam underneath the crystal-clear water for a good, long while, just using up unused energy and taking the minute I needed to let myself feel the rage I'd been hiding.

Felicia

Tension had built in every single cell of my body. This man was an enigma. I didn't know what to make of him. I didn't know what was next for me. I was frightened… I had this horrible, sinking feeling that wouldn't go away.

I didn't do well with the unknown. I mean, this past almost 2 years of my life had been a lot of unknown, but it was formulaic. I never knew what a new assignment would bring but I knew what I had to do to get through it. A to B. It worked.

All that back to back A to B business had brought me to my C. Dario Ferrano was C.

My C.

Eyes like the sea, a beautiful body. He seemed perpetually pissed off but he had been nothing but kind to me since yesterday. Feeding me like I was a starved child that needed nourishment and not taking from my body, even when I begged for it. Waking up in his arms that morning I felt safer than I could ever remember feeling. Even before I got here. He got between me and them and said they weren't allowed to fuck with me because I was his. His.

I didn't know how to reconcile all of this and I knew it could all change in a heartbeat. It could be yanked away from me because he changed his mind or he could reveal his true nature and it could be a mask that, when it slipped, would reveal that he could be even more cruel and heartless than anyone had so far.

But we'd just built a sandcastle together, the best sandcastle I'd ever seen. It had several turrets, a moat, he'd done it all carving and molding the sand with his fingers and palms and small gardening hand tools and it was so attractive to watch him do that with strong fingers and a focused and determined look on his face. Now he was in the gulf, he'd disappeared for a long time under the water. I stood in water up to my waist and felt something swish by me. He was there. He emerged from the water and took my hands and pulled me forward, deeper into the water with him.

"I, I don't swim very well, Master," I warned, feeling panic rise.

"No?" he asked and lifted me, a bit of a devilish smile on his face. I jolted at the feeling of being in his arms and my panicked face made his mischief disappear. He pushed off with his feet and now we were in water too deep to stand in. "I've got you. Hold my neck," he said and let go of me and I started to sink but grabbed on and he was treading water, holding us both up. I was freaked.

"Shh, it's okay," he said. "I told you I've got you." I held tighter and then wrapped my legs around his waist and his words vibrated in every cell. He was holding me up, my only safety from drowning. He was my Master, my savior. I wanted to faint. He became erect against me and suddenly I wanted him inside me with a fervor I hadn't felt about a man, ever.

I tightened my legs around him, leaned in, closed my eyes, and parted my lips, wanting him to kiss me. Nothing happened.

I opened my eyes. He was staring with an angry look on his face. I pulled in a breath and held it.

"We should head back," he said and I saw muscles flexing in his jaw.

"Do we have to?" I breathed before thinking. This wasn't like me. Wasn't like me to ask and wasn't at all like me to want to be in the water. But in the water, he was close to me, I was touching him. He *had* me.

His expression softened. He kept treading and I just held on. "Spin around," he said and shifted me so I was on his back now. "Hold your breath."

He swam underwater for a little while with me on his back. I opened my eyes and it was breathtakingly beautiful, so beautiful that I forgot to keep holding my breath and then took in a mouthful of water. I gripped him tighter and started to struggle and he swam upwards until we broke water. I was gasping and sputtering. He moved us back to where we could stand and put me on my feet.

"You okay?" His eyes had so much depth, so much concern. Water dripped from his hair, his face, and it struck hard that he was the most attractive man I'd ever seen and had been kinder to me than anyone since I'd been in Thailand. And I was his. I said a silent prayer that he wouldn't change his mind and leave without me.

I recovered, pushing away the memories of the last time seawater was forced down my throat and nodded. "Yeah. I'm okay." And strangely, I wasn't lying.

Dare

We hung out in the water for a bit, me swimming and her sitting down in the shallow water just watching me. Then back in the room I got a shower. Then she took one. We had to get ready for the dinner I'd been asked to attend.

I just had to get through tonight and then tomorrow morning we'd be outta here. They'd have her passport ready and then after the 18-hour flight we'd be back on home soil. I'd get her to my place and then I'd tell her that it'd all been a ruse. And then I'd figure out how to keep her safe, keep us all safe, while giving her back her freedom.

Somehow Tommy and I would work to figure out how to gracefully exit this business. At first, I'd thought maybe we could buy everyone out to eliminate the threat and then shut it down so we could deal that way and put all Pop's ill-gotten money to good use. Stan had revealed that there was more off-shore money aside for us and it meant that me and all my siblings were extremely wealthy, filthy rich. We were already quite wealthy with Pop's estate back home but the off-shore money? There was a lot of it.

But, when I found out today what the revenue levels for this place were, and when I found out some of the names involved, I knew that was not an option for us. Not even close. No one would sell this cash cow for any price and even if we'd miraculously been able to pull enough cash together the members would certainly balk at it being dismantled.

But I'd have to find some way to deal, do all this while also finishing the clean-up of the rest of the business so I could sell it all off and move the fuck on with my life. An ugly mess.

When she came out of the bathroom in a short yellow silk robe, she asked me if she could speak and then asked what she should wear for the dinner. I hesitantly reached into the box that Gan Chen had given me that morning when he talked about the dinner.

"Did you bring a collar for your Felicia or should I have one provided?" he had asked.

"I'll need to borrow one for while we're here," I'd told him. Every slave I'd seen so far at the resort wore one.

The royal blue velvet box contained a choker necklace that was bejeweled with three strings of square-cut blue sapphires. It was dainty rather than ostentatious and it looked more like a choker necklace than a dog collar but the intention was obviously still there. The three strands of jewels came to a rectangular platinum clasp at the back and at the front they came to a circle. Dangling from the platinum circle was a heart shaped platinum dangling cutout pendant. Beside it was a matching lapel pin and cufflinks for me in blue sapphires.

"No need to borrow. Please accept this as a gift with my sincere best wishes for you and your Felicia," he'd said.

It was the same shade as her eyes. I opened the box and lifted it out for her.

"It's formal. Choose something formal that goes with this, if you can," I said.

She looked at the collar for two beats and then shook herself free of what looked like a trance. She lifted her hair and tilted her throat and turned her back on me. I took a deep breath and then I fastened it around her slender and beautiful neck, resisting the odd urge to put my lips to her throat. She let her hair drop and then turned and looked at me, tears shining in her eyes. The dainty collar made her eyes stand out in a way that took my breath away for a second.

Seeing it on her neck stirred up emotions in me that I couldn't describe even if I wanted to. It was a beautiful piece of jewelry but what it stood for? Not beautiful. There was a sour taste in my mouth. As I backed away from her to head to the balcony for a smoke, her expression and posture both dropped.

***

In the banquet room I'd been invited to that night there was a table for twelve that was up on a platform three steps up. I didn't know what sordid events were to take place but the whole thing set my teeth on edge. Felicia was on my arm in a little black strapless short cocktail dress and blue strapped high heels, toes and fingernails painted metallic blue and her hair pinned up with curly tendrils cascading down. When we arrived, I saw that we were the last to arrive and that between each chair was a cushion. Most of the guests had a woman on her knees on the cushion beside them. One had a man as his slave. I fought back the rising rancid disgust in my gut at the entire scene.

Their cushions matched their collar colors. Some had leashes attached to their collars. Every one of them wore a collar of some sort. As I approached it, Felicia let go of my arm and let me step ahead and she went right to her knees on the satin royal blue pillow beside my chair, which was at the foot of the table. It was going to take a lot to hold my attitude in check tonight.

Gan Chen rose from the head of the table. "Welcome guests. Everyone, this is Dario, son of Tom, our dear departed friend and partner. This dinner is in honor of the loss of Tom."

I clenched my teeth.

Everyone expressed welcomes and I got introductions. A few that sat close by offered their condolences for my loss. I hadn't known the tone of the evening when invited to this dinner but what Chen said next gave me a sense of relief.

"In light of the occasion this will be a standard meal. We're serving all of Tom's favorites. For anyone looking for play, there will be play in the Townsend room after dessert, also in honor of Tom."

I looked down to Felicia. She was kneeling on the cushion, face pure and sweet like an angel, her expression blank, revealing nothing about what she was thinking.

Thankfully, the meal was fairly uneventful. I had no idea if sex would happen in the room, if the servers would be nude. I had no clue at all what to expect but it was a lot like a formal business dinner like dozens I'd sat through at tables with people I didn't like but with a big exception; slaves at the feet of the businessmen.

Two of the men at the table were partners, then there was Gan Chen, Rafe Ruiz, and several other club members. I had to follow suit and feed her from my fingers like the others. She accepted food graciously from my fingers without looking up at me. I made sure she ate more than I did. I noticed the other "masters" were not nearly as generous with their slaves. I was anxious to get back to the room. I got through the meal as best as I could, trying to be cordial but there were conversations that took place in there that had turned my brain upside down. And a few stories were told about my pop and things that had gone on while he was here that made me feel absolute disgust.

One older guy, probably around 60, who was seated to my left, had looked down at Felicia with lust in his eyes and said, loud enough for the entire room to hear, "Sad to see her go. You'll be very happy, son. Very." He'd licked his lips but I cocked a brow at him in challenge and then he went red-faced. He'd had her. He'd fucked her and he was staring at what he wouldn't have again with lust in his eyes. All of it was a true test of self-control for me.

I'd have liked nothing better than to put bullets in the skulls of every single motherfucking scumbag in that room, him first. I looked around. Every eye in the room that wasn't the eye of a slave was on me and I suspected every eye in that room'd had her. I clenched my teeth and Chen and Ruiz both seemed to read my body language. Ruiz whispered in his boss's ear and that's when Gan Chen had ended things.

Ruiz'd probably told him I was possessive and he wisely ended the festivities.

I declined offers for "play" in the Townsend room, not wanting to fucking know. I needed a cigarette, my smokes were back in the room, and I wasn't about to leave her unattended for a second.

***

When we arrived back in the room it was 10:30 and I knew we were leaving at 9:00 in the morning so after coming back in from the balcony I said, "We should get some sleep. We're leaving bright and early."

Ruiz was to deliver her travel documents to me by 8:00.

"May I speak, Master?" she asked.

"Speak," I answered.

"What would you like me to dress for bed in?"

"Something that makes you comfortable," I answered, taking off my cufflinks.

She looked at the floor.

"What is it, Felicia?"

She kept her eyes on the floor and was about to speak.

"Look at me, angel."

She swallowed hard and her whole body locked tight but she looked at me.

"What is it?" I asked.

"Nothing," she said as she looked at me and then she flinched almost as if I was going to strike her.

I didn't know what was on her mind. I looked at her for a minute, trying to get a read on her.

"Would you choose something for me, please, Dare?" she piped up, finally, breaking the awkward silence. Why was she so pale?

"You okay?"

She nodded. "Yes."

I sighed. exasperated. I walked to her trunk and inspected the contents. There was a lot of lace. A lot of white lace. Fucking figured. Why did this trunk have to be filled with shit that did it for me?

During my tour, I'd been told that if I'd elected to leave her in for further training, I could specify the types of clothing to be sent home with her, my preferred attire. White lace would be my preferred attire if this was what I actually wanted. Since I was foregoing the 'transition training' she was being sent home with me with a mixture of clothes. I found a virginal looking long silky white nightgown with spaghetti straps. I also found a blue crotchless and nipple-less merry widow as well as some other sexy lingerie in just about every color of the rainbow. I passed her the long white nightgown as it was the least revealing.

When she returned from the bathroom, she was in it and she looked even more alluring than I'd expected. I hadn't noticed the nightgown had a side slit almost to the hip and most of the chest area was transparent lace and sheer. Her hair was now down and she still wore the blue collar, which I thought was odd. I tried to deny my brain from thinking about how fucking sexy she looked with her wild curls and that necklace matching her eyes.

"You want help removing that?" I asked and reached for her neck.

She gasped and locked tight.

"What?" I froze in my tracks, my hands in mid-air.

"I don't want it off. I never want it off." Her eyes were wide, frenzied. I was startled at that. It was like she was coming unglued. I backed away and gave her space.

I went to the washroom and saw that some of her things were out on the countertop. A blue stone-handled hairbrush. It looked antique. A toothbrush. Some facial cleanser and moisturizer. I got a twinge at her things sharing space with mine. Her toothbrush was lying directly beside mine. Her hairbrush directly beside mine. Deconstructing it, it was almost territorial. Yeah, she'd probably need some counseling once I got her out of here.

I got ready for bed and when I strode out in my boxer briefs, having forgotten to bring clothes in again, she reacted. She was seated at the foot of the bed and she fisted the bedding. Yeah, that was nice for my ego but I had to pretend not to notice.

It was hot in the room despite the AC so I decided that I'd forego the track pants tonight and threw the blanket to the foot of the bed and then climbed in under the top sheet in my underwear. I thought back to that morning, waking up with my cock against her ass and got instantly hard.

Down boy.

"Come to bed," I said and she spun around, hiked up the nightgown, and was on her knees crawling slowly toward the head of the bed. She looked fucking amazing. Blazing wavy hair falling over one shoulder, her eyes on me and with visions of sex in them, her luscious tits spilling out of the low cut white silky nightgown as she crawled slowly toward me. I turned on my side so that I'd have my back to her when she got to the top and ground my teeth tight as I flicked the lamp off.

She was beside me, under the covers, and I felt her breath on my back.

She was winded. I squeezed my eyes tight and tried to ignore her sweet scent, the warm breath on me, the tingling in my fucking groin. *Motherfucking scumbags in this place.*

***

I was dreaming of her; she was riding me, her gorgeous hair spilling around her shoulders, her beautiful tits bouncing, her eyes on me and filled with want.

"I'm all yours, Master, for forever, and for anything your heart desires," she'd huskily said in the dream and it sounded so hot. So fucking hot.

I had one of her hips in my hand and the index finger of my other hand was looped through the dangling heart pendant, holding on. In the dream, I bounced her on my cock. Fuck, it felt good. Somehow, I knew I was dreaming and had a lucid thought that it felt too intense and real to be a dream. My eyes bolted open and that's when I realized she was under the blankets and she had my cock in her mouth.

She had me deep and she was applying the perfect amount of suction. Fuck. I had her hair wrapped around my fist.

"Felicia," I rasped, "Stop."

She kept going, sucking me deeper. *Fuck* that felt good. I had to make her stop.

"Fuck, Felicia, stop goddamnit!" Because I had her hair, I pulled her back, rougher than I intended. She had a look of shock on her face.

"Get off me," I croaked out. She moved off me with her eyes downcast. I got out of the bed, pulling my underwear up as I stood. She must've pulled them down enough to get to my cock. Fuck, down boy, sorry boy. My cock was fucking pissed at me.

"What the fuck?" I bit off.

Her mouth opened and she looked mortified. Her face was beet red.

"WHAT THE FUCK!" I had to lock my rage down. And now. It was 6:00 in the fucking morning and we were outta here today.

"I just wanted to …" She was trembling like a leaf.

"Stop." I halted her by raising a palm. "Don't finish." She cowered at my hand going up. Fuck, she thought I was gonna hit her.

I stormed into the bathroom and slammed the door. Yesterday's cracked drywall was already staring at me. I couldn't hit the wall again.

Fuck!

I used the john, got in the shower and the minute I got under the water my cock was screaming for me to take care of business myself so I finished what she started in there. Couldn't help it, no choice. Seeing her naked body, having her ass against me yesterday morning, then her legs wrapped around me yesterday in the water, her gorgeous tits against my chest, and then my cock in her mouth this morning? I had no choice but to take care of myself or I'd go in there and throw her legs up over my shoulders and pound her hard until I fucking exploded in her pretty pussy.

I pictured her while I jacked off, I couldn't help it. Wild hair, piercing blue eyes, peach lips around my dick. Hanging onto that fucking necklace. Sweet jesus. I had one hand flat on a tiled shower wall and the other hand in a fist around my dick and it took all of thirty seconds for me to finish, maybe not even thirty seconds.

After my shower I brushed my teeth and when I came out, she was still in the bed, chewing on her bottom lip and not looking at me. I had trouble looking at her, too. Seeing her there made my dick wanna wake the fuck up again.

I was in a towel. I got a suit and shirt from the closet and fished out socks and underwear from my bag and without looking at her I said, "I've gotta get dressed. Before I do, listen to me. You and I have shit to settle about what my expectations are gonna be. We deal with that when we get home. I told you I was not prepared to start this here and I meant that. You pushing like that was not cool."

"You're still, still taking me with you?" She was staring at the bedspread.

I sighed. "Of course, I am."

She closed her eyes and visibly relaxed. She had been petrified that I was changing my mind. She wanted so desperately away from here that she was trying to make sure she secured that seat on the plane with me. I sat on the bed and looked at her.

"I'm very sorry, Master. I just want you to be happy with me," she answered softly, looking up at me with sad eyes.

"I know," I said, clenching my teeth.

"I'm nervous I won't be good enough."

"What?"

"I don't have any directions. I don't know what you need me to be. If I knew, I know I could be that for you." She said it softly, with desperation. Her words twisted my gut into knots.

I sighed. "I'm sorry to put you under stress. I don't like uncertainty either, so I can relate. I don't trust that this room isn't bugged and I'm extremely private. I won't have sex with you here. It could be being recorded. I won't risk that."

Light seemed to dawn for her and she nodded a little. It put her at ease a bit but only momentarily because then she was chewing her lip. I could only guess that she was now wondering what she was in for with me when I was sure there weren't cameras around. I'm sure she'd been exposed to some sick kink in this place and now she had to keep wondering how kinky I was gonna be.

"We'll talk when we get home. Try not to stress. Okay? Let's just get home and then we'll talk more about what I need from you, all right?" She nodded a little. I had to leave it at that. Unfortunately.

I took my suit toward the bathroom. "Order breakfast for us? Pick something that you like." I went into the bathroom to get dressed and shaved.

When I came out at least ten minutes later she was staring at the menu.

"What'd you get for us?" I asked, tying my tie.

She looked up at me, panicked.

"I-I'm sorry, Master. I didn't know what to get." She looked on the verge of a meltdown.

I looked at the menu and it was large, plenty of breakfast choices. But was it really that difficult? This girl had obviously had everything decided for her for the past two years. I had to cut her some slack. I needed her to cool it and stay cool. We were almost out of here. I took a deep breath.

"Okay, what about French toast and bacon?" I caressed her cheekbone with my thumb. Her eyes lit up and she settled at my touch.

"Order us French toast and bacon. Only if it's real maple syrup. If not, I dunno, Denver omelets. Orange juice and coffee. Okay?"

She nodded and had an expression of wonder on her face. Wow. Fucking wow. I slipped out for a smoke.

***

As soon as we were finishing up breakfast there was a rap on the door and I let Ruiz and that woman in.

"Mr. Ferrano, do you need us to see to Felicia before you depart?" the woman asked and he clipped, "Cleo!" He gave her a dirty look like he'd already warned her against asking that or something. She didn't seem to notice.

"No," I answered without looking at her and looked over the documents. It said her name was Felicia Andrews. I knew that wasn't true. Later on, I'd find out her real name, figure out the rest.

"Mr. Ferrano, we appreciate your patronage and your partnership. We hope you'll be pleased with your Felicia but if anything is amiss, when you and your brother hopefully visit in October if there needs any adjustments you can feel free to leave Felicia with us for training for your stay and beyond, if necessary. We want you satisfied. Mr. Chen asked me to send his apologies. He had something arise this morning and was unable to see you off."

"Thanks, no worries. I'm sure I will be."

He nodded and then told me he'd arrange for his driver to take us to the airport. The Asian woman perked up. "Mr. Ferrano, may I please have just a moment with Felicia before you depart?"

"No," I said simply and gave her a dirty look.

She looked taken aback. She glanced at Felicia over my shoulder and then looked resigned.

Ruiz gave me an apologetic look, then reached over and took her by the arm and pulled her out of the room with carefully controlled anger. "Bon Voyage, Mr. Ferrano. See you soon," he said.

After I shut the door, I turned on my heel and I looked at Felicia, who was sitting on the bed, dressed to go in a pretty cream-colored dress with ruffled short sleeves and a square neckline, her hair loose and wavy, wild in a gorgeous way, the collar still around her throat. She was staring at me with shock on her face.

Felicia

I was getting out of here. I was getting to Point C.

Dare had my passport. I was wearing his collar. I didn't belong to these people any longer. I was his. I didn't know yet what that meant and I didn't dare listen to the little voice in my head trying to whisper to me that maybe it was all going to be okay. But when he didn't allow anyone here to fuck with me and when he blocked Cleo and didn't let her sink her claws into me and poison me with her venom one last time before we left, I think I fell in love with him a little.

CHAPTER THREE

Dare

I was not relaxing until I had us on that plane. No, scratch that; I was not relaxing until we were on home soil and even then, I'd only relax marginally. I didn't have a clue when I'd have some actual peace again. After the car brought us to the airport and the chauffeur helped us get our luggage checked I took my carry-on and took her by the hand and headed to where we needed to go. I glanced at her for the first time since leaving once we got to the counter for the airline and immediately took in that her face was ghostly. She was freaked right the fuck out. I guess I'd been stuck in my own head for the drive to the airport.

"Hey?"

She didn't notice.

"Felicia?"

Her attention snapped to me and it dawned then that this was the first time she'd left that hellhole in 2 years. She probably wasn't used to a moving car. She probably wasn't used to the people everywhere in the busy airport. She was also likely deathly afraid she'd wake up back in that prison finding out that getting outta there was just a dream. She was probably afraid of me, too, afraid that I was just another abuser in a long line of people who'd mistreated her in the past two years.

"It's okay. You okay?" I touched her face and she leaned into my palm and closed her eyes and nodded slowly. She seemed a bit wobbly so I got her to a chair and sat beside her, holding her hand in mine and rhythmically stroking it.

"Want something to drink?" I asked.

She shook her head. "I'm okay. I have a bit of motion sickness, I think. From the car ride, and from…" she stopped.

"All the excitement?" I offered.

She nodded a little.

I gave her hand a squeeze, "Stay here. I'll deal with things at the counter and then we'll get to the first-class lounge. Eighteen hours we are not sitting like sardines in coach."

I gave her a smile and then went back to the counter.

The flight was long. It was gonna be long no matter what but this was extra-long because she was not good company. She was trying to be an angel, to behave exactly the right way but she was like a frog in a blender. She was emotional and she was trying to hide it but failing, miserably. Jiggling with nervous energy, trembling, being jumpy, clearly overwhelmed at the sights and sounds all around us. I wasn't breaking any news to her until we were home. It didn't feel safe.

Rafe Ruiz had included a sedative for her in with the travel documents but I'd flushed it. Maybe I should've given it to her.

We watched movies, we slept. At one point she settled down and slept and her head nodded and drifted to my shoulder and I got a pang of something, something fiercely protective. I let her stay there. I played chess on my iPad and then when she woke up, I offered it to her so she could play games on it while I slept a bit.

When we finally arrived, I led her to my SUV, which I'd had dropped off for us. I had no idea what she'd be like when I'd made all my travel plans so I'd done it that way on purpose, trying to keep a low profile, even though I was really too zonked to be driving.

***

"My place isn't fancy," I told her almost apologetically as we got into the elevator from the underground garage, mostly to break that awkward elevator silence, the silence I'd been experiencing for the better part of three days with her, only now it was worse, it was ominous, it was like her fear was palpable.

"My brother bought it ten years ago, his first place, but when he moved to a big house, I took it over. It's close to my office," I shrugged.

I knew she'd been told I was wealthy and powerful, that I came from an important and influential family. I also knew that the resort was luxurious. The place had been five stars, lavish. My place was nice but it wasn't exactly luxurious. It was a typical upper-middle class 2-bedroom condo in a nice building. She smiled without reaction with her mouth, not her whole face.

"I'll get you up and settled and then get our things tomorrow." I didn't want to bring anything into the apartment in case it was bugged.

I noticed her chest was heaving, she was almost panting. She was looking like she wanted out of her skin. I sent a quick text to my brother to say I was home. The elevator stopped on the tenth floor and the door opened and I waved her ahead. My condo was at the end of the hall. I unlocked the door and as I walked down the hall, her following, I sent a text to Zack to ask if the apartment had been swept today. I motioned ahead and she walked in ahead of me and stood frozen in her tracks just three feet inside the door.

I stepped in, stepped around her, disarmed the alarm, and then dropped my keys on the table by the door. I looked in front of me at the view she was taking in.

It was an open concept condo. Big marble island in between the kitchen and living area with pub style chairs with leather backs, stainless steel appliances, brown and cream marble counters with cream kitchen cabinets. Large family room with two brown soft leather sofas facing each other and a glass coffee table between them with an 80" TV over a white brick fireplace. The walls were a chocolate brown with cream trim. The floors were dark hardwood. The apartment had no dining room table. The living area was big enough it could be a combo but I usually ate at the island and didn't have a lot of company so there'd been no need. It had a large master bedroom and a good-sized second bedroom that I used as a den. I had a decent-sized terrace with doors from the living area and from the master bedroom that led to it. It had a good view of downtown. The den had a desk, my Bowflex, a few arcade games I'd claimed when Tommy sold his place, and a futon in it for the odd time someone crashed here.

I figured I'd crash in the den tonight and let her have my room and then tomorrow we'd start to figure out the rest. Now, despite the long flight and a burning desire for a hot shower and sleep, I wanted to talk to her, get this over with. I got a reply from Tommy who acknowledged my, "I'm home. Exhausted. I'll msg you tomorrow." with a quick reply.

I dropped my phone on the island and opened the fridge. There was a note magneted to it by a frame containing a picture of my twin nieces eating from a big double layer birthday chocolate cake with their fingers, chocolate all over their faces. The note was from Sarah, our family housekeeper, she was a nanny to me and my siblings when we were kids. She now bounced between my house and the girls' houses. It said she'd done groceries for me and she'd see me Monday. She had totally stocked my fridge. I'd told her before I left to stock extra and she took that seriously, for sure. She'd asked questions but all I told her was that I might have a houseguest for a bit. I grabbed two bottles of water and passed Felicia one. She was still standing near the door, holding a handbag, and looking pale and lost.

"Sit," I said, motioning to a sofa, "We need to talk."

She sat on a sofa hesitantly. My text alert went off and Zack confirmed he'd been at my condo and left just as he watched me pull into the parking garage.

"Let me see your bag, please?"

She handed me the bag.

I opened it and dumped the contents on the coffee table and then ripped the lining out to ensure there were no bugs. All that she had in the bag was a lip gloss, mascara and eye pencil, package of Kleenex, tin of Altoids, a wallet, and her passport. I went through it all and then put everything back in the bag and put it on the table.

"I need the collar," I said and leaned over, motioning for her to let me unfasten it.

She flinched. I gave her a look. I regretted having to give her that look because I knew it was a threatening look that told her not to give me any hassle but I didn't need her having a meltdown. Her eyes widened and she moved closer to me so I could remove it.

"Shoes."

She removed her heels. I put those, the bag, and her collar all in a plastic trash bag and tied the bag to the arm of a lounge chair out on the terrace. I'd get her other things brought up in the morning after Zack had properly swept for bugs. I had a good idea of what to look for, but wasn't taking any chances. I closed the sliding glass door and came back to the sofa, opened my bottle of water, took a swig, and then spoke.

"My father died right after he bought you for me. My brother and I were loyal to him, loyal to a fault, and we did a lot of his dirty work. A lot. But we did not know the half of who he was. He did some bad shit. We thought we knew what that bad shit was, but turned out we had no fucking clue. I had zero knowledge of Kruna prior to last week. I had zero knowledge that he purchased you for me before he died. As a gift. A surprise birthday gift."

She jolted.

I continued. "My brother and I are gonna determine an exit plan for selling our shares. We want nothing to do with a business like that. Due to the fact that the resort is run by some very dangerous people we cannot do this hastily. When I was told my father purchased you for me as a gift my first instinct was to tell them to cancel the order."

She had a full-on body shudder but was staring blankly at me.

"But I realized that it would be unsafe to do that. I needed to go there and play along. This benefited you because that gave you an opportunity to get outta there. I know they struck the fear of the devil into you to ensure that you coming to me, a perceived important man to them, was risk-free because you had an impeccable record at that hellhole. I don't know how you came to become an asset or a…uh…slave or whatever they call you but we'll get to that part later. For now, for starters, I need you to know that I am not your Master. I do not intend to keep you as a slave. I want sweet-fuck-all to do with Kruna but as it's run by extremely dangerous people, you and I need to handle things very delicately.

I would have liked nothing better than to free every single person enslaved there, but that was not an option for me so because you were sold to my father for me I had an obligation to fulfil that transaction with those men. I did the only logical thing I could do under those circumstances. I went there, met them, let them think I was on board with their lifestyle, and I collected you. I will not hurt you. I aim to hurt no one who isn't a danger to me or the people I care about. I can help you get your life back. Maybe not your old life, exactly, but we'll see what we can do. It may take time and we may have to be creative about it so I gotta ask you to be patient to protect both of us while I figure all this out. No calls whatsoever and no leaving the apartment alone --- for now at least."

She was sitting there staring at me but it was as if she was vacant. Like the lights were on but no one was home. Maybe she was in shock absorbing the news. I could only imagine how big this must be for her.

"We have to play things extremely carefully for damage control so I'm gonna ask you to stay here while I figure things out. Help you figure out what's next. Yeah?"

She said nothing.

"Felicia?"

Her eyes snapped to my face.

"You have questions?"

She rubbed her hand along her throat where the collar had been, a look on her face like she couldn't get enough air. She swallowed slowly and as if she was having trouble doing it. And then she took a big breath as she stared at the ceiling. She started to shake her head in disbelief. She just sat there shaking her head. Her eyes got confused, then they looked angry, she narrowed them at me while still shaking her head. The anger tweaked me for a split second, made my scalp prickle, making me wonder if she was gonna have an issue with my being against them. Then her eyes got distraught-looking. She shook her head some more and then she covered both of her eyes with her palms and she started to shake like a leaf in the wind.

I was sitting opposite to her, on the other sofa. I got to my feet.

"Need something stronger than water?"

She didn't answer me. She just kept shaking her head, her whole body trembling. Her teeth started to chatter. She was in shock.

I reached for a throw on the arm of the sofa I was on and moved toward her, sat beside her and put the blanket over her shoulders. "Hey?" I reached over and smoothed a lock of her hair away from her face. "It's gonna be okay." I put a hand on her back.

She grabbed me. She grabbed me and, in a flash, she climbed me, the blanket falling off her. She was on my lap, her arms around my neck, and she started wailing, sobbing so loud while clutching me that I could do nothing but hang onto her. So I did.

She was plastered against me, wailing into my chest and hanging on for dear life.

And she cried so hard and so long, with her body trembling hard, that she tuckered herself out and eventually the sobs stopped, then the shudders stopped, and then her breathing went soft, and she fell asleep on me, curled up in a ball with her head on my chest, her knees pulled up against her own chest, her dress up around her waist, but she hadn't noticed. One arm was wedged between my back and the sofa and the other hand had been holding tight to my shirt at my shoulder. Her ass was on my lap. I had both arms around her, one hand on the back of her head and the other at the small of her back and my head tilted back on the sofa, eyes on the ceiling. Wow. That was fucking rough.

A few minutes after she went limp, I cradled her tighter into my arms, lifting her and taking her to my bedroom. I yanked the comforter back and then put her in the bed and then covered her up. She didn't wake. She snuggled into the pillow and then in her sleep muttered, "Master."

I felt a muscle jump in my cheek. I shook my head and then reached in between my mattress and box spring, grabbed my gun and backed out of the room, shutting the door behind me.

I re-set the security system. I really didn't think she'd try to take off but who knew what'd happen when she opened her eyes. Maybe she'd be unstable. I checked my gun, finished my water, and then stripped down to boxers and headed to the linen closet for bedding and walked to the den to make up the futon. I tucked the gun between the mattress and the wooden frame.

I'd get her chilled out and get things safe and try to help her move on while I sorted out the craziness that was my life. I needed to sort out the business and then find a way to get my life moving in a better direction. No more scumbags. No more shady shit. Fuck, after this trip to Thailand, more than ever I was so done. But because of this shit it might be a while before I could walk away. A long while. It was a complication… to put it mildly.

***

Something tickled my face. I was flat out, crashed on the futon. It wasn't comfortable by any stretch of the imagination. I wasn't alone. It was still dark and she was leaning over me and her hair was tickling my chin. I snapped up to sitting. Her shoulders were in my hands

"Sorry, Master," she whispered in the dark. "I had a nightmare. I got scared. May I sleep beside you?"

"Felicia," I let go of her and shook the sleep off, "I'm not your Master."

"Please?" Her voice was shaky. "I can sleep on the floor. I just need you near, if…if that's okay."

I got to my feet and grabbed for her hand in the dark. "If that's what you need, we're sleeping in my bed. This futon is shit."

I grabbed the gun and took her back to my room in the dark.

"Nothing to be afraid of, baby. You're safe," I told her and tucked the gun under my side between the mattress and box spring.

I got under the covers and as I did, I felt her shuffling beside me in the dark. I figured she was getting her dress off and then before I knew it, she was snuggled up against me, her head on my shoulder. She draped an arm over me and nuzzled in. Yep, skin on skin.

Whoa.

This was wrong. This was looking like some hero worship and I couldn't allow it. This was indicative of what they'd turned her into. I couldn't deconstruct it right now, though. I needed to crash. I was absolutely exhausted. I started to drift, thinking I should move her off me, set some boundaries. But then she softly said, "Thank you for saving me."

Before I realized what I was doing, I leaned down and kissed the top of her head. "You're welcome."

Tia

Tommy had been jittery, constantly checking his computer, which was on the coffee table in front of him.

"You not into this movie, baby?" I asked.

"Hm?" He looked up at me distractedly.

"What's so exciting on that screen? You get sucked in by one of those candy games, too?"

"Naw. I'm just waiting to hear from Dare. He should be back from a trip any time now and I need an update." He put an arm around me.

I snuggled into him. "Is everything okay?"

He shook his head. "No, it's kind of messed."

"Wanna talk about it?"

"Not sure you wanna be burdened with this kinda shit, baby girl." He leaned forward and grabbed his can of Coke and drank some."

"Kay. If you change your mind…"

His phone made a noise and he grabbed it.

"Kay, he's home. I can breathe now."

"That bad?"

"Oh baby, you have no idea." He shook his head with a grave expression and I felt ice pierce my veins.

"Talk to me," I urged.

That was just before he told me about Dario's problem. Dario's female problem. It was bad. Several times now since Tom Sr. died either Tommy or Dario found out about a new lie or new secret that rocked their world in a bad way. And it wasn't easy for Tommy. I could see that he was feeling guilty about leaving his brother to deal with things and I could guess that he was mulling over us going back so that he could help out more. Dario and he had been working together remotely but I knew Tommy was itchy, itchy to get things over with and itchy to be doing something.

He was building wooden patio furniture out back and alternately working on stripping and redoing a canoe as well during the day in a workshop to keep busy. He did beautiful work. Intricate designs, everything done painstakingly. But I could tell it wasn't enough for him.

That night he made love tenderly to me, holding me close while staring into my eyes the whole time and being my ice cream parlor hottie. It was beautiful. But during pillow talk he told me something that had also been discovered about Tom Sr. that completely shocked me and when the rest of the family found out about it, things might never be the same.

A few hours later he woke up out of breath and covered in sweat. He went up to the rooftop and beat up his punching bag, refusing to come back to bed, and refusing to talk about whatever he'd dreamt about.

When I woke up, Felicia was lying beside me, snuggled into my side with her head on my shoulder and she was awake, looking up at me.

I stretched a little, not enough to make her move. Her warmth felt nice. Too nice.

"Mornin'," I said.

"Hi," she whispered.

"Sleep okay?" I asked.

"Yeah," she replied. And the way she was looking at me, a little star struck or something, made me uncomfortable.

"You want coffee? I want coffee." I motioned to get up so she'd shift. I grabbed a robe from the hook on the door to the master bathroom and put it on the end of the bed, motioning to her so she'd know to put it on. She was just in her bra and panties. I got into a pair of jeans and threw on a tee and headed to the den to get my phone from the charger. I was gonna text Zack and get him over here to check her things as well as mine. I got the coffee started and headed out to the terrace for a smoke with my phone so I could check my messages.

When I came back in she was standing by the island in my black fleece robe with two cups that she'd poured.

"How do you take your coffee?" she asked me.

"Just black. Like my soul," I joked.

She gave a thin smile, a fake smile.

"Sugar's there." I opened a cupboard and pulled out a canister of sugar.

Her eyes widened.

"Milk?" I asked and opened the fridge.

She nodded a little nervously.

I passed it to her and then fetched a spoon from the drawer. She was hesitant for a sec and then she spooned two big heaping spoons of sugar into her coffee, added a big glug of milk and stirred it and then took a small sip, wincing probably at the heat, but her eyes rolled back like it was the best cup of coffee she'd ever had.

"Lemme guess. They didn't allow you to have milk and sugar."

She gave me a little nod. "Or coffee. Green or jasmine tea, mostly."

"Gross. So," I sat at one of the stools in front of the island and motioned for her to take the one beside me, "I know it's still probably sinkin' in but the things I told you last night --- I need to reiterate that we have to play things very carefully. I can't have them at all suspicious about my motives so it's best you stay here and in case they're watching outwardly it'll look like you're here, you're mine. Until I know there's no threat. We've gotta take things one step at a time."

She chewed her cheek, staring past me, into space.

"I'll move my stuff outta the den and get a better bed in there for you. That futon bites. Once we have it all sorted, I'll help you get set up somewhere else. It could take a little while and we might have to get creative but if we play it carefully there's no reason why you can't eventually get back to a regular life. I dunno how long it'll take me to feel sure that they're not watching and we'd be safer to get you a new identity. They wouldn't take kindly to hearing you were set free because that'd put their secrets in jeopardy. And as far as contacting your family…"

She jolted like she'd been prodded with a branding iron.

"You all right?" I put my hand on her arm. She looked at my hand and then at my face, then her eyes shot toward the floor.

"I know this is a lot to take in, angel, but if you can communicate with me it'll put my mind at ease. Try to help me out here."

Her coffee cup slipped out of her hand and crashed to the floor, spilling hot coffee on the both of us.

"Fuck!" I reacted and she hit the deck and turtled, covering her face.

"Whoa! You alright?" I grabbed a handful of kitchen towels from a drawer and threw them on the mess of coffee and broken porcelain. I reached down and touched her on the back. She was trembling. Hard.

"Hey? I'm not mad at you. It was an accident. Come on, up. Are you burnt?" I pulled her up to her feet.

The back of her hand was red. The front of the robe was wet. I took her to the sink and held her hand under running cold water. She was staring at my face. Our eyes met.

Felicia

I wanted to get my head straight. I wanted him to put my collar back on. I wished there were a magic button or a magic pill that could undo the last 22 months so that my brain would be right. It wasn't right. Not even close. My thinking that I was guarding myself and protecting it? I was so wrong. I didn't know how wrong I was until I got out and tried to find function. I wanted to ask him why he called me angel. Did he call every girl that? I wanted him to kiss me. I wanted him to take me. Hard. No. I needed him to take me. I needed sex so bad it was going to kill me if I didn't get it soon.

His scent, his warmth, even the sound of his breathing…when I was in bed with him the last few nights it was so comforting. It was the safest I'd felt in more than 22 months, maybe even ever. But it was like one big long foreplay lead-up. And I seriously needed to have an orgasm.

Yesterday, when we were on our way here from the airport, I was almost jumping out of my skin imagining that when we got in the door he'd throw me down and finally make me his. I was wet, my nipples were hard, and I could…not…wait. It had been a long stretch of deprivation, waiting to give it to my Master, not knowing a thing about that Master but then meeting him and wanting him, wanting him like I hadn't wanted anyone ever. He carried himself like an absolute Dom and

I

could

not

wait.

And although at that point knowing he might reveal himself to be horrible, terrible, sick and twisted and ready to put me through some serious pain after getting me where he knew there would be no Kruna cameras, I couldn't help but think about what I'd seen so far, the sweet, the protective. I was thinking about the sweet touches to my face, the spooning, the sandcastle, the swimming, holding me and the keeping me safe in the water and safe from them and I dared to hope just a little bit that it'd somehow be okay, that we'd get here and the sex would be spectacular and he wouldn't morph into something horrible and cruel. But what had happened when we arrived here turned my carefully constructed universe into an absolutely ravaged war zone.

Yes, it's messed up that I didn't try to make a run for it the minute we got here, but I'd been brainwashed. I was brainwashed to the point that the notion of running would just not happen. Never ever.

People who haven't been in my situation…they do not fully grasp the concept of being broken. I was like a horse who didn't need to be tied, didn't need a saddle, didn't need spurs because I'd been broken. I would not run away. Every once in a while, a rare horse will get his or her spirit back and rear up and throw an owner off out of the blue. But that wasn't me. I didn't think it was possible. I'd been professionally broken by people trained to make sure I didn't rear back ever and they certainly must've believed that or they'd never let me leave the resort with one of their new partners. Not only had they thoroughly broken me but they had an insurance policy that would keep me in line.

I used to be a sassy, fun-loving girl with a filthy mouth and stereotypical ginger bad temper and no fear of anyone or almost anything. All that changed over the first few months at Kruna.

The nearly 2 years there I had a single-minded focus to stay out of trouble and be a perfect slave so that I would not be subjected to the consequences that they'd laid out as well as corrections and re-training. Also, I worked hard to ensure I would get and then stay on the short list of available slaves for sale. Kruna rarely sold the assets. I wasn't advertised. At first I was very sheltered, but after Mr. Frost died I was put into the general slave population and allowed to serve more patrons and without his iron fist ruling over me I found my way to getting ranked among the possibilities for those who were interested in either taking assets off-site temporarily or acquiring them permanently and I made sure that once I got on that list I stayed there. It'd been over two years since someone wanted a Kruna wife but now that there was the demand, I'd been the one chosen.

When I found out that I replaced a slave who had become an owned wife that possibility was the closest thing to freedom I could imagine and so I strived to get on that list. And that was what made me a possibility when they looked for a redhead with a big sexual appetite for Dare.

That's all I knew of what he wanted other than that he planned to marry me. For a request to include a big sexual appetite made me think that I'd be subjected to some serious marathon session sex and I was physically fit, I had stamina, and I had a sex drive that rivaled most of the girls at Kruna and that was what helped me get to where I got to. Point C.

When he didn't lay a hand on me and turned down my advances, I thought I wasn't up to par and that would mean that he wouldn't bring me with him. It'd also mean I'd be off that short list, taking the possibility of life off the resort off the table. I knew I was gambling by aiming for that short list. I knew that because I knew that most girls who left the resort didn't generally get a happily ever after.

A few success stories had been discussed but more often than not we knew who the Masters were and knew their tastes because of what we'd endured at the resort with them. A man who was into severe pain, mutilation, play with body fluids, or who had plans to make his girl the star in her very own snuff film was always a possibility.

Some girls preferred being a Kruna asset to being owned because even if some days were hard they were not endless with one horrible patron. I'd spent months with one horrible man there and knew firsthand how awful that could be. I'd been with a lot of patrons since then and none had come close. I hoped no one in the world would ever come close to that again…

Some dreamed of becoming an owned slave or some even dared to dream about being an owned wife because of the hope that it'd be somehow better. No, you'd never be fully free and your Master or your husband could be the Devil incarnate, but it was life outside of Kruna and the hope ingrained in unknown possibilities…that was everything. That was what gave me my single-minded focus to keep going from A to B and then A to B again and again. The quest for Point C. Sex could get me there so I developed a sex drive because it was my only hope. Sex was what enslaved me, but it was also what could get me out of there.

Dario taking me off the resort was point C and I couldn't help it, when we built a sandcastle and when he swam in the ocean with me on his back, and when he refused to let Cleo be alone with me before we left, hope kind of crept in. It crept in enough that I wanted my Master to be pleased with me, pleased enough to never make me go back.

Cleo hated me. She wanted me off that list. She was constantly trying to trip me up and that was at least partly because one of the VIP patrons, Joseph, had taken a liking to me and had her reprimanded for her treatment of me one night. The VIP owned a girl that came from Kruna and still visited a few times a year and brought her with him and would request group play. The girl he owned was a favorite of Cleo, someone she'd been buddies with.

Cleo had previously been a regular slave and had been promoted to handler when she started to look older because of her dominating personality. If she'd been a submissive, she might've ended up on staff in the kitchen, in housekeeping, etc.

The VIP's girl was jealous of me the first night I was with them because her Master was very enamored with me and she was Cleo's bestie from the days before Cleo was promoted. My guess was that she must've gotten into Cleo's ear about it and that was the start of Cleo's hatred for me. It seemed to progressively intensify from there, especially after Cleo had to endure a correction as a trainer, which was a huge blow to her ego.

But now I was here, away from Cleo and Rafe and Mr. Chen and all of the others, and my Master was telling me I wasn't his slave, that I was eventually going to have freedom again. But that was sort of impossible to comprehend. I'd never ever expected freedom again, never even dared to hope it was in the cards for me. So I couldn't wrap my brain around that right now. I just couldn't.

Right now, all I could think about, was how bad I wanted him to take me, throw me down, and screw the ever-loving life out of me. I was seriously whacked in the head.

Dare

She needed to stop looking at me like that. When she forgot to hide her emotions, she had a very expressive face and it was speaking loud and clear to me right now. She was having some sort of hero worship side-effect or some shit like that and it needed to damn well stop. I was not taking advantage of what those scumbag motherfuckers had done to her for my own carnal satisfaction. No way.

I turned the tap off. "There's probably some ointment in my medicine cabinet. Let's go look."

She followed me into the bedroom and then the master bath and I regretted that because being in there with her … the sexual tension was real. There was a tube of first aid cream in my medicine cabinet. Sarah kept that stocked, too. I smeared some on the back of her hand. I examined the burn. It didn't look too bad; she probably wouldn't blister. Our eyes met again. Okay, I had to make this stop.

Letting it go there was not an option. I wasn't taking advantage of this girl. I wasn't ever gonna be a choir boy but I didn't wanna abandon my new motto of *Man Whore No More.* To take advantage of her in her current state of mind was lower than man whore. It was scumbaggery.

I heard my cell text alert go off so it broke the tension and I headed to grab it, saying, "Put that ointment on your legs or stomach if you're burnt there, too."

It was Zack and he'd pulled in to the underground. I replied to tell him

I'd be down in two minutes. I cleared the broken cup and spilled coffee from the kitchen floor and then poured a new coffee and brought it into my bedroom. Felicia was still in the washroom. I called her name and she peeked out from the opened door.

"There's clean robe or clothes in my closet if you wanna grab something to wear for now. I brought you another coffee. Take a bath or shower if you want. Can you hang in here and watch TV or something for a bit? My P.I. is here and he and I are gonna sweep our belongings for bugs down in my Explorer and then we'll be up. When we come back up, I'll have him double check your bag, shoes, and that necklace."

She nodded, looking shell-shocked, still. I put the coffee on the nightstand and left the room. I set the alarm on my way out. Just in case.

***

Zack had proven himself invaluable over the last several months to the point he'd become a buddy to me as well as our P.I. He checked and said that everything was clear of bugs and tracking devices, including the sapphire necklace, which was genuine and worth a small fortune. I had my luggage checked as well while I filled him in on the details of the trip.

Maybe they weren't suspicious of me. But I wasn't taking chances because I knew they could be watching. I also knew that a select few were at least somewhat aware of the rift in the final days of Pop's life and news could travel that far and if it did, even as a rumor, we'd be under suspicion eventually. As far as the lawyer Stan Smith went, he knew too much and was too far away for me to keep an eye on so I had to bear that in mind. With Pop gone his loyalties could easily change, particularly if he had no ties to me because I'd stopped using him. I needed to retain him as a lawyer at least until all this shit was over with. Pop had another local lawyer and that's who he worked with when he temporarily froze me and Tommy out. He hadn't made any changes to his will so all of that overwrote the temporary orders that had been put in place in the few weeks before Pop died.

Me and Zack talked to my brother on webcam in my den and agreed that depending on how we played out exits from the businesses we did not want to be in, this could mean that transition would take a whole lot longer than we'd hoped. And if it all started to go to hell the whole damn family would have to slip off the grid. Tommy said he'd work on that contingency plan.

Fuck, Pop; you're still fucking with us, even from the grave.

Zack was gathering intel about the people on the list of names I gave him and we were gonna re-group later to come up with a plan. After we said goodbye to my brother, I saw Zack to the door and then I checked on her. She was in my room, watching television in my bed. She was in a pair of my grey on grey checked flannel pajamas, a pair I'd never worn but got given for

Christmas last year. They were huge on her. She was watching cartoons, looking small in my big dark wood sleigh bed buried under my big wine-colored comforter.

I sat on the bed. "How you doin'?"

"Fine."

She probably wasn't fine.

"Is it okay I chose these to wear?" she asked, looking up innocently at me, giving me a pang of something, I didn't know what.

"Sure; I brought your things up. They're in the den and everything is clean, no surveillance or GPS devices. Listen, we have to talk about a few things. You feelin' up to that?"

There was no big rush provided she wasn't in a huge hurry to move on. She winced.

"Will you try for me?" I asked.

She looked at me with what looked like stars in her eyes.

I gritted my teeth for a sec and then forced myself to continue. "I know you've been through a lot. I don't know but I do know, you know? Fuck, okay, first question, are there people looking for you? Family?"

She was quiet a moment, but then answered me.

"No," she whispered.

"No family?" I asked.

She shook her head and looked to the comforter, tried to mask her pain, but I saw it. I wasn't sure if she was telling the truth or not.

"Did they kidnap you while you were on vacation in Thailand or something? Is that how they got you?"

She shook her head. My stomach churned. Did this girl volunteer? There were those that did, those who wanted to be looked after, who came from poverty or who were so damaged they thought that someone making all the decisions for them was their anecdote.

She must've read my sickened expression as she shook her head vigorously. "I was there for work, taken in, blackmailed, and there was no escape."

"Ah," I felt relief. Maybe I shouldn't have but I did. The idea that I'd brought back someone who wanted that for herself? That'd be beyond my comprehension. And for a split second before she said she'd been blackmailed, her behavior flashed in my mind and I was glad to have confirmation that it was a product of her so-called training rather than her behavior being something that was a result of her preferences.

"My private eye says they've probably microchipped you. Do you know if they have?"

She nodded.

"Right. We'll get that dealt with as soon as is feasible. So I wanted to make sure you weren't in a hurry to get back to Alaska. I don't want you to think of yourself as being in prison. We can sort things out for you; I'll help you get on your feet and eventually, not sure how long it'll take, but eventually you'll be able to get on with your life. It'll probably mean a new identity, you might not be able to go back to Alaska, but we have to wait and see what happens. You say there's no family there but are you okay with that?"

"I could live the rest of my life and never step foot back there," she said softly.

"So, you're okay to stay here for the time being?"

She nodded. Then she looked like she wanted to say something else. She didn't.

"Anything you need, you tell me, okay? De-stress, detox, whatever, and we'll figure things out as we go. I know you've probably been through hell so if you want counseling, I can arrange that for you but it'll have to be done carefully for confidentiality. I can arrange counseling over the computer, privately. You wanna go out, I'll have a driver take you, keep you safe while we sort everything. You can't tell anyone where you're from, what's happened to you. We'll come up with a cover story. I'm in the loop, though, on everything with you until I say different. You're not my prisoner Felicia, but you keep me in the loop. I'm accountable for your actions as long as we're on Kruna radar. Got me?"

She nodded.

"Help me out, here, angel. I need to know you get me, that you're not nodding because you've been trained to. This is serious shit we're talking about here."

She stared at me for a beat, just blinking at me, then took a deep breath. "I understand, Dare. I'll be good. I won't try to leave. I won't contact anyone from my past. I'll do whatever you want me to do." Her lower lip quivered. I put my hand on her shoulder and squeezed. She dropped her head to the side so that her cheek was resting on the top of my hand. I snatched my hand back. Her expression dropped.

"Good. Thank you. It's the best way to make sure we're safe. So, uh, help yourself to anything in the kitchen. Watch TV, whatever. Mi casa su casa. I'm working from here today and I've got a lot on the go the next few days so I'll be in and out. Anything you want, need, lemme know."

I headed to my closet and grabbed clean clothes and then headed for a shower.

***

As it got dark, I emerged from my den where I'd been working and found her sitting on a stool at the island staring at the blue sapphire necklace. Zack and I had left it there with her bag. Suddenly, hunger clawed at my gut and I realized I hadn't eaten all day. And although I'd told her to eat, I suspected she hadn't either.

"I was thinking of ordering take-out. You like Chinese food?" The second it was out of my mouth I winced, realizing how idiotic it was. "Wait. Shit. I know that's not the same as Thai but it's probably too close. How about we order some pizza, get you some fettuccine alfredo?"

She smiled. It wasn't one of her fake ones, I don't think. It was beautiful.

"My family owns an Italian restaurant; I'll have food sent over. Anything you don't like to eat?"

"I could go the rest of my life without plain rice but no, not particularly."

"Have you had anything to eat today?" I asked.

She shook her head, not making eye contact.

"Sorry for not taking better care of you," I said, catching her eyes. "I get working and time slips. Don't wait for me, okay? Make yourself at home here. If I'm here we can grab something at night together but if I'm not, help yourself. You can also get food delivered from the restaurant whenever. I have a tab. I'll leave you a menu."

"Thank you."

I almost wanted to take off back into the den to avoid her. This was awkward. But I'd left her by herself all day and thought it'd be rude. Besides, I needed to gauge her frame of mind, too, so I'd know how alert I'd have to be here in my apartment.

"So you wanna watch a movie or somethin'? We can throw something on to watch while waiting for food."

"That sounds good."

I motioned toward one sofa and took the other one.

Felicia

He was in faded jeans and a soft-looking gray t-shirt. He looked good in jeans. He looked good in shorts. He looked good in a suit, man he looked good in a suit. And he looked damn good in those low-rise track pants. It took a lot of hot for a guy to look good in sweats and Dario Ferrano owned hot in those sweats. But most of all, he personified all that was hot in those boxer briefs in the mornings. He was buff. He also had this way, this intensity in the way he carried himself. He drew attention. He had to get female attention wherever he went.

It was a weird day. I was used to being alone. At the resort I'd spend hours alone waiting for an assignment. There was a little socializing with the other slaves, but Cleo hated me so much that the others generally avoided me so they wouldn't get lumped in with me and face her wrath. So I was used to my own company, something I would never have said before Thailand but since becoming Felicia I was used to being alone. Not alone with the freedom to change the channel, not able to eat whatever and whenever I wanted, and so forth. I still hadn't fully wrapped my brain around my new circumstances. It was a lot to swallow. Today had been really weird.

Dare put The Hobbit on. It was a switch to watch something that wasn't porn. I almost giggled at one point because I started imagining the hobbits doing it. I got my mind off that by glancing in his direction and seeing him flex his biceps to put his hands behind his head, which got me thinking about him having sex. Dang. I started to get hot under the collar.

A little while in, I heard a buzzer and he paused the movie and then went to the wall near the door where there was an intercom. A few minutes later he answered a knock on the door and a teenaged boy stepped in, gave me a wave, and put a big pizza box and a large paper bag with twine handles on the island. He and Dare spoke in what must've been Italian for a minute and then Dare reached into his pocket to fetch out some cash and put it in the kid's hand. He then ruffled his hair and then the boy was on his way, waving at me on his way out. Dare brought the food to the coffee table, then brought over a bottle of wine and two glasses, and then he flicked the movie back on while he started putting food out.

I ate while watching the movie, for the first time in almost two years not overly conscious of what I was eating and really enjoying the food. I don't think it was just because it'd been two years since I'd had pizza that this was the best pizza I'd had in my life, hands down.

He paused the film after the meal to step out to the balcony to smoke a cigarette, which was nice since it was his apartment. I didn't know if he did it for my benefit or because he preferred smoking outdoors, but when he came back in he cleared the leftovers away and put them in the fridge. I felt lazy. And full. I felt like I should be doing something. But it all felt so weird. He stretched out on the one couch so I followed suit and lay down on the one I was on.

***

I woke up when the credits were rolling. I was asleep on the one sofa and he was asleep on the other. But there was a soft gray blanket over me so he must've put it on me while I was asleep and the idea of that gave me a twinge in my chest.

He was so handsome. And asleep he didn't look at all pissed off like he usually did. Then again, he was probably pissed off because he had to deal with me. I was a complication in his life.

He was asleep on his back, his t-shirt riding up, his hand flat on his bare chiseled belly. God, he had sexy hands.

I could see his blond happy trail and his jeans were low, showing the start of the V heading down to his groin. His feet were now bare, his socks laying across the arm of the sofa by his feet. My eyes lazily took him in from toe to head and then back down to the happy trail. My mouth started to water and I squirmed. When I'd taken him in my mouth the other morning it was awesome. He was well-endowed. He was well-groomed down there. And the feel of his strong sexy hands in my hair while his cock was in my mouth? It had me wet and ready. More than ready.

But he'd been asleep and my doing that pretty much amounted to sexual assault. It'd been wrong. But I'd woken up to him looking beautiful and sleeping again with me cradled against him and so I wanted to wake him up in a way that showed my appreciation as well as ensured he'd want me. But he'd been angry. And now I knew why. He wasn't there to collect his slave; he was there to deal with a mess put on his shoulders by his deceased father. He gets saddled with me, a dirty and broken human being, and I'm all stammering, begging for sex, and being a pain in his butt.

But sex was all I knew anymore. I knew almost nothing anymore of who I was before Thailand. I only knew A to B. Screw them good and make them happy. Screwing them good generally did make them happy. It meant I didn't get punished, and it helped me get and then stay on course, a course of staying on the short list and not being subjected to corrections or retraining for non-compliance, and because of that, maybe that's why I got off on it.

It was who I had to be and every small A to B victory meant success so I got off on it in some dysfunctional twisted way. I'd always been sexual. Always. Even as a small girl. And the Kruna scouts knew how to spot it and their trainers sure knew how to exploit it. And somehow, I used it. I used my sexuality to get myself out of there.

I looked back up from his happy trail to his face and he was now awake and watching me. He was watching me ogle him. Our eyes locked. I moistened my lips and tried to settle myself down. I was probably flushed. I was so aroused right now. I wanted him, wanted him bad.

"Jetlag," he mumbled.

"Yeah," I rasped.

He stretched. "Wanna crash?"

I think I nodded.

He got up. "You take my bed." He stretched again as he walked to his alarm panel by the door and hit some buttons that beeped and the sight of his muscled arms and back as he stretched revved me up even further.

"But the futon sucks," I answered softly.

"Yeah, the futon sucks."

"I can sleep on the futon," I said but was hoping he wouldn't make me sleep alone in there.

"Naw, I'll be fine." He massaged the back of his neck with a wince and I knew he was thinking about how uncomfortable of a sleep that futon would be. "Maybe the couch is better," he said.

"It's pretty comfy. I can just sleep here. You take your bed."

"Naw, you take the bed." He was staring at me.

"We could both sleep in your bed again," I offered.

His eyes lit with something and he sneered. He looked severely pissed off.

"I'm sorry. I---"

"You take my bed. I'll sleep out here. I'll order a bed tomorrow for the den, move my desk out here, you can have that room."

I wasn't about to argue with that hard expression and those angry eyes. I don't think anyone would.

"Thank you for dinner and the movie. And, um, everything. You've been very kind. Kinder than you should have to be. Thank you."

He gave me a little smile but it had pity written all over it.

"Goodnight," I said.

He gave me a chin jerk but said nothing.

Dare

I woke up to shrill screaming in the pitch dark. It set my fight or flight instinct in motion big time and I reached to get between the bed and box spring for my piece but then I realized I wasn't in bed. I was on the couch. I ran to the bedroom. She was flailing in my bed in a nightmare. I grabbed her.

"Felicia! Wake up!"

She was writhing in agony.

"Hey, it's just a dream." I pulled her up to sitting.

She started to sob and a flurry of words and whimpers came out.

"Master, don't let them get me." She threw her arms over my shoulders and clung to my neck like her life depended on it.

"Shh." I lay down, taking her with me. Her head landed on my shoulder. I stroked her hair and she loosened her grip around my neck and fisted my t-shirt. "It's gonna all be okay, babe. Settle down. I promise it'll be okay. Okay?"

"Okay," she whimpered and her breathing slowed down and I thought she was settling but then she said, "Make me yours, Master. Take me. Make me yours."

I thought the 'master' ramblings were her asleep, still in the nightmare. I guess I'd been wrong.

"Baby, I'm not your Master," I said, shaking my head.

"I want you to be," she whispered. "I'll be a good girl." She squirmed into me. "Your good girl."

For fuck sakes. I had goosebumps everywhere and all the blood in my head rushed straight to my cock.

Her grip loosened on my shirt and I quickly knew why. She slipped her hand into the waistband of my shorts and then she was gripping my cock. Fuck.

"Felicia."

"Please don't call me that," she pleaded.

"What's your real name?" I asked. She hadn't let go of my cock yet and fuck but I was hard. How could I not be?

She was quiet a minute and then said, "Please don't make me tell you. I'm not allowed to."

"Hands off."

She shuddered, then her thumb stroked over the tip. "I can make you feel good."

"I'm sure you could." I grabbed her wrist and tried to pull. She gripped tighter. I didn't wanna be rough with her. Wow. So she was an obedient slave girl but she wouldn't let go of my cock? Just my luck.

"Let go."

"Please, Dare?"

"I'm not taking advantage of you. Let go of it."

"You're not. I'm offering. I need it. I haven't…" she didn't finish.

"You've got some sorta hero worship, babe. I got you outta there and you're developing some sense of obligation here. I don't want that."

"My hair is red and I love to fuck. That's what you wanted, right? I love to fuck, Master. I really, really do. I'd keep up with you, whatever you want, any way you want, I---" she squeezed, stroking upwards.

"Let go of my cock, babe. Seriously."

She took her hand away and moved off my chest but not far away, just beside me. She was quiet for a beat and then said, "You don't want me?"

"I don't."

I could feel her shame. Her distress filled the room. This girl had been assessed and appraised for her sexual value and my telling her she had none to me? It had to hurt.

"Sweetheart, you're beautiful. You are totally what I'd go for. But I won't go there. Not takin' advantage of you. Your head isn't in the right place after all they did to you and yeah, a few months ago you beggin' me like this, I would've. I would've fucked you in a heartbeat but where I'm at in my life right now, I can't. Won't."

"Oh."

"You okay? I'm gonna go back to the living room."

"Can you stay?"

It was a mistake to keep getting in bed with her. I knew it. I told myself we were tired and it was a big bed and nothing was gonna happen but I knew it was a mistake.

"Keep your hands and your mouth to yourself, all right?"

"I will," she whispered. "Thank you."

"Let's try to get some sleep."

Felicia

"Don't cry," he said softly a few minutes later. "You're gonna be okay."

I wanted to believe that. I didn't mean to make my crying obvious. I thought he'd fallen asleep.

"You don't have to fuck to survive anymore."

He sure hit the nail on the head.

"Could I have my collar back, Master?"

"What?" he spat. He sounded disgusted.

"My collar. If you put it back on me, I'll sleep better. I keep freaking out inside and if I have the collar on it'll help me know they can't take me back because I'm yours. In the dreams the collar gone is why they can get to me but…"

He stormed out. I felt my chin trembling.

A few minutes later I didn't know if he had gone to the other room or not. I was driving him away, he'd get sick of my crap, he'd send me away. I squeezed my eyes shut tight and tried to get my heart to settle down, to push the panic away.

The collars at the club that were single strand were the collars for girls available to all patrons. Double-strand collars were slaves booked for the night to a specific patron or party. The triple strand collars were for girls who were owned. Mine looked more like a choker but it had the design of the collars, in essence. Any visitor knew by looking at a woman's throat whether they could have her or not. It was always respected.

My throat had been covered with a different coded collar for the past month and a half, the black X advising that I was off limits, that I belonged to someone who had not yet claimed me. In the past, I'd spent most of my time in single strand collars and plenty of time in double-strand collars. My first seven months there was spent with a double collar and it was often attached to a leash. The minute Dare put that triple strand jeweled necklace on me at the resort it felt different. I'd been waiting for that moment for a long time. It was beautiful; it meant I was at Point C.

I really felt like it might send the nightmares away. I hadn't had dreams in over a year, not since Mr. Frost died. I hadn't dreamt until Dario Ferrano strolled into that room in his tailored suit with his stormy blue eyes, his olive-toned skin, that beautiful body, but now the nightmares were back and they were absolutely horrific.

He was back. I could smell smoke and the outside on him so knew he'd gone out to the balcony. I heard a tinkling and he softly said, "Up; let me put this on. I don't know that this is the right thing to do, baby, but if it chases the bad dreams away…" He let that hang.

A wave of relief washed over me. I lifted my hair as I sat up and he fastened the necklace for me. The feel of his fingers on the back of my neck, it was going to be my undoing. I let out a little whimper. "Thank you." I closed my eyes and absorbed the feel of it and felt my body settle.

"May I speak?"

"Stop asking permission."

"Can you, could you, um… hold me? I'm not still asking for sex, I just, I'm so fucked up…" I asked, knowing I was pushing him but I only hoped I wasn't pushing him too far. What I really wanted, needed, was for him to hold me down and take me, but I knew that wasn't an option. My scalp prickled. I couldn't believe I'd sworn again. I hadn't cussed aloud, or barely even in my head, in almost 2 years, not unless I was instructed to, not since I had my mouth washed out with something disgusting as a punishment for telling a trainer to go fuck themselves.

"Come here," he answered and the sound of his voice, those words, I felt them between my legs and deep in my chest. I rested my head on his chest and wrapped my arms around myself. He was warm and cozy and between being there with him and having his collar on my throat I allowed something that I hadn't allowed in a long time. I allowed myself to hope, and not just a little.

"Thank you," I said, knowing in my soul he was different from the men I'd been acquainted with in the past two years. I'd have never made requests or been so bold otherwise. Bold me today was nothing like the bold me of two years ago but bold me of today was not exactly like Felicia of last week, either.

"Okay," he answered. He put an arm around me. But he did it stiffly.

"Thank you for saving me."

"You're welcome," he answered and gave a little squeeze and kissed my forehead. His body loosened then and his other arm came around me and it didn't feel stiff or awkward any longer. It felt like that was just where I belonged. I fell into a deep and peaceful sleep.

Dare

This was not cool. Not cool at all. I didn't know how to handle this shit. One part of me thought I should start being a dick to her so she'd get over her hero worship. But after what I could only imagine she'd been through I'd be a heartless prick to do that. But I didn't wanna encourage this. Not a bit.

Why? Because it'd be so easy, so fucking easy to take what she was offering. She was beautiful. She was ten times more beautiful than the red-haired girl from grade eleven science class, the one that I let get away in favor of the wild child Debbie was. And the talk about the insatiable sexual appetite? My pop's twisted notions about me having a girl trained to be perfect, being what I wanted spoke volumes, especially with a few things I'd found out about him at Kruna. I shook my head in disgust. But the things she was offering? I was saying No but my cock was fucking pleading with me.

Felicia was asleep, curled up to me, her head on my chest, her leg draped over my thigh. She squirmed, jolting me out of my thoughts, and then she was squirming, no gyrating, right against me. The hand that had been flat on my abs was now under my t-shirt, in a fist over my heart. She opened the fist slowly and her nails skated across a nipple as she flexed her hand. The sensation went straight to my cock. Her nightgown had ridden up and she wasn't wearing panties. Her naked pussy was against my thigh and she squirmed against me. I clenched my teeth but my cock was rock hard. Her hand emerged from the neck hole of my t-shirt and her fingers wove into my hair.

I could whip my clothes off and fuck her brains out. She'd give it to me gladly. She'd been begging me for it. She'd spread wide and let me do her any which way I wanted. She'd be game to any position, any sexual act. She'd let me suspend her from the ceiling, she'd let me fuck her up the ass, she'd let me do anything I wanted.

She'd give me babies, as many as I asked for. She'd be gorgeous on my arm at any family or business event. She'd make herself fit into my life. I wouldn't have to do the work. I wouldn't have to go through the task of finding her, figuring out whether or not she was a psycho crazy bitch, figure out whether or not she sucked in bed, figure out whether or not we were compatible. Wouldn't have to fall for her and then lay awake at night wondering whether or not she'd be faithful to me.

She'd been professionally trained to be the ultimate lay, to be compatible with her Master. She wouldn't nag, she wouldn't whine, she'd take any scrap

I gave her. I could treat her like a princess and lavish her with everything her heart desired. I could use her and abuse her if I wanted to, not that I would, but if I did stupid shit or acted like a dick, I'd never have to worry she'd leave me for it. I could just take her. She was mine. Here she was, in my bed, curled against me, willing to be mine. Wanting to wear a collar that was akin to wearing a wedding ring but even more permanent. She'd probably be missing the spark I wanted in a woman but I couldn't expect everything now, could I? She'd never shred my heart. She'd never ask for more than I wanted to give.

Almost no one would fault me. Outside of the people at Kruna the only ones who knew were Stan, Tommy, and Zack.

Stan, I didn't give a shit about his opinion. He got paid to have no opinion.

Zack, I knew he'd look down his nose at me for it and yeah, he'd probably fault me.

But Tommy? Yeah, he'd tell me it was a bad idea. But he'd be a fucking hypocrite because Pop gave him a girl who didn't even want him and yet he kept her. He got to keep his girl even if she was ill-gotten, given to him out of Pop's fucked up brand of revenge. Why shouldn't I keep Felicia?

Tommy'd give me a look and say it was a bad idea and I'd cock an eyebrow at him and then he'd fucking zip it because he'd know he has no room to judge me.

But here I was, determined I was not doing it. I was better than that. But was I?

I pried her off me without waking her and stormed out of the room, smoked two cigarettes, drank three shots of vodka, and then I went and slept like shit on the shitty fuckin' futon so I could close the door and shut out the world.

Felicia

I woke up alone. I went looking for him and found the door shut to his spare room so guessed he was in there. My heart sank. The sun hadn't yet risen but I wasn't sleepy any longer so I padded into the master bathroom and did my business and took a shower and then because my clothes were in the room he was sleeping in and I didn't wanna wake him I went into his closet and snatched back the flannel pjs I'd worn for just a few hours yesterday.

After a minute checking out some of his other clothes, he had a lot of great suits, I went out to the kitchen and after far too long pondering the notion I finally decided I was capable of making coffee without getting permission first. Then, again after a long pondering, I decided it would probably be okay if I turned the TV on. It was odd making decisions for myself, even small ones. What to wear, what to watch, what to drink. These things don't seem so insignificant when you haven't been able to make those choices for yourself. These things were huge. And Dario Ferrano gave these things to me.

As I was finishing my second cup, watching the news, he came out of the other room and I heard the master bedroom door close as he went in there.

I fingered my collar and closed my eyes, feeling bad about last night and my meltdown. He must've thought I was bat shit crazy. If they had seen me behave that way, they'd have … they'd have… I shuddered. I needed to pull myself together.

I heard him. I opened my eyes. He was looking at me while pouring a cup of coffee. I painted my face blank and straightened up my posture and said, "Good morning."

"Hey." He eyed me cautiously.

He was in chocolate brown suit pants and was carrying a blazer. The pants were slim fitting. He wore a black shirt, black tie. His hair was wet from the shower and he was freshly shaven. As he walked by and I thought about how delicious he looked I caught a whiff and he smelled good, too.

He tossed his blazer on a stool and then reached into a kitchen drawer and pulled out a memo pad and a pen and then started scrawling on it. I stared at his hands, his wrists. He had strong-looking hands. Not rough-looking like someone who works in manual labor, of course, but strong-looking. The knuckles on his right hand were a little bruised from when he'd punched the hole in the bathroom in Thailand. Looking at his hands took me back to watching him work with his hands transforming a mound of wet sand and making it look like a castle. I saw, in my mind, those hands on my breasts. I swallowed hard. His voice jolted me out of those fantasies.

"I need to work at my office today. Got a shitload to do. Here's my cell number. And there's a backup number here for emergencies if you can't reach me. If you call that number it's Nino, he works for me. He doesn't know anything about you. I'll tell him you're a houseguest in case you need him for anything. He's a six-and-a-half-foot bearded bald biker with a lot of tatts so you'll know who to expect if you do happen to need him. Otherwise do not answer the door. The alarm'll be armed, the building doesn't get solicitors, and there's no reason anyone should knock on that door. If there's an emergency where you need out, like a fire, I'm writing down the emergency code to push to get out. This is the fire code only; you don't press it otherwise because it'll dispatch authorities as if you're an intruder. You unlock the door without pushing this code it'll ring as an intruder alarm and won't let you out unless the place is on fire or has a C02 alarm, so don't do that. Once we have things sorted and you can come and go freely, I will program you your own access, which we can do with your fingerprint." He made a face and took a deep breath and shook his head, like he'd just realized something, then he continued. "If my landline rings check the call display. Only answer if it's me or comes up on the call display with my name or the name Nino."

"Okay," I said. Then his words come and go freely echoed in my brain.

"You realize how serious I am about you not being able to phone anyone yet, right?" His brows were up and his vibe was pissed off badass personified.

"There's no one I'd call, Dare. I won't put you at risk. I promise."

"Okay." He stared at me for a beat and then sipped his coffee. "I'll see you tonight. Make sure you eat, all right? Sorry for leaving you without access to your clothes this morning." He motioned to me, clearly talking about the pjs.

"I like them." I shrugged apologetically.

His forehead crinkled and his mouth almost spread into a smile but it looked like he halted it. "You need anything, call me."

"I will. Have a good day."

He took another sip of the coffee, poured the remaining contents of the mug into the sink, said, "Good coffee, by the way," and then went to the door, grabbed his keys, and hit a bunch of buttons on the alarm panel. Then he left.

I sank onto the sofa and wrapped the blanket that he'd covered me with the other night around myself.

Dare

I'd put codes on my home phone making it password protected to dial out to anywhere but me or Nino. I'd forwarded all but my and Nino's numbers direct to voicemail. I didn't wanna mistrust but with what was at stake and what with not knowing where her head was at, I needed to be careful. I considered leaving a guard with her but had a feeling it would be okay, that she'd obey.

It was a busy day but work stress was the kind of stress I could easily deal with. I welcomed it. And having workable problems that I could actually solve put me in a better mood.

I called my place at lunchtime and she answered hesitantly. It was awkward.

"You all right?"

"Yes. Thank you."

"You make breakfast or lunch?"

"I, um, ate the rest of the pizza for breakfast."

I laughed. "Breakfast of champions."

She let out a small laugh.

"I'll be there around 7:00 tonight. You need me to bring anything?"

She was quiet.

"You there, Angel?" I asked gently. She had asked me not to call her Felicia anymore but she begged me not to make her tell me her real name.

"I'm here," she whispered.

"Why're you whispering?" I whispered back.

She cleared her throat and her voice got louder, "Sorry. I'm here."

"What do you need that you don't have? Maybe tomorrow as it's Saturday I'll take you shopping and let you loose with my credit card. Get you some more flannel pjs, girlie shit or whatever, too?" I laughed. "But what about tonight? Anything you need that you don't have?"

"I have everything I need, Master," she said softly and *fuck,* it just about did me in the way she said that.

"Not your Master," I replied.

She was quiet.

"What do you wanna eat tonight?" I pushed the emotions she was stirring in me away.

"Whatever you want," she answered.

"There has to be more than pasta you've craved and haven't had in two years."

She was quiet.

"Babe?"

"PB and J," she said, no sighed, "Thick soft white Wonder bread. Strawberry jam with chunks of strawberries in it. Kraft smooth peanut butter."

I laughed a little. "I think I'll need you to be more specific."

"I am so gonna get fat," she said softly.

"Yeah, you are." I chuckled.

"Hey," she said softly but indignantly.

"Angel, if I can make it so that the worst thing that happens to you from now on is a little junk in your trunk, I'm all over that."

"All over my trunk, Master?" she giggled.

I was surprised at her making a joke but her laugh and easy manner made me smile. That giggle was like music. I'd bet big money that she hadn't giggled like that too much in the past two years.

"Not your Master," I reminded her.

She didn't reply.

"So PB & J for dinner?" I said finally to break the silence.

"Yeah," she said hoarsely and then cleared her throat. "Yes, please."

***

I hadn't been inside a supermarket since… I don't even know. Sarah did all my shopping. It was a weird experience. I seemed to be getting a lot of female attention; shoppers, cashiers, especially at the check-out when I grabbed a bouquet of flowers from a bin. I pushed away the nagging little voice telling me I'd give her the wrong idea and instead told myself I wanted to brighten up the apartment for her since she was stuck there all day.

When I got in, she was watching TV and she'd jumped like a cat that wants to latch itself to the ceiling at me opening the door. I raised a hand. "Just me." I hit buttons on the alarm panel.

She had her hair tied up in a high ponytail and she was wearing my pjs still. Her face was make-up free but she looked fresh and pretty. The apartment smelled like lemons. Everything was spotless.

"Definitely need to get you more flannel pjs, huh?" I jerked my chin up and dropped the supermarket bag and bouquet on the counter.

"I, I washed them and put them back on. I hope that's okay. I did your other laundry, too, from the trip, the, uh, stuff I could wash. I saw a dry-cleaning bag in the master walk-in so I put your suits in there."

"You don't have to clean and do my laundry, babe." I started unpacking the groceries. "I have a housekeeper come by twice a week. Shit, Sarah's due here Monday. We're gonna have to figure out how to play that." I put my index fingers to my temples.

I shook my head at that thought and then pulled out a crystal vase from a kitchen cupboard and filled it with water and then plunked the flowers in and put them in the center of the island. She smiled at the sight of them.

"So why do you like those pajamas so much?" I jerked my chin up. "Remind you of Alaska?"

She climbed up on a stool at the island. "Everything I have is just uncomfortable for lounging. Or inappropriate for outside the, uh, bedroom."

"Ah. Well, tomorrow we can hit the mall."

"You don't have to…"

"Naw, what guy doesn't like being dragged around a mall while a woman buys clothes?" I gave her a wink.

She smiled and it spread to her eyes. They sort of twinkled, the light catching them and her sapphire collar at the same time. My throat went dry.

"I'm really throwing your life into a tailspin." Her expression dropped.

I shook my head. "I do my best work under pressure. No worries. So, why don't you whip us up some PB & J and I'll go get changed?"

She smiled. "You don't mind eating sandwiches for dinner?"

I shrugged. "Naw, why not? Pizza for breakfast, PB & J for dinner, why be conventional?"

"You're amazing," she said and she was looking me right in the eye. She looked serious. Too serious.

"It might look like that after what you've been through, Angel, but you don't know me," I muttered and left the kitchen.

As I passed the utility room, I saw that the dryer was still going and there were folded clothes and towels on top. Shit. Sarah would have something to say about this, for sure. When I came back out, she was finishing putting things away and she'd served up sandwiches.

"What would you like to drink, Ma—Dare?"

"I'll have what you're having," I said and sat down at the island.

She poured two glasses of milk and climbed up on a stool and looked at her plate with reverence. My sandwich was cut in half on the diagonal. Hers was cut into triangles. She closed her eyes a minute and then I saw her mouth an "amen" and then she lifted one of the triangles.

She took a bite and the expression on her face gave me a semi. If her face went like that at a pb&j what the fuck would it look like while she was having an orgasm?

"I don't rate for triangles?" I teased. I reached into the kitchen cupboard and pulled out a bottle of chocolate syrup and squeezed a healthy dose into my drinking glass. Her eyes lit up. I squeezed an even bigger glug into her glass and then passed her a spoon.

She blushed, stirred, took a sip of the milk, and moaned. Then she said, "They taste better when they're triangles. I didn't know if you'd agree."

I grinned. "Does something magical happen to triangular food?"

"Absolutely!" She smirked at me and I felt a pang at that smirk. Fuck, she was gorgeous.

She lifted another triangle and the moan that she made as she ate it, her eyes rolling back, it went right to my fucking cock. Evidently, I seriously needed to get laid.

But how could I get laid if I was keeping up with my 'man whore no more' plan? It'd be complicated to start a new relationship while she was living here, too. What woman who was marriage material would be okay with me having a chick live at my place?

I had to keep her close, though, to make sure that the Kruna scumbags didn't get suspicious. Maybe I needed to push the no man whore plan out a little. Go to a bar, get laid, get sex off my brain for five minutes. A voice inside me said:

Or maybe just take the angel in front of you. Problem solved.

That voice had been nagging at me since the minute my fingerprint opened that tablet and it was getting fucking louder. It was trying to tell me that I could take her, that taking her wouldn't mean I was taking advantage, that I could take her and be gentle with her and she'd get healthy and we'd get what we both wanted. For her, safety and knowledge that she was out of the reach of the Kruna scumbags. For me, my beautiful redhead who liked to fuck, who'd never cheat, and who'd give me a family and be fine with whatever life I made for us, whether it was in a world of shady shit or living in the country or moving to Yellowknife to be a bush pilot, or whatever.

But yeah, taking her? How was I any better than my father if I did that? I'd never have a girl who really loved me, only one who was obligated to pretend she did. Forget that shit.

But Tommy did it.

Yeah, he did. And despite how they got going Tia now loved him. Her world revolved around him. I wanted that. I fucking dreamt about having that and unfortunately, those dreams were vivid and before the wedding I'd even had a few vivid dreams about having it with my brother's girl. But once he slid that ring on her finger and I saw how she looked into his eyes like he was her everything, she started really feeling like family, thank God. And as far as having another girl fall for a Ferrano boy after being thrust at him? Well…lightning usually didn't strike twice.

I pushed my plate with the untouched sandwich back. "On second thought, I gotta hit the gym. Be back later."

Her expression dropped, but she quickly recovered and gave me a nod.

I headed to my bedroom and got my workout gear and threw jeans and a tee into a bag with it and headed out. The gym was in the building. Maybe I'd go for a drink afterwards.

***

"Oh, my, Gaaaawd!"

I looked over my shoulder and saw a skanky-looking bleach blonde in *fuck-me* heels, big hair, and a hot pink tube mini dress approaching me. Aw fuck. Not her.

"Dario Ferrano, slumming it?" Casey was in Debbie's clique in high school. I was in a bar down the street from my building, post workout. I'd texted Zack to see if he wanted to meet me for a drink, thinkin' it'd be good to hang with someone who knew the predicament I was in.

"Slumming it?"

This wasn't exactly a dive bar.

She gestured to me with her hand, "I haven't seen you in jeans since I don't know when. High school? Mr. Dapper Dan is always in a suit. What's up? Leather jacket and jeans? You're like a bad boy or somethin' tonight." She sat on the stool beside me and threw back the last of the pink liquid in her glass and then gave me another once over, her eyes all lusty.

"Just finished a workout." I flashed a smile. She had a great rack, a great fake rack. Casey'd been pretty well flat-chested in grade 12. Now she had double D's, at least. "And I'm always a bad boy, babe."

"So, how about you buy me another drink, bad boy?" she flirted.

A text came in from Zack. "Sorry man, on a stakeout and can't make it. Hit me up next time."

"Bartender?" I called out. "Another vodka for me and another pink sludge or whatever the fuck that was for this lovely lady."

Felicia

After my peanut butter and jam sandwich, I pondered it for a while and then after about half an hour of thinking about it, decided it'd maybe be okay if I took a long bath in Dario's master bathroom. He had one of those peanut-shaped whirlpool tubs big enough for two. He didn't have any sort of frou-frou bath stuff and none had been packed with my things so minus bubbles but the bath was still heavenly.

His mood, as he left the apartment, made it very apparent to me that I needed to give him space. I had to be fair to him. He had rescued me out of necessity, sure, but he'd rescued me nonetheless and had been nothing but kind to me. We were in a sticky situation and it was being made stickier by the fact that my cheese had slipped off my cracker.

I thought I had it together all that time. I thought my A to B plan was what kept me sane because I could lock the real me away and get to it later, if I wanted to. I figured I could turn my emotions off and just do what I was supposed to do. But from the minute he walked into my life and the minute I was getting my Point C, things had gone off the rails and I was having a hard time getting my brain back on the track. I was consumed with the need to spread my legs for him. Completely consumed with it. I'd thought I held it together all that time, compartmentalized things to keep my sanity, but I guess I was wrong. Maybe I was so far off the rails I'd never get back.

After the bath I got into a red silky short nightie and borrowed his robe and then I went to his den to re-make up the futon, which had been folded back upright. I'd give him space to try to make up for the fact that I had been a total pain. I was afraid that if I didn't give him space, he'd send me away or send me back. If his plan was to make them think he was okay with this maybe his life would be easier if they sent him a new girl who wasn't a crackpot, begging and pleading with him to fuck her. But as I started to drift to sleep, I started fantasizing, imagining him romantically carrying me to his bed and telling me that he wanted me, that he'd keep me and keep me safe forever.

I hesitantly slipped my hands under my nightie while under the covers and after a lot of deliberating, a LOT of deliberating, I did something I hadn't done since a few months after I was taken in to Kruna. We were not allowed to masturbate unless it was part of an assignment. Our orgasms were gifts granted to us by our handlers or patrons. There was a camera in my room, which I had not known but had figured out when I got punished for it. The punishment had been severe, unforgettably so.

There were no cameras here. No rules about touching myself here. So I did. I made myself come twice, one huge earth-shattering O right after the other, with my fingers to my clit, my eyes closed and in my mind I was picturing his face, his lips, his tongue, his sexy hands, his gorgeous eyes, imagining his big beautiful hard cock in my mouth, imagining him petting me afterwards, holding me, touching my face in that sweet way of his, and telling me I was his good girl, his angel.

Afterwards, I slid into blissful slumber but then woke with a jolt from a dream, a dream where they'd come in and caught me touching myself. But when they tried to get me, he'd come in and told them to take their hands off. *"She's mine. None of you will fuck with her again."* Then he shot them in the head. Cleo, Rafe, Mr. Chen, and three others. I'd woken up panting but elated. I touched myself again, made myself come again muttering "Master" as I hit it, and then I fell back to sleep.

***

I woke up with a start. Another dream, but I couldn't remember what it was about. I adjusted the pillow and tried to curl back in but felt a chill creep up my spine. The room was dark but the door was now open so there was a stream of light from the hallway over my face. And then I noticed there was a figure looming over me. I caught a waft of tobacco and alcohol and a little bit of sweet-smelling perfume.

"Master?"

He laughed a little. It was more of a sneer. "Yeah, that's me," he said.

I shifted onto my side to face him and fluffed the pillow again.

"Why're you in here?" he asked, but it was sort of slurred. "This shitty futon fucking sucks. You roll to the middle and it dips and buckles. It's like a fuckin' taco. Stupid taco bed."

"It's not so bad," I whispered.

"Forgot to buy you a real bed today. Or maybe I didn't forget."

Huh?

"I was trying to respect you, Dare, give you space. I'm sorry about my behavior last night."

"Hah!" He sat on the futon. "You're fucking with me, right?"

"I'm not trying to."

"Well… you are." He reached down and put his thumb to my lower lip, his fingers along my jaw, his face only inches from mine. "You're fucking with me big time. Do you know what happened tonight?"

I put my palm to the back of his hand and caressed it.

"Shit. You even fucking smell like sex. Aw, fuuuuck me!" He got to his feet. He reached into the pocket of his jacket and then I caught his profile as he lit a cigarette. He took two or three deep hauls off it and then shook his head, uttering more cusswords under his breath as he left.

I stayed still, feeling mortified. After a few minutes I curled up into a ball, closed my eyes and decided to try to go back to sleep. But he came back. He left the door open wider this time and the hall light spilled over the futon again.

He sat on the edge of it. "You're fucking with my head, Angel." His voice sounded sad now.

"How?" I asked, feeling his words vibrate through me.

"I'm a cold-hearted snake. A man-whore. And I've done some bad shit. I've ordered people to take out other people. I've watched people die. Taken lives, myself. Deservedly, but still. I come from a bad fucking seed. I've screwed with lives and just fucked with them until they were unrecognizable. I'm no better than the scumbags who took you. Don't have some twisted hero worship thing, baby, because I'm no better."

"You saved me," I whispered. And I wanted to add *and I wanna be yours* but I didn't say it.

"But don't let that fool you. I did that to save myself," he stated.

"You still did it. And you've been so kind to me."

"Yeah, well a few months before I saved you, I hand-delivered another girl, an innocent girl, to her new Master. Not the same as what you're dealing with, but too damn close. I was totally fine with handing a girl over as a flesh payment on a debt to my own brother. Taking her out of her happy life and saying, 'Here you go.' There's a fucking pattern here with my family, baby, a very fucked up pattern."

He was quiet a moment, then he continued.

"Just before I found out about you, I decided that I was tired of being a selfish prick. Man whore no more! That was gonna be my motto. Karma laughed in my face, though, didn't it? You make me wanna keep being that prick because you and that fucking collar and those fucking eyes and that body, and that angelic face…the things you say to me. I keep trying to stay away, but you make that hard."

I stayed still, not sure what to say.

"I had my dick in a chick's mouth tonight," he said low, and then leaned closer to me, "And I couldn't bring it. Couldn't finish. Never had that problem in. my. life. I was only hard because I was remembering your mouth around it, and then I couldn't bring it with her because she didn't have hair like this." He fisted my hair, but not roughly. "And a mouth like this." His fingertips from his other hand were now on my lips. "And a necklace like this."

His voice had dropped down an octave at that last sentence. He let go of my hair and hooked his index finger into the dangling heart at my throat and crooked it, then pulled. I followed the motion and sat up. He kept pulling with his index finger until my face was an inch from his. "You make me wanna take," he said this with a rasp to his voice that went straight to my clit.

My body went liquid and hot with arousal. My nipples were hard, my heart was racing. He was drunk and pissed off and he wanted me. He jerked the collar again, making me scramble to my knees.

"Stop offering it to me or I'll have no choice but to fucking take it."

"I want you to take it," I whispered a breath away from his mouth. "Please, please take it."

He lifted my right hand and brought it to his nose and inhaled and then let out a slow breath.

"Were you touching yourself tonight, Angel?"

"Yes, Master."

"God damn," he groaned and then his mouth touched my fingertips and he parted his lips. The tip of his tongue touched them. A hot gush surged between my legs.

All of a sudden, he roughly threw me back down to the bed and grabbed me by the calves and then his face was buried between my legs. Oh, my fucking fuck.

His tongue slipped inside me and we both moaned at the exact same instant. He spread my folds apart and then his tongue found its way up to my clit.

"So fucking sweet," he moaned.

"Ah!" I was going to explode in record time. It was going to be huge. I wanted it to last; I wanted to savor it but it wouldn't wait. His tongue swiped over my swollen clit just a few times before I detonated.

I screamed out, "Oh thank you, Master."

I heard him fumble and his clothes started flying off and then he drove his beautiful cock into me. Hard. So hard. He had his fingers between my throat and my collar and he fisted it, using his other hand to brace himself as he rolled his hips and slammed into me over and over. "Ah fuck, baby, you feel as good as I knew you would. Better."

"Oh, Master…" I whimpered, feeling a twisting beautiful blissful ache in between my legs and in my chest.

He hammered hard into me, over and over, and over. He let go of my collar and grabbed my wrists and held them over my head. It was like he'd read my mind.

"Yes! Please keep holding me down while you take me. I'm so lucky to be yours." I was weeping. But I was in ecstasy.

"Mine? Fuck." He was fucking me harder, his hands gripping my wrists painfully tight. Beautifully tight. He brought his lips down to mine and kissed me like his life depended on it, plunging his tongue into my mouth, twisting it up with mine. He was an amazing kisser like I knew he would be.

"Yes, I'm yours, Master. All yours. Please keep me," I said against his mouth and then I licked along his lower lip.

"Stop fucking calling me Master!" he shouted, making me lock tight.

"Like I wanna be called some name you've called every sick fuck that's raped you, hurt you!" He sounded pained and he'd stopped. He was inside me and still had my wrists pinned, but he was still.

I replied and did it with confidence, clarity. "No, Dario, you don't understand. Only you. They were Sir. They were all Sir. I waited 22 months, 19 days and ten hours for my Master, the one who would save me from there, make me his, save me from that hell. Please don't see it as a bad thing that I call you that. I'm so happy it's you that I can call that. You're my one and only Master. I don't even think of you as Sir any longer."

His body was locked tight. Then he sort of growled and then let go of my wrists and wrapped his arms right around me and held me tight as he kissed me and pumped into me slowly, an inch at a time, just a few times and then threw his head back and moaned, "Angel," as he came inside of me.

God, he was perfect.

We were breathless. His hands didn't have my wrists any longer but now his fingers were woven with mine, still pinning me to the bed. His lips were against my collar bone. I wrapped my legs around him tight, kind of hugging him with them. He stayed still for about two or three minutes, just connected with me, and then he slid out of me. He leaned over and flicked the lamp on his desk on, lifted up onto an elbow and looked down at me, the other hand's fingers still weaved with mine over my head. He caressed my cheek with a graze of his knuckles and said softly, "Too fast," then his lips were on mine again, kissing sweetly, softly. I melted into the kiss and moaned.

We made out like teenagers for a while, kissing, caressing, panting. And then after a few minutes groping. He slid back into me, hard again. He started slow, sweet, raining kisses on my face, my ear, my throat, but then he picked up the pace and started fucking me harder, faster, as I arched my back and rotated my hips against his. He was looking down at us, watching his cock enter me over and over. Wow, that was sexy.

Then he rolled and I was on top. He whipped my red nightie off me and began to knead my breasts as I rode him, the sensual look on his face rocking my world as he looked down again, watching my body sheath him. I cupped his jaw with both hands, leaned to kiss him, and put more passion into that kiss than I had with kissing anyone in my whole life. I wanted to show him what this meant to me. I wanted him to feel something so beautiful that he'd never want to send me away.

He rolled back and now he was sitting up, feet swung over and, on the floor, me straddling him, our connection at the lips and pelvises not breaking. He moaned into my mouth as he picked up his pace and then he grabbed my wrists and put them behind my back, transferring them to one of his hands. He held them there. The other hand grazed up my body to my throat and then he held my collar as we, together, set about a faster, more intense rhythm. Me riding him as hard as I could, him thrusting his hips at me, both of us staring into one another's eyes in the lit room. He let go of the collar and put his thumb between us at my clit. "You fuck me so beautifully," I whispered. "Thank you, Master."

He came then, his mouth opening and a big shuddering masculine moan filling the room. He let go of my wrists and his fingers drove into my hair and pulled my head back. He ran his nose from my throat up to my jaw and then his mouth was on my ear. He took my earlobe between his teeth. Sensation exploded in me, too. It was a high I never wanted to come down from.

He flopped to his back, taking me with him. He was breathless. I was on top of him. I ran my palms up and down his face and then my fingers slid through his hair and I kissed his throat and nuzzled in and I said, "Thank you for saving me."

"Yeah," he said, winded.

"Please keep me," I whispered, equally as winded but pouring as much emotion into those three words as I would if I were telling him I loved him.

"Don't tempt me," was his answer and he said it with a fierceness, like he was angry with me, with himself, maybe. But he didn't let go of me so we both passed out, me on top of him still, his arms around my waist, my cheek on his chest, a little smile on my face, the light still on.

CHAPTER FOUR

Dare

I didn't get hangovers. Not usually. I drank a fuck of a lot last night and it seemed I'd dodged another hangover bullet. Maybe that was because I'd pretty much sobered up before I fell asleep. Not sober enough to leave this fucking futon, though. She was curled into the back of me. One hand on my shoulder blade, the other wrapped around my waist and against my stomach. She was breathing against the spot between my shoulder blades. Her pelvis was against my backside and her legs curved into mine, her knees against the backs of my legs above my knees. I put my hand on her hand on my belly and her whole body squeezed as she snuggled in closer. I lifted her hand up so I could get out of bed. As I was pulling my underwear on I glanced at her and her eyes were open and on me. I left the room.

I guzzled a bottle of water, dropped two Advils more for my muscles from that fucking bed than from the booze, and then threw on track pants, sneakers, and a hoodie, grabbed my iPhone, earbuds, and keys, then headed out for a run.

Felicia

I resisted the urge to weep when he left without a word, without barely looking at me. I fell asleep after the second time we had sex feeling safe, feeling blissfully sated and happy. I'd had six orgasms. Six! Three on my own and then three that he'd given me. I knew he was drunk. I knew he'd been beating himself up before we had sex. And now? What would he do now?

Dare

As I was running, earbuds in, hood up, sunglasses on, blocking out the world and rounding back toward the building a block away from home I spotted Pop's widow, Lisa. She was walking out of Bianca's beauty salon and heading toward her car. I sped up and got between her and the car door. She gasped, startled, as my hand came down on her wrist.

"You! We need to have a conversation."

"Dare! Oh my God. You scared the heck outta me!"

"Gimme the keys," I demanded.

She handed me her keys and went around to the passenger side.

I saw Bianca open the door to her shop, looking concerned, her phone in her hand. Bianca was practically a cousin to me. I took my hood and sunglasses off and saluted, making sure she saw it was me and not that Lisa was getting abducted. She waved, looking relieved.

I backed out. I drove for a few minutes, not talking, trying to rein in my emotions. Finally, I pulled up to a park and parked the car and looked to her. She had been sitting in the passenger seat quietly, just waiting for me to address her.

"Out," I said. "Leave your bag in the car." I didn't know if her car had been bugged. I walked about two or three minutes until the car was out of sight and she followed me. I sat on a bench and put my head in my hands, my elbows on my knees.

"Lisa, I know." I glanced in her direction.

She frowned as she sat. "You… know?"

"I found out where Pop got you from."

The color drained out of her face and she clutched at her throat. A familiar vision.

Fuck.

"I know this because he arranged for me to have a Kruna slave before he died.

She gasped.

Yeah, Lisa. Kruna slave. The last one to leave the resort to be married. To my pop.

"Her name's Felicia. At least that's the name they gave her. Don't know her real name. Didn't want her. Didn't want nothing to do with this shit, but if I didn't play along it could put all of us in danger so I picked her up and brought her back with every intention of letting her go once I knew there was no more threat."

"Dare, there will always be that threat," Lisa replied without waiting a breath. "You'd be better off keeping her. For you and her, for all of us."

"Fuck." I closed my eyes and put my head in my hands.

We were both quiet for a minute.

At Kruna, my head just about imploded when I found out that Pop procured Lisa from them. It didn't add up at first because Lisa was friends with my sisters, went to culinary school with Tess. That's where they'd met. Tess started bringing her around and then a few months after Pop's third wife Stacia died Pop announced he and Lisa were getting married. Lisa was a terrible cook; no wonder she'd flunked out of school. She never belonged there. She was only there to meet my sister. It was all staged.

Lisa was almost Stacia's double looks wise. Stacia was a former swimsuit model who died in a suspicious car crash. But Lisa was like Stacia with a personality transplant because while Stacia was a shrew, Lisa was sweet. She seemed totally gaga over Pop. But she also had a personality. She and my sisters were tight. She was there for Stacia's funeral, too, to support Tess and Luciana, or so it seemed at the time.

After the initial shock of the hook-up between Pop and her, the girls eventually got over it. Then Pop got his beloved Sunday dinners with the whole family around him. Pop clearly installed Lisa at Tess's school and orchestrated the whole thing so it'd appear natural. But what he had wasn't just a young and beautiful wife who got along with us but she appeared to worship the ground he walked on, too. The perfect slave. Perfect outside the bedroom so of course I could only guess that for him she was perfect in it, too. Perfect enough to make Pop offer me the same thing.

She got out of life as a sex slave and she got sold to a wealthy businessman in the states with ties to organized crime so he had power, power to protect her. She's married to him about a year and a half and then is widowed, left a lot of money to take care of her the rest of her life. She's in her mid-20s, still plenty of time to fall in love for real, so it would seem. But their remarks on the tour about Lisa had almost made me tip my hand. I held it together as I processed the little bit of info that told me the truth.

Gan Chen casually said, "So, given the unfortunate demise of your father, I take it you are taking responsibility for Monalisa? Your father left that provision, that you and your brother would be responsible."

It took a second to permeate. I had a good poker face and often had to hold my emotions in check in the business I'd been in so I'd replied, "Of course."

"Excellent," was the response. "We need to know that confidentiality continues and so prior to your arrival we've have had our eye on that situation. When there's no suitable surviving family member to take responsibility for a widow in these situations we either take possession of our former asset back or we eliminate the loose end. From the way your father spoke of you and your brother to his friends here and due to the fact he told us you wanted to acquire we suspected all would be well. We were concerned briefly when we found out she left the country a few weeks after Tom was killed but when we discovered you had also gone along, we knew all was well."

I managed to keep my shit together and not tip my hand at that point but it hadn't been easy. You coulda knocked me down with a feather. We'd all gone on a cruise and then took a detour to Tommy and Tia's wedding, doing it that way on purpose so no one would know where Tommy was. Clearly it was the right thing to do as we'd been being watched. Tommy and Tia had done a jaunt on their way there, too, flying to Aruba and spending a week at a resort before chartering a flight under aliases.

Lisa was together. She was Pop's trophy wife without a doubt but she had a personality. She did not come across like his soulless Stepford slave. I'd never seen her give Pop any sass or nag him at all, but she certainly didn't seem oppressed. Why didn't Stan tip me off about Lisa? Did he know?

If Felicia was supposed to be the 'perfect' wife-material slave personified, why was she so out of sorts with me? Maybe because what I brought to her life was outside the norm of what she'd been trained for. Lisa had stepped into a role and knew her part and she fulfilled it. Felicia was likely off-balance because I told her she wouldn't be marrying me and that she was no longer a slave.

When I'd told my brother about Lisa on a brief IM conversation from the resort, he was as shocked as I was. We agreed on our last video call that I needed to talk to Lisa but knew I'd be opening a can of worms so I left it on simmer for the moment. She was pregnant and widowed but young, beautiful, and wealthy. She hadn't taken off the minute Pop died, scared for her life or anxious to move on. She and Tess were living in Pop's house and she was helping raise my nephews. They were best friends and were clinging to one another to heal and move on after all that'd happened. Tess, Lisa, and Luciana were the three amigos. They'd raise their kids together and do their shopping shit and their yoga and their gossiping and reality TV parties, and scrapbooking shit, and they'd be happy. It had all worked out for her. Maybe she could help Felicia heal.

I finally spoke. "I have questions, Leese."

"I bet you do," she answered softly.

"When the time comes, will you help her? Will you talk to her and help her?"

She nodded. "Of course. I don't remember a Felicia."

"She came shortly after you left."

"She probably replaced me. When one goes, they bring another."

I felt nauseous.

"Did they say anything about me?" she asked softly.

"Yeah. They asked if I was taking responsibility. Said I was."

She choked up. "I won't let you down. I tried not to think about *what if*, what if they came for me. It tried to creep in but I just put the baby first, I…" She stopped and shrugged.

"Leese, you're family. You're pregnant with my brother or sister. My sisters love you. Me and Tommy would never let anything happen to you."

Her face went sour.

"What?"

She shook her head and muttered, "Tommy."

My scalp prickled and I knew by her face what she was referring to.

"Hey. You do not speak of that. You do not know. You think you know but you fucking don't."

"I loved your father," she said. "I know what you think of what he did, buying me, and buying her for you. But he gave me so much. He saved me, Dare. I loved him and Tommy took---"

"Shut up," I warned. This was dangerous. "You and I are gonna need to talk about where you're getting your information, but we won't talk about it here and now. All you need to know is that he's gone. You don't need other details, but you need to shut your fucking mouth about my brother."

She stopped talking. Her face went stony. She was guarding her emotions now, doing what she'd been taught at Kruna.

"Fuck," I said and then reached into my pocket for my cigarettes.

"Dario, the baby," she said as I lit one. I gave her an apologetic look and walked in the other direction, taking a few quick drags and then dropping it and stepping on it. I walked back to her and sat beside her on the bench.

"No one's feeding me info, Dare. I have two eyes and a brain. Tessa and Luc know, too. No one talks about it but we can all guess what went down."

"What's your real name?" I asked her, ignoring what she'd just said.

"Shayla Townsend," she whispered.

"How'd they get you?"

She took a deep breath. "They stole me off a cruise ship. I was 17. I had almost no family left, no one really close. My daddy died when I was little. Mom took us on a cruise when they found out her Cancer was inoperable. It was a girls' trip together for us to make memories before her health declined. I checked after your father saved me. She'd reported me missing. They'd said I probably fell overboard. It didn't take long for it to just be a cold case and she died a few months later so there was no one to push for answers."

I put my arm around her and she put her head on my shoulder. But she didn't cry. Poor Leese. Stolen and forced to live knowing her ma was dying not knowing what happened to her. I shook my head and let out a slow breath.

We were quiet a minute. When I asked Felicia about her family, she shook her head. Maybe there was no one. Maybe that was a requirement for these guys before they took a girl. Maybe they made sure a mark had no one to look for her. Felicia had said they blackmailed her. I didn't know the details yet. I'd find out.

I got to my feet. "Carry on as normal. I have to figure out what to do about this situation. I may ask for your help with her. For info about them. I dunno yet."

She nodded. "I am very grateful to be a part of this family. I won the lottery as far as being a Kruna girl goes. I'm sorry for what I said about your brother. You're right. I don't know what happened. I just miss my husband. I know your father was a man with secrets, more secrets than any of us knew about. I also know that he loved you all and wanted you to be happy. He wasn't perfect but family was so important to him. I guess he bought Felicia to make that happen for you. He told me he was worried about how cold your heart was after your engagement broke off. He was so happy that Tommy and Athena fell in love and wanted love for you, too. He got me away from there and made my life better. And I did my best to make him happy. You can do the same for her and she for you. You can give her a beautiful life the way your father gave one to me. You can have that too, be her winning lottery ticket, let her be the gift Tom intended and believe there was nothing underhanded about it." She shrugged and put her hand protectively over her belly, which wasn't even rounded yet.

Nothing underhanded? My father profited off the misery that Lisa, Felicia, and those other girls endured, for fuck sakes. Fucking basement holes and torture rooms and fear and rape. Now I'd imagined Lisa and Felicia in those fucking solitary cells naked, cold, dirty, hungry, and fucking broken. And then I imagined my father sitting in those dining rooms and luxurious suites laughing and drinking and smoking a stogie like king of the fucking world with Lisa at his feet waiting for him to feed her table scraps.

Fuck.

"Let's get you home," I said through clenched teeth and we headed back to the car.

As we pulled up to the house she said, "Look at your brother. It doesn't always start out right… but it can get there."

I didn't reply. I passed her the keys and watched her walk to the house. I texted Nino to ask him if he could swing by and give me a lift home. I video-called my brother from my phone. He didn't answer.

As I was waiting it dawned that when I'd had dinner the last night at Kruna they'd said there would be "play" in the Townsend room. Lisa's real name was Shayla Townsend. I decided to add Lisa's details to the puzzle, to give the information to Zack and see if it helped him get us more information.

Felicia

He was gone until after lunchtime. I'd gotten up, got dressed in a black pair of dress pants and a black blouse, put make-up on and flat ironed my hair. I was sitting on the terrace with a cup of coffee and the cashmere throw from the sofa over me. It was getting chilly. The leaves were starting to change color. I hadn't dealt with cold weather in 2 years and while I'd spent the previous almost decade in the frigid frozen tundra, this was an adjustment. I caught something from the corner of my eye. He was back. He was standing at the patio doors, leaning against the wall, staring at me. He was in jeans and a t-shirt and his hair was wet. He must've been back a while and grabbed a shower.

His face looked hard, pissed. I swallowed past a lump in my throat and got to my feet. He opened the door for me and I went inside. He closed the door behind me. I gave him a tentative smile but my eyes quickly darted toward my feet when the hard look on his face didn't soften. I walked to the kitchen sink and rinsed my cup and then put it in the dishwasher. When I turned around, he was standing behind me, leaning against the island with his arms folded across his chest.

I stood still, eyes to the floor, waiting for him to address me.

"You straightened your hair," he said finally.

I jolted. He'd told me at the resort that he preferred I didn't but maybe I did it in an effort to behave myself. My hair was almost always straight at Kruna unless I was playing the naughty role. I pushed that thought away, avoiding the urge to analyze it, to think about anyone from there.

"Wanna go shopping?" he asked.

I was startled. That was not what I'd been expecting.

I lifted my chin and looked at him and nodded.

"Then let's go," he said softly and went to the table by the door where his keys and phone were.

"Can I have two minutes?" I asked.

He jerked his chin up in a 'yes'.

I hurried to the bathroom and put on some more mascara and lip gloss and then put a few things into one of the purses that had been packed for me, put on a pair of ballerina flats, and found him by the door. He was in jeans and a t-shirt, a leather jacket and sneakers and was standing by the door twirling keys on his index finger.

"You don't have a coat?"

I shook my head.

He reached into a closet by the front door and handed me a black fleece-lined hoodie. It was too big for me but I put it on. It smelled like him. Smelled so good.

"Let's go get you one."

I'd been expecting him to come in and tell me that last night was a mistake and that it wouldn't happen again. Then he'd be distant with me. After all, he was drunk and he didn't mean to take advantage of me. He didn't take advantage of me but I was waiting for him to act like he did. Right now, I didn't know what to make of his demeanor. He was pissed off, as per usual; he'd left this morning without hardly looking at me, but now he was taking me shopping to buy clothes.

The elevator took us to the underground and he opened the passenger door to his SUV for me. When we pulled out of the garage onto the street, I was struck by how odd it was to be in a moving vehicle again. I felt woozy.

He turned the radio on to some classic rock and I just stared out the window watching cars and people go by, living life, living normal everyday lives. We pulled into an enormous mall parking lot and I took the hoodie off and left it in the car, figuring I'd be inside and warm enough in a minute.

As I got out, he came around to my side and reached for my hand. Yes, he still looked pissed but he was holding my hand as we walked inside. My heart was in my throat at that.

"What first?" he asked as we got into the enormous mall. It looked like it had a lot of upscale shops. He stopped in front of the mall directory and map.

"Um…" It felt like I was on another planet. I had spent half my life as a teenager in shopping malls. But after all this time, it was so strange, so foreign. So… normal.

This was a normal I had once prayed for but had long since given up on the notion of returning to my life. This was people, normal and free people around me exerting their free will and they were going about their day: teenaged girls laughing and walking while thumbing away on smartphones, women pushing strollers with babies in them, old people congregated around benches, couples holding hands. I looked down at our hands with our fingers woven together and my heart lifted like a kite being pulled up by a gust of wind.

"Comfortable clothes?" He motioned toward a yoga store on the listing with his free hand. I nodded enthusiastically.

He motioned toward the shop, which was not far ahead of us, let go of me, which meant a small pain in my chest, that I thankfully was able to push back, and then he opened his wallet, handed me a credit card, and then leaned over and whispered in my ear, making me tingle, "Go nuts. Pin 3825."

He sat on a bench and pulled his smartphone out of his pocket and started thumbing at the screen. I think I must've looked like a zombie for a second because he looked up and smiled and then jerked his chin toward the store.

I hesitantly went into the store, pushing back the urge to throw myself at his feet and hang onto his ankle. I took slow breath after slow breath to hold it together. The sales girl totally put me at ease. After buying a few pairs of capri length and full-length yoga pants, t-shirts, tank tops, and hoodies, I went to him and he took my bags and led me to a coat store where he told me to buy two coats while he waited on a nearby bench with my bags. I'd bought a Fall one and then a winter one as it would be snowing in the not-too- distant future. I was kind of looking forward to seeing snow again so I could wear the gorgeous coat. After seven years of living in Alaska, a place I'd never wanted to go, I never thought I'd say that I looked forward to snow ever again.

I didn't want to take advantage, but I didn't want to insult him either by declining his kindness and it was fun. At first, I had trouble deciding what I wanted and all the people around me was a little dizzying, but salespeople were more than happy to make recommendations.

I got two pairs of jeans. I bought a pair of sneakers. And then he let me loose into a higher-end department store and I bought new underwear, some toiletries (like bubble bath), thick fluffy socks, and I bought three pairs of ladies' winter pjs and a bathrobe. I bought 2 pairs of long pjs and one pair of super soft fleece pink and purple striped shorts with a matching hoodie.

"Anything else you want?" he asked as I emerged from the department store. He was seated on a bench with my shopping bags around his feet. He had a cup of Starbucks in his right hand and he held another Starbucks cup on his knee with his left hand. He passed it to me. My heart warmed.

"Thank you. I can't remember the last time I had one of these." Actually, no. I could remember. Suddenly I could remember it as clear as day, so clearly I could smell the November Juneau air. It was on my way to the airport the day I'd left from Juneau airport to leave for Bangkok. Chills ran up my spine. I sipped it. It tasted amazing. It was milky and sweet and it tasted like happiness in a cup.

"Anything else you want?" he asked again. He didn't look pissed off. He was smiling at me.

"No. Thank you for everything. So much. I think I've subjected you to enough torture today and spent enough of your hard-earned money. Thank you, Dare."

He gave me a small smile and then lifted my booty of shopping bags from the floor all into one hand and slipped handles over his wrist so he could carry his coffee in that hand. My non-coffee-holding hand had two bags in it. He took them from me and transferred them onto the already full wrist and then grabbed my hand with his now free hand and we headed back to the car.

"Wanna go eat?" he asked.

"Sure," I replied as he opened the passenger door for me and tossed all my bags into the back seat.

He drove to a little Italian place not far from the mall. He seemed relaxed as we drove, happy even. As we entered, a man in a suit approached.

"Ah, Mr. Dario! What a surprise! We are still getting ready for dinner, but come, sit. We will look after you and the beautiful lady."

"Nice to see you, Augustus. Is Ed in?"

"I don't think so yet, Mr. Dario. He's expected any minute. Please introduce me to this lovely lady!"

"This is…" He stopped and looked at me. His face was blank. I was relieved he didn't introduce me as Felicia, that he remembered I didn't want to be called that any longer.

"Angel," I extended a hand to the older Italian man. "Nice to meet you."

"Angel. Bella! Face of an angel, Mr. Dario. Such a beauty. So lucky, Mr. Dario, so lucky. Right this way."

We were seated and Dario was studying me. I gave him a smile. He didn't smile back. He didn't look angry but he was studying my face, trying to figure something out, I think.

He started talking in a flurry of Italian to a waiter that came over and filled our water glasses. This was a nice place. Intimate. Dim. Red and white checked tablecloths with candles on the tables. I could smell food cooking and it smelled amazing.

We were quiet. It was a little awkward. Then a tall dark-haired and good-looking guy dressed in chef whites came over and put his hand on Dario's shoulder.

"Hey, man. How are you? You okay with a coupla specials since you're here right in the middle of prep for dinner?"

"Sounds good, man. And I'm good. Uh, Angel, this is my brother-in-law, Eddy. This place is owned by my family. Ed's the head chef and manager."

"Nice to meet you," I said. "I've had your food. It's wonderful. Best pizza I've ever had."

Eddy beamed at me. "Thank you; I try. Nice to meet you." He gave Dare a sly look. "I'm sure it's why Dare's sister married me. My cooking." He shrugged. There was a clatter in the kitchen and he said, "Excuse me. I'll get those specials out."

I smiled at Dare. He sighed and shook his head.

"Your Italian is beautiful. Do you speak any other languages?" I asked.

"Spanish, Icelandic, a little French," he muttered.

"Wow."

He took a sip of his water and shook his head at me some more.

"Have I upset you?" I asked.

"What's your name?" he asked me.

"It's Angel," I answered, feeling tingles spark in my chest.

He shook his head. "Sweetheart…"

"Can we leave it at that? Please?"

He was jiggling his legs with vigor, continuing to shake his head at me. Then his gaze sharpened. "I could make you tell me, couldn't I?"

"I know you could," I pleaded with my eyes but my body was suddenly alert with sexuality at that dominant statement.

He shook his head, took a sip of his water, kept jiggling his legs, clearly annoyed with me.

A waiter brought warm bread and a platter with meats, cheese, and olives and put it between us. Another waiter came with a bottle of wine and poured two glasses of red.

We were quiet, eating from the platter and he had a few lighthearted conversations with staff who came by setting up nearby tables for dinner. As the waiter brought over two plates heaped with spaghetti with meatballs three very attractive women rushed toward the table.

"Hi ho, Dariiiioooooo," one of them sang out and Dare looked up and then went, "Ah for fuck sakes." He put his palm to his forehead and stared at the ceiling.

Two were clearly sisters, maybe even fraternal twins, short, almost identical. One was blonde and the other had a blonde on top, dark on the bottom ombre. They were both petite but they looked like Dare. His sisters? Behind them was a tall and strikingly beautiful brunette.

One of the sisters was greeted by Eddy who kissed her and then said, "Sorry, man. They found out."

"They found out," Dario repeated, his voice dripping with sarcasm.

The two sisters were laughing mischievously. The taller brunette was just looking at me. Her eyes were on my throat. My hand covered my collar protectively. It would look to anyone who didn't know better like a choker necklace and it matched my blue sapphire stud earrings and bracelet. They were beautiful pieces of jewelry but I felt self-conscious at the way she was looking at it.

"Luciana. Luc for short. Short like me. I'm Dare's baby sister," The one on Eddy's arm laughed and reached out and shook my hand.

"Angel," I replied softly. I glanced at Dare and he shook his head in dismay.

"I'm Tessa," the sister with the ombre reached over and shook my hand. "That's Lisa. Wicked stepmother." The two girls laughed.

Lisa gave me a nod but she didn't smile. A waiter and a busboy came over with another table and put it against our table.

"Fuck," Dare muttered. The three girls sat.

"Sorry, man. She got it outta me," Eddy said.

I looked at Eddy and then to Dario. He rolled his eyes and drank the balance of what was in his wineglass back.

The waiter came by to fill their water glasses.

"Wine for me," Tessa said and then her eyes got bigger, "What the heck, Dare? Are you…are you in jeans?"

"Holy shit, he is! Cranberry juice for me," Luc said and then glanced to me. "No vino. I'm nursing. It's been years since I've seen you in jeans, Dare. What happened? Drycleaners closed?"

Dare rolled his eyes.

"Just some sparkling water's good," said Lisa.

"She's preggers," Luc added, looking at me.

I smiled and said, "Congrats" to Lisa and took a sip from my wineglass. She gave me a smile but it didn't touch her eyes. I felt a little self-conscious.

"So…" Luc said, looking at Dare, "How'd you two meet?"

"None of your business," Dare answered with an eyebrow raised at her in warning.

Luc looked at me and rolled her eyes.

"Awe c'mon. Is this a first date, third date, what?" She looked at me when her brother didn't answer. His jaw was clenched.

I laughed nervously and sipped my wine.

"It's a none-of-your- business, you pain-in-the-ass date. We need to go, actually. You done, baby?" He looked at me.

My body tingled at the endearment and that he'd referred to it as a date. I had only had a few bites but had already gotten my fill on the appetizers and the bread. Besides, he clearly wanted to go.

"I'm good," I answered and wiped my mouth.

"Get someone to wrap that up?" Dario said to Eddy. "She might want that for breakfast tomorrow." He winked at me and I couldn't help but smile huge, eyes locking with his. His smile spread wide, too. Damn, he was hot.

Luc cleared her throat. "Okay, so you're to the breakfast-planning part of the relationship…"

My eyes darted to her.

"Sorry, Angel, darling. Our brother tries to keep his love life private," she rolled her eyes, "We don't do private in this family. We haven't had the pleasure of seeing anyone he's dating in a very, very long time so we had to barge in and check you out." She looked to her brother. "She has the sisterly and stepmotherly seals of approval… from what we can tell. Right girls?"

"Right," Tessa answered.

"Definitely," said Lisa, which was odd since she seemed like she meant it but that didn't actually go with the looks she'd been giving me.

"Gee, thanks a bunch. Your approval means everything." Dare rolled his eyes.

His two sisters laughed. He got to his feet, reached into his wallet, and dropped several bills on the table. "Dinner's on me," he said this to the girls and then he gave Eddy a chin lift.

"You wait for the food; I'm getting a smoke, all right?" he said to me.

I nodded. He leaned down and kissed my forehead, making me tingle all over, and then left the building. A waiter had appeared with Styrofoam containers and was transferring food from my and Dare's plates to them. I put my new coat on and lifted my purse and then got to my feet. "It was really nice to meet all of you. The food was excellent, Eddy."

They were all smiling at me.

"Hope to see you again," Tessa said.

"Me, too," I returned.

The waiter handed me a twine-handled paper bag with the leftovers and I waved and then another waiter offered me a mint from the big bowl of mints on the bar as I passed so I popped it into my mouth as I left the building.

Dare was leaning against the hood of his car smoking and watching me as I came outside. His face held something intense. I couldn't tell right now if it was anger, frustration, deep thought, but I had to look away from his gaze as it was so intense it gave me chills. He went around to the passenger side and opened the door for me. I gave him a shy smile and got in, then leaned to put the doggie bag into the back seat with my mall loot. He closed the door and put his cigarette out in an ashtray that was affixed to the building.

We drove back to the apartment in silence, but he was fidgety on the ride. When we got inside, he walked like a man with a mission.

"Follow me," he said and marched directly to his bedroom. I put the doggie bag on the island and followed him. He dropped the shopping bags on the floor beside the bed and then spun round and reached for my face with both hands. He pulled me in for a kiss. It was a deep kiss with tongue and a sexy masculine moan and him holding my jaw with both hands. Then he let go of my face and started to unbutton my blouse. Whoa. Yes!

I absorbed the feel of his touch. He started to kiss my throat as he undid the last of the buttons of my blouse and then he found the button on my pants. Goosebumps rose all over me.

"Undo my pants," he said against my throat and then let go of my fly and pulled his shirt over his head. My fingers fumbled with his button fly jeans.

As I got his pants undone and pushed them down over his hips, he pushed my blouse off my shoulders and as the blouse floated to the floor, he quickly got my pants down my hips. I yanked them down the rest of the way and stepped out of them and my shoes. He stepped out of his, walked me back against the bed and then I was on my back and he was on top of me, kissing me. I ran my fingers through his thick blond hair and he let out a deep and sexy moan.

"What's your name," he breathed against my ear and then took my lobe between his teeth.

"It's Angel, Master," I whispered.

"It's not," he grunted and then slid his hand into my panties. "Tell me."

"It is now," I said, my mouth opening into an O at where his fingers just went. He hit the spot. Oh lord.

"Tell me or I'll spank you." He grabbed my collar.

I might come from words alone.

"Oh, please spank me, Master," I whispered, and I had goosebumps everywhere.

"Holy fuck," he answered and his hand left my underwear and then he rolled us, then hauled off and slapped my ass.

I squealed. "Oh yeah."

I was elated. He was absolutely a dominant in the bedroom and I could see he was totally getting off on giving me what I wanted. It got me off. It was perfect. This was precisely what I needed in a sexual partner. You wouldn't think that after all I'd been through, but it still was. Maybe that wasn't healthy for me with what I'd been through but it was who I was, who I always was. I used to be spunky outside of the bedroom but in it I always wanted a dominant male. I wanted to please him, wanted his directions on how to do that. He slapped my ass again and then hauled me back by the collar and his eyes were ablaze.

He was panting, his chest heaving. "Are you fucking kidding me?"

I gulped, thinking he was upset. He wasn't. He really wasn't.

"Your words make me so fucking hard, baby. Keep talking dirty to me."

"Can I please suck your cock, Master?" I panted. "Please? I haven't forgotten how good it tastes. Please can I suck your beautiful cock while I play with my clit?"

His eyes rolled back and his jaw dropped. He regained composure and gave me a heated glare. "Don't you dare make me come before I'm even inside you."

Maybe after having to be submissive for so many men that didn't deserve getting that trust and willingness to please from me, now, having someone who did deserve it? Maybe that's another reason why I was getting off on it so much.

I shimmied down and as I leaned forward to take him into my mouth, he grabbed my collar. He held it while his other hand caressed my hair and then he leaned back and moaned as my tongue touched him. I put one hand to his abs, feeling the ridges of muscle while I bobbed up and down, twirling my tongue around his tip and sucking him deep.

I pulled his cock out of my mouth and asked, "May I touch myself?" and he groaned out, "Yeah, baby. Do it."

I braced myself with a hand beside his belly and slipped the other hand down between my legs and let out a long shuddering sigh. One of his hands traveled up and down my back, the other still held my collar. I got his tip back in my mouth.

It didn't take long before I was shuddering. I came hard and while I was writhing in ecstasy, he let go of the collar but his fingers had my throat instead. I loved the feel of his cock in my mouth and his fingers on my throat as I came. He flipped me and got his cock out of my mouth and then slid down and then drove it into me. His hand went to my breast, tweaking my nipple. I had my head on the pillow and his face was only inches from mine and the room was still light enough, the sun hadn't fully set yet, and I could see he was looking at me with a warmth, no, with heat, with something that made my heart want to explode. I don't think anyone had ever looked at me that way.

He didn't take his eyes off mine as my first orgasm rolled into a second one. He kept fucking me hard while rubbing my clit. He flipped us and I rode him, I rode him hard, throwing my head back, putting on a show and enjoying the sensual expression on his face as he watched me ride him hard. He was gorgeous and he'd made me his last night and again today. I felt euphoric, had to stop myself from telling him I wanted to be his forever and spend every single day of my life thanking him for giving me this.

I rode his cock and his fingers until I screamed out in ecstasy, again. "Oh!" I came so hard. "Thank you, Master," I whispered.

I collapsed forward onto his chest, exhilarated and exhausted and still enduring aftershocks when he flipped me back to my back and then lifted my legs up over his shoulders, slamming into me over and over until he finally came, "Angelbaby," spilling from his beautiful mouth as he did.

He rolled, taking me with him as he got to his back and tucked me in at his side, breathing hard. I curled in and stroked his chest, closing my eyes and soaking in this beautiful, beautiful moment.

He caressed my head, playing with my hair.

"May I speak?" I breathed.

"You don't have to ask me that," he said softly, pulling a lock of my hair to his nose and then rubbing it across his lips.

"Sorry."

"Don't say sorry."

"Okay. What changed your mind about me?"

"A big bottle of vodka and zero self-control."

"I thought after you left this morning that you regretted it and that you'd come back and send me away," I whispered.

I hesitantly looked up at him. My eyes met his and his had what looked like pain in them. "That's what I should do," he said.

"Please don't," I pleaded.

"I have a war going on, babe. Tried to get it on with that chick to get you out of my head and I couldn't because all I could think of was you, here, like this. But I'm not a decent guy. I shouldn't do this. I should be giving you space, letting you straighten your head out."

"You are a decent guy. You're helping me. You have no idea how much you're helping me," I breathed.

"Angel, I fucking ate your pussy before I ever even kissed you on the mouth. Do you not realize how ass fucking backwards that is? You don't deserve that shit!"

I was shocked.

He continued. "This morning I talked to the building manager. Asked if there were any vacancies. He told me the apartment three doors down'll be vacant in a few weeks. The owner of the condo got relocated and asked him to put an ad up. I was thinkin' I'd rent it for you. Get you in your own place and keeping it here would make it so they wouldn't know you weren't living with me. I thought it'd be a good way to get some distance, carefully."

My expression must've dropped. He gave me a squeeze. "I told him I'd let him know. I didn't do it on the spot, probably 'cuz I didn't know if I could let you go. After having you last night, call me a dog, but I wanted you again. Saw you when I got home and was gonna ask you what you wanted. Then the way you looked at me? Fuck, the way you look at me, Angel…

All day I wanted to kiss you, be inside you. Watching you shop, seeing you smile, it got to me. And you taking the pet name I gave you as your new name? Shit, baby.

After getting a taste of you I couldn't stop myself. And now after having you again? You talking to me like that and begging me to spank you, asking me for permission to touch yourself? Thanking me for making you come, for letting you make yourself come? Fuck, baby. This was even better than last night and last night was fuck-hot."

"It was amazing," I agreed, goosebumps all over me, warmth in my chest like I hadn't felt in years, maybe even ever.

"What do you want?"

"This," I answered.

"You've got this hero worship thing happenin' and I am a fuckin' dog for letting it get carried away. I wanna say I really wanted to not go here with you but it's only been a few days. Clearly, I didn't try that hard. But the way you look at me, the way you are when we fuck, it's too much."

I kissed his chin and snuggled in. I couldn't believe I felt so bold to do that. But I did. And it felt awesome to just snuggle in close to him like that.

He put an arm tight around me. "I dunno, babe. I just don't want if this thing with us goes somewhere and for you, as your life gets normal again, to suddenly realize you don't want this."

"I won't," I whispered.

"How do you know that?"

I didn't have an answer for him. I just couldn't imagine not wanting him.

He continued, "Because once I've decided you're mine I won't be willing to let you go unless you do something to shred my heart. Maybe I should give you space, let you figure out what you want before we take this any further."

"Maybe you should," I said softly.

He raised his eyebrows for a second and then moistened his lips and nodded.

"But please don't," I said.

He shook his head and sighed but he looked relieved, I think.

"What do you want outta life?" he asked me.

I shrugged. "It has been a long time since I let myself think about that. All I've thought about for so many months, is this. Getting sold so I could get out of there. That's what I did, Dare. I worked hard to make them trust me so I could be sold. I didn't play them. Please don't think I'm playing you. I didn't play anyone, I just tried really hard to be good enough. And I'd never ever shred your heart. Never ever."

He shook his head and was quiet a minute, studying me, before saying, "So, what if you and I carry on and suddenly you realize what you want isn't this?"

"I don't think that'll happen," I said and my heart wanted to leap with joy because it sounded like he did want this, want me.

"Because you thought you'd have nothing better," he said, "Because you thought this was the best scenario you could get, getting sold. But I don't wanna be someone's best case scenario. I want a woman who worships the ground I walk on. I want a woman who lets me do the same for her and who appreciates that I worship her. I want a woman who wants what I want outta life."

"You deserve nothing less." God, he was amazing. He wanted a relationship, not a slave; a partner in life.

"And if this thing with us goes where it could go, I might always wonder if it's enough for you. And you might never ask for more because you'll think you don't deserve more. What if looking at me always reminds you of how you came to be mine? What if being with me means you can't ever totally forget that hell that they put you through? I know this is a lot but I need this on the table. In the situation we're in we can't afford to just play things by ear. Does what I'm saying even make sense?"

I nodded. "It does. I know my head isn't on straight. But I know that with all that you've given me so far that I have a very good chance of it finding its way to straightening out."

He rolled his eyes. "I feel like a fuckin' dog."

"Listen," I got up onto an elbow and touched his face, "Do you not look in the mirror and see all that is you? Do you not see that you could never ever be a consolation prize to any girl? I won't forget what I've been through whether I'm here with you or totally alone. It'll always be with me. We have to look like we're together so that they don't think you're a threat. So just take me. I'm yours. Won't that make it easier? Then you're not pretending. You're just going about your life. You're just doing what anyone else who had a Kruna slave would do. Instead of adding me to the list of complications, just go about your life. I won't complicate it. I'll enjoy every minute I have being yours as a gift because it is one. You'll be giving me a beautiful gift, Dare. And you've already done so much for me I hate to ask you for a thing and I don't want you keeping me out of obligation and robbing yourself of being happy and being with someone who you choose to be with instead of feeling obligated to keep someone you're stuck with. I'm asking you to try not to feel guilty about what we just did. It was beautiful. Just keep me for now, maybe? I'll work hard to be everything you need and I won't try to make you feel bad later if you don't want me anymore."

"Baby…" he said but let that hang.

"When the day comes that you decide we can safely part, I'll deal. I won't go all stalker crazy on you because I've been trained to behave and I will behave. I won't ever do anything to make you regret rescuing me. And I won't expect you to be mine back. If you want someone else, you do what you want. I'm yours and only yours for as long as you decide but you won't be expected to be faithful to me. You're in charge. If you want me, I'm here. I will have no expectations." Wow, that was a lot. It must've sounded rehearsed to him, like I was trying to sell him something.

"Naw," he touched my face. "If I'm with you, I'm only with you."

I breathed deep and choked up. I shouldn't have done that. It revealed too much.

"See, already you feel deep and I could fuck that up." He ran his fingers through my hair.

"How?" I leaned into his wrist. I kept revealing too much with him.

"Am I always gonna wonder if you really want out?" His eyes roved over my face.

I shrugged. "I don't know."

"Are you gonna want out?" he asked.

"I don't know. Don't know any more than you don't know if you're gonna want out. When people decide to be together, they don't know if it's forever. They only know they wanna see where it goes. I'd love to see where this could go."

He smiled. "That answer is a good sign. A very fuckin' good sign."

"Maybe my head isn't as fucked up as we think." I shrugged. But it probably was.

We were quiet for a minute, cuddling.

"What do you wanna do tonight?" he asked, tucking hair behind my ear.

"Me?" God, he was sweet.

"Yeah, you. You've had your first outing since Thailand, shopping and the restaurant. You wanna go out tonight or you wanna stay in?"

"I wanna stay in," I answered.

"What do you wanna do 'in' tonight?" Dare caressed my cheek with his thumb.

"I wanna please you, Master," I said, "And maybe if I'm a very good girl, after I do, we can eat some more of that spaghetti here in bed while we watch the hockey game?"

His eyes lit up and his hands slid up from my hips to my shoulders and then he pinned me to the bed. "Angel," he breathed almost right against my lips. "I'm not your Master. But is it twisted that I'm totally okay with pretending in this bed that I am?"

"I'm not sure I'm the best judge here but I'm gonna say no. Not twisted at all." I grinned.

He smiled big and then he moaned into my mouth as his tongue dipped in.

I spread my legs wide, arched my back and absorbed the feeling of his cock stretching me. "I've gotta add, too, if you were to choose to be my Master, I have a feeling you'd be very good at it."

Two hours later we'd had sex two more times. He had stamina. Gorgeous and generously amazing in bed. Rough, biting, gripping, dominant, taking what he wanted, not treating me like a piece of china that would break, and giving me orgasm after orgasm. And he was a badass from a powerful family who could protect me. There was a long list of pluses for me to want him, no minuses whatsoever. Sadly, there were mostly minuses on his list of reasons for keeping me. The only pluses were endless sex and keeping the Kruna bosses oblivious. I wished that I could give him more than those reasons to keep me.

He got up and fried up our leftover spaghetti and meatballs and brought it in and we ate it in his bed while watching a hockey game. Damn. Fried spaghetti was the best spaghetti ever. It was buttery and crispy in spots and I ate a massive plate of it. I ate so much of it I think I slipped into a carb coma.

He loved hockey and really seemed happy with the idea that I liked it, too. I didn't bother telling him that I played hockey on a girls' team back in high school. I fell asleep with my head on his belly and his fingers in my hair sometime during the third period.

I heard when he flicked the TV off. He shifted me off his stomach and then curled me up against him, his hand on my bare bottom. He gave it a squeeze.

"Hey Angel?" he called out.

"Yes?" I opened my eyes.

"How do you feel about kids?"

"Kids?"

"Yeah."

"I went to school to be a teacher. Love kids," I said sleepily.

He squeezed me tight, kind of too tight. "Yeah?"

"Uh huh. I taught grade one in Thailand at an English school before… before you know. You like kids?"

He let out a long breath. "You wanna talk about how you went from being a teacher to being at Kruna?" he asked softly.

"No," I answered. "Is that okay?"

"Yeah," he kissed my hand. "you tell me that story later."

"Thank you,"

"What's your name, baby?"

"It's Angel, Master."

"How about when you tell me that story you tell me your name."

"You know my name," I said softly.

"Baby…"

"Dare, if I ever say that other name out loud again something really bad'll happen."

"No, it won't because I won't let it," he said into my ear and kissed my neck.

He didn't answer me about him wanting kids.

"Can't I just be Angel?" I asked.

He sighed. "For now, all right. Goodnight my Angel. Sweet dreams."

"Thanks to you they will be," I said, fingering my collar and curled into him. His Angel. Swoon. I hoped I could be his angel forever.

He gave me a squeeze.

"Dare?"

"Yeah, baby?"

"Do you call all girls angel?"

"Hm?"

"Some guys call all women a pet name: baby, sweetheart, sugar, you know?"

"Ah."

"Do you, uh… do you call anyone else Angel?"

"Never. Why?"

"Never?"

"Nope. Why?"

"Maybe it's not the awesome name I thought it was if it's not just mine."

"It's just yours. You have the face of an angel. You're trying to be a perfect one." I felt him shrug.

"Thank you for saving me. And for giving me that name. Now that I know that, it feels even more like it's mine."

He gave me a squeeze.

"Please keep me," I whispered before thinking, pouring everything I had into the plea. After a too-long pause I wished I could snatch it back. So much for my long logical speech.

But then he said, "I'm thinkin' about it. I'm beating myself up for it but gotta say, I'm tempted."

"Then I have to keep being your angel." I snuggled in closer. "So you won't wanna give me up."

He sighed. "No promises, yet, angelbaby, but you're playing your cards right so far."

"Okay." I smiled.

"But I'd rather you be you," he whispered. "Don't be an angel just because you're afraid. Be you." He caressed my face.

"I'll try," I said.

"That's all I can ask for," he replied.

"Hey Dare?" I asked a minute later.

"Hm?"

"Who won the hockey game?"

"They did."

"Shit," I grumbled.

I felt his body shake with laughter.

"What's so funny?" I asked.

"You actually gave a shit about the game?"

"Uh, yeah."

He gave me a squeeze and then he gave me a sweet kiss on the forehead and I fell asleep in his arms feeling amazing, feeling like I was done with the A to B, I was at C and now I was working on getting to point D. Dare. Getting Dare to keep me. That was my next goal and if I managed that, there would be nothing else I had to sweat and toil over. I could just live my life. Maybe he wouldn't make me sweat for it. Maybe this was it. Could it be? Maybe I could somehow find me or something close to that again.

Dare

I could justify it the same way she had. We had to look like we were together, why not give it a go? Lisa insinuated it was dangerous if I didn't. So why not, right? Yeah, right. I was a fucking dog looking for permission to be a fucking dog. No better than the scumbags that took her. A dirty scumbag taking what shouldn't be mine. Pop was probably looking up at me from hell with a smirk on his face. What the hell was wrong with me? Barely a few days after I get her out of a hellhole where she's been brainwashed to be a perfect sex slave and I'm fucking her brains out, watching the game with her in bed, asking her about babies for fuck sakes.

She felt so good in my arms. Too good. I didn't deserve to feel this. I couldn't sleep. I slipped out of bed and into my den and started up the computer and then buzzed Tommy on video chat.

Tia

Tommy's computer was making noise. I'd been walking by a room that we'd turned into an office for him and saw that it said "D" was calling. I suspected it was Dario but didn't want to take a chance at answering it so I walked away and found Tommy up on the rooftop deck, swimming laps in the pool. I sat down on a lounge chair and watched him swim. It was a nice night. He'd been in a good mood today. We had gone for dinner to this little place not far away that was quiet and romantic and then after dinner we'd taken a walk on the beach.

After three more lengths of the pool he swam closer to where I was and then his arms emerged by where my feet were dangling and he captured me by the hips and yanked me into the water.

"Hey," I said after we emerged from the water. "You got my nightie all wet!"

"I'd like to get something else all wet," he said against my throat and then my earlobe was in his mouth.

He moved us to more shallow water and I wrapped my legs around his waist and he peeled my nightgown over my head. Then his hands were between us. He got his cock free from his swim trunks and then took me by my fanny and fit us together.

"Mm, perfect fit," I said against his forehead and then kissed it. I put my hands into his hair and he put me against the side of the pool and started rotating his hips. A moment later he hoisted me up and planted my fanny on the deck and then climbed up and pulled me to a deck chaise where he went down on me, making me cry out. It was a beautiful night and there were so many stars. I loved this rooftop terrace. We were having sex outside and it was totally private. There was no one here but us. No guards around, no danger. Just us.

"I love you more than anything in this world," I said to him and he moved up my body and then pushed in deep, to the root, inside me.

"Love you more, baby girl." His lips met mine and he kissed me long and sweet and then thrust into me over and over until he came inside me.

Later, I was getting cleaned up and found him in the spare room typing away on email.

"Dare?" I asked him.

"Zack. Why?"

"Is Dare "D" on your video chat?"

"Yeah, why?"

He was buzzing you earlier. That's why I came up to the pool.

"Kay." He kept typing. He was obviously preoccupied.

"Something to drink?" I called on my way back out of the room.

"Yeah, and make it a fucking double," he said.

"What's wrong?" I felt panic rise in me.

"Your foster sister Mia has been digging around, looking for you."

"Oh?" I really should've sent a postcard by now.

"She just bought a plane ticket to come here," Tommy said.

"What?" I was shocked.

"Yeah. She leaves tomorrow."

"Is it a coincidence?" I felt sick.

"She know anyone here that you know of?"

"Not that I know of."

"She in the habit of traveling alone?"

"No. I don't think she's ever been anywhere, really."

"Then it isn't a coincidence. She's been doing serious digging. And if your 17-18-year-old friend can find us, then we aren't doing a very fucking good job at hiding. You got anything to tell me?"

"Like what?"

"Like have you told anyone where we are? Have you logged into social media? Have you done anything that might make it easy for Mia to find us?"

I winced.

"Fuck, Tia. What the fuck?"

"I logged into Facebook. I didn't even post. I was just playing that stupid candy game and I---"

"Fuck!" he roared, "How could you be so fucking stupid?"

My mouth dropped and my chest burned.

He glared at me.

"I was bored and…"

"You were bored? You were fucking bored? So it's okay because you were bored that you put our lives in danger?"

"You don't let me go anywhere and I didn't think it would do anything. I didn't post anything; I just connected the accounts and…"

"You didn't think. You didn't fucking think. Fuck, Tia."

Tears welled up in my eyes.

"Out. I've gotta make some calls."

"Tommy, I'm sorry."

"Out. Fucking fuck!" His fist came down on the desk.

I left the room and closed the door behind me.

Shit.

Shit, shit, shit.

Angel

When I woke up Dare was asleep and spooning me. It felt so good. So right. I hated to leave the safety and bliss of his arms but I had to go to the bathroom. I quietly got up and did my business and then decided to cook him breakfast. It had been a long while since I'd cooked anything. I made bacon on his fancy stainless steel humongous stove and then put it in the oven's warming drawer and then was about to get started on the eggs. As I closed the oven drawer, I felt hands on my hips. I smiled and turned around. Dare was bare chested, sleepy, messy-haired, and totally gorgeous. He was in just a pair of denim-shaded blue boxer briefs that were the same shade as his eyes and his hands were all over me.

"Seriously? Waking up to the smell of bacon and coming out to find you bent over?"

His mouth came down on mine and then we were up against the fridge and he undid his fleece robe that I was in (I was naked underneath) and then hiked me up, hauled his beautiful cock out and then I was impaled on it. I moaned and he carried me, my legs wrapped around his waist, his cock inside me, and we had a spectacular morning quickie where we started out missionary style for a few minutes on his sofa and then flipped me to my hands and knees and finished doggy style on the living room floor while I played with my clit and he held a breast.

Afterwards, I scrambled some eggs and put a mountain of cheese on them, which he teased me for. I made toast with peanut butter and jam, too, cutting his toast as well as mine into triangles and we ate breakfast together while watching Bugs Bunny.

He made me blush when he said, "So now I rate for triangles?"

"Oh yeah…" I'd said flirtatiously, "You rate…"

Dare

Sitting there eating breakfast with her, feeling comfortable, happy, I started getting a nagging feeling, like I was in a dream and was gonna wake up any second alone, sweating, without her. It was almost too perfect. I started to lose my appetite, started to feel sour.

Debbie and I had done a fair bit of role-playing when we were together. Just about the only thing I wasn't down for was her topping me in the bedroom. I just wasn't built that way. She tried one night, dressing in this pleather bodysuit and trying to boss me around, and I'd pissed her off because I wound up hog tying her and then tickling her until she begged for mercy. Then I left her bound and fucked her while she was bent over an ottoman in her parents' basement. She'd been pissed at me for refusing to play along. But I did not play submissive. No way, no how.

But she knew how to play me and get me extra sweet because she'd figured out early on that her roleplaying as a submissive sex kitten was my favorite way to fuck. I liked it. I loved it. A lot. And it got her gifts, too. She wasn't submissive all the time but she tried that role on once in a while, particularly when she was in the dog house with me or when she wanted something that sparkled or to make me do something I didn't really wanna do, like when I had to take her to some chick flick movie or that time she dragged me to a boy band concert. And she tried it on hard when we split up, trying to get me back.

Angel didn't seem like she was trying to lead me around by my dick. She was letting me lead.

My Angel was that way from the start and there was no way she could know that this is what I liked, not unless my Pop asked Debbie and provided that information when he arranged her for me. I couldn't see it. But suddenly I had to know, had to know if I was being played here. I asked her what coaching she'd had about me.

"What did they tell you I wanted before we met?"

She looked startled, probably because we'd been eating bacon and eggs, watching cartoons, and having a nice morning when suddenly my attitude shifted and I had my arms folded across my chest. "What exactly?"

"They…" she paused, toast in mid-air, swallowed a gulp of coffee, and then continued. "They didn't. I waited for instructions. I was waiting for instructions that never came. They talked in front of me saying we had very little information so they were sure I'd definitely be staying an extra month or two once you'd done an interview to list my deficiencies. All I was told was that you wanted a redhead with a big appetite for sex."

"How many redheads there?"

"I'm not sure. Maybe a dozen or so."

"Why'd they pick you?"

"There were only three shortlisted redheads. I don't know why they picked me."

"What does short-listed mean?"

"Shortlisted means I was an option on a small list of possible assets for sale. There's a short list of women who could be sold. Only women the leadership team felt could be trusted outside the resort were on that list. I had enough positive feedback and hadn't had any infractions for behavior in long enough that I was on that list. I don't know all the criteria. I guess essentially they thought I was broken enough."

She was looking at me a little confused, looking more than a little hurt. Her last sentence hit me in the gut but I forged ahead anyway. "Why'd you have a big sexual appetite in a place like that?"

She opened her mouth in shock and then she slumped.

I waited.

Her face went red.

"Forget it." I knew she fucked to survive and it'd had probably twisted into want out of necessity. I was dealing with an internal struggle here and it was making me be an insensitive dick to her.

I felt like I was falling for this, falling for the idea of a girl who worshipped me, wanted me, loved to fuck the way I wanted, wanted a houseful of kids, would lay on my stomach contentedly while watching sports. I didn't wanna let myself get attached in case I was missing something important, like a ploy or plot, like another one of Pop's games. He could certainly be playing me from the grave given the fact he'd put these wheels in motion before he died.

Besides, she could get over this hero worship shit and what if what was left was nothing but pain for me? I became someone I hate after Debbie fucked me over and if I let myself fall in love again and got fucked over again what would I become then?

"Got shit to do today. You need anything before I go?" I downed the rest of my coffee and then headed toward the bedroom, avoiding her face, which I knew was showing hurt.

"No," she said softly as I passed her.

I changed into a suit and headed to my den to send a few emails and get some stuff in motion. When I came out, she was cleaning the kitchen. She looked gorgeous, wearing a pair of black yoga pants and royal blue racerback tank. She had her hair tied up in a messy knot and she was barefoot. My eyes landed on the collar on her throat. I had to resist the urge to take her by it and haul her back to the bedroom or to the kitchen floor, or wherever. Everything that collar stood for was wrong. But the fact that she was wearing it meant she was mine. Not only to her but it looked like it was starting to mean that to me, too. She fucking loved that thing. I loved that she loved that thing. But I was twisted up over the guilt I felt because of it.

I approached her and she hesitated, not meeting my eyes. She was picking up on my mood, evidently.

"I'll be back later." I kissed her forehead. She leaned into my lips and then tipped her mouth up, wanting my lips on hers. I hesitated and then gave her a soft lip touch and let out a long sigh. We stared into one another's eyes for a minute. Then I backed away, shaking my head. She visibly deflated as I did, her eyes downcast. I left the apartment and it left an emptiness in my chest to walk away from her. But I did it anyway.

***

That afternoon I worked on some shit to do with the construction arm of the business, including a meeting with a few of the foreman who weren't happy to be called in on a Sunday, but too fucking bad, and at 2:00 my cell made a noise alerting me to a text from Tess asking me if I was coming to the house for Sunday dinner and if I was bringing my "new girlfriend" or not. It would be just the girls and the kids as Ed had to work, covering for his backup chef who usually worked Sundays. I didn't know if I could handle dinner with them and the third degree about her. Obviously the 'new girlfriend' remark was Tess baiting me to see if I'd agree or say "she's not my girlfriend". I'd be the only male outta diapers in the place if I did go, so I told her I had to work and couldn't make it.

I wished I had my brother here, accessible, so I could run some work shit by him and so I could talk over this Felicia shit. I felt guilty for interrupting him in his new life. I'd told him to let me handle things and now I was feeling like I was in over my head. Fuck. I felt dirty even thinking of her as Felicia. But when I thought of her as Angel I thought of her as being MY Angel and that felt dangerous to me because of what it represented. Me, vulnerable.

Tommy was accessible by phone or computer but it wasn't the same. I wanted to sit down and have a drink with my brother. What I probably wanted most was for him to clap me on the back and tell me Carpe Diem with the girl. She was mine. Seize her. He'd done it and he hadn't regretted it.

When we were having a drink together the night before he got married, he told me that the guilt was there at times but that his need for Tia was always stronger than the guilt. He told me he gave her the option to leave once and she refused to take it and pushed him to prove he wouldn't ever let her go and that's how he knew that he would never want anyone else, ever. At the time it'd hit me hard, made me want what they had even more. And now it was definitely in my brain. Would this girl pick me if she had a true choice? If she wasn't fucking broken? It was too soon. Way too soon for me to start feeling this attached to her. I was just attached to the idea of her, that she was as close to perfect as I could expect to get. Being broken notwithstanding. But she didn't always seem broken. I'd seen glimpses of fire in her eyes, maybe I was catching glimpses of who she used to be.

I had options to consider. Keep her, try to forget about the existence of the club. Let the profits continue to go into an untraceable account offshore and send someone, probably Stan, as a rep to the meetings when I had to. Do what we often did with the construction business; sub it out. Back away. Let it happen for now and just concentrate on the plan to sell Ferrano Enterprises and figure it all out later.

Or, fuck it all. Take the money we had squirreled away and grab my sisters, Ed, Lisa, the kids, and fuck off somewhere, maybe to Costa Rica where Tia and Tommy were living in paradise under fake names.

And her. Leave her a decorative piece in the apartment three doors down. Set her up with counselling. Wait a few months and stage her death, pull that tracking implant and bury it, but really sneak her out the back door and set her up with a life on another continent under a new name.

Or, see where this thing could go. Face the fact that I was too fucking hungry to be reasonable, too infatuated by her and the idea of what she could give me to last more than a few days before I had tasted her, fucked her, fuckin' lapped up her hero worship of me.

What if I just followed Tommy's suit, took what was given to me and kept it, protected it with every ounce of my being, hoping I'd get my happily ever after, too, and that I'd somehow miraculously escape karma for keeping her? I knew what I should do. I also knew I probably wouldn't do it. Not after tasting what she had to give, what she begged me to take.

I worked until after 10:00 that night and then had a video chat with my brother about business until after 11:00. I didn't bring up any personal shit. He asked how it was going with my houseguest and I'd said 'fine' then changed the subject, didn't tell him I'd fucked her, that I was thinking about keeping her, that the dilemma had me twisted up inside. I kept it to myself.

***

When I got home, she was asleep on the futon in my den. Shit.

I'd been an asshole that morning and then left her alone all day without calling and now here I was, standing over her while she slept. When I'd gotten in and saw she wasn't in my bed at first, I panicked. Of course, she wasn't in my bed, she'd never just presume that she was allowed to be there. At first, I went back to my bed and laid staring at the ceiling for 10 minutes. Only ten minutes and here I was. I should leave her, create some distance. But what if she has a nightmare? What if she lets me create distance?

I leaned over and scooped her up into my arms. Her eyes opened and she looked at me with a little bit of fear and then with another emotion; it looked like affection and need. It gnawed at my gut and I felt a mixture of desire and regret. I carried her to my bedroom without a word, put her on my bed, and then I was on her, on her like white on rice, yanking clothes off, grabbing a handful of her hair, which was again curly, thank fuck, but grabbing it probably a little roughly, and slamming my mouth down on hers.

She spread wide for me and moaned into my mouth. I rammed my cock into her, hard into her, and for a minute I held her so tight I was worried I was gonna hurt her. She went from asleep to wide open and completely wet in just seconds. I played with her clit while I fucked her and her hips circled and circled until she convulsed around my cock, crying out a "Thank you, Master" that made me come 2.5 seconds later.

I held her tight, burying my nose into her hair and kissing her over and over, along her jaw, up and down her throat, on her soft lips, on her eyelids. It almost split me in two when she again said, with so much emotion in her voice, "Thank you for saving me."

"You're welcome, sweet Angel," I answered.

"Please keep me," she said, her voice laced with emotion.

I sighed. "You gotta gimme me time to figure this out, baby. My head is fucked over this."

"I'm sorry. I won't ask again. Take all the time you need, Dare. I'm yours for as long as you want me."

Mine. Fuck.

"Sorry I was a dick today."

She snuggled in and said, "You don't have to say sorry to me."

"Yeah, I do."

"You don't. But thank you for saying it anyway."

I didn't fall asleep for a long while. She took every kindness from me as a gift. She deserved to expect kindness. Could she get to where she didn't feel so grateful for any scrap I gave her? I only worried that once she did, she wouldn't want this, wouldn't want me. Not because I wasn't good enough but because she wouldn't need me. She'd start to wonder where her life could go without being owned.

What was she like before Kruna? I wondered if I'd ever see that side of her. I was torn between waiting for her to tell me her story and finding out myself. As I was drifting off to sleep, I heard her whisper, "You're a dream I was too broken to even wish for but somehow you still came true."

Damn.

***

The next morning, I was up before she was and I texted Zack. I told him to try to find out about her but not to tell me the information until I asked for it. I gave him the information I had, which was minimal, that she'd been at Kruna almost 23 months, that she was almost 23, she'd had an Alaska driver's license, and went to teacher's college and then taught first grade in an English school in Thailand before Kruna. He said he'd see what he could find out.

Suddenly I heard keys and my front door being opened and then Sarah Martinez was at my alarm panel, punching in her code. Aw shit; I meant to cancel her today.

"Mornin', Dario. How was the business trip?"

"Hey Sarah, I meant to call. I don't need you here today. You can skip--"

"What? I need to do your laundry and change the bedding, and wow…it's too clean. What's up? You replace me?"

"I have a houseguest and she's tidy. She did the laundry already."

"She? Your sisters said you were on a date Saturday." She was smirking.

"Leave it alone, Sarah."

She laughed a big belly laugh. "I hear she's a pretty little thing."

"Time to go. I'll let you know about the next time I need you. Don't just pop by."

"You need groceries?" She put her purse on my island.

"No. You stocked me up for like a month with enough food to feed a family of six just a few days back." I passed her the bag and jerked my chin toward the door. She put the bag down again and picked up a sponge by the sink and started wiping the already spotless counter. For fuck sakes.

"Where did you meet her?"

"Sarah, I've got shit to do. You can see yourself out."

"Okay, okay. I'll take your dry cleaning with me."

"No, I'll deal with it."

"Don't be silly, I pass there on the way to Lisa and Tessa."

She put the sponge down and started to walk past me toward my bedroom and I blocked her. "I'll get it. She's still asleep."

Sarah grinned like a cat that ate the canary.

I was about to head to the bedroom when the door opened and Angel came out, dressed in my grey flannel pajamas, her hair tied into a ponytail. She'd bought a few pairs the other day but it was pretty obvious that she preferred mine.

Sarah's face lit up.

"Fuck me," I grumbled.

Angel froze in her tracks.

"Good morning! Angel, right? I'm Sarah Martinez. I'm Dario's housekeeper. Housekeeper for the girls, too. I flit around, like a happy cleaning and cooking butterfly. But I'm like more of an auntie to the family. Can I get you coffee or tea?" She moved to my counter and fetched a mug.

I gave Angel an eye roll as she wandered over.

"Nice to meet you," she said to Sarah.

"How do you take your coffee?"

"Extra milky, 2 sugars. Thank you very much."

"Ooh," she winced. "That much sugar is bad."

"Oh, I know it," Angel said. "I gave it up for 2 years. But I've backslid. I'll probably give it up again soon."

Sarah smiled. "Good. Give it up as soon you can, mija, It is so bad. I read this book…"

I took that opportunity to go grab my dry-cleaning bag, kissing her on the forehead as I passed. She gave me a warm look and ran her hand up my chest and sank into me while I kissed her forehead.

"I'll be one sec, Sarah," I said but Sarah was too busy educating Angel on the evils of sugar to acknowledge me.

When I got back to the kitchen, they were sitting at the island chatting and Sarah had her own cup of coffee. Fuck sakes…

"Come for a sec, baby?" I dropped the garment bag on a sofa and led her into the den and shut the door.

"We need a cover story," I told her.

She nodded.

"So," I started. My phone rang. I grabbed the desk line. Private Caller.

"Hello?"

"Dario Ferrano?"

"Yeah?"

"Sheridan Leo. Local associate to Stanley Smith."

"What's up?"

"Stan asked me to meet you and deliver an envelope to you. Says there's time-sensitive information in there for you."

"Courier it to my office."

"I've been asked to hand it to you and no one but you."

I got her address, told her I'd pick it up on my way to my office, and hung up. Angel was still in front of me.

I looked at her blankly for a second. "Right. Cover story. If anyone asks we'll say we met on the plane coming back from Thailand. Stick close to the truth. I was there on business. You and I met on the flight here. You taught there but that ended and you're relocating here. Your plans to stay with a friend fell through when we got to the airport you found out you had no place to stay and were goin' to a hotel but I offered my spare room and you're staying here for now."

"People will believe that?"

I shrugged. "I don't give a fuck. I have had no time or headspace to come up with a better one. The more complicated the less believable. I'll tell my family that you're getting over something, not to ask you questions. It'll make them back off. Except Sarah. Sarah will dig and dig to try to get your backstory. She's harmless, just a den mother."

"Okay."

"But don't give her an in. She'll pick at you like you're a scab until she gets to the good stuff. I gotta go. See ya later on. I'll get Sarah to leave with me. Stay here till we go." I pulled her in for a kiss.

***

Stan's colleague gave me an envelope with another one of those tablets. I sat in my car in the covered parking lot by the Ferrano office and opened it with my fingerprint, again hating with a passion that they had my prints.

A document was on the screen with a note from Gan Chen.

I regretted I was unable to say Goodbye to you prior to your departure. Something urgent had arisen. I was informed that you were not provided with some of Felicia's details prior to pick-up. These would have been provided to you prior to departure but with the rush, typical protocol was broken. I have enclosed them here. If there is anything listed that displeases you, we would be happy to discuss an alternate or enroll Felicia in re-training. Your satisfaction is our top priority. If you require further information please do not hesitate to reach out. Should you require the same information for Monalisa, this can be provided.

This information will expire on this device one hour from opening it. I hope to be meeting with you and your brother at our Partner Summit in October. Kindly RSVP through our mutual acquaintance by September 30.

Regards,

GC

I thought the information would contain her details, details about her past. I braced to find out her name, how they'd gotten to her. But that was not the info I got. I was not at all prepared for the information on the next screen.

The next screen was the Report screen that looked like what came up blank on the last tablet. It was not blank this time. It detailed information gathered through her training. It was like a report card with grades and a few comments sections.

Everything had her individual score as well as a median score for others in the resort. It said she had a high pain threshold, higher than 80% of the other slaves. I didn't even want to know what they used to test that.

It said that she'd taken 19 days to break. The average slave took an average of 3-4 days under their program. 19 fucking days. *Fuck.*

It classified her as a sexual submissive. There were categories: dominant, submissive, and switch. In each category was a graph, a degree, and she graded at slightly more than the 75% submissive mark 22 months earlier and now was listed at the furthest submissive degree.

It said she had no known sexual aversions, that she had the most intense orgasms when experiencing multiple penetration, and that her orgasms were off the chart when she was restrained. She liked it rough. She liked to be bossed around during sex. She had intense reactions to spankings. It said she had panic attacks in her first several months at Kruna but had not had any in over 14 months. Their anecdote for her panic attacks was to restrain her and bring her to orgasm. There was a rancid feeling in my gut and a foul taste in my mouth as I skimmed through the bullet point notes stating that withholding orgasms as punishment worked much more effectively than pain in disciplining her but that she had not required punishment in more than 18 months. Her last infraction was self-pleasure.

It said that she was an exceptional asset who was capable of multiple orgasms that exceeded the average Kruna assets by 400%. She was the most often specifically requested Kruna asset out of the 200 they had by patrons in the past 7 months, prior to that was the second most often requested for the previous 4 months. They had to hate giving her up. My father must've really pulled strings for her.

I reviewed the rest of the information and then closed it off and sat and seethed in my car, chain smoking for the next fifteen minutes before I could head up to my office. I was seething that they'd toyed with her to the point that they could grade her on pain. I was seething because she had endured something for 19 days straight that was designed to break her, that she'd fought so hard to avoid being broken, and that she was now obviously utterly broken because they'd rated her well enough to trust her off the property. That she'd gone from that determined to hold onto who she was before they made her into Felicia but then became so exalted as an illustration of Kruna perfection made me want to fucking puke.

And I couldn't comprehend that she had the insatiability I'd always wanted, that she was a sexual submissive who climaxed the hardest when restrained, and that she was mine, that she wanted to be mine. They gave me this information to optimize her use. They gave me information to keep her under my control.

She only wanted so badly to be mine because they had taken 19 days, more than quadruple of what broke the average Kruna slave, and once she was broken she was so utterly broken that they didn't have to worry about sending her out in the world to be the slave of the son of one of their most important partners. Was she a submissive who loved to fuck so much only because she was broken? If I'd met the girl in Alaska with the piercings and the wild curls and mischief in her eyes would I have wanted her? Would she be so compatible? Or, would she have had that spark, that wildness I loved and still been my Angel, been fucking perfect in every way for me?

I was enraged. Enraged at them because they broke her and enraged at myself. I stomped on the tablet and then walked with it and tossed it in a dumpster behind a nearby fast food joint.

How the fuck could I keep her? How the fuck could I not?

Angel

I was bored. Maybe that was a good sign. Was it a sign that I might be snapping out of it? I was itching to be outside. Back at Kruna I was content when I was in my room or when I had free time with nothing to do. I didn't get to watch TV and I hardly socialized but I was fine in my own company because it was a brief reprieve from the roles I was always playing. There was a quiet courtyard zen garden area we could go to for fresh air and there were common rooms where we could read or talk with other girls. There were some board games, Mahjong tiles, a chess board. There was a gym. I generally spent time alone when I wasn't on assignment. But my mindset had already begun to shift. I didn't feel like I was still Felicia but I didn't feel like me, either. I just wanted to be Dare Ferrano's angel. But him asking me to be me was niggling at me, too. Did I know how to be me?

I'd reorganized everything in his apartment, not that it was messy, and I didn't go digging through his drawers or anything private but I'd washed and dusted everything so often it had become tedious.

He'd said I'd eventually be able to come and go. I wasn't sure what I'd do out there but the idea of taking a walk, feeding ducks in the park, window shopping, people watching, going to the library… it all sounded good.

I wasn't sure where he and I were, though.

He was back just a few hours after he'd left. And he was in a mood. He'd come in, jaw tight, eyes angry, body language rigid, pissed off. He threw his keys on the table by the door, roughly hit buttons on the alarm, walked past me with a chin lift and then slammed the door behind himself in the den. Slammed it hard. I'd been at the island, needlessly wiping it when he came in and now I didn't know what to do with myself.

A few hours later he emerged from the den. I was watching TV. He grabbed his keys and hit buttons on the alarm panel and then headed out the door, barely looking at me. I watched him go without a word.

An hour later he was back, slamming the door, hitting alarm panel buttons, then heading into his den, again without speaking to me.

He hadn't come out by 9:00 at night and so I made a PB&J sandwich and figured I'd might as well go to sleep. I didn't know whether to sleep in his bed or not so I curled up on the sofa. I didn't want to disturb him in the office where my clothes were so I just got under the soft throw and put the TV on and I eventually drifted off to sleep.

I woke up to him carrying me. Again. My heart leapt forward like it'd done last night when he'd carried me to his bed. If I got lucky enough to spend my life with this man, I'd be tempted to fall asleep on purpose somewhere other than his bed every single night if it meant he'd carry me to bed like this every time. It was so gallant, so dominant, so perfect. I opened my eyes and looked at his face and he had what looked like a hard, stone-cold look in his eyes when he looked at me. I didn't know what to make of it.

But he didn't attack me and yank my clothes off. He just put me under the blankets, undressed down to boxer briefs, and then climbed in with me and spooned me. I was in yoga capris and a tank top so I guess they'd do for sleeping. I nuzzled in and pondered it for a minute but then dared to plant a kiss on his forearm, which was across my chest, his hand cupping my shoulder. His lips touched the back of my neck just above the collar and he squeezed me and then gently took the elastic out of my hair and twisted the length of my hair around and around his fist gently, sweetly. He played with my hair until I fell back to sleep snuggled against him.

Dare

I had a long chat with my brother on the webcam before I went to bed.

"What's going on?" Tommy asked.

"With what?"

"With Felicia. Everything okay? You've been off the last few times we've talked."

"I'm not calling her that. She had a bit of a meltdown and asked me not to."

"Meltdown?"

"Yeah. Fucking meltdown mode myself over here."

"Meaning?"

"Meaning…shit…it's gotten complicated. Really fuckin' complicated."

"Uh huh," my brother had replied with a knowing look.

"What?"

"You fucked her; you like the girl."

"Fuck." I had leaned back in my chair and stared at the ceiling.

"What's the problem?"

"The problem? What about this isn't a problem is more like it. Do I really want to take on a girl that's broken? I didn't wanna go here."

"But you went there, anyway."

"Yeah. She's…fuck…she's gorgeous and she's submissive in bed and can't get enough. She begs me for it."

He let out a loud breath.

"She has nightmares, so I let her sleep with me."

He moistened his lips and nodded.

"I called her Angel because she was trying to behave like an angel and because she has the face of one and now, she's decided that's her new name."

He winced and gave his head a scratch.

"Yeah, I know. She won't take off the collar they put on her because it gives her nightmares to have it off. She says she needs it on so they'll know she's mine and not try to take her back. She's begging me to keep her."

He let out a slow breath. "So you fucked her and now you feel bad 'cuz you don't plan to keep her?"

"Fucked her repeatedly, bro. Can't seem to stop. It's feeling like a relationship."

"Shit."

"Yeah."

He gave me a knowing look. "So, we change the plan," he shrugged. "You wanna keep her, you keep her."

"It's wrong."

"Yeah."

"It feels right, though."

"I know." He gave me another knowing look.

"Pop'll be laughing his ass off at me right now."

"For sure," Tommy said quietly. I saw Tia move in behind him and she waved.

"Hey," I greeted.

She put a sandwich and a steaming mug down beside him and kissed him on the cheek. He'd caught her hand as she tried to walk away and yanked her back until she landed in his lap. He planted a kiss on her mouth. She blushed at him, gave him a look of promise, making me feel like I was a fucking peeping Tom on the honeymooners. I cleared my throat. He took her hips and lifted her away and gave her ass a swat. She left the room. His eyes came back to the screen.

I rubbed my eyes. I'd had a fuck of a day putting out fires and shit.

"So, what if as she gets well in her head, finds who she used to be again, she doesn't want this?" I muttered.

"Or what if she falls for you and does?"

"Do I really want someone broken? I grew up with a broken mother, man, you remember. Sometimes Angel seems like she'll get past it. But I don't know if what I'm seeing is her or who they made her into. And I dunno if she'll get past it. I'm not even fucking making sense here."

"I get it," Tommy stated.

"What if her wanting me isn't real, just a side-effect of her hero worship because I got her outta there and then it becomes obligation?"

"Make it good for her so she won't want anything else."

"I'd hate to put myself out there when it could go sour."

"Better to have loved and lost and all that jazz, man."

He was validating it, telling me to keep her. Telling me to take a risk. I figured he'd understand, of course he'd understand, but this wasn't him just telling me to take what I wanted in a caveman, crime boss kind of way; this was him speaking to me from experience. His situation wasn't the same but it was close enough to be highly relatable.

"Send me your counselor's details, okay? I think it'd do her some good to talk to someone. I don't know her backstory yet but I'm guessin' therapy could be good."

"Will do."

"Is it helping you?"

He shrugged. "Still early days, man."

"Yeah. Maybe we should all go. Get the Ferrano family discount." I rolled my eyes.

He rolled his, then asked, "You need me home, man? You're dealing with a lot."

"Naw, it's all good. I thrive under pressure. You know me."

"Yeah, I know you. I know that you'll drown before you lower yourself to ask someone for a life preserver."

I snickered. "Family trait."

"Thinkin' of coming back for a few weeks. While I'm there I can see about lightening your load. Maybe if I make a few appearances it'll prevent red flags. You getting any bad vibes anywhere?"

"None. And it's up to you, man. What do you think about goin' to Thailand for that summit?"

He shook his head. "Dunno, bro. I am not bringing my girl there. No fucking way. I'm also not comfortable leaving her behind. So, I don't know yet. We're dealing with a few things here, too, so a trip home might be good. We can talk when I get there."

"Yeah? Everything alright?"

"Not really." He shook his head. "I'll fill you in later. We'll see what happens in the next few days."

"Zack and I are meeting day after tomorrow to chat. He's been doing more digging."

"Yeah; Ferrano has practically become the guy's full-time job."

"He's good, though. Been a real asset. Well, I'm gonna crash," I said. "I'll message you after I meet with him."

"Sounds good, man. Go chase your angel's nightmares away." He gave me a smile. It looked heartfelt rather than teasing.

Guilt was telling me I should put a stop to this thing with her, that I was putting too much at risk and that I was taking advantage. But I also felt like she was mine already, like it was already said and done. I kept saying I didn't wanna put myself out there but I was pretty sure it'd already happened.

I went to crash, but my bed was empty. I panicked a split second but then found her asleep in the living room huddled under a blanket on the sofa. I lifted her and carried her to bed. She woke. I didn't say anything, just put her in bed, undressed, and then held her. And it took me a long time to fall asleep, but once I did it was because laying there in the dark and holding her close, feeling her breathe, feeling her body heat, running my hands through her hair, feeling her totally soft in my arms, totally trusting, and feeling like she was absolutely 100% mine I'd made a few decisions.

CHAPTER FIVE

Dare

I woke up to her beautiful blue eyes on me. She was flush against me; we were facing one another on our sides and her head was on my bicep, chin tipped up to look at me, one hand on my chest, the other around my waist.

"Hey." I blinked a few times, thinking that waking up like this made me even surer of what I'd decided when I finally closed my eyes last night.

"Hey." she smiled.

Her eyes were shining. Her hair was wild, it was everywhere, a gorgeous mass of waves spilling all over me and my pillows, all wavy and silky and auburn and copper. I looked closely at her porcelain face and could see the scar from the eyebrow piercing, the faint dot from the nose piercing, the dot above her lip where she had a beauty mark piercing. She had a faint dusting of freckles across her nose. I touched each piercing dot individually. "You're like a pin cushion."

She smirked. "Yeah. Real glad I got talked out of those ear spacers." She widened her eyes and for a split second she reminded me of the girl I saw on the Alaska driver's license. That girl looked like she'd give anyone the finger.

"What do you like to do for fun?" I asked her.

She whispered, "I like to fuck, Master."

I snickered. "Other than that." Her words, her tone, her eyes, made me hard. She was in vixen-mode this morning. I fucking liked it.

She squirmed into me. My hand cupped her bottom.

"I'm serious. What do you wanna do today? I'm blowing off work. Let's go do something."

"Whatever you want."

"What do you want to do?"

"Whatever you---"

"Angel." I gave her a look and she swallowed, expression dropping, looking afraid.

"I wanna get to know you. You've gotta wanna do something after two years there and the last several days locked up in here."

"I'd like to know you, too," she said, bright-eyed. "What do you like to do?"

I gave her an exasperated look.

"I don't know me right now, Dare. The things I used to do for fun…that feels a million years ago. How about we get to know you first? Please?"

"What do you think about therapy? Do you think it might help?"

She shrugged. "I can't say. I don't know."

"Would you be interested in trying? It could help."

She studied me for a minute and then nodded slowly. "For you, yes, anything."

I caressed her face, trying to push away worries that she could pull away from me as she starts to heal.

"Let's get dressed and get outta here. We'll go for pancakes, take a walk and see where we end up. I've just gotta send a few quick emails."

"Can we go feed the ducks at that pond across the road?"

"Sure."

I joined her in the shower after dragging her trunk over. That was it, I was done playing. Done waffling. The alternative, putting her in the spare room or in the apartment down the hall? No. I'd be in there every night carrying her back to my bed. It was pointless to keep fighting it. Fighting it was taking too much of my energy and headspace and that energy and headspace could be put to much better use by using it to deal with Kruna and the other loose ends left by my pop.

When I climbed in the shower with her, she'd spun around looking startled.

"Water conservation," I said, matter-of-factly, and then grabbed her by the hips and pulled her close.

I kissed her, we washed each other's backs, and then after washing ourselves got out and got dressed. It was pretty obvious by how she looked at me and how long she took washing my back that she wanted sex in the shower. But, I wanted to let some anticipation build for a bit and get her outta the house. If I started with her in the shower, I'd be in bed with her all day.

"The trunk isn't in there," she said.

"It's in there." I was rubbing my head with a towel. I motioned to my closet. She stared at the closet door and then looked at me, confused.

"You wanna be mine?" I asked.

She nodded hesitantly. "I am yours. For as long as you want me."

"Then you're in here with me," I said. I tossed the towel and slicked my hair back with my fingers.

She teared up.

I walked over to her and held her close. "I don't know that this isn't wrong, baby, but it feels like I have no choice."

"What do you mean?" She sounded crestfallen.

"I'm tired of fighting with myself over this. It feels like a losing battle. You and me have stuff to figure out, but we'll figure it out as we go. I don't know where this is going with us but I'm choosing to do the wrong thing here and see where it takes us."

"Dare," she whispered, "this feels so not wrong I can't even explain."

I nodded, getting her, totally getting her.

"And that's why I'm *all in*, baby."

She melded into my body, putting her arms around me. "Unpack your stuff in there, make room for it. But do it tomorrow. Right now, let's go get you some pancakes."

Debbie never felt like this. She never felt like she was truly mine. Angel felt like she was mine. Could've been because she was so willing to be mine. Or maybe it was because lying there with her in my arms the previous night I decided I was just going to take her, fuck the consequences.

She held her emotion in check. I got the impression that was hard for her, that she was happy, that she wanted to show it but she was deferring to me. I wanted to get her out of the apartment for a bit. We got dressed in jeans and tees and hoodies and went for pancakes.

***

It was nice, it was quiet, though. I wanted to ask her questions, do the things you usually did when you were getting to know someone, but didn't know how to approach things with her. So instead, we were quiet, though comfortably so, and while she was taking in the sights around us, I was taking in her. I couldn't help but wonder what it'd take to see who she was, who she really was.

Afterwards, we were walking through a nearby park and about to feed the ducks. After that I thought we'd walk down to the museum, which was just a few blocks from the duck pond.

"I could see that pond from the balcony, see the ducks. I was thinking it'd be fun to feed them," she told me so I'd ordered an extra order of pancakes to go and we took them with us.

But as we approached the pond and passed a few benches I got my world rocked and not in a good way. I saw the last person I'd wanna see.

Debbie.

It was lunch time and this park was in the business district, walking distance from the condo. Deb worked as a receptionist in a local law office according to what Casey said the other night, said Deb had been working there just a few months. I told Casey I couldn't care less but suspected I'd eventually cross paths with Deb since this neighborhood was where I worked and lived.

And there she was, sitting on a bench with another girl eating sandwiches off their laps and laughing and when we spotted one another her smile died on her face. She had her raven hair pulled back in a low ponytail, big silver hoops in her ears, black nails, black trench coat with high heels. Red billowy scarf the same shade as her lips. I was holding Angel's hand and froze in my tracks.

Angel almost tripped when I'd halted as she was still walking but I caught her by her waist and pulled her back against my side protectively. Deb gave her the once-over and then her eyes were back on me. I turned on my heel and steered Angel the other way.

Angel said nothing. It was pretty obvious that Deb and I knew one another and that I did not want to see her.

I walked, with purpose, back to the car, and opened Angel's door.

"Dario!" I heard Deb, who was following.

I shut the door after Angel was inside and ignored the voice, that fucking voice. I got into the driver's seat. As I was pulling out of the spot, she was only twenty feet from my car, eyes on me. Fuck that. I glared at her and then pulled out of the spot and squealed, fish tailing it outta there.

"Are you okay, Dare?" Angel's voice brought me out of a daze after a minute. An angry daze filled with images of the past.

"Sorry, baby. I'll find us another spot."

"Okay," she said softly.

"Ex-fiancée," I muttered.

"Oh."

She didn't push.

After a few minutes of quiet I said, "Guess you don't have any of those, at least."

"Ex-fiancés?"

"Yeah."

"Well, no." She said that with hesitation.

"No?" I glanced at her.

She looked like she was measuring her words. Her face paled. "I was asked. I, um, I declined."

"Broke the guy's heart." It was a statement, not a question, because I knew any guy who asked her and got told no would have a shattered heart.

"Not exactly."

I pulled in to the parking lot for the park I'd been at with Lisa the other day.

"Care to explain?"

"Turning down the proposal probably started the chain of events that led to me being here with you right now. My saying no wasn't…wasn't taken too well."

It was the start of her revealing things to me. I didn't want to push and make her clam up but didn't want to seem closed-off either. I took her hand across the center console and rubbed it.

"Want to tell me more?"

She chewed her cheek a second and her eyes got a faraway look. Her body went tense. She started to tremble.

"Hey, it's okay. You don't have to." I touched her face with my fingertips. "I can't promise I'll wait forever to push for answers, baby, because if we're a we --- we need everything on the table. But also because I gotta find our way outta this world eventually so I may need information from you to help me do that. But you don't have to do it today."

"Thanks for giving me time," she said and loosened up. "You say you're *all in* and I wanna be, too. I'll try. It's just been such a lot of…" she winced.

"It's okay. Don't worry today," I tried to reassure her.

"Can you tell me? What happened with her? She's beautiful. Um, unless you don't wanna talk about it."

"We were together from 16 until we were 22. She cheated. Few months before the wedding. It'd all been booked. Walked in on her givin' head to the DJ we'd hired."

Angel winced.

"Wasn't the upcoming 7-year itch, either. Found out later that she cheated a lot. She tried to get me to forgive her. Wasn't happening. I also found out a few months after we split that she'd had an abortion. Don't know if it was mine or not. Maybe she didn't know either. Guess I'll never know."

"Sorry."

"It's done. I haven't laid eyes on her in almost three years, since a few weeks after we split. I have no desire to talk to her so I got us outta there. Let's go feed some ducks."

I grabbed the doggie bag and got out of the car and rounded it in time to catch her hand as she closed her door.

She had childlike wonder on her face as she fed the ducks and then I realized it wasn't just the ducks she was looking at, it was the horses on the other side of the fence along the park's border. I leaned back on an elbow in the grass and lit a smoke and watched her as she talked to the ducks she fed, telling one it was being too greedy and telling another to hurry up and "get in there". Then seagulls came and chased the ducks away and she seemed to get off on feeding them, too.

It didn't take long for her to run out of pancakes and when she sat beside me on the grass I stubbed the cigarette out and put my arm around her and we stared out at the pond in silence for a bit.

I was lost in thought but then noticed she was again watching the stables next door to the park. A girl was riding a horse and it was at full gallop going around a track.

"Like horses?" I asked her.

She nodded and got a little mischievous smile on her face. I felt a pang as that expression made me think of her driver's license photo. I watched her for a second, hoping she'd reveal something.

"We had horses," she finally said.

"We?"

"My dad and I. We had two."

"So you can ride?"

"Oh, I can ride."

My pants tightened. "You sure can…" I whispered in her ear.

She flushed but her eyes heated. Then she threw me for a loop. She said, "I…uh…won a few riding awards. For riding horses and uh, riding…um…mechanical bulls."

I just about tripped over my tongue. "You're shitting me."

She got pinker in the cheeks, chewed her lower lip as if pondering something, and then gave her head a shake and said, "Can I see your phone? I don't know if it's still there but…can I?"

I passed her my phone and she opened the YouTube app and typed in "Juneau Ace Roadhouse bikini mechanical bull winner 2012"

She certainly had my attention.

She scrolled and then tapped the screen. I moved closer to her and cupped my hand above the phone to block the sun and get a better view.

It was a loud and crowded bar and the camera zoomed in on the bull and a girl got on. It was her. The filming quality wasn't great but I knew it was her instantly. She was in cut-off jean shorts so short they were practically bikini bottoms and a red bikini top and had bare feet and her hair in ringlets. She had heavy make-up on and a red and white checked bandana around her throat with a tan cowboy hat on. The music started and she threw the hat and then it was like a choreographed number the way she moved on that thing. She gyrated, rode the waves, she whipped her hair around in time to the music, and the attitude on her face? It wasn't super close-up but I could see it and fuck. Ho…lee…fuck. I watched the 3-and-a-half-minute video fucking mesmerized.

That girl, the girl on the mechanical bull with the sass, with the hot body, the wild red hair, she could seriously be my fucking dream girl. Add that girl to the girl I knew here and I'd be golden. No settling. The video started with the bull moving rhythmically to the music, her putting on a sexy show, but in the last minute it really gave her a run for her money the way it spun and jerked but she held on and she fucking owned that thing.

When it ended the crowd roared with applause and started chanting. She stood up on the bull and did a fancy backflip coming off it and the crowd went wilder. I couldn't make out what they were chanting and leaned in to hear better but she exited out of the screen and then handed me my phone. Our eyes met.

Angel

I felt more than a little embarrassed. I couldn't believe I'd shown him that. Maybe I was trying to give him something, since I'd been so closed off about my past and he'd been open with me about his ex-fiancée. I turned it off as the crowd started to chant my name and passed him the phone. When our eyes met, I just about passed out because the look on his face, oh my gosh, he was looking at me like he was going to fuck me right there on the grass in front of the ducks, seagulls, and horses and whoever else happened on by. I felt a hot little whoosh in my panties. He got to his feet and reached for my hand, his eyes holding mine captive.

I started to slowly get up, reaching for his outstretched hand hesitantly, but he grabbed it and squeezed, heaving me upwards to my feet. "We need privacy. Now."

Holy shit.

I guess my Master liked my bull-riding skills.

Dare rushed me to his SUV. I had to jog to keep up with his purposeful strides. He got me to the passenger door and then I was pinned against it and his mouth was on mine and his fingers were forcefully in my hair. I moaned into his mouth. He dragged himself away and his eyes were heated. Holy moly, were they ever.

He shook his head and curled his lips like he was supremely pissed all of a sudden and I felt my body jerk tight as I saw a muscle jumping in his cheek. I dropped my eyes to the ground and felt my shoulders slump.

"I'll fuckin' kill them," he growled.

I let out a staggered breath.

"Get in the car," he snarled and I stepped away and he opened the door and I did what I was told. He slammed it.

He drove back to his condo like an angry lunatic racecar driver. He took my hand as I stepped out of the SUV and not looking at me strode to the elevator, still radiating fury. Inside of it, once the doors closed, he took his keychain and then thrust a key into a keyhole on the button panel for an express ride up and then hit his floor button and we started to go up. He didn't look at me. He stared at the buttons lighting our way upwards, still holding my hand. His hold was gentle but his face was radiating anger more intensely than I'd seen from him so far. The elevator stopped on his floor and then when the elevator doors opened before I knew what was happening, he put a shoulder to my belly and hauled me over his shoulder. I squeaked in surprise as we were quickly down the hall and then I heard him put his key in the hole and then hit buttons on his alarm panel.

The next thing I knew, I was on my back on his bed and my clothes were being ripped off of me. His eyes were heated, hot damn, were they heated. I went to help with my clothes and he ordered, "No. Don't move." I threw my arms over my head, panting with arousal.

In a flash, he had my shoes, jeans, hoodie, socks, tank top, bra, and panties off and I was naked. He ripped his own clothes off and then he was on his back and I was whipped around so that I was straddling him. His angry fiery eyes glinted with amusement all of a sudden.

"Three guesses on what I want from you right now but I don't think you'll need two and three."

I swallowed hard, closed my eyes, and took a deep breath. Then I opened them and looked at him coquettishly and said, in a southern drawl, "Would my Master like me to ride him?"

His teeth skimmed his bottom lip and he shook his head in astonishment. And then his grip on my hips tightened but he said nothing. Oh yeah. That's what my Master wanted.

"Well, he is hung like a horse…" I added and batted my eyelashes, watching a twinkle light his eyes. I reached down and guided him inside of me and I rode my Master. I rode him like I was competing for the trophy not just for Juneau but for the World.

Dare

I couldn't think straight. I was torn between wanting to be in the moment with her, enjoying this beautiful body and her efforts to bring me pleasure and put on a *fuck hot* show for me. She was incredible at it, but I was struggling because I had a war going on in my brain where I saw blood. I saw dead Gan Chen, dead Rafe Ruiz, dead Asian bitch from hell. I saw the security guards

I'd seen, the chauffeur, the housekeepers, bell boy, the gardener, and the pile of fucking sick goofs from that dinner party and on the top of the pile of dead bodies I saw a dead Tom Ferrano Sr. Because in my head I'd shot him, too. I'd shot every single one of them between the eyes one by one for the fact that they had taken 19 days to break her, to do whatever they did to kill the spirit of the girl that I'd seen in that bull-riding video.

I pushed the rage back. I had my dream girl here, right now. She was riding my cock and looking at me with utter fucking devotion on her face and she still had fire. In bed right now she was on fire and I was thoroughly convinced that as far as out of bed went, she had it deep and it was buried under a pile of brutal bone-chilling shit, but it was still there. It was fucking there; I was sure of it as I'd seen a few hints here and there. I never wanted to see her cower in fear from me again.

She was mine because my goddamn father bought her for me. Maybe the fire right now came partly from the fact that she had spent two years fucking in order to survive, but I would make sure it was real for me, that I'd make her feel safe and cared for so she'd have no reason to fake it with me. In my head my father on top of the pile of dead bodies had a knowing smug look on his face because he'd won, proved that I'd been another chip off the 'ole block and would take his gift to me and keep her, keep my very own sex slave.

I decided right then and there that I would find a way to un-break her somehow, even if that meant I had to find a way to completely dismantle Kruna as a wedding gift to her. This was it. This was her. I wasn't settling; she was what I wanted. I knew it down to my bones. I just needed to be patient, make her feel safe, hope that I could systematically work at unbreaking her.

She started to orgasm, still riding my cock, and much like a move she'd done in that video she whipped her hair from one shoulder over to the other and it spilled down her back and shoulders as her lips parted in ecstasy. My right fingers were on her clit and my left ones on her nipple, and as she threw her hair back, she let out a sexy moaning husky, "Dare…" And she said it just the way she usually said "Master" when she came and I fucking loved that. I flipped her first to her back and then over to her belly and took her from behind, a handful of her beautiful hair in my fist and I drove into her tight silky heat over and over until I came undone. I collapsed onto her back and we were both breathless.

Minutes later I was still drifting, not to sleep, but off somewhere deep in thought, when I felt her squirm. I kissed her shoulder and rolled onto my back to let her free. She put her chin on my shoulder and looked at me with a little smile. "Bubble bath?" she asked.

"Mm. Go. I'll join you in a minute." I kissed her forehead.

Her eyes sparkled at me and she nodded and then leaned over and kissed me on the mouth. My hand caught in her hair and I held her to my mouth for a second, feeling emotion bloom inside me. I put my forehead to hers and let out a slow breath. She gave me another smile and then kissed just under my jaw and then got up. I leaned over and swatted her bare ass with a big smile. She let out a sexy "Ooh" and then sashayed sexily to the bathroom in the buff.

I leaned over to fetch my cell from my jeans pocket and texted Zack to say,

"Juneau ace roadhouse bikini mechanical bull rider winner 2012. YouTube."

I put the phone on my nightstand, threaded my fingers behind my head, and stared at the ceiling, listening to the bathtub fill and thinking that I needed to do something about that necklace on her throat. I wanted it gone. I wanted it gone in a way that wouldn't stress her out and bring her nightmares back, though.

Three or four minutes later my phone made the text alert sound. I lifted it. Zack.

My friend, I sure hope U R smart enough to grab the bull by the horns.

I grinned and replied,

"Watch it. That's my future ex-wife you're ogling there. You still good to meet me at the ofc at 9-10 tomorrow? We need to talk about a few things."

He replied with *"yep. See ya at 9. Trenta black double sugar Americano pls & thx."* and there was an attachment. I opened it and it was an ogling googly-eyed happy face. What the fuck was a guy like Zack doing with teenage girl emoticons on his phone? The guy was like a 35-year-old John Wayne, not a tween girl. I shook my head, smiling to myself thinking that my concerns about Zack judging me were obviously not a concern, not that it mattered all that much, but still. The ex-wife comment was my way of telling him I was serious about her without getting gushy. I got up and joined my angel in the bathtub.

Angel

Dare and I had a bubble bath and he was affectionate but quiet. He was definitely preoccupied. When he first came in, he caught me shaving my legs and I stopped when he got in the tub.

"I've not gone this long without a wax in a long time," I explained, a little embarrassed and glad he hadn't come in a minute earlier when I'd been shaving my hoo-ha.

His eyes got broody at that for a second and then he shook it off. "Up the road from here my cuz has a hair salon. She does that shit. I'll hook you up."

I smiled at him. "That'd be great."

"I'll take you this weekend, unless you can't wait that long?"

"That'll be fine. Thank you."

He caught me by my hips and moved me against him. I leaned against his chest.

The bath was nice. Seeing and leaning against Dare's naked wet muscled body was more than nice. When we were drying off he asked me what I wanted for dinner and I followed him, in his / now my pajamas, as I'd pretty much claimed them as my favorite articles of clothing, out to the kitchen where he pulled a bunch of menus from a drawer.

He threw the Chinese food and Thai food menus to the side and then leafed through a few others.

"I could do Chinese," I told him, guessing that's what he wanted but that he didn't want to subject me to any Asian food.

"You sure?"

I nodded. "Like absolutely junky stuff. Like egg rolls and chicken balls with sweet and sour sauce and rice that's fried with soya sauce and scrambled eggs in it. And while you hook me up for waxing maybe you can hook me up with a membership to your gym? I'm sure I've put on five pounds already since being here."

He smiled pretty big and adorably and then grabbed my ass. "Let's get a 'lil more junk in your trunk first, my baby." I nearly swooned on the spot. Then he kissed me quick on the mouth, grabbed a menu from the pile, and then grabbed his phone and as he dialed it he said, "There's a baseball game on tonight."

I smiled. "Good."

"Got an errand so I'll be a few hours and I'll pick up the food on my way back. Can you queue up the game for us?"

I nodded and left him to order the food and went and made the bed and picked our recently strewn clothes up from the four corners of the big bedroom and then put his TV on in there. I switched to the channel for the baseball game. I waited for him on the bed.

***

I'd nodded off but woke up to him leaning over me, kissing my neck.

"Mm," I leaned into his lips. "You smell like Chinese food." He had a small shimmery silver gift bag with white handles in his hand. Purple tissue paper corners peeked out. He put it on the bedside table beside me.

I smiled, asking, "What's that?" and then my heart started beating really loud.

"Presents," he said softly.

I felt my heartrate pick up even more and my chest felt cold deep inside. I hadn't been given a present in a long while, not since…since…I broke out in a cold sweat and started to tremble. Hard. I couldn't take my eyes off the bag.

I heard him, sounding hollow and far away.

"Baby?"

I started to tremble harder. He pulled the blankets back and then got in and pulled me over and then under the covers against him. "You sick? You upset? What?"

"I…" I couldn't form words. All I could see in my head was Jason. Jason's face, his dark hair, his blue eyes, his big smile, and he was holding a gift bag the same as the one Dare had. I tried to curl into a ball. I couldn't get myself together. I was hyperventilating.

"What is it, baby? What?"

"I..."

"Angel?"

"I can't, I can't."

"Can't what? What's wrong?"

"Please. Hurry."

He looked at me like I was crazy.

"Please, please." I clutched at his fly and tried to get it open.

He grabbed my hand. "Angel? What can I do?"

He knew I was having a panic attack and wanted to help.

"I need, I need…" I was in hysterics. "Hold me down. Take me." I was whimpering, hyperventilating, clawing at his pants but I had absolutely no sense of coordination.

He said "Shh" and then he caught my wrists and he held them over my head, then pinned them with one hand. His other hand went down the front of the pajama pants and he started to rub my clit.

"Tell me, order me, please."

"Open up, baby. Stay still." His voice was commanding, perfect, just what I needed.

My legs spread wide. My breathing slowed down and I closed my eyes. "Tighter, please. Please?" I breathed desperately and his hand tightened on my wrists.

"Don't move," he said in a low, husky voice.

I exhaled long and slow and then I started feeling warm again. I started feeling normal again. The sensation between my legs began to build. I started to moan. It took a while and he didn't stop, didn't give up, and then I was there.

"Thank you, Master," I whimpered as I started coming. I came hard, so hard I let out a scream and the sensations went on and on and on even after he let go of my wrists and his hand left my pants.

I shuddered with aftershocks for a minute and then as I started to feel steady again, I realized he was sitting on the edge of the bed watching me. I couldn't read his expression.

I curled into a small ball against him and put my head on his lap, then looked up to his gorgeous face.

"I'm sorry."

His hand caressed my hair and he swallowed hard. He looked shaken.

There was a long moment of looking into one another's eyes and I swear it was like he could see deep inside. I felt naked. Not naked of clothing but stripped completely bare. He laid beside me and pulled me to him and I nuzzled in and inhaled his scent, tried to memorize how he smelled, how he felt. As if I needed to remember it, in case I never felt it again.

Now he knows. He knows how broken I am.

"Hungry?" he finally asked in a soft voice.

I nodded. He got up and then reached for the silver bag and put it in a drawer of the bedside table and then he left the room. I sat up and took a few breaths with my eyes closed and a minute later he was back with a bottle of Coke and two glasses. He put them on his bedside table. Then he left and returned a minute later with two plates of food and sets of chopsticks. He passed me a plate and then un-paused the TV and got in bed and leaned back against the pillows, dropping a handful of soy, mustard, and plum sauce packets between us. I looked at my plate. He'd gotten all the dishes I'd requested.

He started to eat so I did, too. I was careful to not look at him but I felt a tense vibe coming from him. It was angry. Really angry.

"Don't like the eggrolls?" he asked softly, not angrily.

I was scooping the insides out.

"Uh, I like the shells. I don't like what they put in them." I started scooping my fried rice into my emptied shell.

He looked at me like I was an alien but the mood lightened. That was the only conversation during dinner.

We watched the baseball game and we didn't talk. When I was finished my food, I grabbed his plate, which was on the bed between us, and took both plates to the kitchen, rinsed them, and then put them in the dishwasher and put the containers of Chinese food that were sitting on the counter into the fridge. When I came back in he was laying down watching the game, his hands behind his head. His eyes moved to me briefly and he had his jaw clenched. I looked to the floor as I made my way the rest of the way to the bed. After climbing on I put my head on his pelvis. He started to play with my hair. I looked up at him. He had a sad look on his face. His eyes met mine and he gave my neck a little squeeze and then his hand rested on my back. His eyes went back to the screen. I turned over to see the TV, keeping my head on him.

When the game was over, I got up and went into the bathroom to wash my face and brush my teeth. When I returned, he was sitting up, the TV off. He was obviously waiting for me. I'd thought I'd gotten off easy. Guess not.

I climbed into bed beside him and lay on the pillow, looking at him.

"Talk to me," he said. His expression was such that I knew this wasn't optional.

I rose to sitting, crossed my legs, and put my hands in my lap. I took a big breath.

"The gift bag triggered an anxiety attack. I'm sorry. It looked just like a bag that had the engagement ring in it when I was proposed to and I told you that my declining the proposal had a pretty big impact on my life and I… I just lost it."

In truth, I was surprised I'd even been able to tell him about the proposal earlier that day. When it came out without a panic attack, I thought maybe I'd stepped over some hurdle. Clearly, at the sight of that gift bag, I was wrong. *Way wrong.*

He ran his fingers through his hair. "You have anxiety attacks before Kruna?"

I shook my head. "No."

He nodded slowly, eyes looking somewhat far away, then he said, "I'm gonna arrange for counseling. I'll make calls tomorrow."

I nodded and looked down at my hands in my lap. "Yes, Dare."

"Don't," he snapped.

I looked up at him. He looked furious. Not just pissed off, actually furious.

I was taken aback. "Sorry?"

"Don't talk to me like I'm your slaver. It's hot when you do that when we're having sex but otherwise, when serious shit is being discussed, you don't fucking do it. You got me?"

I nodded.

"I'm gonna go to the den and do some work." He got up.

"Dare," I said softly, my voice showing my pain.

He looked down at me.

"Thank you for saving me."

The hardness in his eyes evaporated. He got back in the bed and pulled me tight against him and I started to cry into his chest. He stroked my back and kissed my head and then finally said, his voice sounding a little choked. "You're welcome, Angel. You're very, very welcome."

No doubts in my rattled brain; I was in love with this man. There was not a single doubt about it. My Master, my Dario. My C, my D. My all-the-way-to Z. My chest was filled with so much hope it was almost like a living and breathing thing inside me.

After a few minutes I looked to his face and he kissed my forehead.

"Sorry; you can go get work done. I'll go to sleep now."

He tucked my hair behind my ear and kissed me again. "It's gonna be okay, baby. I promise you it is."

I nodded. "I know." And I did know. He was gonna make it okay.

"I'll stay 'till you fall asleep."

God, he was sweet.

***

I jolted and gasped as I felt him leave.

"I'm just next door if you need me. I won't be long," he whispered and kissed me softly on the lips and then he was gone.

I fell back to sleep wondering about the contents of his silver gift bag.

Dare

I poured a drink. Then I poured another. And then a-fucking-nother. I went out to the terrace and sat and lit a smoke and stared out at the night, my blood boiling, a cold pit in my stomach, and I plotted. I fucking plotted because they needed to be stopped.

I didn't know if I could give her time to tell me her story in her own time or if I'd have to a) get Zack to tell me what he'd found and hope that he'd found out enough or b) make her tell me whether she was ready or not.

Maybe I needed to talk to this counselor, too, to find out how to handle her properly.

I bought her a necklace tonight at a jewelry store down the road and a cell phone from the electronics store a few doors away from the restaurant where I'd picked up our take-out. The phone: so we could text during the day and so she'd get on her way to some semblance of normalcy. The necklace: so I could get the reminder of where she came from off her neck. I figured maybe a new necklace could give her the same comfort because it was from me but it could be a fresh start for her.

But after her attack tonight, I didn't know if it was the perfect time to get that fucking thing off her neck or the worst idea in the world.

And my mind was also on the fact that the report card they gave me on that last tablet, the fucked up data contained on that screen, was actually useful because it helped me see what she needed from me in order to settle her down today.

Yeah, she'd begged me to do that but if I hadn't read that report I wouldn't have picked up so easily on what she needed and I definitely wouldn't have done it. I would've tried to find another way to calm her down. And it had worked. Damn it all to hell, too, because that report's contents meant that it didn't just work because I was there to hold her down and make her come. It probably would've worked if anyone else in the world had done the same.

***

She was quiet, timid with me in the morning when we got up. Maybe she was responding to my mood, I don't know. I'd slept terrible and was in a foul mood. When I came out of the bedroom after showering and dressing for the office, I found her sitting on the terrace staring out at the city with her cup of coffee in her hand. I found a cup she'd poured for me in front of the coffee maker. I drank half the cup while reading emails on my phone in the kitchen and then I poured the rest down the drain. I stepped out onto the terrace.

"You off to work?" She looked up at me with what looked like a hopeful look on her face.

"Yep. See ya later. I'll probably be late so don't, uh, wait for me for dinner."

"Would you like me to cook you something that you can eat when you get back?" she asked with what was definitely hope on her face.

"Naw, don't worry. Don't know how late I'll be. I'll probably just grab something."

She gave me a thin smile. She saw right through me. I felt a pang of guilt. No, I shouldn't push her away. That wouldn't help either of us. I shook my head and changed my mind.

"Can you cook? Besides bacon and eggs?"

"I'm not terrible at it."

"Okay, cook me something. You eat, though, and just put mine in the fridge and I'll reheat it when I get in. Kiss me goodbye."

She got to her feet.

I pulled her in for a kiss and I tried to make it a good one. I ran my thumb across her cheek before I left.

In the elevator on the way down to the garage I texted Lisa and asked if we could meet the following day at the office after lunch. Maybe she'd give me some perspective.

***

I called the apartment after I met with Zack, but Angel didn't answer.

I didn't like it. It had me worried so I called again two minutes later. No answer. Maybe she was in the shower. Maybe she was taking a nap. Maybe she'd taken a leap off my balcony to her death because she was so cracked because of what those sons of bitches did to her. I waited ten more minutes that felt more like an hour and called again. No answer. I had a sinking feeling.

I rushed home, sick to my stomach. When I got off the elevator, music assaulted my ears and it was coming from my apartment. I got in, disarmed the alarm, and found her in the den working out with my Bowflex. She had the door open and my stereo in the living room was on max, playing Gimme Shelter by the Rolling Stones, most definitely drowning out the land line and maybe the landlines of the entire floor.

My heart was racing. I leaned against the doorframe and let out a deep breath.

She stopped exercising, looking a little startled at the sight of me. She had a white towel beside her. She wiped her forehead and dabbed at her chest and then stood up, grabbing a bottle of water and taking a glug.

"Hi," she shouted over the music. "Everything okay?"

"Fine, fine." I raised my index finger to indicate *one sec* and then went into the bedroom and grabbed the cell phone box out of the silver bag in the drawer, circled back, turning the stereo off on my way. I put the phone box on my desk.

"Fuck that was loud!"

Her eyes widened. "Sorry."

"It's okay, baby. That was one of the gifts I bought you yesterday. I've been trying to call and couldn't get you. Freaked me out."

I leaned over and turned the ringer up on the desk phone. It was pretty low. Not that she'd have heard it over that music.

I opened the phone box and took the phone out, "I'll program my numbers," I said and sat down on the futon.

"I'll just…uh...I was gonna grab a fast shower. You'll be here long enough for me to say *bye?*"

I nodded, putting the sim card into the phone.

"I'll be fast," she said and jogged out of the room.

Listening to music blaring like that wasn't something a timid and broken woman would typically do. At least I didn't think so. I got a little smile on my face. I fiddled with the phone a minute and then thought *fuck it.* I called my receptionist and told her to clear my afternoon. I went to the master bathroom, stripped outta my suit, and got in the shower with Angel. I gave her a smile as I moved in and got my mouth around her left nipple, my fingers between her legs.

I pinned her against the shower wall and kissed my way slowly down to her thighs and then got on my knees and hooked one of her legs over my shoulder. As I tasted her, she drove her fingers into my hair and moaned. There were definite advantages to having my office five minutes from where I had my angel.

***

After we went at it in the shower, she went down on me in the bed while making herself come. Then I went down on her again, her ass on the bed, this time both of her knees up over my shoulders until I made her come. Then we fell asleep, exhausted from the exertion.

***

I woke up to loud banging. I sat up. She sat up, too.

Who was knocking on my door? I got into a pair of jeans and stuffed my piece into the back of the waistband. I headed to the door barefoot and bare chested. I looked out the peep hole. It couldn't fucking be…

I opened the door and folded my arms across my chest, a scowl on my face. Fucking Debbie. What the fuck?

She looked surprised. Did she expect Angel to answer the door? I should've been at work so chances were she wouldn't catch me here.

She was wearing high fuck-me heels, a short tight black skirt, her hair down. She had her signature bright red lips all done up. Lots of cleavage popping out of a purple low-cut sweater. Fucking tramp.

"What the fuck? How'd you get in here?"

She shrugged. "I didn't think you'd let me in if I buzzed up so I followed behind someone.

I rolled my eyes and let out a huff. "What do you want?"

"To talk. Can I come in and talk to you?" She eyed me from head to toe and then back up.

"I'm fucking busy."

Her face went sour. "You mean busy fucking?"

Middle of the afternoon, half undressed. I hadn't even gotten my jeans button done up. I probably had just-fucked hair. Angel's fingers had worked my hair over repeatedly.

I raised my brows and waited for her to continue, not saying anything.

"If I can't come in, can we go for a coffee?"

"What could we possibly have to talk about?"

"Are you serious with that girl? The one you were with yesterday?"

I waited a beat and then looked over my shoulder so Deb would know that girl was here. I said, "I am."

She gave me a deflated look.

"Can we have a coffee? It's really important that I talk to you."

"Meet me at the Starbucks on the corner in fifteen," I muttered.

She smiled at me. "Thank you."

I shut the door in her face and went into the bedroom and fished my cigarettes and lighter out of my blazer pocket on the bedroom floor and put my gun back under the mattress. Angel was in the bathroom. I walked out to the terrace and had a cigarette. Then I went back into the bedroom to finish getting dressed. Angel was now in my robe and she was sitting on the bed, the bed made. She looked up at me, looking guarded.

"You heard that?"

She nodded.

"I'm just gonna meet her at the coffee shop. See what she wants."

She nodded again.

"Don't think you have anything to worry about where she's concerned, okay, baby? I promise you that you do not."

"You don't owe me anything, Dare."

I scowled at her. "Are you fuckin' serious?"

She jolted in surprise.

"Are you and me a we?" I demanded.

She swallowed and blinked a few times.

I jerked my chin up, urging her to answer.

"Yes?" Her eyes were huge.

"Yes? Yes! Yes, we fucking are. So I do owe you something. And I'm telling you that with Debbie or with anyone else, even, you have nothing to worry about." I opened a dresser drawer and got out a Henley and then opened another and got a pair of socks.

When I got my head through the neck hole I saw a look of wonder on her face. I sat on the edge of my bed, got the socks on, and then leaned over and pinned her to the bed by her wrists, her arms above her head. I kissed her hard on her mouth. "Want me to bring you back a treat?" I smiled.

She smiled big and nodded and then she gave me a heated look. She squirmed in a very sexual way underneath me. Fuck, how could she be ready to go again so quickly?

I smirked. "Done. Now turn over so I can spank your ass for saying something so ridiculous."

I backed off her. She got a giddy look on her face and turned over onto her belly and put her bottom up in the air. "It's supposed to be a punishment, baby. You're not supposed to be so eager." Instead of spanking her I pulled the pj pants down and gave her a little love bite on her ass cheek. She squealed. I pulled the pants back up and gave her bottom a squeeze.

"Your phone is ready. Start dinner, yeah? Let's eat early. Thanks to all those calories you made me burn I'm half starved. I'm not going back to the office today after all. Be back in half an hour or sooner. Oh, and I'm programmed in your new phone if you need me. I'll hook your app store up to my credit card later if you wanna download anything." I winked at her and buttoned my jeans, went to the closet for a pair of shoes, and left. She was laying on the bed on her belly, still, her chin propped up on a pillow, hair over one shoulder but fanned out, a beautiful smile on her gorgeous face. I'm sure I had a smile too, as I left, until I got to the elevator and realized who I was walking away from and who I was walking toward.

As I was getting out to the sidewalk in front of the building my phone made a text sound and it was Angel texting me.

"Thank you for the cool phone. Xoxo"

"You're welcome, angelbaby. Xoxo"

"and I'm very sorry you were worried about me."

"Okay my baby."

My smile returned.

***

I saw Deb when I entered the Starbucks, sitting at a corner table for two with two coffees in front of her. I sat, giving her what I imagine were dead eyes.

"I got that for you." She motioned toward the large cup in front of me.

"What do you want? And before you tell me, lemme just say don't even think about approaching someone I'm seeing. Ever. It's not lost on me that you probably expected her to answer the door today, not me. If you wanted to see me in the middle of the day, we both know you woulda come to my office. No games, Debbie. Make this quick. She's at home waiting for me. In bed."

Shot to the heart. Deb's expression dropped.

"Do you ever think about us? About how good it was?" she asked, giving me that submissive sex kitten look. That look she used to give me.

I narrowed my eyes.

"I do," she continued, then licked her lips and gave me a few slow blinks, "I think about it. A lot."

I shook my head and folded my arms across my chest.

"Don't go back to her at your place. Come with me instead. Come to my place. Please?"

I let out a laugh. This was fucking rich.

"You talk about me with anyone, Deb? You ever have a conversation with my pop in the last three years?"

She shook her head. "No. Why?"

"No reason."

"But I saw in the paper he was murdered. I'm very sorry about that, honey." She reached across the table for my hand. My arms were still folded across my chest. I looked at her hand and shook my head, disgusted.

She pulled her hand back and got a desperate look.

"I never got over you," she said quickly. "I haven't stopped thinking about you for three years. Then I heard about Tom dying. I wanted to come to the funeral but I heard it was private. Then it hit me extra-hard when I saw Luc the other day. She just joined my gym and I approached her to give my condolences about your father and she tried to rip me a new one and then she told me you were with someone else and that it was serious. Then the next day I saw you and it felt like fate. My chance to do something about it. It hit me really hard to see you with someone and I knew I had to act fast before I blinked and suddenly you were married with kids and it'd be too late. I know your sisters hate me because they said I froze your heart. I've changed. I was too young to settle down but after all this time not having you? I've grown up. The guy I've been seeing, he asked me to marry him." She looked down at her lap. "I told him I'd think about it. But I don't wanna say yes. No one compares to you, Dario. If I'm ready to get married, and I am, it has to be you. I messed up so bad. I don't deserve this, but you have to know I think about you all the time. About how lucky I'd be if I were your wife, what beautiful babies we'd make together. I---"

I shot to my feet so fast that the chair fell down behind me and then people were staring.

"Go fuck yourself, Debbie. You think I don't know that you killed the baby we might've made together?"

She flinched like I'd slapped her. I leaned forward and said in a low voice, almost a growl, "And it's already too late. I don't think about you at all. In three years, I haven't thought anything about you except for thinking I was lucky I caught you sucking that goof off because you are one skanky bitch that I was lucky to get rid of. I plan to get married just once and if I'd married you it would not have been forever. It would've been a huge mistake. Don't darken my door again. Ever. If you do, I'll fuck your life up so bad that what I did to that pencil dick DJ will seem like nothing. Do not underestimate me."

Her mouth was wide open and she looked like she was gonna shit herself.

I left and didn't look back.

I didn't head home. I went in the other direction. There was a bakery a block away that I was heading to instead. I was picking up dessert. Then I stepped into a jewelry store next door to it and bought two more necklaces for Angel. In case the first one I bought wasn't right. I told them not to put these ones in a gift bag; I slipped the necklace boxes into my jacket pocket instead.

***

When I got into the apartment, I smelled food. It smelled good.

"What's cookin'?" I came up behind her; she was at the sink washing mushrooms. I kissed her earlobe.

"Loaded baked potatoes and pork chops with mushroom sauce," she said.

"Mm." I put the bakery box on the counter and said, "And angel food cake for my Angel."

As I kissed her temple she smiled and said, "Mm, can we skip dinner and do dessert first?"

"That dinner smells too good to miss. We'll do dessert later in bed. How 'bout that?" I winked suggestively. "I'm gonna go check in on some work shit in the den. How long till dinner?"

"Twenty minutes," she said, with a smile. "I'm not much of a cook but I did this meal for home ec and aced it. So we'll see if I remember the recipe." She chuckled.

"It smells like another A+, to me," I told her.

I went into the den and reached into my jacket to pull out the jewelry store boxes. I stuffed them into my desk drawer. I flicked the computer on and saw a message from my brother waiting for me.

As I opened it I thought about the fact that Angel hadn't even quizzed me about Debbie. Was that because she was trusting or was it because she was still under the mindset where she wouldn't question her Master?

***

She made us a really nice dinner. Afterwards, I loaded the dishwasher while she changed and then we went out for a stroll, walking off the dinner and getting her out of the apartment. I wanted to start her on a path to getting toward normal. I figured it'd be good to make sure she got out of the apartment every day. We stopped at a store and bought a loaf of bread to take to feed the ducks at the park where I'd seen Deb. Angel didn't ask me about Deb so I brought it up.

"So, you didn't ask me about coffee with the ex."

She looked at me carefully for a moment and then said, "I figured you would tell me about that if you wanted to."

"Not that you didn't have a right to ask?" I cocked an eyebrow.

"You told me I had nothing to worry about and so I'm not worried. If you want to talk about it, I'm happy to listen. If you don't, I respect that."

"Because that's what you're trained to do?"

She shrugged. "Believe it or not that's always how I've kinda been. Sometimes people don't feel like talking, especially about stuff bothering them. I don't push. You've given me no reason to mistrust you."

"And I never will. She wanted me back. She wanted me to go back to her place and fuck her. She heard I'm serious with you and told me to forget coming back to you, to come back to her place instead. Said she wished she was my wife, talked about the beautiful babies we'd make together. I think she showed up at the apartment today hoping to intimidate you, scare you off. She got a big surprise when I answered the door instead."

Angel's eyes changed. They went kind of fiery there for a sec. It looked like anger, jealousy. It revved my engine up, actually. But then her fire flickered out just as fast. If I hadn't been watching her, I would've missed it. That was promising, though. And if that's who she always was it was a rare quality to be so trusting. Most women I'd been around were jealous, territorial.

"What'd you say?" she asked softly.

"I told her never to darken my door again or I'd fuck her life up."

Angel got a small but satisfied-looking smile. And I'm sure that as we went around the block toward home, I probably had one, too.

I had no intention of continuing to be the kinda guy to fuck someone's life over out of revenge if I could help it, but by the look on her face (I didn't know if that was pre-Kruna mindset or post-Kruna or both) we were simpatico about the fact that sometimes you had to fuck people up. Sometimes you had to retaliate. It was good to see that smile because sometimes tough choices had to be made. And in my position right now I had some major work ahead of me to get my freedom from the mess Pop left us. Seeing her reaction told me she'd probably be okay with my decision to have to go to the dark side on occasion, if needed. And to get us out of the mess that was my life right now, that might be more than necessary.

CHAPTER SIX

Tommy

Tia was crying when I found her shortly after reading Zack's email and I didn't have it in me to be supportive at that moment. I stood over her, she was in the bed. I said, "Tomorrow morning you get up and you phone Mia and you call her off."

She nodded at me, tears in her eyes.

"I need to do some serious fucking damage control, Tia. Thanks a *fucking* bunch."

She'd covered her face, sobbing. I stormed out of the bedroom and went to the rooftop to beat the fuck out of the punching bag. And I didn't sleep that night. I didn't sleep because if a goddamn teenager could find us then so could my enemies and that meant that I couldn't sleep, couldn't feel safe, so I stayed up all night stressing about it.

The next morning after prepping from me and some more harsh words that she probably didn't need to hear, she called Mia from a burner phone on hands-free and I listened.

"Hello?" the female voice answered.

"Mia? It's Tia." Tia sat on the sofa, hands fidgeting in her lap. She looked like she hadn't slept much either.

"Tia? Holy shit. Tia?"

"Yeah, it's me."

"Wow, Tia. Are you okay? Are you still in Costa Rica?"

"I'm fine. What's new?"

"What's new? You've been gone since grad and you ask what's new? What the hell is new with you?"

"I'm, uh, on my honeymoon."

"Your honeymoon."

"Yes. I'm on my honeymoon and…"

"And you're calling me out of the blue three hours before I'm supposed to leave to come to where you are? Right." She was full of skepticism.

"Right. I need you to not come to where I am, Mee."

"Why?"

"Because I'm on my honeymoon."

"Your honeymoon. Your honeymoon with Tommy Ferrano, Jr., son of murdered businessman by the same name. You can't see my air quotes around the word businessman, Tia, but I say that knowing that the businessman your new husband is was your ice cream hottie and that he has kidnapped you and is holding you against your will. We are going to get you out of this. Got me on hands-free? Your darling demonic husband there listening? Listen, you sonofabitch, you let her go. I have connections, too, and we are going to get her out of there and your Italian mafia ass is gonna rot in jail."

"Mia!" Tia shrieked. She looked at me, mortified.

I shook my head, eyebrows raised, and folded my arms.

"Tia, we are going to get you out of there. Ferrano? You listening? Let's negotiate. I have leverage, believe me when I tell you I have fucking leverage."

"Mia, I am happily married. Happily. I'm on my freaking honeymoon. I don't want you to rescue me. I am deliriously in love. What on earth? You've got the wrong end of the stick, Mee…"

"Tia, Beth heard Rose and Cal talking to the cops. We later found out your father is in jail. We know that you were kidnapped. We know a lot about the Ferrano family."

"We? Who's we?"

"Me, Beth, Ruby, Nick. We've been working together. Nick's uncle works at an IT security and online forensics company and he's been interning there. They've been watching for you."

"Oh my god, Mia. You're so off base it isn't even funny. Don't come here. Don't worry about me. I'm on my freaking honeymoon. I'm in love. I'm happy." Tia looked frantic. Her hands were in her hair and she was looking pleadingly at the phone sitting on the sofa between us.

"Oh, alright…" she let that hang. "I won't rescue you. I can hear how happy you are. I'll just back off." She was full of shit.

Tia took the phone and took it off hands free, giving me a raised index finger. "Mee, you're not on hands free anymore. I am serious. Things aren't always what they seem, okay?" She listened for a second, her eyes on me.

"No," Tia continued. "I am serious. I'm in love. We're happy. We're just on our honeymoon. You don't know the whole story." She glanced at me and chewed her lip. "I don't know yet. It's open ended." She shrugged. "No, you can't come here. Listen Mee, if you follow us, there are people who could follow you and put Tommy and me in danger…"

"Fuck, Tia!" I hissed. She winced. I grabbed the phone from her.

"Mia? Tommy Ferrano," I said, giving Tia a shake of my head. She paled.

"Tommy Ferrano?" she said. "I'd say nice to meet you but I'm sure it's not. We are onto you, you motherfucker. You hurt a hair on her head and you will go down."

"Listen Mia, Tia and I are on our honeymoon but there are people we don't want to know where we are. You come here you could be followed. You might have compromised her safety already and you'd definitely compromise your own safety. I need you to not fly here. I'll have you reimbursed for your ticket and whatever other expenses…"

"You seriously expect me to believe that you forced my friend to be with you and that she's okay with this? I know she was forced. I know this for a fact. I visited her father in jail and he enlightened me. He also gave me his login for Facebook and I saw the message Tia sent him after grad."

Fuck. Fucking Greg.

"You think you know everything but you only know the half of it. You don't know what you're dabbling in here and if you care about Tia's safety you need to stand down."

"You're threatening me?"

"No. I'm telling you that I don't want you putting her in danger. Stand down."

"I don't believe she's okay and I won't believe it until I see it with my own eyes. I'll cancel my flight but only if you produce her. I need to see her and talk to her so I can determine for myself whether or not she's actually okay. Get on a plane today."

"Fine."

"Fine?"

"Not today but I'll get her on a plane soon," I said.

"How soon?"

"We are not dropping things and running back there. You'll see us in a couple weeks."

"Three days. And I get twice daily phone calls from Tia until then so I know she's okay and you haven't done something to her. Morning and night."

I gritted my teeth. "Fine. I'm sending someone to meet with you today to find out everything you know and where you got the info. You need to share this so that we can determine whether or not you've put us in danger. Got it? He'll meet you at your place in two hours."

"Who are you sending? One of your wiseguy thugs? Sending someone to rough me up?"

"No. Zack Jacobs. Look him up. He's a P.I. You'll need to meet with him today so he can do damage control."

"Fine, but in public. Give him this number and I'll meet him in public and I won't be alone. Tia calls me tonight before midnight my time and then tomorrow by this time or I'm on a plane, Mr. Caruso."

Yep, she proved she knows exactly where we are.

I got off the phone and glared at my wife. Then I got on the phone and sent Zack over there.

Dare

Lisa walked into my office looking as put together as she always did but this time her face was solemn.

I invited her to sit on the sofa with me.

"What's wrong, Leese? You got morning sickness?" I gave her shoulder a squeeze.

She shook her head. "No. I've just…" She swallowed hard. "Since finding out you know … and finding out about Felicia … I've just been thinking a lot. It brought stuff back to the surface for me. I guess I've buried a lot and now um…" She paused.

"You're facing it?" I tried to help her along.

She shrugged. "I'm thinking about therapy maybe. I feel stressed, panicky all the time; I'm not sleeping. I don't think it's good for the baby."

"Let me arrange the counseling. Due to the sensitivity of the issue it has to be someone we trust."

She nodded. "I've been thinking about Tess and Luc and what they'd think if they knew."

"Hang tight, please. Tommy and I need to talk about how to play this."

She nodded. "Why did you wanna see me?"

"Angel and I; she's decided it's Angel. As you know, we're giving things a go together and…she's not handling things so well. I wanna help her. I was gonna ask you to talk to her. And I was gonna ask you some questions that might help me know how to be with her. Did you have trouble adjusting when you got here? Did you have panic attacks or anything like that?"

She snickered. "I'm having more trouble adjusting now, now that I've been thinking about it. They program you, Dare. They do it in a way where you just go on about your day, do what you're supposed to do. If she's showing you she's broken it's because the truth broke her. The truth being that she's not a Kruna slave any longer. It's almost easier to function on autopilot, I'm starting to figure out. You've gotta imagine how she feels. She probably feels like a fish out of water, not sure how to act."

I nodded. "I figured that. If I'd been what she thought she was getting she'd have functioned as well as you did?"

Lisa nodded. "When I got here, I just did what I was told. And I was so grateful for being here, so grateful at how kind your father was to me. I felt like I was so lucky." She shrugged. "Dare, if she's having trouble, she needs you to be decisive and guide her. Wean her into making her own decisions slowly."

"That makes sense."

"That's how it sort of worked with us. As time went by your father gave me more and more freedom. Not because he seemed to be hanging onto control with me, more like he was helping me adjust slowly. They had me in a training program to transition me from slave to wife and that helped. It was a lot being in public after all that time at Kruna. When I first got here, I spent over a month in a hotel suite just seeing him when he had time. Then he started to take me out in public slowly, then he put me in culinary school, and you know the rest."

I blew out a breath. "I just took her right out of there. They wanted her in a wife training program, but I said no. Said I'd train her. So, maybe this has been too hard on her. Too much too soon. Can you see her tomorrow? Come by the condo?"

"Yeah, she's shell-shocked for sure. She doesn't know who I am, does she?"

"No. I should talk to her first."

She nodded. "I think so. I don't think you should make me blindside her. Handle her with a firm hand and that'll help."

"Meaning?"

"Meaning she might need more direction from you. You have a lot of power, whether you want it or not, and it doesn't have to just apply to the bedroom. Your power can help her. Your words, the way you treat her." Lisa shrugged. "This might not make much sense but praise from a Master means a lot. She's going to take all her cues from you."

"I get it. Thanks, Leese." And I did get it. The way she'd acted when she was afraid or stressed, she looked to me as her protector. She'd done that probably both because I was her "Master" and because I'd taken her away from there.

Angel

Dare came back after work with a pizza. We ate on one of the sofas together while watching the news and then I hesitantly asked if he wanted to take a walk as he was coming back from putting our paper plates in the garbage.

"I need to talk to you first," he said as he pulled me onto his lap. "My brother Tommy's coming home tomorrow and staying for a bit. He's got stuff to handle plus he's gonna help me sort out some business shit our pop left us with. And while he's here we'll strategize on what to do about our Kruna shares. They're having a partner summit in a couple weeks and he and I have gotta talk about how to play things. See, I'd been hoping that within a few months from now I'd be totally out of most of the business my Pop dealt in. I had plans to start fresh, get my pilot's license, decide whether or not to fly commercial, be a bush pilot, something. Something different for a while."

I nodded, feeling a little pang of fear. I was trying to listen to what he was saying but I was stuck on the partner summit bit. I hoped he wouldn't go to Kruna. I hoped he wouldn't take me back there. Before the panic had a chance to set in he continued talking. "Tommy's new bride, Tia, I want you to know a bit about her. I also wanna tell you about something else."

He had my attention again. I shifted on his lap and put my arm around his shoulder.

"Tia's father was an enemy of my father. Tia's mother was Pop's first love. Pop went on a revenge spree and screwed Tia's father over a period of two decades in order to break the man because Tia's mother chose him over Pop. His last-ditch effort was forcing the guy to give Tia to my brother as a payment for his debts. Tia and Tommy are happily married, newlyweds. It didn't start out happy, especially not for her. I told you I delivered her to him. I never let myself think deep on it but from the start didn't think it was okay to pay a debt with flesh unless it was your flesh, you know, not deciding that for your kid. Anyway, I went along with what Pop said because that's what I did. I was loyal to him even when I didn't agree with all the things he did. It's how we were raised. Pop was demanding and loyalty to him was first. My brother and I had plans to take the company legit once Pop retired so I was biding my time. I went through the motions and tried not to overthink things. We knew we were in gray areas and Tommy and I were fully entrenched in a lot of it. I'm no choir boy. I've done shit I'm not proud of. Turned a blind eye to shit I knew was wrong more often than I can count. But we were planning on transitioning it to something cleaner when we found out Pop was playing way dirtier in the world than we'd ever realized. Through a series of events after a shit storm that put the whole family in danger we decided to break away from Pop. His actions cost Tess her husband and my nephews their father, made Luc go into early labor and almost cost us baby Nicky, and my father's actions almost cost Tommy and Tia everything. We're talking kidnappings, shootings, a lot of bad shit. Most of the world doesn't know that at the end, just before Pop died, me and Tommy forced his hand. He pushed back because he saw our mutiny as the ultimate betrayal and it didn't end well."

I listened without saying anything. I wasn't sure if he was telling me he killed his father or his brother did it or someone else on their orders but he was, in essence, telling me that he and his brother were responsible.

Dare seemed to be studying me and the effect of his words.

"This is something that's not talked about. Ever. There are people in my family that suspect why Pop really died but it's not discussed. Don't bring it up. Don't ask questions. It will never, ever be discussed. You're going to be around my family so you need a little of the backstory."

My heart lifted. Maybe it should've dropped because of the secrets he was revealing. But it lifted because this meant he saw himself with me long-term. That's what it had to mean. He was telling me his secrets and hoping I could handle them. Could he handle my secrets? Could I bring myself to tell them to him? I didn't think I could.

"You don't want a bunch of gory details but you know my pop was a partner at Kruna so you can imagine the kind of man he was. Let's just say he was dark. He was power-hungry and did not hesitate to snuff enemies out. He didn't care if you were blood, if you were one of his children even. If he saw you as anything but loyal you were dead to him. My sisters don't know a whole lot about the details and they, Tia, and you don't need them but know that our family is on the road to change. I'm in the middle of selling off most of the family business piece by piece to get us out of being so closely tied in with organized crime, racketeering, you get the picture."

I nodded.

"Okay, here's where you're gonna be a bit shaken up, I think."

I braced. He put a hand on my cheek and didn't let go. I leaned into his palm.

"I found out when I came to Kruna for you that Lisa, Pop's widow, she was a Kruna slave. I never knew. Pop didn't tell us." He stroked my cheekbone with his thumb, staring right into my eyes.

I blinked. Then I gasped as it sunk in. Monalisa. I said it out loud. "Monalisa?"

He nodded solemnly and rubbed my back with his other hand.

"I asked her to come over tomorrow. I thought you two could…you know, talk."

I was dumbstruck. Monalisa was like a celebrity to me.

"All this, does it make you wish you never met me?"

My eyes darted from the floor to his face. "Oh god, no. No way." I wrapped my arms tight around his neck and put my head on his chest. He leaned back and spun so he was lying on the sofa and I was on top of him. I curled up on top, my cheek to his chest, and I closed my eyes and listened to his heart beating.

I didn't know how to feel. If he kept me, I'd have someone nearby who knew what my life was like. Would that help me heal? Or would Monalisa and I just remind one another of who we really were, how dirty and tainted we were? She'd probably know some of what I'd been through in being broken. I'd know that she'd been through at least some of those same things.

I thought back to that day I met her, the way she stared at my throat, the way she didn't smile. Now it made sense. I'd heard about her. I'd heard a lot about her. I modeled my A to B in the hopes of becoming like the girl that was my predecessor. I was told she was beautiful, graceful, could command a room or be completely obedient, she was a favorite among the patrons and the staff and other slaves, and her reward was to get married off to a powerful, wealthy, and handsome Master who never brought her back, who never even came back after he acquired her.

And here she was in Dare's family, living a life, a real life, out on the town with Dare's sisters, free. She didn't have a husband any longer and she hadn't been sent back. Dare's sister had said she was pregnant, too. I don't think she even had anything on her throat when I'd seen her.

"They didn't want her back?" I asked, in awe.

"Pop specified Tommy and me as guardians in case of his death. Kruna bosses found that acceptable."

"What did you specify?" I asked softly.

"I didn't. Pop arranged you and they never asked me. I guess I'd better find out." He reached to the coffee table and grabbed and then started to fiddle with his phone. I went to climb off him to give him space but he gripped me tighter. "Don't go," he said softly. I closed my eyes and nuzzled into his chest as he thumbed away on the phone.

I didn't want to even think about him being gone. He was amazing, thinking about making sure I didn't go back to them if something happened to him.

"A girl whose Master died was brought back," I said softly into his shirt. "He hadn't made a provision so she was brought back. She committed suicide not long after returning."

He put his phone down and put both arms around me and gave me a squeeze and then kissed my forehead. Against it he said, "I will make sure that they can never hurt you again, baby. I promise."

I nodded.

He tipped my chin up so that I had to look at his face. His handsome strong jaw, his stormy blue eyes, his beautiful mouth.

"I don't make promises lightly. You should know that. But I promise you I will do everything in my power to keep you safe. Okay?"

"Okay." I closed my eyes and lay on him while we quietly watched TV for the next little while.

Dare

I texted Stan and told him to call me from a secure line the next day at 9:am to find out about provisions made for her. He called me back a few hours after that to say that Pop had listed himself for her and since Tommy and I were his heirs it'd default to Tommy if something happened to me. Stan asked me about the upcoming partner summit and I told him I'd get back to him in a few days with an update about whether or not Tommy and I would attend. He said he'd attend for us if we couldn't make it. Then he and I discussed some of the business he was working on dealing with for us. Stan was proving himself to be valuable, at least. We needed to keep him busy and on our payroll so that he'd be loyal. At least I hoped he would be. I had to play my hand close to the vest in case he wasn't. I considered asking him about Lisa and why he'd never said anything about the fact that she'd come from Kruna but decided to talk that over with my brother first, to ensure he and I were on the same page about how to play that. If Stan couldn't be trusted I didn't want him to know I had suspicions. Maybe Stan didn't even know. Pop never let anyone in the world have all of his truth. You got bits and pieces, no matter how close to him you thought you were.

Things were shaping up all right with a few other areas but Tommy would help when he arrived and that'd make things a little easier on me. He was arriving the next day. Lisa would be spending time with Angel in the afternoon and then we were all having dinner at Luciana's and Ed's after Tommy and Tia arrived. After dinner, Tommy and I could sit down and strategize about Kruna and a few other matters.

Lisa arrived just before noon. She came in with food from the restaurant for them for lunch.

Angel was sitting on a sofa when I answered the door and Leese and I hugged and then she went right to Angel and opened her arms while I put the food on the island.

Angel stood stiffly and let Lisa embrace her. She looked to me with her lip trembling. She held it together.

"You okay, baby?" I leaned over and put my arm around her shoulder as

Lisa let go of her.

She nodded.

"I'm going to the office and then I'll be back to pick you up later for dinner at my sister's. Okay?"

She nodded and put her arms around me and sank in. I kissed her.

Lisa gave me a smile and I left the two of them alone.

Angel

Lisa and I sat quietly for a few minutes after Dare left.

"Wanna grab food?" she finally said. "I'm just so starving all the time so I brought salads in case you're watching what you eat but I also brought stuffed cannelloni and bruschetta for me and for you, too, in case you're not."

"Mm," I said, "I've eaten non-stop since I got here. No salad for me, thanks."

She gave me a knowing smile. "Food back there was not good. I was a glutton my first few months out."

I pushed the pang away at the mention of there. "I don't even want to step on the scale. I'm afraid of what I'll see."

She nodded. "Throw that fucker off the balcony. You owe it to yourself to never step on a scale again."

I smiled big at her. The morning ritual with Cleo at Kruna included weighing us as well as inspecting for adequate grooming and hygiene.

"I, unfortunately, have an OB/GYN who wants me on the scale at every appointment."

"At least you'll get something awesome out of the deal at the end," I said.

She put her hand to her belly and she beamed with joy. "Yeah."

We walked to the island and unpacked the food.

We ate quietly but there wasn't any real awkwardness. Afterwards, she said, "I am here if you ever want to talk. I don't know if I'd have any real words of wisdom for you but if you have questions or want to talk about anything, I'm here. I was there nearly six years and I've been out over two so if I can help, let me know. Even if you just wanna talk, vent, whatever."

"Same," I said.

She broke into tears.

I panicked a little and then rounded the island to go to her and put my arm around her. She put her head on my shoulder and started sobbing.

"I'm su-supposed to be here h-helping you," she sniffled.

I patted her back gently, not sure how to reply.

"I've had a really good life since getting out. Tom was amazing to me. I loved my life with him so much. I'm so glad that I get to have a piece of him, you know? This baby? I can't wait to be a mother and have someone to really love. And it's so hard because I miss him and what we had but no one wants to talk about him because of some of the things he did. But I was his and he treated me like gold."

"I'm so sorry for your loss," I said.

"And I get to have his baby and I get to stay here. Dario and Tommy are making it so that I don't have to go back and now I have you, you'll be like a sister of the heart, someone who knows my secrets. Secrets I haven't been able to tell my best friends, Tess and Luc, because of what it'd make them think of their father." She was crying harder. "Fucking pregnancy hormones," she said while wiping her eyes with her napkin.

"It's okay," I said.

"I've been holding it all in. Tom and I never talked after the wedding about Kruna." She whispered the word Kruna like it was a dirty word. It was.

"He told me on our wedding night that it ceased to exist for me. And that was an order. He wanted to pretend it didn't exist so that I could be healthy, move on, you know? I got to bury it and pretend the cover story was the actual truth. But now meeting you and knowing Dare and Tommy know…" She sniffled. I passed her another napkin from the napkin holder on the counter.

"Thanks," she said. "It's so hard. Part of me wants to keep it buried and another part is so glad that I have people in my life who know the truth, who know who I really am. My name isn't Monalisa. My name is Shayla. I've said that name twice in five years, you know? Only twice. But that's who I am. I should be Shayla Ferrano, not Lisa Ferrano. My mother is dead. My father is dead. My husband is dead. But I have this family here and half of them don't know who I really am."

I nodded.

"What's your real name?"

I shook my head. "I can't."

"You're not ready."

"I don't know if I'll ever be ready. They said if I ever uttered that name again…"

I let that hang, unable to finish that sentence.

"I know," she said and was quiet for a minute. "When I told Dare my name the day he confronted me to tell me he knew the truth I felt my whole body shiver. Like they could hear me say it and would swoop in any second and take me back."

I shuddered.

"Want to tell me your story?" she asked.

"No."

"It's okay. Do you want to know mine?"

"No."

She could've gotten upset at that but she didn't. She nodded and patted my shoulder. "Ever want to, you've got me. You ever want to ask me questions, do it. You ever want to sit and pick over the bones of the bad guys? I'm all for talking smack."

I was quiet for a beat and then, "I could maybe do that," came out in a whisper.

She laughed.

I laughed.

"You wanna start?" she invited.

I shrugged and winced. "I don't know if I can even…"

"C'mon, it'll be therapeutic for us both." She dabbed at her eyes.

I chewed my lip for a second and then I mouthed, "Cleopatra."

"Cleo? Fucking demon bitch," Lisa said.

"Oh my god!" I breathed and covered my mouth, my whole body tense.

She sat up straighter and with her palms she pulled her cheeks back so that her skin was super tight and she pursed her lips, "You? You up two pounds, you fat pig. Oh my god, two pounds! You fucking cow, you. You drink too much cum, you dumb bitch, you?"

She did Cleo to a tee. I laughed so hard it hurt. I hadn't laughed like that in two years.

"That's her to a tee. Oh man. Rafe," I whispered.

"Small dick, huge stupid diamond earrings. Sweats profusely while you do him."

I cackled. "So much sweat."

She shivered and took a gulp of her water.

"Orianna," I said softly, feeling so naughty and a little bit scared that somehow Orianna would know about this conversation.

"Oh fuck." She threw her hand over her forehead, "That Domme could make me come just looking at me. Holy fuck. Is it wrong that my nipples just got hard thinking about her?"

I snorted. "She could make anyone come. And if you didn't come on demand, you were sorry."

"Lola," she said and she smiled with what looked like fondness, which I found odd.

I shook my head. "She finally retired. She works in laundry."

"Seriously?"

I nodded.

"She was such a whore," Lisa said.

I snorted. "She really liked attention, didn't she?"

"I hated being paired with her for threesomes. She had to yell the loudest, had to suck harder, had to come longer, you know?"

"Oh, I know." This was fun.

"Donavan," she said and opened her mouth about to say something bad about him.

I threw my hands over my ears and shut my eyes tight, "No!" I shrieked.

I felt her hands on my wrists gently. "Hey? Sorry…"

"Oh god." I was on my knees on the kitchen floor. "Oh god. Oh god."

"Oh fuck! I'm so sorry!" she said.

I was sobbing and my hands were back over my eyes.

"Angel, I'm sorry!"

I couldn't get myself together. I buried my face in my knees and then I was sobbing uncontrollably on the kitchen floor.

"What can I do? Can I get you something?"

I couldn't answer. I saw his face, I heard his voice, I felt the lash of his belt, the bite of the shackles. I smelled the stench of death. I couldn't stop crying. I gagged a few times, bile rising in my throat. It'd been more than a year since I saw his corpse but the mere mention of his name and I was a total mess.

The tears wouldn't let up, the shaking wouldn't stop. Lisa reached over to touch my shoulder but I completely lost it. "Don't, don't, don't." I scurried to the corner. It felt like I was back in that room, chained to that bed, smelling that smell, feeling his cold body against mine.

I heard Lisa on the phone.

"Dare, can you come back? I talked about someone at the resort and it triggered an anxiety attack or something. She's on the kitchen floor. No, just crying and rocking. Okay. Angel? He's coming. It's okay."

Dare

I burst into the apartment and Lisa was standing at the sink with a helpless look on her face. When I got closer, I saw that Angel was huddled in a ball on the kitchen floor against the corner cupboard. I reached down and touched her and she flinched.

"Baby, it's okay. You okay?" I scooped her up and gave Lisa a nod. "I've got this. Can you wait a few?"

She nodded.

"We'll talk in a few minutes," I said and took Angel, who was holding herself and shaking hard with her eyes shut tight. I took her into the bedroom and got her on the bed.

"Baby?"

"Oh god, oh god, oh god."

"Angel!" I got louder. She didn't reply. She curled into a ball on her side on the bed.

"What is it, baby?"

She took handfuls of her hair into her hands and the pain on her face hit me right in the gut.

"Help," she pleaded in a small voice.

"What can I do?"

"Help. I can't, I can't, I can't…"

I reached over and took her wrists away from her ears and pinned them over her head.

"Need me to make you come, baby? Will that help?"

She nodded a little and was shuddering from all the crying.

"Lay down." I sat.

"I need it to hurt, Master. Can you please make it hurt first?"

What the fuck?

"Please make it hurt, Master. Make it hurt."

Fuck. *What the fuck do I do here?*

"Please!" she cried out in a shrill voice and then whispered, "Hurt me."

I was stunned.

"Dare," my name was a prayer on her lips. "Please. I can't… take it. Take it away."

"How?"

She was trembling so fucking hard and it was freaking me the fuck out.

"Please, Master!" she cried out in a shrill voice again. The look in her eyes was gutting me. She looked frightened out of her mind.

Lisa was in the doorway with the door open. I was about to holler at her to get the fuck out but she said, "Spank her."

I was stunned. Lisa looked to Angel.

"Felicia!" Lisa shouted and Angel went completely stiff. Lisa continued in this deeper, huskier, more authoritative voice, a voice I'd never heard from her before. "Get over your Master's lap right now." Angel immediately threw herself over my lap and lifted her ass.

"Tell your Master what you need, Felicia!" Lisa demanded.

"I'm sorry, please spank me, Master. Spank me and take me and show me I'm yours. Not his. Yours. Not his. Yours. Cover his hurt so I don't feel his pain."

I looked to Lisa with what was probably shock on my face. She nodded at me and then left the room, shutting the door.

"Angel, I can't hurt you."

She whimpered, "Please. Yours. Can I be yours? Can I be yours?"

Fuck.

"Yes, you're mine. You're mine, baby."

"Not his," she cried out, in hysterics, "Not his."

"No. Mine, Angel. Not his." I stroked her hair.

"Please!" she whimpered and lifted her ass higher.

My hand, of its own volition, yanked her yoga pants down and then I grabbed the back of her collar with one hand and that other hand quickly came down on her ass and smacked it.

She groaned. She groaned long and deep and like she was gonna come any second. My cock got hard despite my brain feeling like I was in the middle of a sick fucking scene.

"I didn't mean to see his face, didn't mean to see it. I need to feel you so I don't feel him. Sorry for being naughty."

I slapped her ass again.

She whispered, "Please tell me. Tell me, tell me."

"You're mine. You're my girl and you'll only be naughty for me."

"Yes, Master. Only for you."

"I want you to be naughty, Angel."

"You do?" she sobbed.

"Yes. I want you to show me who you were before Felicia. I want that girl."

"Master…"

"I mean it. I don't want this broken girl, I want *my* girl, the girl from the bull-riding video. You were wild before Kruna, before you were Felicia, weren't you?"

"Yes."

"You be that girl for me, okay? You don't have to be Felicia ever again."

She choked and sobbed and it broke in the middle.

"You're my girl, Angel. No more Felicia."

"Yes, Master. Your Angel."

"No more spanking. You okay?"

She sighed in disappointment.

"You want more spanking?"

"Yes."

"Not today. Right now, what else can I do to make you feel better?"

"I need your cock, Master. Please give me your cock. Let me be your good girl."

I flipped her onto her back and unzipped my pants and drove inside her hard and fast, digging my fingers into her hips and after just half a dozen hard strokes she came all over me, instantly, screaming out her "Thank you, Master." And it didn't take me long to finish, either, and I told her she was my good girl as I came inside of her.

We took a minute to catch our breath. I felt dirty and kind of sick in my gut.

"Are you back?" I asked softly.

I felt her nod.

"Did I make it hurt enough?" I caressed her hair.

"More hurt would've been … but it was still good," she answered softly. "Thank you."

"I don't know how to hurt you, baby. You'll need to tell me what you need when you can tell me so I'll know next time. What happened? Is it gonna set you off to tell me?"

She froze and then started to tremble again. I held her tighter.

"I just don't want what he made me feel. I wanted you to cover it."

"Who?"

"Please can we not talk? Please, Dare?" She was sniffling with broken breaths.

"We'll talk later. I gotta go see Leese out. You okay for a minute?"

"Yes," she said softly. "Can you please tell Lisa I'm sorry?"

"Yeah, my baby, but don't be sorry, okay? It's not your fault."

She didn't answer.

I found Lisa sitting outside on the terrace staring out at the city. It was raining pretty hard. She looked deep in thought.

"Hey." I wanted a smoke but it'd have to wait since she was out there.

"They really did a number on her. And for me to think that… whoa."

I nodded. "What happened? What caused that?"

"Well, the tables got a little turned. She didn't wanna talk. But I guess I did, so I did. I cried a little and didn't say a whole lot about Kruna but I sort of talked about how hard it was to keep my secret and how everything I'd buried was now eating me alive. About how much I miss my husband. She was trying to comfort me. She's really sweet, Dare. She really is a great person, I can tell. Anyway, I joked that if she was ever up for some trash talking of the people there, I'd be game. She actually liked that idea so it started off kinda funny, names she was speaking were ones I hadn't uttered out loud in over 2 years but she was laughing, loving the shit I was saying, the impressions of them. It was inside jokes that only her and I would get but it was awesome. It felt like a release for me and I could tell for her too but then I said a certain name and before anything else came out of my mouth, she had a flip out."

"What was the name and what's the story?"

"Donavan. Donavan Frost. He's very high up at Kruna. One of the highest, if not the highest. He's cruel. He's relentless. He's a severe sadist. He put everyone on rotation so you'd get him every few months and trust me when I say you needed the break in between. He must've been particularly awful to her, deeply traumatized her. Just the mention of his name…" She trailed off and got a faraway look.

I clenched my teeth. "What else do you know about him?"

It took her a second to reply. She was clearly digging through some not-so-nice memories.

"He's probably late 30's or early 40's. Handsome. Looks a bit like Rob Lowe, tall, likely 6 foot 5, built. Twice that I know of he took it too far and really hurt girls. One died from asphyxiation. The other wound up with several broken bones and they had to bring in a surgeon for her. He is vicious. He sprained my wrist. You'd spend time with him and you'd be black, blue, and emotionally traumatized."

"Okay. You okay? Seeing her flip out like that must've shaken you up good."

"I'm okay now. I'm sorry to say this but you have to control those outbursts. You can stop them from happening or you can nip them in the bud quickly if you see one coming on. You need to. If she has those freak-outs in public it won't be good. You say she was considered exemplary. She's not being exemplary. She's broken and her Master is probably the only one who can fix her. You'll do that with a firmer hand."

"What the fuck?"

"I know how that sounds but you have power over her. You're her Master. She will do what you tell her to do. That's why I waited for you to get here and just stayed near. She needed you. You. You getting her out of there and taking a fish out of water so fast like that… it fractured her armor and she's cracking under the pressure. She needed prep. She will act how you tell her to act. You order her not to freak out and it'll stop. I'm telling you this because it will. You have to be her Master, Dare. She needs that."

"So you're saying I need to control her, keep her broken? The fuck, Leese?"

"No, listen…you have the power to fix her. You just have to take your time doing it. They systematically broke her. She became a robot. You rescued her and got her out and she's trying to adapt but you have no idea what it's like for her to be out of there, trying to function after all that. You can systematically put her back together. I've done reading on this and I experienced it. I'm a switch, Dare, and back at Kruna for a while before I left, they had me work with their trainers to help work on broken subs. I went through their slave-to-wife transition training too, and I had a slow transition back into society when your father brought me here. Tom knew what he was doing and I transitioned well. Be firm, be caring, give her what she needs from you and then wean her off it with more good, less discipline, more freedom. You have to look at this the way you'd train an animal because that's what she was reduced to. Reacting and staying in line to avoid punishment plus getting positive reinforcement as well. She needs you right now. I know you don't want to cause her any hurt, but she's hurting more this way. You can do this in a way that will rebuild her. Think about what I've said. If you need me or if she needs me, I'm there."

"Thanks. Ditto."

She gave me a kiss on the cheek. I saw her to the front door and then I went back out and had a cigarette, astonished. The authoritative tone Lisa had taken and telling me she was a switch, meaning she could be domme or sub was a mind-fuck for me. But it was obviously my good fortune because Lisa's insight could maybe help me get Angel better.

I went back into the bedroom. Angel was asleep. I glanced at the clock and saw we didn't have to be to Luc and Ed's for dinner for hours. That whole event was fucking exhausting. How did I even get hard in the middle of that? How the fuck could I be her Master, her actual Master? Was it possible to do that, be that to her and slowly wean her off that behavior? How long would it take? And at the end what would I be left with? I had to try. I'd get her better, wean her off that slave mindset, and maybe it'd mean I could also get some of the information I needed, too.

I shook her gently. "Baby?"

"Yes, Dare?" she answered sleepily.

"Tell me right now who Donavan Frost is. Do not freak out."

"Dare, please, I---"

"Tell me. Right the fuck now. Don't 'Dare, please' me. From now on when I ask you questions, I need answers. I know you're having trouble but that's how it's gotta be. I'll be as gentle as I can, baby, but tell me. Now. Right now."

She didn't hesitate. "I was his full-time personal slave for my first seven months at Kruna."

"Seven months?"

"Yes."

"In seven months, you were only with him?"

"It wasn't always just him but he was always there, always making me---" she stopped.

"Okay, I'll be back."

I phoned Lisa from the living room.

"She was his personal full-time slave for her first seven months at Kruna."

"Oh my fucking god."

"Yeah." I put my palm on my forehead and squeezed my eyes shut tight. Then I let out a long sigh. "Leese, I need you to be there tonight for this dinner so we can have another chat, so you can give me some more tips."

"Maybe she needs to not see me again so soon. After this afternoon…"

"No. Be there. She needs to start healing. She starts tonight."

"Dare, that's really, really bad."

"Yeah."

Angel

He climbed in bed and held me close.

"Okay, here's the thing."

I braced.

"We're gonna work on fixing you," he informed me. "I want you. I want us. I want you better. I told you I am in this, all in, but I'm telling you now, it's for the long haul. You got that?"

"Yes." Oh god. Long haul? My heart swelled.

"We need to get you better so we need to turn the clock back and get you in a different mindset. Right now, you forget about Donovan Frost and everything else you and Lisa talked about today. We're taking an hour and a half to nap and then we're getting up, we're getting a shower and going to my sister's for dinner. No freak outs tonight. You be my perfect Angel and we'll have a good night, okay? No freak-outs. No anxiety. You're my perfect Angel. We'll have fun. You won't feel embarrassed or anything when you see Lisa, and we're gonna just chill out, have some good food, and some laughs. Okay? Then we'll come home and if you pull all that off… I'll make you come real hard, baby. All right?"

Whoa. What?

"If tonight doesn't go good, if you aren't a perfect Angel, maybe we'll just go to sleep and you won't get to come. How about that? Will having that in your head help you get through the rest of today?"

Wow. Oh my god. I felt a gush in my panties.

"Master?"

"Yeah?"

"Master." I sighed and nuzzled into him. I felt this overwhelming peace surround me.

"Yeah." He pulled me closer and kissed my temple. "We get to play the master and slave game for a bit to see how that goes, baby. We do this with you knowing that I won't ever really hurt you. You mean something to me. You mean a fuck of a lot to me already. What I think we can have, if we get through all this shit, which we can and which we will, it means everything to me. But Lisa and I talked and she gave me the lowdown how she acclimated after Kruna and we're gonna give her method a try. Do you trust me with this power? Is this okay with you?"

"100%. I'm all in, too." My voice was laced with emotion.

"Good. I don't know yet that it's okay with me, Angelbaby, but I'll try. For you. For now, nap. Then we wake up, get a shower, and maybe you straighten your hair for tonight. Okay?"

"Good idea, Dare." That was a good call. He was intuitive.

"Sleep, baby. When we get up you'll be my girl, my good girl, and we'll go out and have fun. Okay?"

I nodded.

He pulled me closer and I closed my eyes and took a nap. It was a really, *really* good nap.

CHAPTER SEVEN

Tia

It was weird being back. It was weird enough being back on home soil but what was even weirder was being in Tom Ferrano's house, the Tudor style mansion that was where, on my high school graduation day, I found out my dad sold me to Tom Ferrano and where I found out that I was to be presented to Tommy as potential marriage material. It had only been a few months since that day but it sort of felt like a lifetime ago. It was also the place where Tom kissed me in front of his whole family and then kidnapped me from the driveway. I shuddered in memory of all of that.

It'd been tense with Tommy and me for the past few days. I felt really stupid for putting us in danger because of connecting my Facebook account with a stupid game in order to get to the next level of the game. I didn't realize how that small move alerted people who were watching for me, telling them where we were. He was still angry after my phone call with Mia but in the end, he said coming back and dealing with shit at home would be good for both of us. It wasn't easy to keep my distance from him when we were under the same roof with nowhere else to go, especially considering he didn't let me leave the place without him.

The night of the phone call to Mia was the first night in a long time that we hadn't had sex. But in the morning when I woke up I had my arms wrapped around him, my head on his shoulder, and my leg draped over his thigh. I could feel that he was hard and so I woke him up with my mouth. I made him come and then leaned up, kissed his owl tattoo (like I did each morning if I woke up and he was still in bed with me), and rolled away from him to get out of bed.

He caught my wrist and pulled me back, then with a tender look on his face he used his hand to make me come, not letting me look away, holding my eyes with his the whole time.

That day was quiet, with him in his shop and me in the house getting ready to pack for home and as I went through the motions of feeding the houseplants, clearing out the fridge of whatever might spoil in the next few weeks, and getting things done I thought about what I'd say to the girls.

I had to say enough to get them to back off without revealing too much. Tommy didn't ever want me talking about him to anyone. His rule #2 was to not discuss him with anyone. But he'd have to bend enough to let me get the people that cared about me to chill out.

I felt bad that they'd worried all that time and went on a campaign to rescue me. I felt more than bad about that. I wished I could rewind things so that they didn't have to worry about me like that. I was so conflicted between feeling selfish for taking off like that but after everything that'd happened, I had just hoped the note I'd sent Rose and Cal would be enough. I guess I took it for granted that they'd handle things with my friends. I never should've assumed that Mia and Beth would sit back and take Rose's word for everything. Ruby would. Mia and Beth? Nope, as evidenced by the fact that we now had to fly home and that my totally awesome but sassy and tenacious friend Mia had demanded that my husband produce me by a certain deadline.

Somewhere down the road, when all this was behind us, I might look back and laugh that my badass Dominator got bossed around by one of my besties. I wasn't ready for laughter yet, though. He certainly wasn't.

Dex and Nino's twin brother Tino (who was identical to Nino but not bald, not bearded, and not the biker type, more the burly Men-in-Black suit / goon type) had picked us up at the airport with Tommy's BMW convertible and then they left together and followed us back. Tommy and I drove to the house and got settled in a guest room that Sarah had directed us to. Tino and Dex were on duty outside. Tommy had said that Dario had hired a few guys back from before plus were using a few of Zack's guys because security would be important for now, while everything got analyzed for risk mitigation.

It seemed that no one was home but Sarah, who lived here with Tess, her boys, and Lisa. She'd greeted us enthusiastically, grilling me to ask how soon we were gonna have babies. While she was doing that Tommy kissed me goodbye and he left me there in the kitchen with her so he could meet Dario at the office. It was the first time I was without Tommy other than my brief stint at the fruit market since before we left, the day he'd gotten my name tattooed on his chest.

I was pleased about getting a minute apart from him but I wasn't pleased about being left for an inquisition. Sarah and I hung out drinking sugarless coffee, which she was very proud to gloat about, the fact that she'd gotten me off my 3-sugar coffee habit, and we chatted for a while until I went upstairs to get unpacked and get a shower and ready myself for dinner at Luc and Eddy's. Bianca and Nino, Dare and Angel, Lisa, Tessa, and Sarah were all coming, too.

As I passed the master bedroom, I heard noise so I knocked. I guess Sarah and I hadn't been here alone after all.

"Lisa?"

She opened the door. Her eyes were bloodshot.

"Oh! You're here. Sorry I didn't greet you. Welcome back."

"What's the matter!?"

She waved her soggy Kleenex. "I'm just having a moment. I'm gonna skip the dinner thing. Sorry."

"Oh no! It'll be fun to have everyone together. You should come."

"I'm gonna stay in, honest, Tia. It's not a good day for me today. I've had some stuff to deal with and…" She hiccupped and then tried to pull herself together.

I reached for and then squeezed her hand, "I know. Tommy told me. And no worries. I'll just tell everyone you're a little under the weather. Blame it on morning sickness. Do you need anything?"

Her chin trembled and she shook her head.

"I won't tell anyone; don't worry. You can talk to me if you ever need to."

"I need to talk to Tess and Luc eventually, but Dare wants me to wait. God, what'll they think of me?"

I nodded in agreement. "They'll be shocked at first, it'll rock their world. But they love you. I think after the shock wears off you guys'll work it out. You can talk to me any time, okay? Don't be afraid to reach out to talk to me. It's not good to hold it all in."

"I talked to Dare's Angel today and I messed up. He asked me to help her and I went over there and started making it about me and then I upset her and she had a panic attack. It was fucked up."

"I'm so sorry."

"Yeah. I feel awful. I think holding all my stuff in the last two years made it easy but now it doesn't feel so easy anymore."

"You are allowed to feel upset, Lisa. Just because you've had more time go by doesn't make what you went through less than what she's going through. And you're dealing with the loss of your husband. I'm sure she probably understands."

She nodded.

"Do you want something to drink or eat? I can make something for you before I take my shower."

"No, Tia. You've gotta be tired from all that traveling. And I'm okay. I ate a huge lunch a few hours ago with Angel."

"What's she like?"

"She's gorgeous. She's nice. She's broken. Understandably. But Dare is head over heels. It's good to see. I think he can help her heal."

I smiled, "I'm happy for him."

"They have a long road ahead of them."

"I bet they do."

"How's your and Tommy's road? Things okay? You take your own advice and talk it out if you need to, too, babes. Okay?"

I waved my hand, "It's not exactly okay but it will be. For better or for worse, you know."

She nodded, "Till death do us part." She choked on a sob.

I hugged her. I felt so bad for her. She was so young and beautiful both inside and out and she'd been through so much in her life so far.

"I'm gonna go lie down," she finally pulled away.

"I'll check on you when we get back."

"Don't. You guys'll be exhausted by then, especially with how full you'll be. Ed really knows how to feed people."

"That, he does."

"See you at breakfast."

"Okay, Lisa. Feel better."

She nodded.

I went to grab a shower and unpack what we'd brought. The rest of our things were here, the things we hadn't gotten rid of or brought with us, our clothes were in the closet and Sarah had stocked the bathroom with toiletries for us. Tommy's cars were here, my personal things. It was nice to be close to those things but it felt weird.

Tonight, we were doing this dinner thing and tomorrow I was going to be calling on Mia and the gang at the Crenshaws. She said Tommy and I were expected for dinner at six o'clock. I'd talked to her before we'd left for the airport and she sounded skeptical but yet excited at the idea of my coming to see her. I was both looking forward to and dreading that at the same time.

Dare

We got to Ed & Luc's and Lisa hadn't shown up. I was asking about her when Tia embraced me at the front door and I introduced Angel to her. Two seconds into that introduction Luc and Tess grabbed Angel and brought her to the family room and Tia hung back and told me Lisa wasn't feeling good but when I asked if she looked like she'd been crying Tia nodded with concern etched on her face.

I sent a text to Lisa.

"You need anything? You ok?"

She answered right away.

"I'm fine. Sorry to bail on you tonight but it was a bit much. I'm okay, though. Just wanna have a quiet night alone. I'm gonna eat some ice cream and watch a comedy."

"Ok. You need anything, you tell me. Ok? You sure you're ok?"

"Yes. Totally fine. Have a good night."

I went into the family room and Angel was sitting on the sofa getting passed a crying baby Nicky. He settled instantly. Serena and Katrina were both playing with her hair.

She smiled at me. I couldn't take my eyes off her. She was gorgeous all the time but right now, a baby in her arms and toddlers all over her? Fuck.

Tommy clapped me on the shoulder and jerked his chin toward the other room for us to step out and talk.

Angel

Almost as soon as I was in the door Luc gave me her fussing infant son so she could check dinner. The gorgeous chubby baby boy stopped fussing instantly and was all gummy smiles and cooing. Her two girls were all over me, too. Kids flock to me like flies to horse poop; it's always been that way.

The place was a bit of a madhouse. Luc, Tessa, Eddy, and Sarah were in the kitchen bickering. Not really fighting but arguing over who gets to do what, who does what better, the right way to grate the parmesan, the right way to slice the bread.

Tessa's boys were on the floor like total angels doing a large wooden alphabet puzzle together and Luc's girls were all over me talking a mile a minute.

Dare came in from talking to Tommy's wife Tia by the front door. Tia is a knockout, but she has a sweet demeanor about her. She put me at ease completely, despite the fact that I can tell she knows the truth about me. It was obvious in the way she smiled at me. But it's like she's not judging me. And I know that she can kind of relate to my and Dare's unusual situation in a way. When Dare looked at me with the baby in my arms and got this sexy and intense expression? Wow… if a look could get you pregnant I'd be pregnant with quintuplets right now. Boom! Pregnant. There were goosebumps all over me.

And Dare's brother Tommy was there. He said *Hi* to me and kissed my cheek when we first got in. He is really tall, dark, and looks a bit like Dare in the facial features but has light brown eyes and light brown hair. After Dare and Tia came into the room, Tommy pulled Tia into his lap on the sofa and started whispering quietly to her, making her smile and blush. By the way he touched her and whispered to her, it made me go damp in the panties.

Dare's brother is hot. Like… *hot, hot, hot.* Oh, my. I can tell by just looking at him and seeing how he and his wife act toward one another that he's 100% Dom. Phew. Is it hot in here?

He looks at her the way James Deen looks at the women he's fucking in his porn movies. Such intensity. James Deen? The way he fucks? Holy moly. I bet Tommy fucks like that. *Okay, I need to stop thinking about Dare's brother and his wife fucking.* I shifted in my seat.

Another couple came in. The guy was a mountain of a man, a bald biker type with a reddish beard. She was a tall brunette with a killer body. They were introduced to me as Nino and Bianca. Bianca and Tia embraced and then I stood, still holding the baby, shook hands with Bianca, and then her husband kissed me on the forehead and gave Dare a high five, glancing at me with approval. Bianca rolled her eyes, but smiled good-naturedly. They have a little boy, maybe in first or second grade. He smiled at me, gave me a hug around the legs, told me his name was Joey, and then he dashed to the kids playing on the floor. Luc's girls rushed to him, fawning over him.

Then Eddy called out, "Dinner is served", from the kitchen and we made our way to a big eat-in kitchen with a huge table for the adults and a small table set up for the kids.

This was a great house. Big and open-plan, and not just a house, it was very clearly a home. Kindergarten paintings decorated the refrigerator as well as hung in frames on the walls. The kids' table was colorful, chosen for kids rather than matching the décor. The baby was put into a swing between the adult table and kid table. We all sat down and Eddy said grace over the meal. The meal ensued with laughing and joking and shenanigans, and there was almost a food fight between Luc and Tessa who giggled uncontrollably about something I missed with Sarah holding Tessa back from dumping a dish of grated parmesan cheese all over Luc.

It's the kind of mealtime that reminds me of when I was a kid, back with my dad. It was just us two but he had a farm and there were always farm workers there so more often than not there'd be a lot of people at our dinner table. Dad cooked on the grill as much as possible and we'd often finish those big extended family dinners with campfires with guitar-playing or stories by the fire. My childhood was filled with hayrides and barn dances and playing outside and it was bliss. I had a pretty blissful life before my dad died. His best friend Charlie and his wife Betsy wanted to take me in. They couldn't have kids of their own and were crazy about me. The feeling was mutual. They stayed at Dad's farm when I went to Alaska to look after it for me. Dad should've made them my guardians. Because he didn't plan well enough for his death, being he was just in his 30s at the time, I had to go to Alaska and be with my mother, who got Dad's life insurance policy.

Mom blew through the insurance in no time, complaining about the money she had to shell out for his final expenses as well as my plane fare. The only thing that made Alaska bearable was Holly, my half-sister. I hardly knew Mom before I was sent to live with her. She didn't seem to want to know me and couldn't be bothered much with my little sister, either, so I took care of us while she partied and went through men the way most women went through clean underwear.

We didn't even eat dinner together at Mom's house because it was always a 'fend for yourself' kind of thing and not long after I arrived the food got sparser and sparser until I was old enough to get a job and then most of my earnings went into the pantry. Then at Kruna, meal time (if alone) was uneventful and quiet most of the time and when you were entertaining it consisted of sitting at someone's feet, waiting to get scraps from their fingers or you'd have to perform sex acts in order to get fed a bite of food and at times, it was disgusting. The night I ate from Dare's fingers, though? Not disgusting. It felt erotic to me. Him feeding me, providing for my needs? It was something that I now ached for. I ached for Dare to be my Master, to keep looking after me, to cherish me.

The farm was a provision that Dad did manage to make and it was to be given to me when I turned 21. I had planned to claim it after my Thailand adventure as I was turning 21 in Thailand and had planned to do the teaching gig for a year. Holly talked about moving down after she graduated high school but obviously none of that had happened. I wondered if the farm was still being looked after by Betsy and Charlie, who were happy to look after the place until I was of age. I'd emailed them before leaving for my teaching job and they told me it was all in good hands. I wondered if they had tried to find me after all this time.

"Hey? You look a million miles away," Dare whispered into my ear.

"Sorry. I was. I'm okay."

"Gone to a good place?"

"Yes. A very good place. Dinner was good." I hadn't let myself think about my dad much, but being here around a real family, it sort of made me feel like it was okay to think back.

"Yeah, I'm stuffed," he said, putting his hand on his stomach. I reached over and rubbed his belly. He smiled at me and tucked a lock of my hair behind my ear. His smile told me he was pleased with me.

"Dessert is coming," Luc announced. She and Sarah went to the kitchen to get it.

"Need help?" Tia asked.

"Nope, stay there. We've got this under control," Sarah called back.

"Welcome home Tommy and Tia!" Luc called out bringing out a massive white cake. It was huge and it had been painted with icing in the image of Tommy and Tia holding one another, Tia in an off-the-shoulder ruffled wedding dress, Tommy dressed in a white tux. They both looked gorgeous and in love.

"That's beautiful," I breathed, dreamily.

Sarah announced, "And I have gifts for them." She thrust a silver bag at Tia with white handles and purple tissue paper sticking out of it. Oh no. That bag again.

I felt Dare's hand land on my leg and his fingertips dug in almost painfully. "Keep your cool," he growled into my ear and his other palm landed softly on the back of my neck, massaging, fingering my collar.

I took a few slow breaths while Tia dug into the bag. That jewelry store really needed to change their signature wrap for the sake of my sanity.

She pulled out a silver baby rattle and it was engraved with the name Ferrano.

Tia rolled her eyes and put it on the table. Sarah beamed at her. Then Sarah handed Tommy a gift bag that was black with red handles, red tissue paper sticking out.

He opened it and let out a hearty laugh. There was a black pair of handcuffs with red frills around them and a bottle of wine in the bag as well as a blue plastic ice cream scoop.

"Get her drunk, cuff her to the bed, and knock that Chiquita up!" Sarah shouted.

The room burst into laughter.

"I was gonna put in a box of ice cream to help things along but it woulda melted," Sarah added with a cheeky shrug. Tommy let out another burst of laughter. Tia went beet red in the face.

"Oh, what's this?" Luc asked.

"Nevermind!" Tia glared at Sarah. Tommy kept laughing.

"No parents around to bug you two for grandbabies so I'm taking that job and I'll be the granny. Okay?" Sarah looked on the verge of tears. "I love all-a-you like you're my own kids. So there."

The room hushed.

"You're not old enough to be a grandmother," Dare broke the quiet.

"You're too sexy to be a grandmother," Eddy added.

Sarah snickered and wiped the tears away.

"You are way too stingy with the sugar to be a granny!" Tia threw in and everyone including Sarah laughed.

"Stepping out for a smoke, Angelbaby," Dare said to me. "Get me some cake." He kissed me on the mouth and softly whispered, "Good job. Keep being my good girl." And then he backed away.

My heart tingled in a happy way.

He walked over to the other side of the large table and whispered something to Tommy and then Tommy grabbed the two empty gift bags and followed Dare out of the room, carrying them with him. I was glad to not have to stare at that bag for the rest of the evening.

Dare

"Thanks, man." He handed me the empty gift bags. I put the black and red one on the counter but stuffed the silver one with the purple paper into the trash bag, "Fuck. I bought her a gift in a bag like that and she had a panic attack. Reminded her of something bad." He followed me out to the back yard where I lit a cigarette.

"Good that she held it together tonight. No?"

"Yeah, it's good but it's only because I had to threaten her before we got here."

"Threaten her?"

I explained to Tommy about the report I'd gotten with instructions on how to manage her, how they offered the same for Lisa. Then I explained how Lisa pulled some dominatrix shit in my apartment when Angel had her meltdown, and then I told my brother that I had to assume the "Master" role to try to help her. He completely agreed that it sounded like a logical way to handle things. I told him about her needing to be held down, about wanting to be spanked. He joked that it didn't sound too taxing to have to use it to my advantage in the bedroom.

"I know you'd be all over that, man, and I won't lie; some of the shit we've gotten up to so far has been fuck-hot. But I've gotta handle her with care. I want this girl. I want her whole. Not a shell of a person, you know?"

"Submissives aren't shells, man. They want to please their Dom, ache for it even. A submissive can feel whole when they connect with their partner. They place a huge amount of trust on you and it's a big responsibility. It's really easy to fuck it up so you gotta be careful but if you do it right, she'll get off on it."

I nodded. "I know submissive doesn't mean broken. But because she is, maybe it'd hold her back in future."

"You'll have to see how it plays out. Me and Tia have had a rocky road in the bedroom. It's a work-in-progress keeping myself in check, not fucking it all up. At times I go too far but sometimes that's because she pushes the boundaries. I created a monster, but I fucking love the monster," he shrugged. "Nothing's really wrong between two people in bed if it means you both get something out of it."

I shrugged as well. "We'll see how it goes. Not gonna lie, it was hot when my ex used to play the submissive sex kitten. Angel ain't playin', though. It's her. But that's because they broke her. She took 19 days to break, man. 19. Most of those slaves were broken in 3-4 days. What does that say about how strong-willed she was before? If she were well, she probably wouldn't want this. When she gets well, maybe she'll be disgusted with the shit we did when she wasn't, and what if she hates me for it. Fuck, that's why I hesitated, man. I didn't want to get in deep with someone broken because if they can be fixed, how do you know how to be? How do you know you're not keepin' them broken?"

"You're overthinking it. Just take cues from your girl. Lots of strong women are submissive in bed. Believe me, I've seen it. You see how it goes. You see how she is as she gets well and then you two decide if that's the way you wanna keep playing." Tommy's eyes shot up to behind me. I looked over my shoulder.

Angel was in the doorway. She had a little frown on her face. I didn't know how much she'd heard.

"Hey, baby," I said hesitantly, stubbing out my cigarette. Tommy clapped me on the shoulder and then went back inside.

"Hi," she said softly.

"Get over here." I could see by her face that she was trying to mask how she felt about whatever she'd heard of our conversation.

I pulled her against my chest and then she softly said, "If anyone can fix me, it's you. But if you don't want the job, I won't hold it against you. I really won't. I don't want to be a ball and chain for you."

"Baby, I'm sorry you heard that. I already told you I was all in. I am. I wanna be. I just wanna do right by you. I feel like a heel for getting involved with you in a way that may make you later think I took advantage. You gotta see it my way. I was absolutely not going to go there with you because I didn't wanna be like my old man. But you and me, we have something. I want this. I just want to do this right. I'm doing things blind here, baby."

"I was always a submissive, Dare. Always. Always liked it rough and I don't think that'll change."

"Okay, baby. It's premature to talk about this but you might be different, want something different when you're past the trauma. And if you don't ever wanna be submissive again, it's not a deal breaker for me. Okay? We'll just take things a day at a time. I don't want you thinkin' you've got to be something specific to keep me happy. This relationship has two people in it. We will find our way together."

"And I don't want to make you be something you're not just because I'm so broken. It's good to know that you like it, though. I know a Dom when I see one and it comes natural to you. That makes me feel a little better about things. Please don't feel guilty for dominating me. It's what I want. It's what I need."

"Things are beautiful between us in the bedroom, Angel. I just wanna keep it that way. I don't generally share details of my sex life, you should know, but Tommy and I, we're close. He used to frequent the BDSM club scene and he's been around the slave trade more than me; my experience is limited to picking you up at Kruna. He's the closest to an authority on the subject I've got and he has insight here. And having advice from Lisa, too, hopefully I can help you."

"Dare, it's fine that you talk to others about it. It doesn't bother me."

Yeah, probably because she isn't used to having any privacy where sex is concerned.

"You wanna head home?"

"Yeah, if it's okay. They're about to play Pictionary, I was sent to get you two for it, and I kind of feel like that's too extroverted for me right now."

"Yeah, uh… no to Pictionary. It's highly competitive in my family on any day but when that fuckin' game comes out, the gloves come off and the Ferrano genes bleed through. My sisters are serious about their Pictionary. Serious as a heart attack."

She chuckled.

"I like them. I like all of them."

"Good." I smiled at her and put my arm around her and led her back inside so we could say bye. "They like you, too. Let's get them to wrap up some of that cake for later."

Angel

My heart sank when I heard him talk about me being broken. I didn't wanna be broken. I wanted to be whole. I wanted to be the girl he wanted in the bull riding video.

He knew it took them 19 days to break me? I was shocked at hearing that it was only 3-4 days for the average Kruna slave. I felt broken on day 2 but evidently the breaking crew didn't agree. I wondered what else Dare knew.

When we got back to his apartment, I followed him into the bedroom.

"I want you to take a shower and then wait for me, in bed. Spread wide for me," he said without looking at me and then he left the room.

I swallowed hard, feeling liquid with arousal, and did exactly what I was told.

After I got into the bed he returned to the bedroom, went to the bathroom, and I heard the shower turn on. When he walked in, naked, and very ready for me, my eyes traveled the length of him. His gorgeous blond hair was wet and messy. He had some scruff on his face and it was rugged and handsome. His defined chest, arms, and abs were the epitome of beauty. The sexy v that led to his cock belonged on the cover of romance novels. His cock was big, hard, beautiful. His legs were muscular. His whole body was this tanned olive tone. From what he'd said, he was three quarters Italian, a quarter Icelandic and I'd give him a total of 100% Adonis.

He climbed on top of me and hovered over me. "Were you a good girl tonight?"

"I tried to be, Master."

"I think you were a very good girl tonight," he said and touched my lips softly with his. "I was very proud of you tonight, my Angel."

"Thank you, Dare."

"Now I want you to show me you're a good girl some more."

"I would love to, Master."

"I want you to suck my cock while I suck your clit, baby. Open wider." He rolled off to the side and turned around and then he was hovering over me with his cock in my face, his face buried between my legs. I opened wide and he slid in as far as he could. I didn't gag. I squeezed my thumbs inside my fists, which was a trick I'd learned long ago, before Kruna, even. Whether it really turned off the gag reflex or was mind over matter, I didn't know, but it worked. He groaned and dipped his tongue between my folds and then sucked hard. My pelvis shot upright. I grabbed his ass and massaged it while he fucked my mouth and he kept on sucking and lapping, tongue pushing hard on my button, and in no time flat, I was moaning and gasping and I was done. Dare sent this angel to heaven.

He pulled out of my mouth and spun around and then drove his cock deep inside me. "You suck so fucking good, my baby. And you taste amazing. See how you taste?" He dipped his tongue into my mouth and held my face with one of his hands while he devoured my mouth with his.

"Mmmm, Master. You fuck me so good."

"You came hard, baby, think you deserve to come again?"

"Oh yes, please let me come again."

"Tell me something first," he said.

"Okay," I whispered.

"When's your birthday?"

I was taken aback.

"Tell me," he demanded and then twisted my nipples ever so slightly.

"October 3."

"Good girl." He got a finger inside me.

He started to work my g-spot and still sensitive from the orgasm I'd just had I started to ride his hand.

"Middle name," he said against my breast.

"Please…"

"Right now," he growled and pulled his finger out.

"Elizabeth," I said on a whimper.

"Good girl," I got his finger back.

He grabbed my clit and pinched as he slid his cock inside me and then he thrust into me over and over and over while working my clit until I exploded around him, hard, my nails digging into his back. He came hard, too, and then I fell asleep, exhausted, happy, feeling his juices coating the area between my legs. It was bliss.

***

The next morning, I woke up with his mouth around my nipple. I ran my fingers through his soft blond hair. He sucked hard and my back arched.

"Open your legs."

I did.

His thumb found my clit and he started circling. I was on the verge of coming and then he stopped. "Where were you born, baby?"

I hesitated and his thumb left.

"Charleston," I said quickly and his thumb came back.

"Good girl."

He let me come.

That day I stayed at the apartment as he was off with his brother at the office. I cleaned, I worked out, I blared music (but kept an eye on the cell phone in case he called), and I watched TV.

That night he didn't get in until late and when he came to bed, he woke me with his mouth between my legs.

"How's my girl?" He asked against my clit.

"I'm good, Master," I answered sleepily.

"Yeah?"

"Soooo good," I moaned, fisting the sheets.

"Do you wanna come, my baby?"

"Yes, Master. I wanna make you come, too."

"Oh, you will." He climbed up me and got his cock in my mouth, straddling my face.

"Can I touch myself, Master?" I asked a moment later, squeezing his tip and then planting a kiss on it.

"No." he answered, "Stay still and suck. Be a good girl and I'll let you come after." He held my wrists in his hands above my head, hovering over my face.

"Okay." I sucked him good and it didn't take long for him to come down my throat, the sexy moan he let out as he came lighting my body on fire.

He climbed back down below and leaned his head on his palm, which was supported by his elbow dug into the bed. His fingers leisurely circled my nipple and then worked their way down to between my legs. He gave me a sexy grin.

"Saw you in my bed and I couldn't wait for mine, but we're gonna take our time with yours tonight, Angel, let the burn build."

"Okay," I breathed.

He leaned down, kissed my navel, and then trailed kisses up to my throat and his hand was against my pussy but he barely moved it. I wanted to squirm.

He passionately kissed my shoulder, my throat, my earlobe, and I was covered in goosebumps.

"Can I jerk you off, Dare?"

"Yeah," he whispered, so I quickly reached for him. He was only semi-hard, but it took about 3.5 seconds for that to change.

One and then two fingers entered me and he crooked those fingers and kept crooking them softly against my g-spot. I let out a long moan. He then got his other hand under my bottom and then I felt his middle finger exert just a little bit of pressure against my back entrance.

"Oh!" I was melting.

"You like that?" he asked.

"Mmm hmm. I do. I do. Ah!" I spread my legs wider and squeezed his cock harder.

"Put your hands above your head, Angel," he told me.

"But then I can't touch you. Can I suck you again?" I was squirming.

"No. Stay still. You're breaking my focus." He pushed a finger just inside me, to stretch me in the back, and continued hitting my g-spot in the front and then added his thumb and hit my clit. *Oh!* I thought I was going to explode. My body started to tremble. Then he added suction on a nipple and I started to hit it.

"What's your name?" He slowed. I'd been almost there. I moaned in protest.

"Tell me!" he demanded.

I gasped, "Angel."

"Fuck!" he shouted and broke contact completely.

I jolted in surprise.

"God fucking damnit!" he yelled right in my face.

I started to cry.

"Fuck!" He left the room, yanking up underwear as he left and slamming the door hard.

I curled up in a ball and I was trembling. I was fucking this up. He was having to do so much, put so much effort into this, and I was just a total fuck-up. A broken woman. Ruined. Filthy dirty. Empty.

A few minutes later he was back, leaning over me.

"I'm sorry," he said. "I'm really sorry, baby; open up, let me in."

I uncurled and laid on my back, legs spread. Tears still streamed down. I felt so empty inside.

He was on top of me and then he was rubbing his cock between my legs against my clit and teasing my entrance, and then he got himself hard again and plunged into me. I was crying silently.

"Baby?"

"Yes?"

"I'm sorry. That was dickish of me. You tell me when you're ready."

"I don't mean to hold anything back from you. You don't understand. You…" I was gonna tell him. Somehow, I'd get it out. It was time. I pushed the void away and dug deep, ready to talk.

"It's okay, Angel," he stopped me. "I'm sorry."

"No, I'm sorry. I just didn't…"

He stopped me with his palm over my mouth. "No. I'm sorry. Quiet. Let's get back to where we were. Unless you're too mad at me and want me to stop?" He lifted his hand off my mouth and looked at me, waiting for me to answer.

"I'll never ever ask you to stop," I stated. "Never. Ever."

He got a supremely pissed off look on his face but then he flipped me over onto my tummy and then he took me hard, rough, and beautifully.

Dare

When I'd left the room in the middle of that… I called Zack. He answered on the first ring.

"You get my message earlier?"

"Which one?"

"Charleston," I said.

"Yep. It was good. I've got her."

"You have her name?"

"Yeah, man," Zack replied.

"I want her to wanna tell me." I squeezed the bridge of my nose and shut my eyes tight.

He was quiet a beat before resuming. "I have a lot of info here now. You want it, I spill. You don't, I'll hang onto it."

"Wait. You need more info or you got everything?"

"I've got enough. You confirming where she was born got me the confirmation I needed that I have info on the right person."

I pondered it a second. If he didn't need me to dig any further for her name then I should just let her tell me when she's ready. I wanted it from her. It was something she was holding back and I knew there had to be a damn good reason for it. Maybe when she was ready to tell me it'd mean that we'd passed a milestone closer to her healing.

"There any reason you can think of that I shouldn't just wait for her to tell me herself?"

He was quiet a few beats. "Naw man. You can wait." There was something in his voice that made me think there was definitely a damn good reason why she wasn't telling me.

"You sure?"

"Dario, I'm sure. You wanna know, I'll tell you. But you wanna let her do it, there's no reason I need to give it to you instead."

Good enough for me.

"All right. Call ya tomorrow."

I'd gone back to the bedroom, finding her curled up in a ball and I felt like a fucking heel holding back like that, stopping when she was right on that edge, punishing her by stopping before she could come.

That's what they did, held back orgasms to punish her, and I didn't wanna abuse the power. That's what I'd essentially done, though. Backed off with her all worked up out of anger and that's not what I was trying to do here. So, I went in, got her to open up, and I put everything I had into making her come, not for more information, not to keep her in line, but just to give her what she needed. She was petrified of telling me her name. I had to make her feel safe, not more afraid. I had to wait.

Angel

I'd gotten his fingers, his mouth, and his cock. I was full in my pussy with his fingers and when he got his cock into my ass, I came so hard that one orgasm rolled into another and it was so amazing that afterwards I bawled in his arms. He held me and stroked my hair and I fell asleep holding him as tight as I could.

In the morning, I woke up to the smell of toast and coffee. He brought me a tray with breakfast in bed.

"Good morning," he said cautiously.

"Hi." I sat up.

"Breakfast is ready," he said.

"It smells good. You cooked?"

"Kind of. I made toast. I'm sorry about last night," he said, looking remorseful.

I shook my head, "I'm sorry about last night, too. I know you're just doing what you need to do to get me…better."

He frowned and sat down, setting the tray beside me. There was toast cut into triangles with peanut butter and jam on it with a coffee and a banana.

I wanted to cry. How did I luck out like this?

"What's the matter?" he asked me.

I shrugged. "I just feel lucky."

"Lucky?"

"Lucky that I got sold to you. It could've been anyone. It could've been anyone else and then I wouldn't have you. You're amazing, Dare."

He gave me a tight smile and ran the back of his thumb along my cheekbone.

"I got lucky. I joked with Pop that I wanted a mail-order bride not knowing anything about Lisa's truth or about Kruna. His gift came from a fucked-up place, my baby, but he did give me a beautiful gift. I feel bad one minute that I let it go here with us but a split second later I am relieved that I opened my eyes and got my head outta my ass where you're concerned. You and me, we're gonna be happy; I promise you that."

I wanted to melt. He pulled me into his arms and held me tight.

I wanted to explain about holding back my name, about the threats and that being broken through 19 days of torture kept me from being totally open, about how I felt about him calling me his Angel and how I didn't want the reasons for that to change, but I couldn't find the words or figure out where to even start. So I just let him hold me for a few minutes and then he left me to have breakfast, putting Bugs Bunny on for me and telling me that Tommy and Zack were going to be over any minute and that they needed to talk in the den privately. The toast he'd made me was cold by the time I ate it but it was still the best pb & j toast I'd ever eaten in my life.

CHAPTER EIGHT

Tia

Tommy didn't sleep much the night before so I didn't sleep much either.

He came into the bedroom and then he tied me to the bed with neck ties and the handcuffs Sarah had given as a gag gift. I was on my belly with one of my wrists cuffed to the headboard and my other wrist tied with a black necktie he'd fetched from somewhere (his father's office?) that was fastened to the headboard and feet spread and tied to each of the cannonballs at the foot of the bed. Once secured where he wanted me, he did me hard via anal sex. As much as I was in the moment when it was happening, I was not having very positive effects from it in the morning. It was a little too rough with not quite enough lube and now I was paying the price of not speaking up about it. I took a long soak before breakfast, wincing through the burning and hoping the swelling would go down soon and then as I headed downstairs, he was just waking up. I met Lisa and Sarah in the kitchen. Tessa was still upstairs getting the boys dressed.

Lisa seemed in pretty good spirits while we helped Sarah make breakfast but then she locked tight when Tommy came into the kitchen.

"Mornin' girls," he said and she paled and froze in her tracks. This was the first time she'd seen him since the day after our wedding when we saw them off.

"Mornin' Tommy." Sarah passed him a cup of coffee.

"Hi," Lisa said, not looking at him, awkwardly looking anywhere else but at him.

I gave Tommy a shrug as he kissed me.

"What's up, Leese?" Tommy asked.

She shook her head, looking at her nails. "Nothing. Sleep okay? Uh, welcome back."

He eyed her warily. "Fine, yeah. Thanks." He took his coffee to the table and grabbed the newspaper.

We had a pretty quiet and uneventful breakfast. Tommy kissed me goodbye as he was heading to Dare's for a meeting and then that afternoon, he'd be picking me up to take me to Rose and Cal's for dinner.

After he left, I got a moment alone with Lisa. "Everything okay?" I asked.

"Sure, Tia. Yeah." She was tidying up the table.

"You sure?"

She nodded quickly, not looking at me, and left the room mumbling that she had to get ready for an appointment.

Alone, as Tess had taken the boys to the library for story time and Sarah was gone to clean Luc's house, I picked up the phone and dialed Rose and Cal's number.

Ruby answered.

"Hello?"

"Ruby?"

"Yeah?"

"Hi."

"Who's this?"

"It's Tia."

Silence. She *totally* knew it was me.

"Rubes?"

"Yeah?" She didn't sound good.

"I, uh, I just wanted to confirm it's still okay to come over today. We're back. I assume you know all about my conversation with Mia and everything."

"Yeah, I know, Tia. Ma's expecting you so, yeah, see you at six."

"Okay. Um, see you then. Can you tell Mia I checked in?"

"Uh huh," she replied, her voice sounding hollow, "Bye."

The line went dead and I was left sitting there holding the phone and feeling sick at heart.

***

When Tommy and I approached the house, Cal came out and greeted us. He gave me a hug and shook Tommy's hand and waved us in. Everyone was already at the table.

The problem was that it wasn't just Mia, Beth, Rose, and Ruby. Nick was there, too. And when we entered the dining room, I felt a really uncool vibe coming off Tommy at the sight of my ex-boyfriend.

Rose folded me into her arms, but didn't say anything. She just squeezed me hard. She smiled at Tommy a little. *Actually smiled. Weird.*

I looked around. The rest of the girls were at the table, not speaking. Mia looked pissed off. Beth looked happy to see me but nervous. Ruby was staring at the table cloth with tears in her eyes. Nick looked like he was filled with nervous energy. He was staring at me. He'd cut his hair short. That was surprising.

"Okay, sit everyone," Cal said. "It seems there's been some things happening that we should get out in the open so that we can move forward and have a nice meal together. Everything is ready and I've already had a conversation with these folks but we'll all have a little talk together first."

Tommy and I sat down at the table. Rose was at the foot, Cal was at the head, Tommy and I to Cal's left and across from me was Nick, across from Tommy was Mia. Ruby sat beside Nick. Beth sat beside her. The other chairs on the side Tommy and I sat on were empty. Everyone else in the house was absent.

"It seems," Cal continued, "that everyone was a little bit worried about you, Tia, so they put their heads together, did some snooping and eavesdropping and found your last letter to us, and then went on a mission to find you. I've had several telephone conversations plus one long in-person conversation with your husband, before you both left the country, and I have to say that if anyone had come to me or Rose instead of going maverick, we could've saved a whole lot of angst. I won't say that I don't think you two didn't jump the gun getting married so quickly but I will say that the few conversations I've had with your husband, Athena, have been good ones. He has earned my respect."

Everyone in the room looked contrite, except Nick. He looked angry.

I was surprised. I had no idea Tommy had been in touch with Cal. I felt Tommy's arm go around my chair and I felt my heartrate settle a little at feeling his support. I put my hand on his thigh and squeezed. He put his free hand on top of mine.

Mia spoke up, looking at Cal. "We know our friend, our *sister*, and we know that it's not her to vanish without a trace. One phone call to Ruby in all that time? One. And it was vague. You and Rose were not you and Rose. You were both worried sick. Secret meetings with social workers, the police, Tia's father. It was all very weird and we are not small children. We wanted, no needed, to know what was going on. We could tell by how you behaved and by the limited things you did say to us that we wouldn't get straight answers and so we took matters into our own hands. We found her and we had every intention of saving her because that's what she'd have done for any of us." Mia circled the room with her index finger on the word 'us'. "Am I right?" she was looking right at me, finally.

I let out a deep breath. "I am sorry for worrying you. In the beginning there were a lot of things happening that I can't talk to any of you about. My father is a piece of work. He put things in motion that put him and I in danger and I had to play things very carefully. In the process of a really messed up situation I fell in love."

Nick snickered. I glanced at him and then continued.

"I am sorry that I made you all worry but I was in the middle of a dangerous situation that I can't talk about even now. Now we're under heavy security because we had to come back before we could confirm that it was safe. I am here to tell you all that I'm sorry you were worried. I am fine. My husband is keeping me safe. I need you all to back off whatever investigations you've been doing and to please cooperate with Zack. Mia, he told Tommy you are being very tight-lipped. He's a good guy and he's a professional who is helping to keep us safe. In doing that he uncovered your plans to find me and the way you did things could seriously put us and the rest of Tommy's family now also my family in danger. You guys are still my family, I love you so much, but now that you know I'm okay you need to stop. And you need to give Zack all the info you have."

"Can I talk to you privately?" Nick interrupted to ask me.

"No," Tommy answered for me, leaning slightly forward in his chair and exuding a serious bad-ass vibe. "If you need to talk to my wife you can talk to her right here."

Nick glared at me and didn't meet Tommy's eyes.

"Nick, thank you for your concern. I appreciate that you tried to do what you thought was helping me but as you can see, I'm good."

"Tia…your dad says these guys buy and sell women, drugs, have politicians in their pockets, are into all kinds of bad shit. I know that's not the kind of life you want. Your father says that's not the kind of life your mother would want you in and---"

"Shut up," I blurted. "You don't know what you're talking about. If you've been listening to my father as an authority on my husband then that was your first mistake. Nick, I'm good, I'm more than good. You don't know what you're talking about and you don't even need to be here. I'm here to talk to my family. Not my ex."

Ruby snickered. "He's not here just for you, Tia. He's here for me, too. He's really been there for all of us through this. And if it wasn't for him, we wouldn't have found you."

Nick glanced at Ruby and then back at me and he shook his head. "Ruby and I aren't seeing each other, Tia."

Ruby looked at him with incredulity. Clearly, where he and where she saw their relationship was very different.

"If this guy is forcing you to stay with him, I won't give up." Nick folded his arms across his chest. "Please, can we talk privately?"

I shook my head. "No. There's no need---"

He cut me off. "I still love you. I'm not afraid of him."

He was such an idiot.

"Is this guy for real?" Tommy laughed.

High school drama shit. I was so past this.

"Nick, even if I wasn't happily married, which I am, we were done a while ago. The fact is that I am happily married. Deliriously happy. Maybe you should go. This is not cool. You're being disrespectful to my husband."

"I'm staying for Rose's veal parm." Nick said, folding his arms across his chest and then he leveled his gaze on Tommy and did it in a way that was seriously stupid.

I rolled my eyes. Then I glanced at Tommy and Tommy's eyes on Nick's were glittery and fricking scary. Tommy's chest was rising and falling rapidly and his upper lip started to curl. Nick looked away, looking frightened but trying to hide it.

Rose got up. "Let's have some of that veal parm now, shall we? I made you chicken parm, Tia; I know you won't eat veal."

Bethany leaned over. "Tia, if you're happy and if you're safe, that's all I need to know." She squeezed my hand. I smiled at her.

Mia still looked skeptically at Tommy, who was radiating barely-restrained fury.

Ruby still wasn't looking at me. She was staring at the table cloth.

"Thanks, Beth. Guys, my father lies. He's in jail for selling drugs. He's a gambling addict. He's a junkie. He knows very little about my life and even less about the kind of man I married. He's grasping. He tried to get me to lie to get him out of jail and it backfired and now you're giving him the time of day so he's milking it; he's lashing out. I need to know you're done with all the investigating. I need to know that you aren't putting me and my husband in danger out of misplaced concern. If you can do that, if you can please love me enough to trust that I'm being real here, I'm happy to stay for dinner. If you are going to sit here and disrespect Tommy and show lack of respect for me and my intelligence then we need to go. I will leave it up to you."

There was silence for a moment, then Cal spoke. "Girls?"

Mia spoke up, first. "We love you. We have questions and we're nervous for you after some of what we found out but if you can't answer the questions and you ask us to stand down, we will. We're sorry we put you in danger. You have to understand our perspective, we were just…"

"I know. I appreciate it. I appreciate your love and your concern and whatever lengths you went to in order to try to help me when you thought I needed it. If I could've let you all in on what I was dealing with I would've. But, I couldn't. I still can't. I'm sorry about that. But seriously, I'm good. I'm happy."

"He's good to you?" Ruby asked, finally looking up.

"Do you remember our talk when I told you he proposed?" I asked her.

She nodded.

"Every word was true. I am madly, deeply in love. Soulmate, Ruby."

Tommy kissed my temple.

Nick got a disgusted look on his face and got up. "I'm outta here."

"Nick?" I got up.

I felt Tommy stiffen and he caught my wrist.

"Give me one sec," I said to Tommy.

Tommy's jaw got tighter, but he let go.

I followed Nick out to the front room.

"I'm happy. Please be happy for me. Please call off your uncle."

"How can I be happy for you?" He spun around to face me. "That's supposed to be me. Fuck, Tia."

I was surprised.

"Nick, we broke up. Before I even met Tommy."

"I wanted to win you back. I wanted to be with you. You were more than a girlfriend to me, Tia. You were my future. That's why I started working at my uncle's company. I was trying to change for you…" He took a step toward me. I put my palm up and took a step back.

"I'm sorry, Nick. Tommy is my future. But thank you for trying to help me."

"He's dangerous."

"He loves me and you don't know…"

"He is dangerous, Tia. The stuff my uncle found out… I didn't even tell the girls the half of it."

"Stop."

He was being too loud.

"I can help you get away from him. Come with me right now. I'll get you hidden. I'll…" He reached for and caught my wrist.

"No, Nick. I'm good. Seriously." I shrugged him off and shot him a warning look. If Tommy had seen him put his hands on me, that would not be good.

He blew out a long breath. "Don't lose my number. You ever need anything, you call me."

"Thanks. But, I'm good. Have a nice life, Nick. I mean that."

He left, slamming the door.

I headed back to the dining room. It was quiet and awkward in there and I knew they'd heard everything. Tommy's expression was hard but he made no moves. I sat beside him. Rose, Mia, and Beth went to the kitchen to get food. Ruby excused herself and I suspected she was chasing Nick down.

Dinner was weird but Rose tried to make nice. She asked us about our living arrangements.

"We're staying in the house I grew up in for now. We weren't planning to be back this soon from our honeymoon so I'm not sure about our long-term plans yet. We may travel some more first," Tommy told her.

Tommy asked Cal about his work and they talked for a bit but the whole meal was forced, uncomfortable. Afterwards, I was in the kitchen with everyone clearing up, and as soon as Rose left the room Beth and Mia cornered me.

"Tia," Mia whispered, "Are you really okay?"

I nodded. "I really am."

Beth got right in my face. "We were so worried about you. Don't ever do that to us again."

I rolled my eyes and shook my head. "You guys don't know what I went through and I can't go there. Let me say now that I'm done apologizing. I've done it. If you can't accept it, there's nothing more for me to say."

Beth put her arms around me and so did Mia. I spotted Ruby in the corner of the kitchen. She moved in and bridged the gap. We had a group hug and Ruby choked first. That led to all of us getting sniffly and watery-eyed.

"He is fucking gorgeous," Beth whispered.

"So much," Mia added.

Ruby butt in. "He usually gives her 2 orgasms each time. Two!"

We all giggled.

"Is that actually true?" Beth gasped.

"Sometimes even three," I whispered.

"Holy shit!" Mia squealed.

"And you know what he can do to a cherry stem…" I added.

"Wow," Ruby said and they all got dreamy-eyed. We all started giggling louder.

Tommy stepped into the kitchen and saw our huddle, heard our girlie cackling. "Baby, sorry, but something's come up. We've gotta go."

I sobered, wiped my eyes, which were wet from both laughing and crying and hugged the girls. Then I hugged Rose and Cal and thanked them for dinner, promising to see them again soon. Rose made me promise to come or at least call if we had to slip off the grid again. And then she hugged Tommy. Hugged him! He looked shell-shocked. Whatever impression my husband made on Cal had obviously transferred to Rose.

Mia gave Tommy a shrewd look and stated, "You be good to her!"

He gave her a salute and led me out.

***

"Fucking bullshit," Tommy said as soon as we were off their street. "If that was any other scene, that fucking punk would've been toast right then and there." He picked up the phone and dialed.

"Tino? The punk's uncle? I want him interrogated. Find out what he thinks he knows." He ended the call.

"Thanks for keeping your cool," I said.

He'd obviously made up an excuse to get us out of there as, clearly, he was having trouble keeping it cool.

"Fuckin' guy," he was getting louder and even more livid and it showed in the erratic way he drove the car. "Tries to get my fucking wife to leave with him with me in the room and after saying he knows who I am. Does he have a death wish?"

"Tommy, please." I massaged my temples. "Slow down. You're driving crazy. And shh, I have a wicked migraine. That was seriously awful. I wanted to puke that whole time."

He reached across the console and gave my leg a loving squeeze and said, "Loved hearing you defend me, baby girl. Every single time you said 'my husband' I felt so much pride." He gave my leg another squeeze and then turned the radio on low.

I slouched in my seat but glanced over and gave him a half a smile.

It'd been too long being out of touch since I'd sent that goodbye letter and although I thought about them often, I had been self-absorbed and hadn't thought about what they'd be thinking all this time. They were the only family I had and I abandoned them, leaving them to worry about me. I had told myself it was better to cut ties and keep them safe from the truth but bottom line, I hurt them. I felt like crap.

***

"What could you have done differently?" Tommy said to me later on that night when he saw I was still feeling low. "We had to be careful. You didn't mean to hurt anyone, baby. You didn't vanish without a trace; you did what you had to do. Your safety is way more important than their feelings, Tia. Don't let them guilt you. If they care about you, they'll get over it. I told your foster dad we were going, told him a lot about what we were dealing with, more than I'd generally care to reveal, but I did that because you care about them. It was up to him and his wife to smooth things out with the girls and all this happened because of how they chose to handle things. That's on them, not you."

That night it took me a long time to fall asleep even though my husband had worn me out with a fast, hard fucking that was definitely about him being pissed at Nick and needing to show me that I was his. Three times during the sex he demanded that I tell him who I belonged to and was supremely pleased with my response of: *You, baby. Only you. Forever you* as illustrated by his "Fuckin' right!" But it felt like as soon as I did finally fall asleep, I was woken up. Tommy was thrashing in bed beside me, having a bad dream.

I backed out of the bed and started to call his name, seeing it was a bad one and knowing from recent experiences, particularly the one where he grabbed my throat and squeezed until I started to turn blue, that keeping my distance until he was fully awake was important.

He rocketed upright and after a split second he seemed lucid and then apologized for waking me.

"It's okay. You okay?"

"Yeah, baby," he breathed out hoarsely.

"Wanna tell me?"

"Nope, it's okay; go to sleep." He got out of bed and left the room.

***

He woke me up at dawn with sweet kisses on my earlobe and warm minty breath whispering my name in a husky voice. "Wake up, wife. We have plans today."

I stretched. "What plans?"

"We need to see a man about a hog," he said.

I smiled big. "Are we going to the loft?"

He wiggled his eyebrows. "Even better than that."

I got up and excitedly dashed for the shower. What could be better than that?

CHAPTER NINE

Dare

Angel and me were taking a walk after going out for lunch near my building and we were holding hands. She was smiling at me, laughing at a story I was telling her about one of my Viking cousins and how I'd gone over a year ago to be in his wedding and we lost the guy during his bachelor party and wound up finding him only 2 hours before the wedding, still drunk as a skunk, wandering outside in his underwear. Her laughter was gorgeous. Her eyes were lit up and she had a huge smile on her face. She looked carefree.

"Is it beautiful there? I'd love to go. I've always wanted to do loads of traveling."

"It is. We *should* go." I smiled and squeezed her hand. Suddenly she paled. We were walking by a crowded restaurant patio and she froze in her tracks.

"What's the matter?" I frowned.

She shook it off and then resumed walking.

"You okay?"

"Uh huh," she replied but she clearly was not. I was hoping this wasn't another panic attack coming on in the middle of the street.

"Tell me," I said, eying her seriously and giving her hand a squeeze.

"I thought I saw someone I used to know. It probably wasn't them. It's okay."

"Where? Who?"

She dared to glance back over her shoulder and then visibly relaxed. "I don't see them now. I must've been mistaken."

"You sure? You're all right?"

She took a big breath and beamed at me. "Yes. I'm sure."

"Who was it?"

She shook her head, still smiling, not wanting to tell me. I glared. She was not about to get away with a dazzling smile to get me to let it go.

"Now, baby," I insisted.

Her smile slipped.

"Jason," she replied softly. "The guy who asked me to marry him in Thailand. But it wasn't him, obviously." She shrugged.

Angel

I thought I'd seen him at a table for two sitting alone, looking right at me over a menu. I'd been afraid to look back, afraid to find out whether or not it'd really been him. But when I looked back there was no one there. That table was empty. Either it was a lookalike or my mind was playing tricks on me.

I pushed away thoughts of him and just focused on the footsteps Dare and I were taking, heading back toward his building. He didn't go back to his funny story; instead he was quiet the rest of the walk back and the vibe coming off him was tense.

As the doors closed inside the elevator, Dare's phone made a sound. When he read the text, his expression dropped.

"Awe shit," he grumbled.

"Everything okay?"

"No. That was Tess. They took Lisa to the hospital. She started bleeding. Had a miscarriage."

"Oh no." My stomach dipped and I felt cold envelop me. Lisa would be devastated. Absolutely gutted. My hand covered my mouth.

"Can we go see her?"

"We'll go tomorrow. Give her today. Okay?" He was replying to the text, his jaw tight.

I nodded.

We got to the apartment and he went to work in his den for a bit. I curled up in bed and watched TV but thought about Lisa. Poor Lisa. She wanted that baby so badly, was already in love with the idea of being a mother before she'd even started to show.

Poor Shayla.

Tommy

I pulled up the driveway at the farm and watched Tia's face as the house came into view.

"Oh, my goodness!" Tia exclaimed, "Holy shit!"

We stopped in front of the house and she threw the car door open, giddy with excitement. She ran toward the front steps.

Just before we left to go get married, I met with a contractor and went over specs with him to fix up the farmhouse. When I planned it I didn't know when we'd be back here but knew that whenever we did I'd be bringing her up here. She called it our 'happy place'.

It'd been a small stone farmhouse with a gutted kitchen and walls filled with graffiti as the place had been empty for a few years before I bought it. But now it was covered in a soft grey board and batten with a lilac colored shingled roof and lilac colored shutters flanking each window. I'd had the roof, siding, and front porch redone and a back deck and gazebo added.

The day before, I'd paid someone to come cut the grass and put out pots of colorful fall mums around the front of the house as well as a big vase filled with two dozen pink roses on the kitchen counter. I followed her to the porch and found the key in my pocket and opened the door.

"Wait," I told her as she went to go in and then I lifted her up and carried her over the threshold. Excitement was written all over her face.

Inside, the place had been converted to open plan. It was now one main room with a country kitchen opening to a great room with the big stone fireplace, staircase right up the middle to the second floor. I hadn't put her down yet when I said, "You can pick out furniture for the place. I just had them move over the bed, sofa, and table and chairs from the loft for now."

She tightened her arms around my neck and kissed me, kissed me big.

"You're the best husband ever, my husband."

"Mm, Let's go christen the new bedroom," I answered and carried her upstairs where we found the two bedrooms and a bathroom. They'd been painted a soft blue and I'd had the pine floors refinished and new walls put in up there. I'd had the bathroom redone, too, adding a big soaker Jacuzzi tub plus a new shower, toilet, and sink.

The smaller room was empty but the larger room just had the brass four poster bed from the loft in it. It wasn't made but there was a new bed-in-a-bag set with blankets and sheets plus four new pillows, still packaged, on the end. Clearly, my wife didn't care to stop and make the bed before christening the new room. My text alert went off but since my shirt was getting unbuttoned by her as I put her down on the mattress, I decided that the text could wait.

Dare

I called Zack.

"Hey bud, the guy who proposed to her was named Jason. I'll try to get his last name."

"Okay, man."

"She thought she saw him today at the bistro on Canal Street with the big outdoor patio."

"You get a look?"

"Naw man. She said maybe she didn't see him after all."

"All right, man. I might already know. Call me if you get anything more. I'll do the same."

***

He called me back just a half an hour later.

"Man, where are you? Are you with your girl?"

"Yeah, I'm at home. She's here. Why?"

"You ready for this?" Zack asked, obviously putting me on alert.

"Ready? For what?"

"Gan Chen and a few of his goons are on a plane on the way here and I just got a lock on where Frost is. She did see him today. He's here."

"Frost?"

"Jason Frost. The guy your girl was dating before she got pulled in by Kruna."

"Jason Frost? Connected to Donavan Frost?"

"Jason Frost is Donavan's nephew. Donavan was another of Gan Chen's partners before he died. The way it's looking, Jason Frost was seriously into your girl. See, Kruna scouts spotted her at a nightclub owned by Donavan Frost, managed by Jason Frost. They wanted to bring her in and involved Frost. It's looking like he worked on the outside with scouting and helping organize bringing people in. Guy's good-looking, smooth with the ladies. Seems like Jason tried to date her not to lure her in but tried to put the kybosh and keep her for himself. I haven't figured out yet what transpired between the proposal and her becoming a Kruna slave. Three days after Jason Frost bought an engagement ring your girl was supposed to fly to South Carolina but she never got on the plane and hasn't been heard from since."

"Donavan Frost is dead?"

"Yeah, died at 40 years old over a year ago under mysterious circumstances. After his death Jason Frost inherited his money, sold the bar to some other Kruna partner, and moved to Philly. Appears he wasn't involved in the Kruna world any longer, really, but recently got very involved."

"Very?"

"I'm assuming so. He's had phone calls and face-to-face meetings with Gan Chen. He flew to Thailand just a few days after you got her home and was there less than 24 hours. He went home to Philly for a couple days and then he flew here yesterday. I know you've got a good security system there but I think you need to grab her and go to your safe house while I dig further. It's looking dangerous."

"How'd you get all this info?"

"I have reliable sources. Can't divulge that right now, Dario."

"My safe house is out, man. I boobie-trapped it when all the shit went down with Jesse Romero. It blew up. I haven't sorted out another one yet."

"Find another safe place and wait to hear from me. Just go to ground a few days so I can watch these guys while we see if they reach out or make moves. If Gan Chen gets ahold of you let me know before you meet with him."

"I'll call you back," I said and hung up. I left the den and went to the bedroom where Angel was watching Bambi on TV, tears in her eyes.

She smiled nervously at me and wiped the tears away with her sleeve. "I'm such a sap."

"Hey, can you pack a bag for you and me for a couple days? We've gotta take a little trip."

She got out of the bed. "Okay."

I kissed her on the forehead and wiped a stray tear from her cheek away. "We're going to a cabin so bring jeans, warm clothes, bathroom stuff and phone chargers for both of us. But I also need a suit, shirt, tie, and dress shoes in case I have to leave for a meeting while we're gone. Maybe a grey 3-piece suit, white shirt, black tie. Okay? Gotta make a few calls. Can you manage? Can you do it quick, please?"

"Yes, no problem." She sprang into action and dashed toward the closet, looking a bit tweaked, probably picking up on my mood. I phoned Eddy. I couldn't get him. I left him a voicemail.

"Shit has heated up, bro. Can I use your cabin for a few days? Call me. I'm heading toward the restaurant now if I don't hear from you. If you get this, call me and tell me if you can meet me at the storage unit."

Angel

Dare was on the phone in his SUV.

"Hey man. Yeah, can you meet me at the unit? Cool. Okay, bye."

Then he dialed another number and said, "Bro, some shit has hit the fan. You and Tia stay at the farm tonight. Call me and I'll fill you in. We've got some unwanted company. Two potential threats. Ciao, brother."

He dialed yet again.

"Nino? Me 'n Angel are heading to Ed's family cabin as a precaution on some stuff I have to fill you in about. I'm gonna get Sarah or one of the girls to shop for food for a few days for us for there. Can you or Dex drive it up? Quietly. Make sure no tail. I'll call you back. Right. Bye."

He hit buttons on his phone and then started talking again.

"Hey, me and Angel are heading to a safe house for a few days. You got time to shop for us for three to four days? Now. Okay, good. Nino or Dex will come by in about 2 hours if you can hurry. Text me when you're back and I'll send one of them."

He put the phone down, lit a cigarette and opened the window. "Sorry, baby, I can't wait till we get there. Having a nic fit."

I opened my window wide and watched him, chewing my cheek.

He turned the music up. It was *Send me an Angel* by *The Scorpions*. I chewed my cheek harder.

I kept watching him. He knew my eyes were on him, but he wasn't enlightening me. So, I didn't ask. I stared straight ahead and got lost in the song.

A few minutes passed and then he pulled into a gas station, got out, and started pumping gas. "Grab my wallet and go pay?" he said to me through the window and I was sort of surprised. I saw his wallet on the console between us, so I picked it up and went into the gas station.

I was feeling on edge not knowing what was happening. Maybe he was keeping it from me so I wouldn't have an anxiety attack.

I found cash in his wallet so paid for the gas and when I got back out to the car he was ending a phone call saying, "Yeah, man. See you in about fifteen."

We got back on the road. The vibe coming off him was setting my teeth on edge. Finally, I worked up the nerve to ask, "Dare?"

"Yeah, baby?" He didn't look at me. He was focused on the road and smoking another cigarette.

"Everything's not okay," I said simply because it was obvious and therefore it'd be silly of me to ask, "Is everything okay?" What was not obvious was why but what was kind of obvious to me was that he probably wasn't filling me in because it was bad. Real bad. But it wasn't me to demand answers, at least not anymore.

"No, my baby. It's not. I'll fill you in later. No stress, though. I've got you."

Uh oh. Me of two years ago would've demanded answers. Me of today just sat and stared straight ahead. I felt his palm on my cheek. I closed my eyes and leaned into it. It always brought my anxiety levels down when he did that and I think he knew it too, because he often did that, ever since the second day he was in Thailand.

We pulled into an industrial plaza marked as 'mini storage' up beside a blue pickup truck. Dare got out of his SUV and approached the truck. I saw him talking to someone who handed him something. They talked for a minute or two and then Dare approached an orange garage door and unlocked a padlock on it, hauled the door half way up, then went inside. The blue pickup truck stayed put. I started to feel vulnerable. Out of Dare's sight out in public, someone could swoop in. I hit the lock button on the door to lock all four doors. "Roxanne" by The Police came on the radio. Oh, the irony.

A moment later, Dare came out with a black knapsack, spoke into the window of the blue pickup for a moment, and then returned to his SUV and went to get in. I unfroze as he jerked his chin at me to get me to unlock the door. He got in but said nothing. As we pulled away, I saw the blue pickup truck leaving. It was Eddy. We were back on the road.

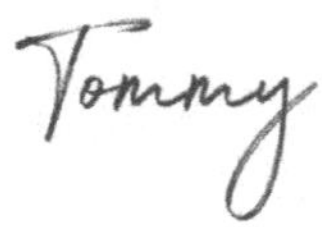

I climbed into bed, rolled Tia onto her side, curled against her back and then put my lips to her head. My arm was around her. She stretched and then lifted my hand and sleepily asked, "What happened? Your knuckles are all bruised."

"Mm," I grunted, surprised she hadn't noticed on the drive up.

"What'd you do?"

"Mm." I closed my eyes. She rolled to face me.

"Don't *Mm* me. What happened?"

"Don't worry about it."

"Husband?" She poked my chest.

I smirked and kissed her nose. "Shh. Let me sleep, wife. You wore me out." I gave her ass a swat.

She snuggled in. We slept for a while and then my phone was making noise again, waking us, so I grabbed it.

There was a text from Zack.

"Talk to your brother?"

I replied, *"Not yet today."*

"Where are you?"

"Farm."

"Good. Stay there if poss. Check your messages from Dario then call me. Btw, in addition to what's going down with Dario (Thai drama) cops are looking for you."

"Why?"

"Nick Gordon is in hospital. Told cops you beat the snot out of him at 4:00 this morn."

"Thx. I'll deal when we're back."

"Call me after you chk msgs with your bro on conference. We need to talk."

I wasn't sure how Zack knew that the cops were looking for me. But he regularly proved he was worth his hefty retainer.

When I woke up from a nightmare last night, a nightmare that Tia was gone, that the punk had kidnapped her, I got into my car and drove to the punk's apartment, busted down his door and hauled him out of his bed so I could bust his face. Then I came back and crawled into bed beside my wife and slept for three hours before waking her up to drive here.

I texted Dex, "Nick Gordon, Tia's ex, is in the hospital after getting a much-deserved beating. He needs to drop the charges. Bring Tino with you."

Twenty seconds later Dex replied, "I'm on it."

The Dex and Tino team worked well in terms of persuasion. Dex was the baby-faced fast talker and Tino was the intimidating muscle. I wanted to curl back into Tia. The nap hadn't been enough considering I'd barely slept, but I had to check my voicemails.

Two minutes later I was outside, walking by the pond, on the phone with Dare, ready to conference in Zack.

"I'm on the road, man. Can't talk but will call you back in 10 minutes when I'm at Ed's family's cabin. You still at the farm? If so, stay there."

"Got it. Yeah, I'll stay put."

Dare

I got us into Eddy's family's cabin. It was remote, wooded, and a nice little place on a great piece of property. Ed's dad used it as a hunt camp years back but he'd died and Luc and Ed had since done some work, put on a second story plus an addition, and made it into more of a cottage. It had a wood stove, big back deck overlooking a forest with a stream, three bedrooms. It was close enough to get to the city in a hurry, but away enough to feel like a haven.

I'd stopped at our storage unit and got a bug-out bag and keys from Ed on the way. Tommy and I each had bug-out bags there, one for each of us, plus a bag covering the whole family should the shit ever hit the fan in a way where we'd all need to be gone. I needed to update that bag to cover Angel now, too.

We got our things inside and then I told her I had to step out to make a call.

She was looking a little hurt, probably because I was keeping her in the dark but she was keeping as tight a rein on it as I guessed she could manage. I didn't wanna keep her hanging for long but I needed to brief Tommy and follow-up with Zack before I could take the time to sit down and talk to her. If she had a flip-out I needed time to devote to getting her chilled out so if I got these calls out of the way first there was more of a chance of me being able to give her whatever time she needed.

Suddenly a sick feeling crawled up my spine and I texted Zack.

"Just dawned that Angel's got a fucking chip. They put a tracker in her so if there are bad intentions then this place isn't gonna be safe for long so I'm adding security. What's the status on everything?"

I had a few guys I could use. I'd need a few more to make sure the house back home was safe, too.

I texted Eddy. "Get Luc and the kids to Pop's house. We need to go on lock down. I'll keep you posted."

"Got it," Eddy replied a minute later.

I called my brother. As soon as he answered I launched in:

"We have people on their way from Thailand, including Gan Chen. We've got another visitor who's here already, Jason Frost, Angel's ex, an ex who's looking like the reason she was at Kruna, the ex who I just found out is related to one of the former big wigs from Kruna, a now dead former bigwig who fucked my Angel up royally. Angel saw Jason this morning and he didn't approach, he took off, so he was stalking us. Zack confirmed it's him and he's been on radar after being off for a bit so something's up his sleeve. I'm at Ed's family's cabin but Angel has a tracker implant so if we're on Kruna's hit list, we're not safe. I'm getting supplies dropped here by Nino or Dex soon and I need to get some security here."

"I mobilized Dex already," Tommy said. "I had to get him to visit someone at the hospital and get them to drop assault charges."

"What?"

"Tia's ex. More later. Not important right now."

"Alright, so I'll get Nino here with supplies. I need security here in case they track us down. I'm gonna call Nino and get a couple guys here and get a couple to watch the girls. Ed's taking Luc and the kids to be with the other girls. Is Lisa home from the hospital yet?"

"Tino's going with Dex. Hospital?" he said. "She has an appointment?"

"Shit. You don't know."

"Don't know what?"

"Tess messaged me this morning to say she was at the hospital with Leese. She miscarried, man."

"Shit," Tommy replied. "I haven't read my texts from her or Luc yet. They've both texted. Okay, you call Nino back, I'll call Tess and make sure she and Leese are home. If not, I'll get Dex and Tino to escort them after dealing with the punk. It's probably the same hospital. Same neighborhood."

"Got it."

"Call you back soon."

I got a text to Nino and then I went back inside. Angel was looking out the window at the forest out back. I stepped in and took her into my arms.

"Okay, babe, come sit down. I had to get a few things done first and now I can tell you that we need to chill here for a bit while I see what's what."

We sat on the sofa and I kept her close. "You did see Jason this morning. He's in town."

Her eyes went wide and she started to shake her head in a No.

"Yeah. There's more but that's all I'm saying this second because I don't want you to freak out. What you've gotta know right now is that I'm taking care of you; I'm keeping you safe. How dangerous is this guy?"

She stared off into space for a second.

"Baby?" I prodded and stroked her cheekbone with my thumb.

"I don't think he's very dangerous. But… I don't know."

"No?"

She shook her head. "He didn't ever seem like he'd really hurt me or anything, but I don't know. I saw him shoot someone once but it wasn't a … it didn't seem like his usual thing. But I didn't know him long. I don't know…"

"No?"

She shook her head, looking like she was shaking off a trance. "Why would he be here?"

"That's one of the things I need to find out. Who did you see him shoot?"

"How did you know it was him?"

"Zack has been digging."

"Digging?"

"Yeah. We need to pull together an exit strategy for Kruna. Zack's digging around, getting intel, so we can figure out the best way forward. Who did Jason shoot?"

"Do you have a lot of intel?" She was looking at me with huge eyes.

"I don't yet. Zack does. Who did he fucking shoot, Angel?" I snapped.

She started to shake.

"Hey?" I pulled her closer and put my hands in her hair. "I'm not going to let anything happen to you. Nothing. Do you believe that? Do you trust me?" I caressed her face with both thumbs and she nodded and sank into me.

My phone made a text sound so I reached for it. It was Zack.

"Chen arrived and is checking into a hotel now. Stay tuned."

My phone rang while I was replying to Zack. It was a local number but not one I recognized. I answered it.

"Hello?"

"Mr. Ferrano?"

"Yeah?"

"Gan Chen. I'm in town. We need to meet."

I let go of Angel and stepped outside.

"Where? When? Anything I should know before we do?"

"I'm staying at the Hilton downtown, near your office. We can meet in my suite or in your office. You should know we have a minor problem with someone from Felicia's past. I'm here to ensure, personally, that it's dealt with. Our relationship is important to me, Mr. Ferrano, and I wanted to make sure I spoke to you personally to notify you of the problem as well as to assure you that it is in hand."

"I see. Okay. I'm a little out of town. Do we need to meet immediately?"

"We can meet tomorrow. I can work on the situation in the meantime."

"All right. How about noon at my office?"

"Perfect. I want you to know, Mr. Ferrano, that I will ensure the situation is handled."

"Just call me Dario, Gan. And good. You need help with this situation? You need manpower?"

"No. If I do, I'll let you know."

"Gan, Felicia told me when we were out earlier that she thought she saw someone she knew. Is the person you're here to deal with named Jason?"

"Yes, it is."

"Well, he was seen in a restaurant on Canal street but he disappeared as soon as she saw him. You sure our meeting can wait? I can come sooner."

"It's fine. It's in hand. I just wanted you vigilant. Jason was a little put out that Felicia left Thailand and based on his reaction I had him watched. I found out he'd flown to your city so I'm having him apprehended. I recommend you have someone watch Felicia until I update you."

"She's safe. And all right. See you at noon tomorrow. You need anything in the meantime, you call me."

"Thank you, Dario. All's well with your Felicia?"

"Exceptionally well," I replied.

"Good. Until tomorrow."

"Right." I ended the call and then I let out a long breath and phoned Tommy and conferenced Zack in. I informed them of the latest and Zack told me he had Chen under surveillance by someone on his team. He said they were working to track Frost down, too.

I reached into the truck and got another pack of smokes out and as I lit one I got another text from Tommy telling me that Dex was escorting the girls from the hospital back to the house. I got a text from Sarah that she'd just helped Nino load his car with groceries and now Nino was on his way with supplies for us.

I had just a few drags and then went back inside and she was sitting on the sofa looking lost.

"It's all okay, baby." I tucked a lock of her hair behind her ear. She'd been wearing it straight in order to keep herself together and while it looked beautiful, sleek, shiny, and gorgeous, it was the hair of "Felicia". When it was wavy it gave me the promise of who she was before she was broken. One day soon I hoped we'd be able to toss that fucking flat iron off my balcony. Together.

She snuggled into me and it started to rain and it was heavy, coming down in buckets. We sat quietly for a while, watching the rain out the big picture window. I rubbed her back and rained kisses all over her face. She made contented sounds, arms around me. I was gonna ask her about Jason Frost and the shooting again but before I could, I heard a car. I jumped up, pulled a gun from my knapsack, and stepped out with it, catching her face as she saw and watching a horrified look spread across her face. "It's probably Nino with our supplies but stay here."

She nodded and I stepped out. It was Nino. He and I unloaded about a dozen grocery bags into the kitchen and she started unloading food from bags into the fridge and pantry.

"Sarah must've shopped for a month instead of a few days," I muttered, carrying in two stacked cases of bottled water. Nino followed with the last of it, a case of 24 rolls of toilet paper and case of 12 rolls of paper towels.

"If you don't need to be up here that long, me, Bee, and little Joe'll come spend a weekend and finish up the food," Nino joked. "Been a while since we had a getaway."

"Yeah, well with the state of the union, might not wanna get too excited. It could be a while longer," I mumbled and saw Angel's eyes get bigger. "I'll walk you to the car, man."

Angel waved at Nino, saying, "Thanks very much, Nino."

He gave her a smile and said, "You're welcome." He followed me outside where he clapped me on the shoulder and said, "Good to see you shacked up, man. She's a beautiful girl. How'd you meet?"

I gave him the quick and dirty low down on Angel, Kruna, and where things were at with the threat. He listened, looked pissed, and said he was committed to helping me eliminate any and all threats. He was heading home to take care of organizing security for us so that I'd have someone here to watch over us tonight and to watch over Angel while I was at the Gan Chen meeting tomorrow. It sounded like Gan Chen wasn't here to be an enemy but I wasn't taking chances. Nino said he'd also been organizing security for the farm where Tommy and Tia were as well as Pop's house to watch over the girls and kids.

When I got back in I suggested she make us something to eat, said I was stepping back out for a smoke. I needed to make a few more calls and didn't want her to hear.

Angel

I was having trouble holding it together. He was being super-secretive, making calls out of earshot, looking angry and stressed, smoking like a fiend. I got the groceries all away and after sitting for a long time doing nothing because he was outside in his SUV on the phone because it was raining outside, I decided to put a movie on. There was an old floor model television that had to be circa 1980 along with a VCR with a bookshelf filled with dozens and dozens of old VHS movies. The rain kept pouring and nearly the whole length of a movie passed before he came back inside.

I'd heated up a big family-sized lasagna. There was enough food here to feed us for weeks. I'd taken the pan out to cool and I was setting the table.

He went to the bathroom, came out, got a bottle of Gatorade from the fridge, and then he looked at his phone again just as it made a text sound.

He headed toward the door again.

"Dinner is ready," I told him as he went out.

"One sec." He kept going with the phone.

I finished getting the table set and waited. And waited.

When he came in, I looked at him. He looked to the table and gave me a smile. "Dinner ready?"

It'd been cooling nearly half an hour and I'd already told him it was ready but I didn't fuss; obviously he had stuff going on. Stuff he wasn't telling me…

Strange how *this quickly* I could feel like I had a right to know.

"Yep. You ready to eat?"

"Starved, babe." He opened the fridge and got out a bottle of wine and poured two glasses.

I served up the lasagna and we sat.

His phone kept going off while we ate and he replied to texts while we re-watched the John Candy Summer Rental movie as it had rewound and started playing again.

After dinner, he washed the dishes and I dried them and then he started a fire in the wood stove for us while I picked out a movie for us to watch. I figured after his choosing The Hobbit that first night that he'd like something along those lines so I picked *Ewoks*, thinking that someone who liked Hobbit movies might also like Star Wars type movies.

I watched it and he was texting and emailing for the most part but had his arm around me, my head on his shoulder, so it was still comforting. I felt taken care of, if confused, but I settled against him and just decided that I was going to let my Master take care of me.

***

I woke up in Dare's arms. He was carrying me up the stairs.

"Hi," I mumbled sleepily.

"Hey sleepy girl," he said and then he put me down on the big old-fashioned canopy bed with the patchwork quilt. I had admired it earlier when I'd had a look around. There were three bedrooms and another bathroom up here. The one bedroom was half pink and half blue. On the pink side were bunk beds with pink comforters and the blue side had a crib. The other room had a futon and a few air mattresses so I wasn't surprised Dare put us in the master bedroom as he hated sleeping on futon mattresses.

He held me and I drifted back to sleep.

***

When I woke up, I was alone in bed. I used the bathroom and then went down the stairs and it seemed I was totally alone. There was a note on the kitchen counter.

Angel,
Check your text messages.
XO
Dario.

I found my purse and the phone he'd bought me was inside but it was dead. I'd brought two phone chargers so I plugged it in and poured some coffee that was already made. I caught something from the corner of my eye. I looked out the window and saw two guys outside. One was Nino. They had holsters over their shoulders and they were armed. I got a sinking feeling.

As the phone powered up the text message alert went off.

"Angel, I have a meeting this morning. I have Nino and Luke here to keep an eye on you. Stay inside. Don't worry. All is fine. It's just a precaution. I'll text if I don't think I'll see you by dinner time. XO."

I answered.

"Ok. XO."

I sat down with my coffee and tried to not freak out. I had to keep my cool. I was away from my Master and he'd told me Jason was in town. He'd said on the phone to his brother that there were two potential threats. And he had Zack digging around and I didn't know what Zack would find, but if the digging had to do with Kruna and with me it could put the one person on this planet that I loved, other than Dare, in danger. I said a little prayer.

CHAPTER TEN

Dare

I left early to deal with some stuff at the office and then to meet with my brother and Zack before the Gan Chen meeting. I'd left her in bed, but Nino and another security guy were there. Tommy had dropped Tia off with the girls so we wouldn't have to worry about security at three places. He asked if I should bring Angel to the girls but I didn't know that she could handle that yet. She was fragile and the last time I'd left her alone with Lisa things had obviously not gone well. With Tess and Luc having no clue about Angel's past, Lisa's past, and added to that the fact that Lisa was apparently a fuckin' mess over losing the baby it seemed like a bad idea.

I was concerned about Lisa and therefore glad she was on lockdown. Tommy tried to approach her with condolences when he dropped Tia off and said that Leese had a fucking meltdown when she saw him. Tommy left her there but called me before he left the place and we agreed he'd tell Dex to make sure that Lisa stayed in the house. And then I told Tommy about Lisa's comments. I hated to do it, to bring up that shit for him, but told him that she blamed him for losing Pop. He needed to know, especially with the fact that she was now having this reaction to the miscarriage.

"She what?"

"She blames you. She didn't out and out say it but eluded and was just about to when I told her to shut her mouth and said she had no idea what happened and didn't need to know."

Tommy was shaken up at that and it took a lot to rattle my brother so him being rattled told me he'd been torturing himself over his actions since they'd happened. We knew that the girls all suspected that Tommy ended Pop's life but no one asked and nothing was said. Tommy had no choice. I knew that and I had a strong feeling my sisters knew that, too. It'd be suspected to those not in the know that the death was due to blowback after taking out Jesse Romero and that's how we left it. The papers made that sound like the case, too.

Tommy and I had been interviewed by the police and we had alibis. Our contact JC and his cleanup crew, along with someone we had on payroll in the homicide department, made it so the whole thing was tidy. Not too many questions.

But Luciana, Tessa, and Lisa? Yeah, not much was said other than the fact that Pop and some of his guards were shot at one of Pop's safe houses. The girls never asked Tia what'd happened. Tia never offered info, according to Tommy, and no one asked. But everyone knew Pop had kissed Tia in front of the family out of being angry at Tommy and at least a few people knew that a few of Pop's men pulled Tia from Tommy's Jeep after I put her there and took off with her.

Tommy showed up at the office and then me, Tommy, and Zack talked for a bit. When Tommy left the office at 11:30, it gave me some time to do a bit of work while waiting for noon for Gan Chen to show up.

I got my poker face firmly in place.

Tommy

I stepped out onto the street outside the Ferrano offices and that's where I was greeted by two uniformed cops who arrested me for the assault of Nick Gordon. Dex told me Gordon was gonna stand down but either he didn't do that or the cops hadn't yet gotten that message.

Tia

Tommy didn't say much about the latest drama we were in, but told me to stay vigilant with Luc, Tessa, and Lisa at the house. We spent a great night in the farmhouse before he found out about new drama and then dropped me off with the girls.

When we'd first arrived at the farm, I was excited about the possibility of decorating it. We wouldn't live there but it'd be our place whenever we were here, if we continued to live overseas, and if we decided to move back home, we would have a country getaway, a getaway where I'd fallen in love with him and shared some amazing moments.

We'd taken a walk on the property and we'd gone up to the loft, which was mostly empty but we'd still made out like crazy up there, in memory of the fun we'd had there before. And then just as he was getting ready to close the loft up, I said, "Bet you a dollar you can't catch me." I was near the stairs and he was on the far side of the loft, closing the doors that opened out to the back, facing the pond.

"How about we make it a little more interesting than a dollar?" he had offered.

"Hm. Okay. Bet 'cha you can't catch me before I get to the front door of the house and if I win, I get to tie you to the bed and have my wicked way with you. And you'll owe me a dollar."

"And if I win?"

"Then you can do whatever you want to me. And I'll owe you a dollar."

He'd smirked. "I already do whatever I want to you on a daily basis, baby girl."

I'd smirked back. "Are we playing this game or are you too afraid to lose?"

"I'll give you to the count of five."

"Five? That's not enough."

"One…"

I dashed down the stairs as fast as I could. I got to the door of the house and waited a good minute before he emerged from the barn. He strolled out of the barn and sauntered over.

"Hey! You let me win. Why?" I huffed.

"I've gotta let you win once in a while, wife. And besides, I'm a little curious about what you'll do to me after you've tied me up."

I giggled. "Well then… how's about you get your sexy ass up to bed and let me show you?" I swatted at his butt but he caught my wrist and then he threw me over his shoulder and carried me up toward the bed. I was upset for a minute, thinking he'd changed his mind, but we got to the bedroom and he set me on my feet, then he threw his shirt off, kicked off his boots, and flopped onto the bed, throwing his arms up over his head.

"Ravish me," he challenged.

I chewed my lip and then straddled him and started unbuckling his belt. Once I got it undone and off him, I proceeded to use it to restrain him. I wrapped it around the brass headboard rails and then took his wrists, crossed them, and worked at weaving the belt around them. It wasn't looking too secure so I undid it, took off my own belt and used his belt on one arm and my belt on the other. Since I'd undone my jeans, I decided to take those and my shirt off, leaving me in a red demi cup bra and red cheeky panties.

Tommy looked totally relaxed, totally amused, and very interested in what I had planned. I never figured I'd win this challenge. So, I'd had to wing it.

I got his pants undone and down over his hips but then I decided I wanted to touch and kiss his gorgeous chest so I started at the owl tattoo and then tongued the nipple just below my name. I felt him flex his hips and I smiled against his chest and ignored his crotch area. I kissed up to his throat and tongued his earlobe, then I sat up and leaned back onto his thighs so that I wasn't anywhere near his cock. I ran my hands up and down his torso and his expression was heated. He was staring into my eyes and practically into my very soul.

I leaned up, still avoiding his crotch, and got my boobs in his face. He nuzzled in between my cleavage and I squeezed his shoulders and ran my hands up and down his arms.

And then I backed away, down to his thighs again and watched him bite down on his bottom lip, staring at my boobs. I cupped them in my hands and then ran my thumbs over my nipples. He shook his head, watching intently as my right hand slid down into my panties.

"Oh wow," I breathed. "I wish you could feel how wet I am, husband."

He smirked. "Come up here, wife, and let me feel how wet you are. Let me feel it with my cock."

"Nuh uh."

"Or come way up here, wife, and let me feel how wet you are with my tongue."

"Mm." I inserted a finger inside myself. "Wow, I'm wet and tight, husband. Bet you'd love to feel how tight I am, too."

"You gonna let me feel or taste or are you gonna be a tease?"

"Teasing you is fun."

"Mm. Touch me, Tia."

I touched his cheek and then scrubbed it with my fingertips and leaned up and kissed his mouth. He tried to give me some tongue, but I backed off.

"My cock, Tia," he said. It sounded like an order. I knew him well enough to know it was one.

I shook my head. "Naw. I wanna tease you a bit more first."

I got on my knees so my face was hovering over his stomach. I kissed his belly button. He arched so that his cock was at my chest. I grabbed my boobs and squeezed them together, getting his rigid cock between them for just a moment and then I backed off and kissed his abs, getting back on my knees between his legs. He lifted his feet and then crossed them at the ankles and trapped me between them. His amused look had faded and now he looked like he wanted to devour me. I stayed still, trapped between his legs, but with his hands restrained above his head it didn't look like there was much he could do about it. I tucked my hair behind my ears and then reached for his shoulders, getting my fingertips under his arms. I began to tickle his armpits. This earned me a scowl. He pulled on the restraints a little.

"Oh? Don't like that?" I asked as I tickled his stomach. I didn't think it was very effective, he'd just tightened his abs so probably couldn't even feel it. I squirmed out from between his legs and got off the bed.

"Get back here, wife!" he demanded through gritted teeth.

"I'm thirsty. I think I'll go grab a drink. You thirsty?"

"No. Not even a little," he replied, looking like he was getting more than a bit impatient with me.

"I'm a lil' peckish, too. Did we bring any food? Anything I can make a sandwich with?"

"Tia…" Tommy was definitely losing patience.

"I'll just go look." I left the room, calling back, "Man I miss Nita's cold breaded chicken."

I went downstairs and took my time perusing. I found a few bottles of beer and water in the cool retro powder blue with a pearl finish fridge. There was a matching Aga cooker. This was a great country kitchen. Not too big, but definitely cool. I took a few sips of water and opened and closed a few cupboards, which were all empty, then sauntered back upstairs, trying to be all sexy in my red undies and bra. I leaned against the doorframe and took in the delightful sight of him lying there looking almost helpless with his pants down below his hips, his underwear tented in a delectably mouth-watering way, and his arms over his head, still fastened by two belts to the brass headboard.

"Hey, my husband," I breathed huskily and swallowed a sip, purposely letting a few drops of water trail down my chin and between my breasts. I pulled one strap down, letting one of the 'girls' out and put the sole of a foot flat on the door frame so that my knee was bent.

"It's hot up here, isn't it?" I poured just a tiny bit of the cold water over that breast, not enough to soak myself but enough to make that nipple pebble. I arched my back.

He shook his head at me. "You're so gonna fuckin' get it."

I giggled, shrugged, pulled my bra strap back up and walked over and put a knee to the end of the bed.

"It? What *it* am I gonna get?"

He shook his head. "It."

"Promise?" I prodded.

"Oh, I promise."

I put the water bottle down on the floor and straddled him again. Leaning down, I kissed him on the mouth. His tongue struck out like a vicious viper and he was ravishing my mouth. I backed up.

"Get back here. Undo the belts, Tia." He was panting.

"I'm in charge and I say I'm not done playing yet," I said, totally enjoying the power.

I grabbed his cock and squeezed. "I may not be done playing for a long, long while."

"I don't fucking think so," he said and I saw his biceps flex and then heard a series of pings. The brass headboard quite literally came apart at the seams.

His wrists still had the belts around him but they were no longer attached to the no-longer-together headboard as there were pieces of it on the bed and the floor. Suddenly, I was roughly flipped onto my back, my wrists pinned above my head by one of his hands, and he reached down and ripped my panties to the side and he rammed his cock hard into me.

"That's not fair. You're reneging…" I started to say but I was interrupted by a piece of leather going in between my lips. Oh, my Lord! That was Tommy's belt and he was getting it off his wrist and gagging me with it. It was quickly fastened around the back of my head.

"Who's in charge?" he snarled and tightened the grip on my wrists. I couldn't answer, obviously, as I was gagged. His face looked absolutely furious. There was a vein popping in his forehead. I gasped in fear and he rammed in again and again, holding my eyes with his and then he let go of my wrists and flipped me so that I was on my belly and got back inside of me. He had my hair in his hand and he was pulling. And I was moaning, tasting the leather, feeling drool trickle out. The sound of skin slapping on skin pierced the air and then it was Tommy grunting, me grunting, and the bed banging into the wall. Then one of his hands grabbed my hand and took both our hands under my hips and he cupped me with both our hands and started using my fingers against my clit.

I moaned, and the orgasm gripped me. He was slamming in over and over while we circled my clit together and I clenched hard around him and listened to his masculine moan fill the room. What a beautiful fucking sound. He took the belt away from my mouth and moaned, "Who?"

"You're in charge, baby," I breathed, while continuing to come hard. Then not long later, we were snuggled up together falling asleep.

"Hey?" I whispered, kissing his owl tattoo.

"Hm?" he replied.

"You owe me a dollar."

He laughed and then he kissed me breathless.

***

We hadn't wanted to come back to the city so soon but found out that a) there was potential trouble brewing to do with Dario's relationship and the sex slave resort and b) Lisa had lost her baby and was home. Tommy needed me locked down and safe while he helped Dare ensure that whatever threat there might be was neutralized, if needed, and I needed to be there for a member of our family if she needed me.

When we got back to the house Lisa, Luc, and Tessa were all in the family room. I didn't see Sarah and none of the kids were around so I assumed Sarah had them out somewhere.

Lisa was sitting on the sofa under a fleece blanket and her eyes were red. I stepped into the room and went to go to her but as Tommy stepped in behind me, she made a horrible sound that sounded like it rumbled up from her gut.

"Noooo!" Lisa screamed and pointed at Tommy, her beautiful face contorted into an ugly hate-filled scowl. "Get away from me!" She threw the blanket and dashed from the room, slamming the door of a nearby bathroom. Smashing glass was the next sound we heard. Tommy moved quickly, pounding on the door, calling, "Lisa!"

"Youuuuuuuu!" she howled from the other side of the door.

Tommy backed away, looking ashen. I knew, then, that she blamed Tommy for the loss of her baby and I could only guess that she was stressed at seeing him. The way she'd acted when she saw him the morning after we'd arrived? I had a horrible sinking feeling.

What brought this on, though? She wasn't like this at our place in Costa Rica, during the wedding.

"Tommy, you go. We'll settle her down. Be safe." I kissed him. He gave me a little nod, gave me a squeeze, and left, looking visibly rattled.

It took a long time for her to come out. When she did, me, Tess, and Luc were sitting with a pot of tea, talking softly. No one was saying much of anything, though, certainly not what we were all thinking. We'd just sat quietly while the girls asked me where we were and I'd told them a bit about the farmhouse and the surprise Tommy'd given me.

Lisa emerged from the powder room, finally, and she glared at me.

"He killed my husband. I know he did. You know he did. We all know it. I want you to tell me exactly what happened."

Oh shit.

Dare

Gan Chen arrived at noon sharp. Leanne, my receptionist, saw him in and offered refreshments. He was with two men, one Asian and one who looked Italian. Bodyguards. I was packing heat but had no one at my back. I had

Zack and three of his guys in the boardroom and Zack was listening on an intercom and recording the meeting.

Gan declined the refreshment offer and I told Leanne not to allow anyone to interrupt us.

I reached for his hand and we shook. He asked his men to wait in the waiting room and to leave us alone. I guess he'd assessed my office and felt safe enough to converse with just me.

"How are things, Dario?"

"No complaints," I said.

"And your Felicia?"

"Keeping me busy." I smirked.

"I gathered that. No transition training? That's taking a challenging road."

I shrugged. "I guess I was a little anxious to get her home. She's somethin'."

He smiled, looking pleased. "Your father said you'd never taken a slave before but that you'd be a natural. If you are having any difficulties but don't want to have anyone else work on the training, I'm happy to give you advice. Any time. I, too, prefer to train my own girls. Once I bond with a girl it's hard to imagine anyone else giving her a correction. I think you and I are probably alike in that regard."

I forced a smirk. "Sounds like it. Thanks for the offer."

"I've spent time with your Felicia. She loves to be spanked. Throw in a little face slapping, too. She responds exceptionally well to that. It's better to use spanking as a reward than a punishment. If you want to punish her, withhold---"

I cut him off by saying, "Thanks Gan, but let's not go there. I've grown attached very quickly and the idea of anyone else spending time with her, even prior to her becoming mine, it gets me riled. I'd hate to put our relationship in jeopardy, but I know myself."

He waved his hand. "Absolutely. Let us carefully back up."

I poured two glasses of vodka from the sidebar behind my desk. "Five o'clock somewhere, right?" I needed that drink during this conversation like I needed my next breath.

"I'm still on Thai time so let's."

"Salut."

He and I raised glasses and drank.

"So Gan, not to dampen the mood but please tell me more about why you're here. This Jason situation? What can I do to help?"

Gan took a breath. "He and Felicia were in a relationship prior to her becoming a Kruna asset. For a variety of reasons, most due to potential security breaches that we foresaw with his relationship with her, he was cut out of her life and she was brought in. Jason's uncle was an important partner. He took control of Felicia and kept her for himself for the first several months she was with us. He did that mostly to punish Jason and so made his escapades with Felicia very obvious to Jason. It was ugly."

Gan shook his head in memory. "He mysteriously died and we suspect but cannot prove that Jason had a hand in poisoning him. After Donavan's death Jason tried to acquire her from us a number of times, which myself and the other partners decided was a bad idea. He tried to push around the time your father expressed interest in helping you acquire. Felicia met the specifications and we decided it was serendipitous as we'd meet your needs, help your father, and remove this pesky problem. If she was no longer available Jason would cease to be a pest. See, if he'd been anyone else it wouldn't have gotten that far but Jason's grandmother is a senator. She's very aware of our resort, one of our original seed partners, in fact, rarely involved in the past decade. Unfortunately, he got emotional when he discovered she'd been sold. He did some research and got someone to turn over information and found out where she went. We had a breach of trust at the resort but that breach is in the midst of being dealt with. This is not something that typically happens; I want you to know how seriously security and privacy are handled. As a result, we're here to apprehend him. He's enough of a thorn that he is a thorn that will need to be extricated."

"What can I do to help?" I asked.

"For the moment, just be watchful. We expect to have him apprehended within twenty-four hours."

Tia

"I think you need to have a conversation with Tommy, Lisa," I suggested.

"No. You tell me. What happened after Tom's guys drove off with you?"

"You need to get those hands bandaged," Luc said. "You're bleeding. You might even need stitches."

Tessa dashed into the bathroom and returned, looking horrified, shaking her head at me. Lisa had obviously hit the mirror or something.

My phone rang; it was Dex.

"I'm outside, Tia, but Tommy's gonna be there in two minutes. He wants you to tell the girls all to go to their rooms. Separately. Luc with Tessa. He wants you in your bedroom, too."

"Why? What's going on?"

"Those are the orders, Tia," Dex replied. "Need me to come in and enforce?"

"I think I'll be okay. Thanks, Dex." I hung up.

"Tell me," Lisa said. "I want to know exactly how it happened. I need to know."

"Lisa, I'm sorry but I have orders that we're all to wait in our bedrooms. Separately. Luc, can you please go to Tessa's room?"

Luc and Tessa both looked confused. Tessa had a broom and dustpan and started to head toward the bathroom.

"Guys!" I exclaimed, "Seriously. We're under some kind of threat right now. You know we're on lockdown. We need to follow Tommy's orders and go to our rooms. I'm sure there's a reason for this."

Tommy was already coming in the doorway. "What the fuck did I say?" He looked incredulously at me and at the others. Lisa was standing by the sofa looking at Tommy with hatred on her face.

"Go!" he shouted to his sisters. They both started to move toward the stairs.

"You killed my husband, didn't you?" Lisa said and the sisters both stopped in their tracks and stared at Lisa and then looked to Tommy in unison.

"Go," Tommy repeated, through clenched teeth.

"Lisa…" I started.

"Tia, stop," Tommy snapped.

I looked to him and didn't know if I should stay or go.

I stood there and waited.

"I loved him." Lisa started to cry.

Tommy sighed and thrust his hand through his hair. "You don't want to have this conversation. Trust me."

"And at least I was going to have a piece of him, you know? But now my baby is dead and so is my piece of him."

"I'm sorry you lost the baby. You need to chill out, though, Lisa. You need---"

"I need to know what happened."

"Fuck." Tommy's face was so filled with pain it hurt me like a physical blow.

Lisa sobbed. "I tried to forget, I tried to bury the pain like I bury all my emotions, but I just keep…feeling. I keep feeling so much." She looked at me, eyes pleading for me to understand.

"He tried to kill us," I blurted. "Tommy had no choice."

"Tia!" Tommy stared at me and shot daggers from his eyes.

I continued anyway. "It was self-defense, Lisa. It was. Tom had me taken to that cabin and he was going to kill me in front of Tommy. He was gonna shoot Tommy, too. It was self-defense. It was like a quick draw race. Tom was about to shoot and Tommy drew on him to save us."

"Tia, shut it."

"No Tommy, it was. You need to hear this, too. You did the only thing you could've done. Lisa, he's not sleeping. He's tormented. He is in so much pain over losing his father but it's not his fault. It's Tom's fault. You loved Tom and I'm sorry but Tommy loved him, too. Tom did this, not Tommy."

Lisa covered her face and fell to the floor and wept into her hands. I went to her and put an arm around her. She cried into my shoulder and put her arms around me.

I looked up to Tommy's face and he was staring at the ceiling, flexing his jaw. I looked past him and saw that his sisters were in the doorway.

"Tommy?" I called out. He turned around and put his fist into the wall. I jolted. Then he did it again and stormed past his sisters and he left the house, slamming the door on his way out.

"C'mon. Let's get that bleeding stopped."

Angel

"Roll over," Dare told me and I rolled to my belly. It was late and I'd fallen asleep waiting for him through an endless day of worrying about him. He'd carried me upstairs just like last night, just like most nights, and as usual, it was a wonderful way to wake up.

He pulled my yoga pants down and off. He took my socks off. Then he pulled my hoodie and tank top over my head, leaving me in a white bra and white lace thong. He made a deep *mm* sound that reverberated all through me, raising goosebumps.

His hand was on my ankle. He caressed it. Then his hand moved up to behind my knee. I felt his lips on my behind and he kissed upwards, slowly, kissing the small of my back, my spine, my shoulder, my neck. He swept my hair to one side and then said, "Up, on your knees. Cheek stays on the pillow."

I put my rear up in the air and then felt both of his hands on me, caressing up my legs toward my bottom and then grasping my hips.

"My beautiful angel," he said and I looked back at him in the lamplight of the room. He was still fully clothed in a suit and tie and looking at me with passion.

I smiled at him. "I love being yours. It feels like I was born to be yours."

His expression went heated, so heated. He leaned over and whispered, "You were." and then his lips touched mine and his tongue swept in.

One of his hands was kneading a breast and the other was gripping my ass. I was waiting, hoping. And then my hopes came true because the hand on my ass left it and then came back with a whack. I groaned right into his mouth. He whacked it again and I whimpered. Then his fingers dipped between my cheeks and down and then Dare found how wet I was. Dripping wet. I got flipped and then I was on my back and his fingers were between my legs, his mouth on a breast and he sucked deep while also pushing two fingers deep. I had goosebumps all over my body. I was panting. I wanted to touch him.

"May I touch you?"

"No. Lay on your back. Hands above your head. Hold the headboard."

I did. I lost his fingers. I lost his mouth, but then I caught sight of him undressing, taking off his button-up shirt, taking off his suit pants. He ran his fingers through his hair with both hands and then his warm strong hands were on my knees, lifting them up and opening my legs wide. His head descended right between my legs and his tongue hit the bullseye immediately. I let go of the headboard and grabbed his hair and moaned. His head lifted and he slapped my leg and then grabbed my face. "I said hold the headboard. Don't let go."

Holy fuck. Holy fuck, fuck, fuck. I was gonna come without him even touching me again.

I shuddered and grabbed the headboard.

"Naughty girl. Now you don't get my tongue. Now I get to fuck your mouth." I whimpered and he climbed up and got his knees under my armpits. Oh yes, I wanted it in my mouth. Bad.

"Oh, Dare. Please fuck my mouth."

"Oh, you want that?" He pumped his cock in a fist a few times and the tip touched my chin but then he moved back, just out of my reach.

"I do."

"Say please."

"Please, Dare."

"You're a naughty girl. You're my naughty girl."

"Yes, Dare. I'm your naughty girl. But I'll be a good girl. Please may I suck that beautiful cock?"

The second the word 'cock' left my mouth his cock entered it. I grabbed his hips with both hands

"No." He pulled out and slapped my breast. "Hold the headboard, Angel."

I was panting. I was soaking wet and I needed him soon or I'd combust.

I held the headboard and waited, panting like a bitch in heat.

He moved down and leaned over my face and got his mouth by my ear. "Be good and you can have it. But be naughty if you want more spanking, baby." He whispered this and I immediately let go of the headboard and scampered until I was at his crotch and I flipped him so that he fell onto his back and then I was straddling his face and had my face down at his crotch. I got his cock in my mouth and then I got his hand hard across my ass. I moaned. His other hand came down and he grabbed me by the hair and roughly pushed my head so that his cock went deeper. That hand stayed on the back of my head fisting my hair while the other slapped me right on the pussy. I started to tremble, hard.

He came down my throat and I came with his tongue inside of me, his mouth working by sucking my clit.

Wow. Amazing. Every day with my Master kept getting better and better.

***

The next morning, we were eating cheese omelets and his phone started again. He went outside with it for a while and came back in and told me he needed to take off for the day. He pinned me against the wall with his hips and said into my ear, "While I'm gone you be my good girl, okay?"

I nodded.

"But tonight, when I get back, I want your hair curly. And I want you to be naughty. All right, my baby? Very naughty."

"Okay," I whispered, feeling my nipples get hard at the words and at the look in his eyes. He kissed me deep and for a long time, and then he left.

Dave

I had to get back to where Tommy and the girls all were. Shit had hit the fan the night before and Tommy needed me. He, Lisa, and I were sitting down and having it out. Lisa had a meltdown and had gone off on Tommy, screamed about him killing Pop in front of the other girls, shattering a mirror, and Tommy said it'd been a nightmare. Tia had spewed the truth out to settle Lisa down and it did but Lisa hadn't spoken a word since.

What'd happened to the sweet girl? Was she having an Angel-style meltdown? Taken out of her carefully constructed world of pretending and after the miscarriage now she couldn't hack it? I threw her life into a tailspin, ripped her world apart by telling her we knew her secrets. And it made everything unravel for her. Poor thing. Poor thing, yeah, but we couldn't let her put our family in jeopardy, either. Tommy and I needed to do damage control.

As for my Angel, I was trying out a new method. Getting her to be naughty. I was keeping her obedient during the day and naughty when it was the two of us, using sex. When all the drama bullshit was over I'd opt for naughty more and more until eventually I just let her decide who she needed to be. If I did that and eased her out of the slave world but kept the Master card in my back pocket and saved it in case she had a meltdown it could work. I hoped it would. The night before had been fucking hot, her going crazy like that to get a spanking. I got hard while driving just thinking about it.

Gan Chen had his resources working hard to get Jason Frost in. I had a quandary there, though. If I analyzed all that I currently knew it could be that Frost simply wanted to save her from that slave life.

Could he be a good guy stuck in a bad situation? If he saw that she was okay with me would he be able to let go of the guilt of her getting pulled in to Kruna because of his failure to keep her safe?

If that's all that this was, I could conceivably get him off our backs. But then again, how would I do that without revealing my cards? If I revealed to Jason Frost that I wasn't Angel's Master but a guy who'd fallen for her and a guy that wanted out of the Kruna association, that could put Angel, me, and my family in danger with Kruna. It was a fucking conundrum, for sure.

Maybe I should just let Gan Chen catch him, do away with the guy. After all, he was connected to Kruna, the nephew of the sadistic prick who'd fucked her up for seven months and even if he was trying to save her now, he'd waited almost two years to do it so he couldn't be that concerned with her welfare.

But I could also look at it like this: I was Tom Ferrano's son. I shouldn't be persecuted because of my father any more than Jason Frost should be persecuted because of his uncle. Was letting Gan Chen and his guys catch him the best thing to do or if I did, would I accrue more bad karma? What to do?

***

When I got to Pop's place, I heard Tommy and Tia arguing in the kitchen.

"You didn't have to break his goddamn face! It's not like I was gonna leave with him. It's not like he's any real threat to our relationship, Tommy."

"No?" My brother's voice boomed. "The fucking guy is digging around in my family's business; he's trying to get you to fucking betray me. He disrespected me. He needed his face fucking smashed in. He's lucky he's not in the fucking ground!"

Tia's muffled voice grumbled. "No! Don't touch me right now. I'm not fucking happy with you."

"Don't tell me not to touch you. I'll touch you if I wanna fucking touch you," he growled. "I'll do whatever the fuck I wanna do to you."

I caught sight of Sarah and Tess in the family room, both with horrified looks on their faces. Sarah was holding baby Nicky.

I stepped into the kitchen.

"Hey guys. Chill. Ears out there."

Tommy had her pinned against the wall and his hand was on her throat. He let go of her. She was red-faced. She gave me a relieved look as she passed me. She stormed out of the kitchen. Tommy put a hand to his forehead and stared at the floor.

"Hey, man. Let's go talk," I said. "Let's talk first and then we'll talk to Lisa. She still in her room?"

"Yeah," he nodded and followed me out to the back yard. Luc was out there with the other kids. I motioned for her to take the kids inside.

***

He wasn't interested in talking to me about his fight with Tia at first but clearly, she was pissed about finding out Tommy'd been arrested for assaulting her ex-boyfriend. He'd only been in for a few hours as the charges had been dropped but Tia had found out. Between him being pissed with her for what'd happened with Lisa the day before and her being pissed with him about beating up the ex and getting arrested, plus the whole lockdown scenario and Lisa's state of mind things were heated. I talked to him about a few things businesswise and he seemed to plug into the discussion and put his beef with Tia aside.

Then, once he was a little calmer, we tried to talk to Lisa. She was little more than catatonic, though. I spoke gentle words, told her I was sorry about the baby, but that she needed to talk to us. She just stared off into space. I didn't have a good feeling about this. We had Dex stay in the room with her, telling him to restrain her if she tried to leave or hurt herself and to keep phones and computers away from her.

After we left Lisa, Tommy told me that he was discussing the Nick Gordon thing with Zack outside when Tia'd overheard him through an opened window. Although the charges had been dropped the cops tried to make Tommy's life miserable and not before some cop who was evidently unsatisfied about how the Pop case was handled tried to quiz him about Pop's murder. It hadn't been a good day for Tommy. Then he came back to the house to Lisa freaking out and calling him out about Pop's death right in front of our sisters and Tia.

My brother said he just needed some space and to spend time with a heavy bag. He also said he was gonna hole up in a bedroom later on and get on Skype with his counselor as it was time for his weekly appointment anyway. I figured that was good timing.

I got back late and without any word from Gan Chen about Jason Frost. Zack was digging deep and told me he was getting some good info and would update me in the morning with where things were at.

So I drove back to the cabin and got there as Nino and Luke were swapping out with two other guys for the night shift to keep watch.

***

"Are you hungry?" she asked me after I kissed her hello.

"Yeah, I didn't get a chance to eat."

"I just made a clubhouse sandwich. I can whip you up one if you want?"

"Sure." I sat on the sofa and checked my emails on my phone. Then I jerked my chin up at her and said, "Your hair? Why is it straight?"

She smiled seductively at me and my pants tightened at the promise of that smile. That smile was very much like her driver's license photo.

"Maybe I should be punished for not following your directions. Over your knee, maybe?"

A smile spread wide on my face.

"Oh, you will be. You make me that sandwich and then you go get a bath and bring those curls back. Then you and me are gonna have a little chat about you following my instructions."

She chewed her bottom lip and then whispered, "Yes, Master."

Mm. *Oh yeah.*

Angel

I made him a sandwich and then took a bath and got my hair wet and shaved my legs, underarms, and my hoo-ha and I did all of this as fast as possible because I was very anxious to have our little 'chat'.

The whole time I flat-ironed it that day felt like foreplay because that was about all I could think to do that'd be considered *naughty*. I couldn't backtalk or anything super-naughty. It just wasn't in me. Every pull through of that iron got me thinking about getting dominated by him. He was always dominant when we were having sex but the few times we'd really played, I'd been lit on fire.

When I got out of the bath and was in the bedroom getting dressed, I heard him turn the shower on. I dropped my towel and reached into our bag to get out some undies and then felt his presence at my back. He had my hips.

"You, my naughty Angel, no clothes. Wait on the floor bent over on your knees for your punishment." He slapped my ass hard and I groaned. Then he went into the bathroom and shut the door.

It took forever for the shower to turn off. I was on all fours on the carpet waiting for him. My hair was still dripping as I'd been so excited that I had dropped to the floor immediately after getting his directions before even finishing getting dried off.

I heard his footsteps and then I heard,

"This is how I like my baby." I felt his hand go flat against the small of my back and he gently caressed up to my head and then he had my hair. I felt the head of his cock tease my entrance, felt his pelvis against my backside. My nails dug into the thick carpet and I took a deep breath. On the exhale, he entered me hard and fast. A ringing slap landed on my backside, making me groan. After a few strokes of his beautiful cock inside of me he backed away, took my hand and went toward the bed. He sat and hauled me across his lap.

"You naughty?"

"Yes, Dare."

"You need a spanking?"

"Yes, Dare."

"Your ass is beautiful, my baby."

"Thank you. It's all yours, Master."

"Mm. Are you ready for a spanking, my naughty girl?"

"Oh yeah."

"How naughty were you?"

"About ten slaps, Master."

He hesitated.

"I can take it. I want it," I whispered.

Then he slapped my ass.

It burned. It burned so good.

Then he stroked my stinging cheek gently for a second, like he was trying to make it feel better. Then he hauled off and slapped again, on the other cheek. I groaned pretty loudly, fisting the quilt at the foot of the bed with my right hand and grabbing his ankle with my left hand.

He slapped again and I moaned. Then he did it again and I felt like I was going to climax because then he dipped his fingers between my cheeks and rubbed my slippery seam for just a second. It was as if I was boneless. My pussy was throbbing. I ran my hand up and down his leg.

"Thank you, Master…"

He slapped again and then I was being pulled up onto the bed and flipped onto my back, his body covering mine. "That's enough." He caressed my face and I nodded, euphoric. He kissed my lips softly and then he was inside of me, being gentle, fucking me slowly while kissing my mouth, looking at me like he owned me.

I started to weep; it was that beautiful. I put my hands on his face. He kissed my wrist. Then he took and then held my wrists above my head and picked up the pace, rotating his hips in big circles so that he was hitting my clit at each rotation. I came hard, shuddering loud, so loud I'm sure the guards outside would've heard and then he came inside me, collapsing on me. I felt his heart racing, I felt up his back and there were goosebumps all over him. I kissed his throat.

He stayed still. He stopped breathing heavy. His body went tense. He backed up and gave me a small smile as he exited the bed with, "Be right back." He leaned over and kissed my lips softly before he left the room.

I covered up and turned onto my side. He seemed conflicted. He hadn't hit me ten times. It'd only been half that. Was he too excited to go that far or was it actually a turn-off?

Dare

I sat out back, away from the two guards, and I smoked a cigarette. I felt tormented. I had almost slapped her face, in the moment of passion remembering Chen's words and thinking that she'd like it but I couldn't fucking do it. I couldn't slap her face. I liked the submissiveness, the trust; it was hot. I liked the spanking, too, especially liked how she responded to it. But right now, I was feeling a little gross because some of what we'd done made me think about her being abused. I never wanted her to know that I felt this. I didn't want her to remember any of the abuse, didn't want her to associate anything she and I did together with anything she'd done with anyone else.

When I got off on slapping her it flashed that someone else doing the same would mean her coming hard, not fighting it. Then I'd feel like I was sick in the head for getting off on it. I wanted to give her what she needed but I also wanted her whole. I wanted her to be mine. But I didn't want her to stay in that place where she got off on pain. If I did what the sick fucks who hurt her did to her and she got off on it, what did that make me? How was taking their advice on how to get her off from a founding partner of the place that also fucked her, who probably helped or gave orders to fucking break her gonna help either of us? I wish I'd never read that report and that Chen had never said those things to me. Things were pretty fuckin' screwed up in my head.

I went back to bed and she was asleep. I pulled her to me and held her tight. It took me a long time to crash. There was a shitload of crap in my life right now and part of me wanted to say Fuck It and take her and just fuck off somewhere away from all of it.

Part of me thought about just taking off alone and asking my brother to watch out for her until we could fake her death. Maybe I should take off and try to forget her. Let her find her way to being healthy. Away from organized crime. Abuse. Filth. Despite telling myself that though, I didn't let go of her. I fell asleep holding onto her for dear life.

***

In the morning when I opened my eyes, she was beside me, watching me sleep.

"Mornin'," I greeted.

"Hi." she smiled.

"Would you mind goin' down and making us some coffee, baby?" I stretched.

"If I refuse, would you spank me again?" She gave me a mischievous look and my face split into a grin.

"Do you want another spanking?" I asked.

"Maaaay-be." She drawled, snuggling in and then gave me another smile.

"How about you make me coffee and I'll reward you for doing it instead of punishing you for not doing it?"

"Okay. Can I get an advance?"

I rolled her and got on top and she wrapped her legs around my waist. I grabbed a handful of her hair, loving the curls and loving the gorgeous smile on her sleepy face. "You're beautiful." I said.

"You're beautiful," she returned.

"You're mine." I slid my cock inside her. Who'd I been trying to kid last night? There was no way I'd give her up. Broken, not broken, she was mine.

"You're mine," she said fiercely, and her eyes were full of fire when she said that, which stoked my fire real good. I grabbed her tight and held on while I gave her that advance on the coffee. That advance was a good one and it was a good thing, too, because it'd have to last me a while.

***

Hours later I was getting antsy. I didn't like that Chen hadn't caught Jason Frost yet.

Tommy was getting his counselor to fly in from the UK for Lisa because she hadn't budged yet. He said things were tense with him and Tia, that they weren't really speaking to one another and he admitted to me that he felt like he was unraveling. Add to that the fact that my phone was ringing off the hook with work shit, shit that I'd been neglecting because of all the drama I'd been entrenched in.

I was in and out of the cabin on the phone, texting, and trying to deal with a dozen things at once. I was in a bad fucking mood.

As I headed out the door with a new pack of smokes, I heard Angel say, "Maybe you shouldn't smoke so much."

"Yeah and maybe it was better when you asked permission before you spoke," I snapped.

Her expression dropped, her shoulders sagged, and I wished I could snatch it back. "Angel, I'm sorry. I'm so sorry. I didn't mean it." I rushed to her and pulled her tight against me. "Forgive me?"

She shook her head a little. "No, Sir." She said it with pain rather than venom.

My heart hit my gut. I deserved that. I deserved the 'Sir' because I'd just treated her like they treated her. I scooped her up, took her upstairs, and lay her down in bed, climbing in beside her. I caressed her face. "Too much goin' on. Bad fucking mood today. I'm so sorry. I'll never say anything like that again. Ever. Promise. So sorry, baby."

Her eyes were cold. But she didn't pull away. It killed me that she would never pull away from me even if she wanted to, but like a selfish prick I took advantage of that sad fact and held her close to me.

"You're allowed to be mad at me," I whispered. "Go ahead, pull away. Call me a fucking bastard. Smack me in the face."

She stared at the ceiling, hugging herself while I held her.

"If I told you to spread your legs for me right now, you'd do it, wouldn't you?" I growled in her ear, "You'd do it despite the fact that I just cut you deep with my words. You'd do it and you'd get wet for me, wouldn't you?"

Her lower lip trembled.

"Baby, you have every right to be pissed at me. You have every right to call me out on my shit. I need someone to do that, you know? Call me out when I'm being a prick. Tell me to fucking cool it. I need that."

She choked on a sob but held it in, best as she could.

"You are supposed to be everything I need, Angel, and I need that. I need you to be real with me. I need you to dig deep and find the girl you used to be and show her to me. I am crazy about all of what I've had from you so far. You're in here." I thumped on my chest with a fist. "I want the rest of you, too."

"Can you please leave me alone for a while, Dare?"

That was a start. It wasn't yelling and screaming and pounding her fists on my chest out of anger, frustration, and pain, but it was a start.

"Sure." I let go of her and kissed her forehead. "Again, I'm sorry. I really mean that."

She shook her head at me, pain in her eyes. As I left the room, I called back, "I will do my best to keep giving you what you need. I need you to give me what I need, too, baby. This relationship needs to go both ways."

I stepped outside but didn't light the cigarette. I grabbed a long stick from a brush pile and a hunting knife from the nearby toolshed and started to whittle it. It was a skill my Icelandic grandfather taught me. It'd been a while but years ago it'd always been something that relaxed me. Maybe taking it up again would help me quit smoking. She was right. I'd been smoking a pack and a half a day the last few days and I was wheezing.

I sat for a while outside and whittled and then when I went back in I found her reading a magazine up in the bedroom. She didn't look at me but I felt her go tense when I stopped at the foot of the bed, about to talk to her.

My phone rang. It was Zack.

"You ready for this?" is how he greeted me.

"Yeah man." I sat and braced.

"Gan Chen is in the hospital. Multiple gunshot wounds. Not sure if he'll survive. His body guards are dead. You out there in the woods with just two guards, I don't think it's a good idea. Your father's house might be better. You should probably try to get there. You're too vulnerable."

"Fuck. Fuck fuck fuck!" I winced. I looked at her. She looked alarmed.

"I think you need all the info I have, man."

"Yeah?"

"Yeah."

"Lay it on me." I left the room, heading down the stairs and out the back deck.

"All right. Your girl's mother's name is Felicia Mooney, father's name David Macleod. Sister, Holly Mooney. You want your girl's name or you still waiting for her to tell you. If you come in contact with Frost there's a chance he'll use her name, anyway."

"Fuck." I didn't know what to do but made a snap decision, "Lay it on me."

"All right, her name's Angie Macleod. She was born in South Carolina but at 13 she moved to Juneau to live with her mother after her father died in a work accident. Mother had Holly by another guy. Angie's father had custody of her from age 4 but the mother got custody after he died."

"Angie Macleod?" I whispered, in complete shock.

"Yeah."

"Angie?" I repeated.

"Yeah. Angelica Elizabeth Macleod."

"Angelica?"

"Yep."

Holy fuck.

"Angie graduated high school early. Smart girl. Mother's a raging alcoholic and pill popper, still in Juneau. Before your girl left for her teaching job she arranged for the sister to live with the paternal grandmother because the mother was abusive. Angie practically raised the sister. But…oh shit, we just got a lead on where Jason is. I'll call you back." He disconnected.

I took a minute staring out at the woods beyond the deck. I heard noise in the house so I stepped in. She was at the sink filling the tea kettle.

"Angie," I said. She spun around and it took a second to penetrate. When it did, her eyes were wide. Her mouth dropped open.

"Yeah, I know," I said. "We need to talk. There are some things going on. Gan Chen and a few of his people are here to try to catch Jason because Jason wanted to buy you and got pissed when he found out you were sold to me. But Gan got shot. He's in the hospital. Zack told me your name because---"

Her hand clapped over her mouth and she started to tremble, so I stopped talking, got to her, got my arms around her, and she shrieked, ducking to get under my arms and away and then she ran around to the other side of the table.

She pointed at me. "N-no. No. Stay back. I have to go save her."

I stopped and put my hands up, "Baby, listen…"

She backed up until her back was to the door and then her hand went to the doorknob.

Fuck, for some reason she was having a meltdown. But, worse.

"We have to talk, Angel. I know some of your story. I need the rest."

"Oh God!" A sob tore out of her mouth. She turned the knob.

"Don't, baby. Come here."

She sprinted out, making a run for it. She ran toward the woods.

Fuck! I started running for her. Then I heard a gunshot. It whizzed by me. What the fuck? I heard another shot. Angel was down. I dropped to the ground. I saw movement from the corner of my eye. He was on the other side of my car. Where the fuck were the security guards? Thank God I was still packing; I fired my gun and clipped him on the shoulder. I ran for him and he shot but missed me. I shot again and the bullet hit him in the face. He dropped. I ran and then I was standing over him. He was Asian. He was dead. I shot him again to be sure. Then I ran for her, watching in case there was anyone else. She was lying on her stomach on the grass.

"I guess your angel is getting her wings," she said when I leaned over and examined her. She was shot in the calf. She'd be okay.

"Not yet you aren't, let's go." I carefully lifted her up and carried her to my Explorer. She passed out.

CHAPTER ELEVEN

Angel

I woke up in the hospital. I was on an exam table and they were telling Dare they were going to take me into surgery to get the bullet out but that I would be okay.

The nurse and doctor started to talk to me, noticing I was awake and I started to feel the blood thundering in my ears, the panic setting in. He was sitting beside me. He had my hand in his and he gave me a look, a look that snapped me into behaved slave mode. But it felt like I was splitting in two. Slave girl and scared girl who needed to fucking save her sister from the fiery pits of hell.

The nurse and doctor left the exam room and Dare said, "Hey."

My eyes widened and I started to feel the panic rise.

"No. Chill out," he leaned over me, seizing my wrists, "You can't freak out, baby. You freak out and they put you in the psych ward. Chill the fuck out."

"I gotta go, I gotta go. Holly. Holly."

I realized my throat was naked and I started hyperventilating.

"It's gone. It's gone. My collar; oh my God!"

"Baby!" His voice got very stern. "Chill out now before things go really fucking wrong."

Dare

They'd taken her collar and other jewelry off in prep for surgery to remove the bullet, but I had it all in my pocket. She was freaking the fuck out and if I didn't get her chilled out, they'd notice her behavior and undoubtedly commit her. I did what I had to do then so that I could keep her settled. I couldn't hold her down and rub it out here in the hospital room, so I got my mouth against her ear.

"Angel, do you hear me? This is your fucking Master telling you to calm. The fuck. Down. Now."

Angel

I froze.

"Deep breaths," he ordered. He grabbed my hands and held them over my head.

I took a slow and deep breath. And then another.

"Again. Keep doing it. Keep breathing."

I complied.

"I didn't want to keep going backwards, baby, don't want to keep taking you back to what you used to be, but if that's what it takes to calm you the fuck down right now, so be it. I'm your Master and you fucking behave and do every single thing I tell you to do. Got me?"

He transferred my wrists to one hand and then his other hand cupped me between the legs.

"Be a good girl," he commanded and exerted pressure with his middle two fingers against me for a second and my body went lax. "I can't give you what you need right now but be good and you'll get it soon."

I stayed still, willing myself to breathe another breath. And then another. And then another.

A few minutes passed and he let go of between my legs but he kept hold of my wrists, both crossed above my head and braced under his other palm.

We heard someone coming in so he let me go but gave me a warning look. It was time for surgery.

Dare

All we needed was for her to have some freak out in the hospital and them commit her. Then if other Kruna scumbags got wind of it she'd be in serious danger, meaning we all would be as I would not hesitate to go Rambo on them if they so much as messed up a single curl on her beautiful head again.

The two security guys at Eddy and Luc's cabin had been gunned down and one was dead. The other we got in to the hospital. Of the gunmen, I killed one but the second gunman had been injured, not killed, by the security guard that had died and as I drove us to the hospital, I'd called Nino, who was already on his way. He'd gotten there, got the injured guy into the toolshed and then got his brother there. Nino and Tino got creative and then got the guy talking and the guy sang like a canary.

Jason Frost was now in our custody. Tino, Nino, and a few of our guys got to his location and they got him to Tommy's farm, locked him in one of the stalls in the horse barn. I hadn't talked back to Zack yet but had texted him that Angel had been shot in the leg and that we were at the hospital, that we had Frost in custody.

He replied with an "Okay. I'll call you soon."

Tommy's counselor was due to arrive that day and would be staying at the house with the girls and was reportedly going to be working with Lisa. I texted Zack to send people to Alaska to scope out Angel's family situation. Gan Chen was in critical condition but had made it out of surgery.

Angel

I was awake. The bullet was gone from my leg and there was a big bandage. Dare barely left my side and though he didn't say much he had a fuming angry demeanor that kept me on high alert, kept me quiet, and kept me in slave mode, behaving myself.

A full day had passed since my surgery and he'd only ever stepped out of the room for about an hour, the longest he'd been away from me since I got shot, and while he was gone Tommy had sat in the room with me, watching me with a cold 'don't you dare try anything' look on his face.

Dare came back. Tommy stayed in the room but leaned against the door.

"You good?" Dare sat on the edge of the hospital bed.

I stared wide-eyed.

"I'm telling you, baby, I need you to listen and stay calm. Be a good girl. Got me?"

I nodded.

"I'm getting you out of here today and taking you to my brother's farm for a few days so you can recuperate. When we get there, I'm going to update you on where things are at. In order for me to do that you need to listen and you need to behave so they'll let you out of here. Got me?"

I nodded.

"Answer me."

"Okay."

"No, answer me properly."

A tingle worked its way from my scalp to my nipples and then straight between my legs, "Yes, Master."

"Good girl."

From the corner of my eye I saw Dare's brother shift uncomfortably from foot to foot and blow out a slow breath.

***

We were at his brother's farmhouse. I was in a double bed upstairs in the spare room. There was nothing else in the room. After a brief chat with the doctor where Dare did most of the talking. He got me here and carried me upstairs and put me to bed, slept beside me, holding me close, and now it was the next day. I was awake, eating toast with PB & J in triangles that Dare had made me and I was drinking coffee. Then he started to talk to me.

"You okay?"

"Yes…" I hesitated. I didn't know whether to call him Master or not.

He squeezed my hand reassuringly. "I'm sorry that I had to take you back to that time like that in there, Angel, but I couldn't let you freak out like that in front of the doctors and nurses."

"I know." I wasn't angry. It'd given me a sense of calm and I didn't want to delve too deep into that but frankly, it was a sense of calm I could use right now. I just did what I needed to and let him worry about everything else. It was easy. I wanted it now because I had a feeling that whatever he was about to say would be big. I didn't want to ask for it, though. It was time to put on my big girl pants.

He started talking.

"Hold it together now, 'cuz this is big. You good?"

"I'm good."

"Jason Frost was responsible for that. He tried to have me killed."

I jolted but held myself together.

"No one is after your sister. Everyone is all on the same side right now and while that means me and my brother are on the same side as the bad guys, me and my guys apprehended Jason and took down his snipers. That sniper only meant to injure you. Frost wanted me dead, you delivered. He had login details for your tracker, which is how he found out you left Thailand. And how he found you here. He tried to kill Gan Chen. Chen is in the hospital recovering from multiple gunshot wounds. He's gonna live.

I've now got Frost in a holding area. You wanna talk to him you can. You can think on that. He tried to buy you a number of times after his uncle died. He found out that you were recently sold and quietly lost his shit and began plotting so he could get his hands on you. He hired someone to take me out and deliver you. I took down the assassin. We caught another gunman and had him interrogated, which led to finding Frost. We haven't interrogated him yet. I haven't gone there yet. Before I proceed, I need answers. I need all the answers, baby."

"He proposed to me. He…he…" I started to panic.

"Chill out, baby. I've got you."

I scampered off the bed onto my knees, a little too hard for the sake of my leg wound, but I ignored the pain and wrapped myself around his leg. He started to stroke my hair and shh'd me. Like this, at his feet, his hand on me, now I felt like he had me.

"I need a collar," I whispered and his hand went into his pocket and he pulled out a box, "You're not getting that blue collar back. I refuse to put it back on your throat. What about this necklace. Will it do?"

I glanced at it as he circled my throat with it. It was a thick silver choker with a heart pendant with a keyhole.

"It's beautiful," I whispered, "Thank you. But it's not right."

"Why?"

"It needs three strands. One means I'm available. Two means I'm booked to a patron or party. Three means I'm owned."

He reached into his pocket and pulled out two more necklace boxes and put them on me. One was a flat choker necklace with a bow pendant and the other was a longer necklace with charms, like a charm bracelet. It had a little horseshoe pendant, a tiny angel, and a little duck. He stroked my hair, playing with my curls, "We'll figure something out. These okay for now?"

I leaned into his leg, "Yes. Thank you." God he was sweet.

After a minute of more hair stroking, he continued.

"He can't hurt you; he's locked down. I had my liaison Stan tell the other *powers that be* about Chen's injuries and that we have Frost. Chen said before that Frost and you have history and he suspected Frost was making a move so he came to meet with me. You need to fill me in, Angel. I need your story. I know you've been through a lot but I need details and I need them now so that I can figure out what to do to keep us safe. At this point the Kruna big wigs still think of Tommy and I as friends. That has to stay that way for now."

"Dare, I… it's so..."

"Please, baby. I need details. I need them now. I know it's probably gonna break you to talk about this shit, Angel, but I'm here. I won't let anything happen. You need to enlighten me so that I can deal with this shit. Give it all to me. Let me take care of you. I've got you. You break and I'll help you get back together, okay my baby? It's okay to break. I'm here. Trust me to look after you."

He leaned down and took my hand and got me to my feet. He kissed my forehead. "C'mon, let's get into bed."

He held me close. I slithered down to his belly and planted my cheek on it and stared up at him. He had such a gentle and caring look on his face. It was hitting me straight in the soul. He tucked my hair behind my ear and jerked his chin up, urging me to start. It took me a minute but I found my voice.

"I do trust you. I do."

"Okay, baby. Go." He jerked his chin up.

"I was having fun in Thailand. Teaching, hanging out with other teachers, some other expats my age. We hung out in this nightclub and a lot of Americans, Canadians, and Brits went there. That's where I met Jason. He managed the club. He was handsome. He liked me. We started to date. He wanted to get serious like really fast. It freaked me out but we were having fun so I kept trying to keep it light. He was more serious than I was, though. This Thai woman who was the cleaning lady for the nightclub pulled me aside one day. She was always giving me weird looks and stuff and then one day Jason and I fell asleep in the office after the club closed. That's the night he proposed. I laughed it off, thinking he was just drunk, and then he got emotional about it. I calmed him down with sex and we fell asleep.

Anyway, the next morning he was in a mood because I hadn't accepted and said he had to run an errand so I went to leave to go back to my place and the cleaning lady warned me. She told me that Jason's family was involved in slavery and that I should steer clear. She begged me not to out her. They didn't know she spoke English so spoke freely enough around her to tip her off, I guess. She said she thought I was a nice girl and didn't want to see me tied to that. So I tried to back off from Jase and then he proposed to me again, sensing I was pulling away. He was really desperate the second time. It was creepy. He was talking in riddles and saying things to the effect of that I'd be sorry if I didn't pick him because that'd change everything.

It started to freak me out so I was gonna quit my job and get out of Thailand. I told no one. They must've been watching me because I got flagged at the airport, put in this little room, and the next thing I know I'm in that little room with Jase and his uncle, who I hadn't met yet. They were trying to play things carefully with me, see what I knew.

I told them I had an emergency back home and was just flying back temporarily and they didn't buy it. The woman who warned me was brought in and I knew that they'd figured out she'd told me. Mr. Frost left me alone in the room with Jason and Jase tried to sweet-talk me. Obviously, they weren't convinced that I didn't know anything so then his uncle took over and told Jason I was off limits, that they had to pull me in. Jase freaked and grabbed the gun from a guard and shot the woman in the head who told me. Right in front of me. He pointed the gun to his uncle and his uncle talked him down but then overpowered him and pistol whipped him until he was knocked out and then took me. I tried not to break. I used to be so strong, but then they showed me---"

I was shaking. He pulled me up by the armpits so I was beside him and tight against him. I couldn't see his face for the last part because I was right against his chest.

"They had Holly. My 15-year-old sister, Dare. They fucking had her bound and gagged on a plane and were threatening to bring her to Thailand. That's when the name I was born with, that person, she ceased to exist. That's when I became Felicia. I had to be Felicia so she wouldn't have to be. Please don't make me tell you the rest. Please. Mr. Frost kept me to teach Jason a lesson and I didn't think Jase was all that dangerous. I thought he… he…"

"Okay, baby. That's enough for now." He stroked my back. I was trembling hard.

"They're gonna get Holly if they find out I'm not behaving, Dare. Please…please. When you said Jason was here and Mr. Chen and you called me that name, I thought they'd think I told you and that'd mean I wasn't behaving and they were gonna gonna g-get her, take me… I never want to run from you, I want to be yours forever, but I thought… I don't know what I was thinking. Maybe I ran thinking I had to get to her first. They said if I ever uttered that other name outloud again that Holly would be theirs. Somehow, they knew I hated my mother so they made me take her name. You started calling me Angel and at first I thought you knew who I really was and then I realized that's who I was to you, an angel, and Dare, that's who I want to be. It's me but a version of me, the me before Alaska, before all the ugliness, before Kruna. Daddy called me Angel. Oh God, I miss him. It was like you saw who I really was under all that ugly dirty ugly dirty…if they find out…oh god…"

"Shh, they won't. It's okay. I won't let them. Breathe, baby, breathe."

"Dare, please don't let them. Don't let them take me. You take me. Keep me. My head is so…I need, I need…"

My words were all screwy.

He didn't make me keep begging. He didn't wait until I made sense because he knew what I needed. One of his hands slid into my pajamas and then into my panties and then I threw my hands over my head and he pinned them with his other hand. I tested by lifting and his grip tightened. "Don't move. Be a good girl, Angel."

I whimpered.

"Isn't this good, baby?" he asked a few moments later, continuing to rub me.

I was having trouble letting go and he obviously knew it.

"What do you need, my baby?"

"I need your cock, Master. In my mouth. Rough. Make me. Make me do it."

He let go of my wrists, grabbed my hair, and roughly pulled my head down toward his crotch. I flipped onto my side so that my crotch was up near his head and one of his hands was fisted in my hair and the other went to my pants and hit the spot instantly.

Yes.

This.

"Suck it good, baby. Be my good girl."

Fuck yes.

I got his pants undone and couldn't get my tongue to the head of his cock fast enough. I whimpered again, feeling sensation build as he fucked my mouth, pumping forward into me. He had his thumb on my clit and at least two fingers inside me and I was about to combust.

His phone rang.

His hips and his fingers stilled and I stopped bobbing.

"No, ignore it. We're almost there, baby. You're such a good girl."

I tried to find it.

His phone stopped ringing and instantly started ringing again.

"Fuck," he grunted and pulled away.

He reached for the phone from the nightstand.

"Bro? Right. Yep. Okay, two hours. Right." He hung up and looked at me.

"I need to go to the office for a conference call with Chen's partners."

"If they find out you're not and I'm... if they do, they…" My words were screwy again.

"But you're behaving, baby. You're my perfect Angel. There's nothing to be afraid of, okay? Nothing? I own you. You're mine. You've done everything right. You're allowed to tell me everything. I mean that. You're mine, not theirs. So you can tell me everything because you're my girl. My good girl. Forget them. You're not theirs. You're mine. They don't matter."

Oh my god. He was it. He was it for me. I felt a surge of emotion and peace rush within me and wash over me.

He reached for me again. "Let's get you that release, Angel-baby. I could use one, too."

God, I loved him.

As I came, I couldn't stop the words "I love you" from tumbling out. I said, "I love you, Dare," and then I closed my eyes and drifted to sleep. He was against me, holding me. He didn't reply. But that didn't matter. I just needed him to know. He held me a while and then I felt him tuck me in and tell me he'd be back later.

Dare

Does she love me? She's so fucked up right now. She's regressed so deep into her slave behavior and she's so fucking fragile that I need to handle her with care. I don't know what more I need to know from her in order to move forward but she's given me enough for me to go into this meeting.

After I was sure she was asleep, I moved carefully out of the bedroom and headed downstairs. I phoned Tommy and asked if he could have someone bring Tia to come hang for a few hours with her so that if I was a while, she'd have someone to talk to besides security. If Lisa hadn't fallen apart it'd be better if it were her but Lisa wasn't an option right now.

When I got to the office, my brother arrived and then we headed to the board room to put on our game faces and talk to the Kruna scumbags. I had the phone call recorded.

Angel

I dreamt about Thailand, about the time before Kruna.

Jason was tall, dark, and handsome. He was rich and charming and obsessed with me. He was a devil in disguise. He liked the power of running the bar and his powerful uncle at his back. But I didn't think he was a bad guy. It was like he'd snapped, been pushed when he got aggressive about me marrying him. Like he was stressed to the limit. And when he shot the cleaning lady? It threw me. For all this time, I hadn't allowed myself to think deeper on it. I think he was a little bit of a spoiled rich kid caught up in things. And he tried to stop them from taking me in, but they thought I knew too much. And because of that they punished him by making him watch them work at breaking me that first day. Jason cried that day. I saw him crying.

And then his uncle repeatedly brought him in to watch while I was abused.

I dreamt about the few dates we had, the laughs we had. And then I woke up. I stayed in bed.

I thought back to when he proposed to me and wondered if I'd just said yes if he could've protected me from what'd happened over the next two years. But if he'd done that and I'd somehow managed to stay in the dark about the existence of Kruna, my life would've been a lie. I'd have been married to a liar. And I'd never have met and fallen in love with Dario Ferrano.

I let my mind wander even farther backwards for the first time in a long time.

Two Years Ago

"Angie! There's mail for you!"

My little sister Holly thrust the envelope at me, saying,

"It's thick. It's gotta be a yes!"

My application to teach in Thailand had been accepted. I was stoked! I was leaving in two weeks. I'd arranged for Holly to move in with her grandmother in Anchorage a week later and I was getting the heck out of Alaska.

I met up with some of my friends at a bar that night and we toasted my journey. When I got home, I was a little tipsy, but I'd taken a cab. No harm; no foul. My mother, though, she was not impressed.

"So, you're leavin' now and you think you can break all the rules, huh?" she sneered at me, clearly way drunker than I was.

"I decided you can go now," she mumbled, staggering to the sink to put her glass in. "I started packing for you."

She wandered away, bouncing off walls all the way to the staircase in her threadbare cotton nightgown. I flipped her the double bird behind her back, took a deep breath, and walked into my bedroom, which was off the kitchen.

Everything from my closet and from my drawers was piled on my bed. Every drawer in my nine-drawer dresser was open and empty. Books, clothes, shoes, papers, all on the bed. Posters from the wall ripped off and thrown on top. Curtains from the window? One half hanging by one remaining hook, the other on top of my bed.

I texted my best friend Laurie. "Can I crash at your pad tonight? She is off the charts."

She replied straight away. "Come! Slumber party. Yay!"

I snuck quietly upstairs to Holly's room and shook her gently," Holl, c'mon. We're sleeping at Laurie's." I had to get my sister to come with me. If Mom came back out, something she often did before finally passing out, and couldn't find me, she'd start on Holly. The only reason I hadn't moved out already was because of Holly. She was 15. She was from Mom's second marriage and I hadn't met her until I moved here when my dad died, but she was the reason I stayed. I bought groceries, helped her with her homework, and she and I did our best to stay out of Mom's way. Her grandmother promised that Holly could live there with her when I went to Thailand and said she could stay there until I finished my teaching contract. After that was up, we'd go and move to the farm my dad had left me down in Charleston. The farm was being looked after and it was all organized.

I suppressed the urge to go to Mom's room and scream in her face. I suppressed the urge to scream at the top of my lungs at how awful of a mother she was. I just got an overnight bag together and me and Holly took off to walk to Laurie's studio apartment about five blocks away where we could crash on her pullout sofa bed.

The next day, I went home first to see what was what, and Mom had trashed my room further as well as trashed Holly's room. So I got my stuff packed and packed up my car with my sister's things, leaving Holly at Laurie's so she wouldn't have to deal with the arguments and then I drove her to her Gran's early. Mom didn't care. She said, "Good riddance to bad rubbish!" as I left.

Holly's gran put in an application with CPS to be on the safe side and I gave them a statement before I left for Thailand hoping it'd mean that Mom wouldn't get her back. Holly and I promised to Skype every night.

I almost didn't go before knowing if the CPS stuff was sorted, but she encouraged me to live out my dreams. She and her gran assured me all would be well.

***

Thailand was a blast at first. I had enough English-speaking people around, lots of spare time, and had loads of laughs. And Jason and I had fun. Great sex, nothing deep or meaningful, but fun. He liked to party. He had a big dick and he knew how to use it just the way I liked it. Rough. He said he loved my spirit. We laughed a lot. It was great. But then it all went wrong. It all went horribly wrong when he shifted from fun, on a dime, to suddenly way too serious about commitments we were too young (and too new) to make.

When he'd asked me to marry him the first time, I told him I was too young to get married but that I was having a blast with him. He got all sensitive with me and told me he wanted more than to have fun with me. He said he wanted to own me. I thought it was just a macho possessive thing at first and things got too heavy so I lightened the mood by giving him a blowjob and then we smoked a huge blunt together and passed out on the couch in his office. When I woke up the next morning the gift bag containing the engagement ring, I'd already rejected was beside me. When the cleaning lady told me about Kruna, that bag was still in sight.

After I got pulled aside in the airport, I got taken to Kruna, a beautiful 3-storey lavish resort that looked like paradise but that was hell on earth. And that's when I endured the first 19 days of torture. On the night of day 19 I was moved to Donavan Frost's quarters. Mr. Frost took me as his own personal sex slave for the first several months. He did this to punish Jason for the fact that the cleaning lady had warned me, that she'd learned so much because he was careless.

At first, he had Jason there often. At first, after I was broken, he made Jason watch us have sex while a guard held a gun to Jason's head. I never looked Jason in the eye after he'd shot the cleaning lady but felt his eyes on us when his uncle was punishing him and I felt his hatred focus on his uncle.

Mr. Frost was horrible. He was handsome and charming, looked a lot like his nephew, and he was pure evil. Pure. Evil.

He couldn't ejaculate unless he was hurting you and he ejaculated a lot while I was his slave. He died one night in his sleep, mysteriously. I'd been in the bed beside him, naked and bound to the headboard, and knew he was dead for over 24 hours before anyone came for us, which was something that I'd tried to push out of my mind ever since. Being chained in bed beside a corpse whose mouth was open and whose opened eyes were bleeding for all that time, a corpse who spent 7 months torturing you after you were already broken, it can fuck a girl up.

After that, I was put into the Kruna equivalent of a psych ward, put through some training, and then put with general population slaves and that's where I first heard the legend of Monalisa. I listened to a conversation between a few girls one day where they talked about her. She'd been a slave who everyone loved. Everyone. And she got sold and became a wife to a handsome American businessman who never brought her back and who never came back. I went on a mission to get what she got. I went on a mission through following my A to B plan over and over so I could get sold, point C. Jason didn't come back after Mr. Frost died. I didn't know what happened to him.

Tommy

I watched my brother's expression turn ugly as he listened to the guy talking on the loud speaker.

"Donavan's scout spotted her and wanted to bring her in. Jason tried to stop it by revving up their relationship and trying to get her to marry him.

Things went wrong, she found out too much, and we had to bring her in. Frost taught his nephew a lesson by making your girl his, by using her roughly in front of Jason. We were concerned. It was brewing hostility that didn't need to happen. A decision was made and we were looking at a number of options with respect to Donavan Frost as he was a problem for a number of reasons. Before we had a chance to act on our decision someone beat us to it. They had him poisoned. It was definitely an inside job and we suspected but couldn't prove Jason had paid the person who did it. Unfortunately, your Felicia got caught in the crossfire. She was with him when he died and she was in a precarious position. It was about 24 hours she was alone with his corpse, restrained in the bed beside him.

We didn't know if we'd bring her out of that. She was traumatized. Her trauma was from a combination of being Frost's full-time slave for several months and that. He was very dark.

Surprisingly, she did come out of it and she became exemplary once she was in general population. How resilient she was is one of the reasons she was on the potential acquisition list. Jason caught wind and tried to purchase her. We didn't think that was a good idea. He repeatedly tried. It was decided he would not be permitted to visit Kruna. When your father requested a redhead for you. we determined it would be in everyone's best interests that it be Felicia. She would be out of bounds for Jason, who we'd hoped would stop being a thorn in our side. And we knew she was exemplary and would meet your needs. A win-win.

We are very sorry for this inconvenience. Had we known Frost would become a problem for you, we would have taken action sooner. If you'd like to turn him over to us, we would be happy to ensure the problem is no longer a Ferrano problem. Permanently."

"I'll be interrogating him today. I'll either dispose of him myself or we'll arrange for a transfer," Dare said to the guy on the phone.

"We will leave that decision up to you. Let me know."

We said our goodbyes and then I looked at him and his expression was cold, calculated. It didn't sit well. It reminded me of myself.

Dare and I were heading back to the farm so I could pick up Tia. Tia and I had barely spoken in the past few days. She wrapped around me at night and it was a soothing balm for me but during the day I'd been wrapped up in this stuff and all my shit and she'd been keeping busy with my sisters. And I was pissed at her and she was digging in her heels with me so we'd yet to hash things out.

Lisa was gonna be spending hours each day with Oliver, my counselor, and he was trying to spend time with me, too, but I'd been dodging him with excuses so far. He was staying in the pool house. He'd be here a week or two and recommended I meet with him daily. He recommended that we send Lisa to a special retreat for intense therapy for a few weeks after he left but we weren't sure about that. He also recommended to me that Dare do the same for Angel but I hadn't approached that subject with my brother yet.

***

When we got to the farm I waited in my car and Dare sent Tia out.

"Hey," I said as she got in.

"Hey," she replied.

I leaned over to kiss her. She moved in and our lips touched.

"How is she?" I pulled out of the driveway.

Tia shrugged. "She didn't really come out. She came down for a drink and I asked if she wanted to talk and she didn't. She went back to bed. I checked on her a few times and she was either sleeping or looking out the window. I think she needs Dario. How is everything?"

I blew out a breath. "We probably won't get out of this association any time soon, unfortunately. It's gonna take time. We have to play their game for now. We might have to go to Thailand in another couple weeks for their partner summit. I don't know yet."

She made a face. "God, no."

I shook my head. "Baby, let's save this until we know what's what."

"If you think I'm going to be okay with you going to a sex slave resort…"

"Baby. Seriously. Not now. I'm fucking tired. Let's go back to the house; I need to sleep."

She folded her arms across her chest. Great. More fucking attitude.

We got back to the house and the place was quiet. Sarah was in the yard with Luc, Tess, and the kids and I didn't see Lisa or Oliver. I grabbed Tia's hand and pulled her up to the bedroom we were staying in.

I slammed the door, locked it and stalked her as she backed up, looking a little freaked out.

"So, we're doing this now, are we?" She folded her arms across her chest and tried to look tough.

"I am not fucking happy about what you said to Lisa," I said. Tia and I needed to iron shit out.

"I know. But it needed to be said."

"That's not an apology, Athena."

"No. It's not. It's all out in the open now and we can all move on. You've been beating yourself up for this. Part of moving on, I think, is talking things out with those who were involved and impacted by what happened. You're getting therapy. Lisa's getting therapy. Your sisters don't understand the full scope of what Lisa has been through so they need her truth, too. That's next, I think."

"Hey! You don't fucking decide that shit."

"I know. But that's what I think."

"Fuck."

"I have a right to voice my opinion so that's what I'm doing."

"Yeah, well you already made a decision that wasn't yours to make by telling Lisa about Pop so don't you fucking dare cross that line by telling Lisa's secret."

"I wouldn't do that."

"But yet you did it to me…"

"You're my husband. It's our story, not just yours. I was there. I had your father's gun to my temple. I saw him point his gun at you, too, and I've watched you torment yourself every single day since. It's our story, not just yours." She had tears in her eyes.

I shook my head and ran my hands through my hair.

"I need to do something, Tommy. I need to help us move on. We can't stay in this trap where you are angry at yourself and what happened and where you stop me from living because you're afraid of more blowback."

"You not happy with me?" I felt my gut twist.

"It's not that."

I felt sick. I sat on the floor in front of the door and leaned back against it. I pulled a knee up and let out a long breath.

"You could've had me from the start, you know?" she said. "I would've been yours from the minute you tied that cherry stem into a knot. You could've had me and played your cards in such a way that you'd never have had to hurt me, you'd never have lost me. But you didn't wanna court me. No, you had to claim me. I'm yours anyway, it was just a lot more painful and traumatizing of a journey this way. I know that this is who you are. And I love you. I don't want anyone but you, all of your many layers and flavors. But I don't want to keep living like this. I don't want to live in fear." Her voice cracked and she whispered, "Fear of you strangling me in your sleep. Fear that I'll have to watch you wake from nightmares every night because this is eating you up inside. Fear that I'll have no choice but to run away from you if I want a normal life. Fear that I'll never ever leave because I can't imagine living without you so instead I'll doom myself to being cooped up walking on eggshells because you're in so much pain and won't do anything about it."

"I'm doing therapy, Tia. I'm trying, god damn it."

"And I don't want you to stop trying. You're barely trying, though, honey. I know you hate the therapy. You do one hour a week because that's the minimum you can get away with. But I don't think it's enough. Oliver is here now. Spend more time with him. Don't just give up and let the pain eat you up until you're a shell of a man."

I sighed. She walked over and sat beside me and put her head on my shoulder. I put an arm around her.

"I love you. I want to help you. Let me help you."

"I love you, baby girl. And you are helping me. I wouldn't even be here if it weren't for you. I'd be dead or rotting in jail. Come here." I put my arms around her and then we got up and I hiked her up so her legs were around my waist.

I carried her to the bed and then I gently made love to her, slowly, showing every inch of her body my full attention. Then, after she was asleep, I went down to the kitchen. I saw Oliver heading into the pool house so I grabbed two beers and knocked on the door to the pool house.

Oliver seemed like the kinda guy you could sit and shoot the shit with and chatting with a couple beers might be a whole lot easier than sitting at the computer staring at the guy's mug on my screen.

Dare

I found Angel in bed, staring off into space.

"How are you?" I asked her.

She shrugged.

"Angel, do you want to see him? This could bring you some closure."

"Do you think I should see him?

"I don't know. Maybe?"

"What's going to happen to him?"

"I don't know yet. I just had a talk with Joseph Lucas. I told him I hadn't decided. I haven't talked to Jason myself yet."

She shuddered and then asked. "Where is he?"

"Here."

"Here? Joseph Lucas is here?" She looked horrified.

"No, Jason's here. He's in a horse stall in the barn. I've got six guys watching him.

Her eyes widened.

"You wanna talk to him, it's a one-minute walk. You don't, I go talk to him. From there I decide whether or not to turn him over to Kruna or I take him out myself."

I knew my expression was hard and some guys would never tell their girl that this was something they'd do. But she needed to know who I was. At my core, I was a Ferrano and I would not allow anyone to fuck me over, to take what was mine, to threaten my life or the lives of people I loved. Whether this guy started out as a good guy, whether he was just dealing with the hand he was dealt, or was a serious bad apple, I'd have a conversation with him and then I'd make my decision. I'd let her have a conversation first, if that's what she wanted to do.

"I'll talk to him," she said softly.

"Let's go. Baby, you can't tell him anything about me and Tommy wanting out. You can't let on that---"

"I know, Master," she winked at me, "I'll be your good girl."

I smiled and took her hand.

Angel

We walked hand-in-hand from the house to the barn, which was only on the other side of the driveway, and I saw that there were, indeed, men surrounding the barn.

Nino winked at me and opened the door and then I walked down a path with stalls on either side, down to the middle where another guard, a young and good-looking blond guy with a wholesome boy-next-door face smiled at me.

"Please don't go," I whispered to Dare as he led me closer.

"I won't," he said firmly.

We approached the stall. It was gated with thick iron, unlike the other stalls that'd been traditional horse stalls.

I saw Jason sitting on an overturned milk crate in the back corner and when his eyes met mine, they were filled with pain. He looked the same though. In two years, he hadn't changed. Tall, dark, handsome, well-dressed. I hadn't seen him in over a year but hadn't looked him in the face in almost two.

"Angie!" he exclaimed, and then his expression dropped when he saw Dare at my back.

"Jase," I said softly.

He got to his feet, moved toward the gate, grabbing it. I stepped back and landed against Dare's body. Dare's arm curled around my belly and he gave me a little squeeze, kept holding on, gave me support.

Jase launched right in. "I've been trying to figure out how to get to you. He was a horrible bastard, Ang. It took time but I was trying to find a way to get you out all that time. I had to end his life so I could get you out. I had him poisoned. I figured it was a deserving death after what he did to us."

I got a shudder from head to toe remembering the stench of death.

Jase continued, looking proud of himself.

"He had to pay, sweetie. But I think they suspected I had a hand in it because after Uncle Donovan died, they wouldn't let me on the premises and they watched me. I was heir to his shares but they kept me on a need-to-know basis. I already tried to buy you, to get you out of there. But they blocked it and wouldn't even let me see you. I got adamant about it, especially with what percentage of that place I own, and I think that's one of the reasons they let you go to him---" He jerked his chin at Dare. "---so I'd give up. When I found out they sold you to Dario Ferrano, I figured I could save you, finally. I know of that family. I met his father many times. I didn't mean for any of it to happen, Ang. I didn't. I love you. You were supposed to be mine, not Uncle Donavan's, no one else's." He gave Dare a dark look.

"Jason…" I started but I started to choke up, "I'm good now. I have a Master and he's good to me. You don't have to rescue me. What's done is done."

"Well, clearly I failed again. I failed to keep you safe from Uncle Donavan and I failed to rescue you. And now I'll probably pay with my life."

I started to feel bad for him.

But then he said, "I was supposed to be your Master," dejectedly and my blood ran cold. He kept talking. "Watching them break you? I watched hours of footage of how they broke you over and over. I wanted to kill him. I wish I could've seen him die. He made me watch as he beat you, as he made you beg, as he fucked you and made you come. I wanted to kill him for stealing that from me. I got him out of the way so I could take his place at Kruna with you. But fucking Chen, Lucas, Delgado, and the others? They fucking blocked me."

I felt weak. I leaned against Dare. "Master, could we go, please?"

Dare turned me to face him and looked right into my eyes and answered, "Absolutely, my Angel."

"Angie?" Jason called my old name, but I walked faster and faster and then I broke into a run and I ran back to the house and right upstairs and threw myself into the bed where I wept. I wept hard.

I didn't love Jason. I knew love at first sight was real because with Dare it'd happened, within 24 hours. With Jase it was just some fun. Good sex; he was rough and I liked it rough. He liked it often and I liked it even more often. He joked that I was a dream come true. He called me his spirited sexy submissive who he could barely keep up with. Seeing those traits in me and living in the Kruna world? Of course, he wanted to take ownership of me; I'd be the envy of the resort. I'd thought, at first, that it was so he could keep me safe but it evidently was just so he could keep me for himself, break me himself. How could he watch that footage over and over? I wanted to puke remembering some of what'd be on those recordings.

Eventually that's what I'd become, broken, though not under him. His uncle took this broken girl and kept me broken until I got into general slave population and started to find my feet. Sometimes in the early days when I knew Jason watched his uncle fucking me, I'd think that maybe Jason was just a victim like me. But I now knew that he wasn't. He was like a spoiled child whose toy got taken away before he was finished his game and he was still in a hissy fit about the fact that his uncle kept giving him his lumps.

I felt Dare's hand on my back. I rolled over to look at him. He sat on the edge of the bed.

"You okay?"

"I can't believe him," I answered.

Dare swallowed hard and looked sad.

"Are you sad for me? Don't be sad for me. Be sad for him. He isn't sorry that happened to me. He's sorry he lost. He wanted to be his uncle. He wanted to help run that place with me at his feet. He is evil.

I didn't love him, Dare. I never loved him. I dated him and yeah, I felt bad that he got punished having to watch them break me and watch his uncle…watch him abuse me, but Jase wasn't distraught because he loved me. He was distraught because his toy was taken away. And he poisoned his uncle out of revenge and then he tried to take me from you. He could've killed you. You! Fuck, that motherfucking bastard could've hurt you!" I got to my feet and started bawling my eyes out. But this wasn't broken tears; I was fucking pissed.

"That motherfucker!" I hollered and whipped the pillow across the room and then I whipped the other pillow and then a magazine, too.

"Baby," Dare said, but I was in a blind rage, pacing.

"I need to hit something."

"Angel, come here."

"No Dare, I need to hit something and I need to hit it hard."

"Let's go run. Running is good. It's better than hurting your knuckles. C'mon, baby."

Rage was bubbling, boiling over. I was having trouble thinking straight.

"Let's put on your running shoes and run. C'mon." He grabbed my hand, reached into the suitcase on the floor and grabbed sneakers for me and put them in front of me. He was dressed in jeans and boots. He kicked his boots off and got into a pair of sneakers, too.

I got the shoes on and then I started stretching as we descended the stairs and he grabbed two bottles of orange Gatorade and then we went outside. I glared at the barn where Jason was, and then focused my gaze forward, toward the trees. And then, we ran.

And as I ran, I felt angry, so angry, but I also felt free.

Dare

She had defied me when I said to *come here*. She said *No* to me. I'd never been so happy to hear the word No from a woman in my life. She was fighting mad. She was showing signs of not being broken but of having fight in her instead. And it was fucking awesome. It made me feel good. It gave me hope.

I ran a slow jog behind her and two of our guys took a slow jog behind me. I hoped this was the start of a turning point for her.

After a good hour of running we were back at the farmhouse and she was in the shower. I left her to it so she could get a few minutes alone.

Nino stopped in and told me he had Frost's belongings from the guy's room at the B&B he'd been staying at picked up. He handed me a suitcase and briefcase. He said there was a laptop and clothes, weapons, and cash. A lot of cash. I sent him with the laptop back to the barn so he could get Frost to give his login. It might help us to know what was on that laptop.

He came back ten minutes later and it was open.

"It opened with his print," Nino said. "I've adjusted the settings so there's no longer a password." He put it on the table.

She came down in those pjs of mine that she'd claimed and I got my shower and made a few quick calls upstairs. When I came down, she was on the back deck with Nino laughing and they were at the barbecue. He was flipping burgers and sausages.

She saw me come down and came back in and went to the counter where she was making a big salad. I kissed her and she smiled at me and then went back to chopping vegetables. We ate outside with Nino and Tino at a picnic table and she was lighthearted with them and a good hostess. Then Nino and Tino walked over to the barn with food she'd dished out for the other security guards and for the prisoner. I didn't bother telling her that Jason Frost wasn't getting dinner. Instead, I talked to the guys outside for a few minutes and then said goodnight and went inside. She was finishing up cleaning the kitchen.

"I'll make a call and have them pick up Frost tomorrow morning. He made his bed with them so they can deal with him. You okay with that?"

She nodded.

"We need everything else on the table. Tell me everything else."

"You don't wanna know."

"I do. I wanna know it all. I need it all."

Her gaze went razor sharp. "No."

"Angel…"

"Why? Why would you want to know about the abuse I dealt with? It won't help me to relive it and it won't help us when you can't get those images out of your head." She threw the tea towel on the counter and folded her arms.

I was proud of the fact that she was feeling brave enough to say No to me but now wasn't the time for it, not in this situation.

"I need to know it all so we can move forward. It could take a while before we're out but the more info I have, the better. Their partner summit is coming up and---"

Angel

"You're going?" Horror swept through me.

"I might have to," he answered. "It's gonna take time to get out of this business without making enemies so I have to play their game for a while."

I swallowed hard and started to tremble, imagining being back there after my teensy weensy taste of freedom.

"So, information is power, Angel. I need you to trust that I can take whatever information you have. What they did to you, all of it."

No. No way did I want him knowing about the horror they'd put me through. No way did he want all that in his head. He would never look at me with love in his eyes again. He'd look at me through a tainted lens. He'd see worse than the broken slave on her knees begging him to be her Master. He'd see how dirty and broken and unfixable I really was, how broken and unfixable I'd always be, and he'd know that he deserves better.

"Please, Dare."

"Baby." He grabbed me and put his arms around me. "I need you to come clean about it all. You need to come clean. You've already come so far. You're transforming before my eyes. You're not Felicia."

"Well, I'm not her, either."

"Her?"

"Her. That other name. I'm not her, Dare. She was crushed into dust. She's gone."

"Maybe you're not Angie anymore. But you're my Angel. You're my beautiful girl who survived all of that."

"I'm a fucking mess!" I shrieked.

He smiled. "Yeah. But you're showing some good signs. You've been damaged but you're not broken, babe. Now, tell me. Let's sit down. I want to know the rest of your story."

"I can't. I can't." I shook my head and cross my arms, backing away from him. Damaged? Damaged was an understatement.

"Baby, listen…"

"Can I go to bed? I want to go to bed."

He sighed and stared at me a beat. I pleaded with my eyes.

"Okay," he relented. "For tonight we'll leave it on ice. We need to talk this out, though. Kiss me goodnight. I've got a bit to do and then I'll be up."

I went to him the table he sat at, with a laptop. He put his arms around me and I sank into him. He pulled me down onto his lap and held me tight. My chin trembled.

"I'm tired, Dare. Can I go?"

"Go. I'll be up soon."

I listlessly climbed up the stairs, crawled into the bed, and got under the covers, completely under the covers, head and all.

Dare

I found a folder on Frost's laptop that said Angie. It was filled with video files; Bile bubbled at the back of my throat. I didn't open them. I paced the floor instead.

There was no way in the world I wanted to watch her get abused, watch anyone lay their hands on her. The fact that Frost could watch that shit? Repeatedly? What the fuck? I stormed down to the barn, telling the guards to get out of earshot.

"What's in those video files, Frost?" I greeted. He was laying on the floor against the wall on some hay. He propped his head up on his palm.

"That's a lot of footage of Angie's first days at the resort. It's also some footage of her and me before she found out about Kruna. And Donavan gave me footage of her from about three months in. Quite a transformation."

"You videotaped sex with her without her knowledge?"

"I'm glad I had spank bank material all this time without her. I needed it. Once you have a girl like Angie you don't wanna forget. I know you know what I'm sayin'. Of course you know what I'm sayin'. That's a ten-million-dollar cunt you've got yourself in there and I know she's worth every penny your old man paid."

I ignored the urge to crush the guy, it wasn't easy. "So, you inherited Donavan's stock and thought you'd take over his position?"

"That was the plan. But obviously that's out the window. Listen, can we make some sort of deal? I know I've got balls to even ask since I shot first instead of approaching you, but we're reasonable men, aren't we? We're business associates at this point, co-shareholders. How about we strike a deal?"

"What kind of deal?"

"I'd make a two-part deal, part one being for her but I can guess you wouldn't be interested in selling her."

"She's not for sale."

"Then one part only. You buy my Kruna shares, help me get gone so that they can't take me out."

"You think these guys would be all right with a partner buying up shares behind their backs? I doubt it."

Frost shrugged. "They just want me out, man. They loved your old man. They wouldn't have any problem with Ferranos holding a bigger stake."

He sure *did* have balls trying' to bullshit me. Or more likely, he was off his rocker. "They want you dead, man."

"And I'd like to not be dead. How do we make that happen? Fuck, I'll give you my shares. Draw up the papers."

"If I let you out what's to stop you from killing me and taking her?"

He shook his head. "I won't. I'll go and you'll never hear from me again."

"No, you'll go away and plot some more to try to find a way to take her from me. You can't get a girl like that outta your head; you said it yourself."

He got a desperate look. "I love that girl. But, I also love breathin'."

"You loved her so much you wanted to break her and make her yours."

"Man, you ever break a girl?"

"No."

"It's a thing of beauty. Killed me that they stole that from me and a girl like Angie? She was amazing. She was the perfect blend of wild and submissive. She was wild on that dance floor, out in the world. And then in the bedroom, she was a goddamn goddess who did whatever I wanted her to do. You don't find that every day."

"No, you don't."

"And creating it yourself? It's a rush like no other," he said and we stared at one another a beat.

"So, what can I do? What can I give you that'll make you let me go?" His eyes turned desperate.

My phone rang. I glanced at the screen. Zack.

I answered. "Hey man."

"Where's Jason Frost?"

"I've got Frost."

"Shit. Where?"

"In front of me, in a cell."

"What are you doin', man?" Zack was tweaked.

"Havin' a chat. Gonna decide whether or not to hand him over to them or take him out myself."

Frost's eyes grew bigger.

"He's trying to make a deal with me to let him go. Offering me his Kruna shares."

"Dario, man, can you hang tight? Can you hang tight till I get there? I need to talk to you. It's important. Don't do anything with Frost."

"When?"

"The morning."

"I think I need to settle this tonight." I wasn't sure if I could let this slime ball live to see one more sunrise.

"Dude, I'm on my way. Wait. Don't do anything. Okay?"

"What is it?"

"We've gotta talk in person. Don't make any moves. None. Just wait for me."

"Fine."

***

An hour later I was sitting on the front steps of the house with a stick and a knife and Zack pulled in on his Harley. Behind him was a car that had three guys in suits in it.

"What the fuck?" I said aloud as he approached me. Two of my men emerged from the barn and stood sentry in front of the barn. Two more materialized from the rear of the farmhouse and flanked me.

A guy in a suit stepped out of the front passenger seat of the car and then he stepped in front of Zack and flashed his ID at me. He shone a flashlight on the ID.

Interpol. Fuck.

"We need to take custody of your prisoner," the ID-flashing guy said.

I looked to Zack.

"We need to talk," he said.

"I'll say we do," I replied.

"Step aside, boys," I said to my guys and then watched as they took custody of Frost.

Zack and I had not more than a quick chat before he left. He told me we needed to talk in the morning, that he had a lot to explain, asked me not to jump to conclusions, and then he left with them. To say I was pissed would be putting it mildly. I went in the house and stared at Frost's laptop, sitting on the table. I bet Interpol would love to get their hands on that. I texted Nino and he came in from outside and I handed it to him and told him to leave with it, to put it some place safe.

"What was that scene all about?" he asked me.

"Don't know yet; guess we'll find out." I answered and then went in and phoned Tommy with the quick low-down. He replied through gritted teeth that we couldn't do much but wait for more intel from Zack unless we wanted to jump ship in the middle of the night. I agreed that if we were gonna be arrested we'd be in custody now so we'd wait. I went up and found her asleep. I climbed in and did nothing but stare at the ceiling for the rest of the night, listening to her breathe, pondering everything going on in my life.

In the morning, I got a text from Zack addressed to me and my brother telling us that he had to leave town for a few days but would meet with us when he got back. He said it was important, he knew that he had a lot of explaining to do, but asked that we trust him. He referred us to his partner, a guy named Hal, who could help with any PI / security needs until he was back. *Right.* As if we'd continue to use his services not getting a full explanation from him. His text directed me to tell Kruna that I'd taken out Jason Frost, that he was dead.

I was not happy. I didn't know if Zack was a Fed or if the Feds were gonna be back to discuss Jason Frost or everything else further. I didn't know if we should just stay vigilant or if we should take off. It didn't sit well being in the dark, being vulnerable. My brother was as livid as I was.

Angel and I packed up and headed back to the condo. She was quiet all the way back, likely picking up on my mood in addition to dealing with her own emotions.

I took her upstairs and then told her I was stepping out for a few hours.

"Do you want me to have someone come sit with you?"

She shook her head.

"I'll be back soon."

I left.

Angel

He'd been distant that day. I didn't know the status with Jason. I didn't know what was on his mind, I didn't know much.

He left the apartment and I curled up on a sofa under a blanket and watched cartoons.

Much later, he was back. He kissed me hello and then went to his den and was gone for a long time. I fell asleep on the sofa, hoping he'd carry me to bed, but at four a.m., I woke up on the sofa and he was asleep in the bed. My heart ached. I went back to the sofa and couldn't fall back to sleep.

The sun came up and I smelled coffee. I sat up and he was in the kitchen,

"Hey," he said. "Why're you out here?" He sipped his coffee. He looked ready for the office, dressed in a dark blue suit.

"I fell asleep, I guess," I muttered and went to the bathroom. When I came out he was on the phone and gathering up his keys and heading out the door. I stepped to the island and he rushed back over, still talking on the phone, telling someone off by the sounds of it, saying "I don't fucking think so! Find out where he went!" and he kissed me quickly and then he left.

I stood there for I don't know how long, sadness enveloping me. Did something change with him and I? Did he feel differently about me now? What was going on? Did Jason get away or something like that?

If he did, would he find me and take me?

I tried not to let horror wash over me. I tried hard.

CHAPTER TWELVE

Tia

He came home late. I heard him come in from where I was on the sofa in the dark and he walked right by me, heading straight to the master bedroom. I held the tears back. A few minutes later I saw a light go on in the hall, maybe the den. Then I felt his presence. He sat on the edge of the sofa, "Hey, baby?"

My throat and chest twinged and I had trouble swallowing.

"Angel?"

"Yeah?"

"What are you doin' out here again?" I guess he hadn't seen me.

Words wouldn't form on my tongue. He hefted me up into his arms and carried me to his bed. I wanted to fall apart; I felt such relief. My back landed on the soft mattress and then his lips were on mine. His hand touched my face.

"Why're you crying, my baby? What's wrong?"

He sounded so gentle, so concerned. His baby. A sob tore out of me.

He flipped us so that he was on his back and I was on him and he held me close. "Talk to me."

I shook my head and kept crying into his chest.

"Babe?"

"You left me on the sofa last night so I thought you didn't care and I…"

"Huh?"

"You always carry me to bed and last night you didn't and so I thought you didn't care…"

"Baby last night I don't even remember hitting the bed I was so zonked. I'm sorry. I didn't know you weren't there. Shit. Do you wait for me on the sofa on purpose all the time?"

I felt stupid. Stupid and needy. Why did he even want me?

"Angel?"

"Kind of."

"Why, baby?"

"That first time you carried me to bed I'd fantasized about that before it happened and then you did it. And it was beautiful. And then the next night I didn't want to presume to climb into your bed and you did it again. And the other times were just flukes most of the time but last night you felt distant and I wanted you to carry me, so you wouldn't feel distant, and you didn't and I…" I didn't know how to finish.

"Thought we were havin' problems? Thought I was pulling away?" he offered.

"The K-kruna stuff is so ugly, Dare. I started to wonder if you knew more, if you'd seen Jason's tapes. If you knew how bad, how dirty I am."

"What?"

"I'm tainted. I'm dirty. I'm too dirty for you." Too needy, too broken.

"What the fuck? You can't be serious."

I sobbed.

"I haven't watched any of Jason's tapes. I wouldn't ever watch them. Never. I'm not some sick fuck who gets off on watching people hurt you. That motherfucker is whacked, baby. I wouldn't ever watch them. And if someone tied me down and made me watch them it would not ever mean that I'd look at you as dirty. You're not dirty, baby."

"I am."

"You're not!" he said fiercely. "Tell me. Tell me all of it and you'll know it won't affect how I feel."

"It will."

"It won't."

"It has to."

"Try me."

"Fine. Wanna hear how they waterboarded me for hours with seawater? Do you know what torture waterboarding is? It meant I never wanted to be in water again. I panicked for months even in the shower, Dare."

"Baby."

"It's torture, Dare. But that doesn't make me dirty, that just makes me messed up in the head. Need to know the details of being locked in the dark with a rabid priapic monster for four days while he fucked me repeatedly in every hole, not feeding me, not giving me more than a few sips of water per day and the only other thing I had to drink was his cum?"

His eyes were hard and he was working his jaw muscle.

"Wanna hear how I got my mouth washed out with piss for swearing at a trainer?"

"Okay, enough."

"No. Not nearly enough. You didn't really know what you were asking for but I'll tell you what you need to know. 'Cause you need to know how I got tortured for hours with vibrators tied to me in punishment for making myself come, how my ass bled for two days after being double anal penetrated by two men. Do you really wanna know about me being suspended upside down and hog tied while no less than a dozen men took turns fucking my mouth? And don't even get me started on Jason's uncle. You want a play-by-play?"

"Stop."

"No, I thought you wanted to know the truth, Dare. Does all that help you feel like you know me better? How about I tell you how I felt when they finally broke me by doing all sorts of horrendous things to me after over more than two weeks, almost three, and the final breaking straw was them showing me that they had my 15 year old sister hog tied in a cargo plane and in the photo frame were no less than seven naked penises surrounding my blindfolded child of a sister and they were about to take her virginity on camera and make me watch if I didn't finally give in. They were then going to bring her here and make me watch them do to her all the things they'd done to me and they threatened to tie a Hitachi between my legs so I'd have no choice but to come over and over while I watched them ruin her. Now that you know that stuff, that stuff that only gives you the quick and dirty, only the highlights of things that were done to me while they were breaking me, tell me, Master…how filthy and tarnished am I to you now? You can't tell me you'd even think of making such a broken, dirty, ruined shell of a woman the mother of your babies. Right? Am I right?"

"Shut it. On your knees in front of me right fucking now." He was completely furious.

I wanted to ask, "What?" but I didn't dare. I stared at him for a beat and the look on his face was scary. Crazy scary. He pointed to the floor, a scowl on his face.

"Now!" he yelled and I dropped to my knees in front of him and stared at his feet. My heart hammered hard in my chest.

He dropped to his knees too, surprising me. Then he spoke and he did it gruffly.

"I do want to know everything. I want you to know everything, too. All my secrets. Believe me, I feel dirty sometimes, too, baby. But I want you to own me, too. So, here." He pulled an envelope out of his jacket pocket and spilled the contents on the rug between us.

It was a folded piece of paper and two ring boxes.

"Marriage license. Wedding rings. I was planning to do this with hearts and flowers and some romantic grand gesture but you need to know right here, right now that I'm all in, no matter what, Angel."

I choked on a sob. He wasn't done.

"Will you own me? Let me be yours, your husband? Will you be my wife, make babies with me, lay on my belly and let me feed you fried spaghetti while we watch sports? Will you let me try to be what you need, whether that's to be your Master, your equal, a bit of both, whatever helps you feel safe? I want everything you have to give me and that includes your truth so that I can help you through healing from it. Will you be what I need, too? Sweet, beautiful, funny, submissive, wild? I want it all."

I did a face-plant into his chest and his arms came around me. I felt his fingers in my hair.

"You can heal, baby. You are resilient. I know you are. You're all I want and all I need and that's despite what they did to you. I look fucking forward to watching more of that experience peel away. It'll always be with you but it doesn't have to cover you. I will do my fucking best to be all you need. You, Angelica Elizabeth Macleod, my Angel, need to be the mother of my babies. No one else. You. I want to keep seeing your spirit shine through, I want to have thousands of hours with your legs wrapped around me, I want redheaded or blond baby boys and girls that look like a perfect mix of me and you. I want you, your sexy white lace, your cowboy hat, and everything in between. I want to make you feel safe, collar, no collar, whatever you want, whatever you need."

He let go of me, reached to the floor, and then he opened a ring box and showed me a man's platinum band with the inner inscription, "Owned by an Angel" with a tiny pair of engraved wings. And then he showed me the other ring box's contents, it had a big diamond ring and beside it was a blue sapphire crusted eternity band with three rows of gems.

"I had a jeweler friend take apart that first collar and make that for you. At first I never wanted to see it again but it's part of our story, our truth, my baby."

I choked on a sob. "It's perfect. You're perfect."

"I know we have a long road ahead for you to heal but I want to walk that road with you. I want to help you heal. I have all the patience in the world for that because you're my end game, Angel. You're it for me. Will you marry me? Before you answer, I know you're feeling broken. I know this probably goes against what any therapist would recommend, but you're mine. I'm yours. Marry me?"

"Yes. Yes, I'll marry you. I would be the luckiest girl in the world to make a family with you. Do you know why?"

"Why?" He smiled at me.

"Not because you're my Master. Not because you own me. But because when you took a wet pile of dirt and formed it into a castle in front of my very eyes it was then that I knew that you could build, with your hands, a place where I'd want to live for the rest of my life. You did that. You brought a broken girl back to life. You took a wet pile of dirt and formed it into a castle for me, Dare. You did this with your bare hands. With those hands you also took a broken girl and you glued her back together, too. I want to spend the rest of my life making your dreams come true. All of them."

"I love you," he said and then his lips touched mine as he slid the engagement ring on my finger.

EPILOGUE

Angelica Elizabeth Ferrano

We got married in a beautiful little church with his family around us. He wore a tux. He was beautiful. I wore a white strapless wedding gown and a veil and left my hair loose and curly. He'd also bought me a new necklace for my birthday a few weeks before, which I wore on our wedding day. It was simple, white gold, and consisted of three chains with a pendant of two hearts linked together. When he lifted my veil, he fingered a curl and gave me a dazzling beautiful smile as he gently poked the side of my nose on the tiny diamond. I had put my nose piercing back in the night before.

Maybe after everything I'd been through, I wasn't Angie Macleod any longer but I was looking forward to being Angel Ferrano.

The wedding happened a month after he'd proposed. He'd been busy with work during the day and at nighttime he was always there, always attentive. Sometimes we played rough and sometimes we played gentle. He seemed okay with the rough, okay with my submissive tendencies. We were very compatible sexually.

I was thinking about my future. I wanted to get back to teaching, maybe. Dare asked me to hang tight while he finished sorting out some business stuff. He didn't know how long until they'd be free of Kruna. He said there'd been complications with a few business areas that he was trying to get out of but was kind of tight-lipped about it. I didn't push. I was busy trying to find myself in my new life after being a sex slave. I didn't ask him about the partner summit but that date had come and gone.

I took an art class a few blocks away. It was only once a week but it was fun. I walked there and back alone and I often walked to the library, to the park to watch kids play, to feed the ducks by myself, and occasionally I stopped by the office to bring Dare lunch, a cup of his favorite coffee, or just to give him a kiss.

One day just a few days before our wedding I walked through the park at lunchtime and saw Dare's ex there. She was sitting with a few girls eating lunch. It was the same place I'd seen her the first time. She glanced at me. She recognized me. She looked to her lap and said nothing to me. So I kept walking. I glanced over my shoulder when I was almost past her and saw her looking at me, a sad look on her face. She really screwed herself when she screwed him over. At least she was smart enough to heed his warnings to stay out of our lives. Poor stupid girl. But it was my boon. If she hadn't shredded his heart, he'd never have been at Kruna, picking up his birthday gift.

Me.

Lisa wasn't at our wedding. She was away at a retreat but she and I had been texting. She phoned me the night before our wedding, when I was having a girls' night in with Tia, Tess, and Luc for my bachelorette party. Lisa phoned me and I slipped into a bedroom at Tessa and Lisa's place to have some privacy. She said the therapy was helping and said that she wanted me to do the same, to not bury what we'd been through. She said she was getting so much out of it that she was thinking that after Dare and Tommy were clear of the Kruna world maybe she and I could start up a charity of some sort to help those who'd been through what we'd gone through.

I didn't know how soon the guys would be clear of Kruna. I didn't know if it'd ever happen, and if it did, I doubted we could be so public about our truths but I didn't want to burst Lisa's bubble. She seemed confident we'd find our way out. She told me she couldn't get into details about how she knew we'd get out but said for me to think about it. She wished me a happy wedding day and said she'd be home as soon as she could be.

The wedding was a dream come true. We had a little reception afterwards where we danced together to the song "Make Me Do Anything You Want" as our wedding dance. It was perfect for us. And then the music got upbeat and me, Tia, Luc, and Tessa danced our asses off until my new husband whisked me away for our wedding night, which had a whole lot of loud and energetic drunken marriage consummating. And for some odd reason there was nothing submissive about me that night.

The next day when I woke up my Master, my husband, the love of my life was coming into the hotel suite. He sat down in front of the window looking like the weight of the world was on his shoulders.

"Good morning, hubby." I stretched and smiled, wondering where he'd been. "Guess what?"

"What, baby?"

"I did something as a wedding present."

He looked at me but he wasn't smiling.

"When I had the stitches out from my leg and I told you the doc referred me to that plastic surgeon? I didn't tell you everything. I also got a referral to another doctor and the day Luc took me to the appointment for the plastic surgery consultation I had another appointment, too. I had the doctor take my IUD out. Surprise! Never know… we might've made a baby on our wedding night."

He was looking very troubled.

My heart sank. "I thought you'd be happy. Is it too soon for that?" I couldn't wait to give him babies. Maybe I shouldn't have made that decision on my own.

"I am happy. I'm gonna be so happy when we start our family, my baby. I'm sorry for my anticlimactic reaction but I got a call a little while ago and had to go down and meet with Zack in the lobby. What I've gotta tell you is gonna be hard. I can't keep it from you. That wouldn't be right."

I sat up. He put his hand on the back of my neck and squeezed reassuringly.

"I wanted to find a way to get you and your sister in touch safely like. So I got Zack's team on it weeks back. Told him to look her up and feel out the situation. Would've loved to have had her here for yesterday, baby."

My mouth dropped open. I felt the panic trying to set in. I pushed it back. He kept talking.

"Zack couldn't find Holly in Alaska anywhere so he did some looking. As it turns out, her grandmother got sick and your mother got wind of it and called CPS and CPS had returned her to your mother before the Kruna scumbags had people kidnap her."

"She…" I could barely breathe, "She's not in Alaska?"

"Whoever picked her up from your mother didn't return her. Your mother never reported her missing. The grandmother didn't get better. Died a few months later. Your mother figured Holly ran away. Holly has been gone for almost as long as you have."

The world stopped turning. Holly. Oh God.

"We think we know where she is, though. I'm gonna find out, Angel. I'll do everything I can to find her for you."

He pulled me into his arms and I grabbed him and held on tight.

Tia

Tommy has to be here for now so we're staying and I'm totally okay with it. We decided to go back to Costa Rica soon to close up the house, keeping it for now. Tommy and Dare are working together at Ferrano Enterprises. A few of the subsidiaries were sold but they haven't finished their clean-up. Tommy rented a house a few doors down from his father's house. It's just for now, while we figure things out, but I love the house and love that it's just down the street from family.

He's doing therapy and he really seems like he's doing better. He's busy with work and he's on the webcam with Oliver three times a week. I see a difference in him. It's good. Really good.

I've been hanging out with the girls and with Angel, too. She had me, Tess, and Luc be bridesmaids and it's been nice to have friends again. Now that I know we're staying put here for at least a while, I've called Ruby and she, Mia, and Beth are coming for a girls' night while Tommy is out of town on business. He's going to be gone three days and then when he gets back, we're going to Costa Rica. While he's gone, he'll have Nino and Dex doing shiftwork staying with me here (and had a state-of-the-art security system put in); and even though that's overprotective, believe me, for Tommy it is huge progress.

***

The day after Dare's wedding when I woke up, I felt something warm on top of me and something wet on my face.

I opened my eyes and was greeted with a big pink tongue. I winced and then realized it was a puppy's tongue. I reached forward and grabbed the big yellow fluff ball and saw my husband sitting on the edge of the bed, a huge smile on his handsome face. The puppy was a golden retriever, maybe about six or eight weeks old, and he was furiously licking the air and whining while I held him at arm's length. He had a big pink bow around his neck.

"Oh, my gawwwwd!" I squished the puppy against me. "Tommy!"

"Like him?"

"I love him! I love you!" I put the pup down and threw myself at Tommy.

"Follow me." He backed off the bed, putting me on my feet.

I scooped up my puppy and followed him downstairs and out the front door. Our house was similar to his father's house. An older large Tudor style home, it had two big gates out front, which Tommy liked for security reasons.

I liked it because the place had character. Big rooms, architectural details. Gorgeous gardens. Apparently, I had a bit of a green thumb. I'd been spending time tending the flower beds and really enjoying it. Tommy said we'd see what was what, and maybe we'd buy it.

Out front was a brand-new metallic orange Jeep. It had a big black bow across the hood.

"What?" I stared at it. I put the dog down. He went to a tree and lifted his leg and peed. "Good boy, Marley!" I said and leaned over and patted his head.

"Marley?" Tommy asked.

"Of course. What else could it be?" I replied, staring at the Jeep.

"Is that for me?"

"It is. It comes with driving lessons so you can finish your license."

"Really?"

"Really," he replied and put his arms around me. "Time to start livin', baby girl. I'll be a nervous wreck for the first bit so be patient with me, okay? And go slow. Don't take off every five minutes or I'll have to drag you home and tie you to the bed. Alrighty?"

"Alrighty." I put my arms around his neck. "I love you. I need to run to the store now, actually. Do you mind if I dash out?"

"Uh…" he looked a bit flipped out. "You don't even have your full license yet."

"It's just the drug store around the corner," I said. "It's like… two minutes."

"What do you need at the drugstore? Maybe me and Marley will just tag along."

I smiled, took a big breath, and then I said, "I think I need to buy a pregnancy test. I'm a week late."

His eyes bulged.

"I did the math and my birth control implant has been in now for over three years so it's possible it's stopped working."

His eyes bulged some more.

"Are you okay?" I reached for him. He grabbed me, squeezed, and swung me around. He said nothing, but his eyes were filled with wet. He reached into his pocket and handed me the keys and then whistled. "Marley, come. We need to go to the drugstore. And then maybe the cigar store."

I opened the door to my new Jeep and turned the ignition while my husband put our puppy in the back seat.

Tommy

While Tia was in the bathroom doing the pregnancy test, I got a text from Ben Goldberg with confirmation of the final date for Fete's grand opening. He wants me and Dare there. We own 34%, Ben owns 34%, my buddy John Lewis owns the rest. It's happening a week before Christmas, two weeks after the Kruna partner summit, which got rescheduled due to Gan Chen's injuries.

I replied to say I'd be there and I paced, waiting for my wife to come out and tell me whether or not we were going to be parents. Me, a father. The idea of sharing Tia with anyone else doesn't sit well. But the idea of being a father, being responsible for molding a kid into the kind of person he's gonna become? That's fucking huge. Am I really ready for that shit? I'm still trying to keep my head together after the events of the last few months. And there are going to be some rocky months ahead what with the Kruna bullshit. But the idea of her carrying my baby? The idea that our love created life? It's fucking beautiful.

As I'm pacing, I see the pup has something. I lean over. Shit, Tia's not gonna be happy. The dog has chewed one of her favorite red-soled heels. I grab the shoe from the dog. "No. Bad!" I tell him and hear the bathroom door open. She's standing there, flushed, smiling, holding the stick.

"It's positive," she says. "It's supposed to take two minutes but the second I peed on it, it went positive. Do you think it's right?"

I smiled. "With my strong swimmers, no surprise. Oh yeah, it's right."

She wrinkled her nose at me, looking adorable. "You're so full of yourself."

I laughed. "Come here, wife, so you can be full of me."

She walked over, blowing out a long breath. "We're gonna be parents, Tommy."

"I know, baby girl. You're gonna be an amazing mother. Come here." I dropped to my knees, tossing the shoe behind me and lifted her sweater to kiss her bare belly. She put her hand in my hair and smiled, eyes shining with tears.

"I love you," she said.

"Love you, too, baby girl."

"Thanks for the puppy."

"You're welcome."

"Thanks for the new wheels."

"You're welcome."

"Thanks for the baby," she giggled.

I smiled. "Thanks for loving me despite my flaws. There's a lot of them."

"You're welcome. Now go buy me some vanilla ice cream. And some pastrami."

I laughed. "You're the boss."

Zack

"Dario, I might know where Holly Mooney is but I need your and Tommy's help. There's a very good chance she's in a Mexican brothel. It's run by the cartel your brother worked with to take down Juan Carlos Castillo."

"Fuck, seriously?"

"Yeah, man. One of the partners of Kruna is part-owner in this one, too. It's very likely that's where they took her after they blackmailed your wife. Listen, we've gotta talk, too. I'm in the lobby of your hotel. I know it was your wedding night last night but can you come down?"

"Yeah man."

When Dario Ferrano walked into my office three weeks earlier and sat with me I told him the truth. I'm affiliated with a government task force, an organization working to take down places like Kruna. I admitted I made myself available to the Ferrano family due to Tom Sr.'s suspected ties with human slavery. I'd been undercover for 2 years, working for the Ferranos for 8 months and befriending them as well as working with them to figure out the inner workings of their father's business as well as his leisure activities.

"I'm not out to put you or Tommy in prison, Dario. You've both been products of your upbringing and I can see, my superiors can see as well, that this is not who you are anymore. Being close to you both throughout the mess with your father has been very enlightening. We can get you both a deal where you're immune to any prosecution if you both act as freelancers and help us out with bringing the Kruna resort down."

Dario glared at me, shocked. And then he said,

"If you weren't such a good friend and such a good guy, you'd be a double-crossing traitor who needed to be killed."

Without missing a beat, I replied, "If you weren't such a good friend and such a good guy, you'd be sitting in a jail cell awaiting indictment. Now, are you gonna help me recruit your brother? We are going to shut down Kruna. The intel you got me throughout all this, the names, all the shit I recorded, Jason Frost, it has been huge. We're ready to take this to the next level. That next level starts at their partner summit."

"If I say no?"

"If you say no you can't help me bring down the organization that broke your girl. If you say no, maybe the organization I work for sees you and your brother as threats instead of friends who can help us. If you say yes I also go above and beyond to help you find your sister-in-law."

Dario let out a big breath and told me he'd talk to his brother after the wedding. Then he said, "One more thing…" and he punched me in the face and left the office.

We were cool now, though. I let him have that.

Liza

November 1st

I'm back. I'm doing a lot better. And I'm ready to tell Luc and Tessa my truth. I've already told it to Zack; he showed up at the retreat I was at. Tommy and Dare don't know yet but even Oliver, my counselor, is affiliated with the organization Zack works for. I know that Zack has plans to shut Kruna down and with my testimony a part of their case, I'm sure they can do it.

The girls are meeting me at Venetia for lunch. The restaurant is closed so it'll be just us. Tia and Angel are coming too, to support me. I hope that Luc and Tessa can handle it. I hope that I can handle it. I'm ready to live again, putting my past behind me but not burying it.

Dex knows my truth. Either Tommy or Dare told him. He picked me up at the airport. He's cute. He's tall, blond, he's sweet. He's my age. He's seen me at my worst. Well, my worst post-Kruna. They had him guard me for a few days before I went away and that was rough but he is a good guy, I can tell. Dex wants to take me to dinner. But one thing at a time.

I know telling Luc and Tess that their father bought me as a sex slave and had me befriend Tessa as a ruse will hurt them but I know them and I know it won't take them too long to forgive me. And maybe someday soon I can be Shayla again. Like I said to Angel, she might not feel like Angie any longer but coming out the other side, she doesn't have to keep being Felicia, either.

Dare

I have my dream girl. She's beautiful. She's mine. She worships the ground I walk on and I do the same for her. She wears sexy lingerie, can't get enough of me in the bedroom, and she wants kids, too. And Pop gave her to me. Crazy. No settling for me.

Every day she seems a little less broken. There are still moments where I see it, see what they did to her, but I also see the future and it is bright. As bright as her piercing blue eyes.

I had my brother back, too. He and I were running Ferrano together and we were still cleaning up but it was already on its way to being something that we'd either be able to sell for a decent price and a clearer conscience or it'd be something we could pass onto our kids without setting them up for lives of crime. I've also enrolled in pilot school, which is part-time, but leaves that option open, for down the road.

I've got a lot of money in the bank. I've got my health. I've got good friends, even if one of my best friends is a double-crossing Fed.

But I also had a missing sister-in-law, which Angel is distraught about.

I had to tell my brother that Zack had played us. Zack had been awesome. He had helped us through some really rough times. Tommy was shocked that Zack played us but in hindsight, we figured it'd all happened for a reason and the fact that he was in our lives meant that there was a chance we'd actually find our way out of the world of human trafficking.

I had to break the news to Angel that we'd have to go to Kruna for their partner summit and that I'd need her to come with me. She'd be able to give me information while we were there that would help with Zack's case. It'd be the beginning of the end. Kruna was told I'd killed Jason Frost. But the organization Zack was freelancing for still had him under lockdown. They were still pumping him for information.

I'd been thinking about whether or not to turn over Frost's laptop. It had information to help bring them down but it also had footage of my wife being broken and raped and abused. I was having a hard time reconciling what to do about it. The best thing I figured I could do was to talk to Angel about it and see what she wanted to do. For now, Nino had it somewhere safe.

It wouldn't be easy. We were gonna be putting our lives at risk by double-crossing the Kruna scumbags. A lot of people would be brought down if the people Zack was working for got their way.

But like I'd vowed to myself, I'd un-break her and I'd gift Kruna's demise to her, if I could. I wanted to find a way to succeed at both and the unbreaking part was already well on its way.

When we got home from the hotel the day after the wedding, we chucked that hair flat iron down the garbage chute together. I was looking forward to watching more of her spirit shine through. Soon, when things were settled, we'd take our honeymoon in Italy and then head to Iceland, where we'd do the tourist thing and also see my Ma (she couldn't make the wedding as her husband was in palliative care) and then visit some of my cousins. And I was also looking forward to the honeymoon and life after that honeymoon because after we got back, I'd be buying us a house with more than a few bedrooms in it for our future babies and somewhere in that house, maybe in the basement, I was absolutely going to be installing a mechanical bull.

The End

AFTERWORD

Hey!

I hope you enjoyed Dario's story.

And it seems the drama isn't over…

The Dominator 3, Unbound is next.

And then a spin-off, Holly's story. Saved is also available.

Thanks for reading my books and for making my dream come true. I hope I've entertained you.

Thanks for supporting indie authors!

Thanks so much to those who volunteered as beta readers for this book. I didn't have beta readers for The Dominator but did for Nectar and it really helped so I reached out to people on my newsletter and got some great feedback and some encouraging support, too.

Thanks to: Hannah, Katrina, Christine, Tiff, Molly, Tabitha, Heather, Divya, Pauline, Kat, Andrea, Rebecca, Stephanie, and Kimberly.

Some of you gave me amazing feedback. Some of you helped me find mistakes I'd overlooked after staring at this document for so long that I started to miss mistakes.

And some of you just loved Dare and Tommy so much that it was simply a joy to make you happy by giving you the first look. Thank you for all your help!

I started working on The Dominator when I was 15 years old. I could never seem to finish it. Through my teens and early 20's I stopped and restarted and started over multiple times. The idea for this book got put away until finally, in my early 40's, I sat down and re-started and then finished it. When I was 15, I was in love with the idea of a tough badass mafia man taking care of me. I've ALWAYS been partial to dark romance.

Dare didn't exist in the previous incarnations of the book at all. Tommy was an only child.

But I'm so glad he exists now!

I didn't know there would be a sequel to Tommy & Tia's book until I typed "The End" and then my fingers typed, "Or is it?" I guess I wasn't ready to say goodbye to Tommy and the other characters yet.

The story of Dare and his Angel soon came to me and it felt meant to be based on some of the areas of Tommy's book that just fit in. I was stoked at how excited people who read Tommy & Tia's story were for the continuation of books based on the Ferrano family.

There are a lot of people who have cheered on my writing in my lifetime. Teachers, co-workers, friends, family, loves, and now fans, too. I have fans. Me! Holy crap :D Thank you all!

Thank you for helping me live my dream!

ABOUT THE AUTHOR

DD Prince is a Canadian author who has been writing ever since she learned she could put pen to paper and create with words. She loves to read and write dark, contemporary, and paranormal love stories, especially when love --- whether dark, sweet, or co-dependent is the anecdote. She is passionate about faith, family, friends, food, and words.

Since writing The Dominator, she has gone on to publish more Ferrano family books, a dark and taboo vampire romance trilogy, a steamy biker romance series, contemporary enemies-to-lovers romance, and more.

TRUTH OR DARE PLAYLIST

Make me do Anything You Want: A Foot in Cold Water
Gimme Shelter: The Rolling Stones
Send me an Angel: Scorpions
Roxanne: The Police

Bonus:
Angie: The Rolling Stones

ALSO AVAILABLE

The Dominator Series:
The Dominator
Truth or Dare:
Unbound
TNT
Saved – A spin-off dark romance.

The Nectar Trilogy
Dark and taboo vampire romance. You've never read a vampire story like this!

The Beautiful Biker Series
Detour, Joyride, and Scenic Route (more books coming!)
A biker romance with steam, love, banter, grit, laughs, and a little bit of darkness…

Sci-Fi Romance
DD Prince also writes sci-fi 'out-of-this-world' romance as Scarlett Starkleigh. Read Hot Alpha Alien Husbands (Daxx & Jetta).

Alphahole
An enemies-to-lovers, roommate, and office romance. You're going to love to hate Aiden Carmichael!

DD's list of books may have grown. Check out her website (below) or her Amazon page for more information. Sign up for the newsletter to ensure you don't miss new releases or sales.

Follow DD Prince on most social media sites as DDPrince or DDPrincebooks

Facebook: Facebook.com/ddprincebooks

Twitter: twitter.com/ddprincebooks

Website: ddprince.com

Follow on Amazon to be notified about upcoming releases and books sales:

Amazon: www.amazon.com/author/ddprince

Newsletter: http://ddprince.com/newsletter-signup/

Nice reviews are like a gratuity for authors.

Thank you very much for reading my words! Thank you for taking a chance on me by reading this book. I truly hope you enjoyed it. Please leave a review. If you can, please leave a review on Amazon (and Goodreads and Bookbub, if you use them). It truly does help me.

Even a short one with just a few sentences saying that you liked the book --- it helps me so much. It's like tipping your server.

Thank you!

CPSIA information can be obtained
at www.ICGtesting.com
Printed in the USA
LVHW050416210520
656158LV00016B/1305

9 781099 866869